FIVE
WINTERS

FIVE WINTERS

A Novel

KITTY JOHNSON

LAKE UNION
PUBLISHING

Published by Lake Union Publishing, Seattle

www.apub.com

Amazon, the Amazon logo, and Lake Union Publishing are trademarks of Amazon.com, Inc., or its affiliates.

ISBN-13: 9781662508004
ISBN-10: 166250800X

Cover design and illustration by Philip Pascuzzo

Printed in the United States of America

In memory of my lovely mum,
who was my number one fan

WINTER ONE

❄

1

It is a truth universally acknowledged that if you have a crush on your best friend's brother when you're eleven—flat chested and too shy to say boo to a goose—he is always going to see you that way. I'd been in love with Mark for as long as I could remember, but now here I was, at his wedding reception in a posh hotel in East London, and Mark was officially off the market.

Mark, with his jumpers that always go bobbly because he keeps them far too long.

His "fun" facts about maths—*Beth, did you know, if there are twenty-three people in a room, there's a fifty-fifty chance two of them will have the same birthday?*

Mark, with every bit of his lovely dad's kindness but absolutely none of his practical DIY skills.

Hooked up. Hitched. Espoused.

Married.

"She looks cold," Rosie said of her new sister-in-law.

"A shoulderless, backless dress in December will do that to you."

I was acting my poor pathetic butt off in an attempt to convince the world, Mark, and my best friend on earth that I was okay. Trying not to glug my champagne too fast while I watched Grace fitting into Mark's side like a jigsaw piece.

Actually, she didn't look cold at all, despite the wedding dress maker skimping on fabric. She looked glowing. That's what they say about brides, isn't it? That they glow. As if the happiness of getting what you want plugs you into some kind of blissful circuit board.

"I wasn't talking about her dress," Rosie said, helping herself to another glass of champagne from a passing waiter's tray.

My ears pricked up. This was the first hint Rosie had given that she wasn't especially keen on Grace. But then again, Rosie had been travelling a lot with her new job, so I supposed she hadn't really had the chance to get to know Grace that well, what with the romance being such a whirlwind thing.

I wondered why Rosie had reservations about her brother's new bride. I mean, I knew why I didn't like her—she'd just snatched the only man I'd ever really loved right out of my dreams. But if Rosie didn't like her either, maybe there was something else wrong with her apart from this one glaring fault?

"What d'you mean?"

Rosie shrugged, already almost halfway through her new glass of champagne. There was no point trying to keep up—Rosie always had been able to drink me under the table. "Oh, I don't know. Just a feeling. When she smiles at you, her smile doesn't seem to quite meet her eyes. But then, maybe she's shy or overwhelmed by us or something. Who knows?"

I stood next to Rosie, watching the happy couple. Grace's arms were wrapped around Mark's neck now, and she certainly didn't look very shy as he bent to kiss her. I'd seen Mark with numerous girlfriends over the years—long-term relationships that had lasted until the girl in question realised he was never going to settle down with her—but I'd never seen him as smitten as this.

"You do think she loves Mark, though, don't you?" I asked, because despite the fact that Mark getting hitched was breaking my heart, I didn't want him to be unhappy. Couldn't bear the thought that Grace might not feel the same way he obviously did.

"Oh yes. Look, don't listen to me. I'm sure she's fine. Mark's not a total idiot. Like I say, I probably just need to get to know her better. She's obviously very fond of her grandmother, anyway. Someone who loves their gran must be all right, mustn't they?"

"Yes," I said, remembering seeing Grace hugging an ancient-looking lady earlier in the proceedings.

Richard and Sylvia, Rosie and Mark's parents, were heading in our direction. They were dressed to match, the yellow polka dots on Richard's pale grey tie complementing Sylvia's dress. With it being December, the venue was decorated to be festive, and Sylvia was an unseasonal daffodil amongst the swags of yule greenery and holly. Richard's pale grey suit may have been more restrained, but his expression was pure sunshine, just like Sylvia's.

"Hello, darlings," Sylvia said, scooping both me and Rosie up into a hug. "Isn't this just fabulous?" Her waving hand indicated the swish furnishings, the Christmas decor, the buffet, and most of all, the bride and groom.

"Yes, Mum," Rosie said, kissing her cheek.

"And doesn't Grace look divine?"

As Sylvia released me, Richard caught my eye. I may have been able to fool everyone else, but I'd always instinctively known he was aware of my crush on his son, even though we'd never had an actual conversation about it. For a heating engineer, Richard was incredibly in tune with emotions. Or maybe it was just the emotions of the people he cared about, because I hadn't actually seen him in action in his customers' houses. He had a very loyal customer base, though, so for all I knew, he dispensed counselling while he fixed people's boilers. It wouldn't have surprised me. The man was a gem. I loved him to pieces.

When he hugged me, I could smell cologne and fabric conditioner. Fresh air and salmon sandwiches. Comfort. "All right, Beth?"

I clung to him for a moment. Rosie and I have been best buddies since we were four. As little kids, we were inseparable. I was an only child, and Mark was three years older than Rosie, so from the moment we met at school, Rosie and I were unofficial twins, always together, whether at her house or mine, forcing our mothers to have playdates and picnics in the park even though they didn't have that much in common. Richard wasn't around much back then because he was always out at work the way my own dad was. It wasn't until my parents died that I really got to know him.

When I was foisted on a bewildered aunt as a grieving nine-year-old, Richard and Sylvia willingly became my surrogate parents whenever Aunt Tilda had to work or just needed a break. I never thought of Mark as family, though. But he sort of was.

"Any nice boys at your work, girls?" Sylvia asked. "I couldn't decide which outfit to wear, so I ended up buying three, if either of you fancies getting hitched soon."

"I don't work with boys, Mum. I work with men. And they're either already married or total dorks, so no."

Sylvia turned her attention in my direction. "No one new at the vet's?"

"We had a new vet start the other day," I told her, causing her eyebrows to rise hopefully.

"She's called Freda, and she's from Sweden," Rosie said.

"Ah," said Sylvia, deflated.

When they moved on shortly afterwards, Rosie told me, "I have met someone, actually. But don't tell Mum. It's very early days."

It was a welcome distraction. "Ooh. Who? Spill everything."

"He's called Giorgio. I met him at a sales conference last month. But don't get too excited. It's just sex. Good sex, though—when he can get over here from Italy."

I looked at her sceptically. "Are you sure you're not really madly in love and just pretending it's casual?" I knew my friend well.

Rosie shook her head. "Positive."

"And he's not married?"

"Nope. Listen, quit worrying. Worry about yourself. What's it been? Two years since you last dated anybody?"

Mark and Grace were dancing now, their bodies melded together.

"And forget about my brother once and for all," Rosie added, the rather stern command tempered by a caring hand on my shoulder.

Ah. Maybe my acting skills weren't going to earn me an Oscar anytime soon after all.

"I'm thirty-five, not thirteen," I told her.

Rosie just lifted her eyebrows at me.

"D'you think your parents will be too upset if I don't come for Christmas this year?" I asked, imagining what it would be like with Mark and Grace freshly back from their honeymoon.

"You know Mum needs ten months' notice if you're going to miss Christmas. Of course they'll be upset. Anyway, what else are you going to do? Volunteer for sick-dog duty?"

Volunteering to take care of the dogs and cats who were too ill to be sent home from the veterinary surgery where I worked was exactly what I had intended to do over Christmas. I hadn't said anything to my boss yet, but I knew he'd be only too ready to bite my hand off if I offered.

"Sorry and all that," Rosie said, "but you have to come. Unless you want Mum's bitter disappointment on your conscience all over the festive period."

She was right, of course. If I didn't join them all, I would feel bad. When someone's done as much for you as Richard and Sylvia had done for me, it's not right to disappoint them. I just hoped I could handle it.

I felt exposed and vulnerable when Rosie went off to the loo shortly afterwards. Looking round to check on Mark's whereabouts, I spotted him with Grace's grandmother. She was seated, and he was squatting so that their heads were on the same level, clearly listening to what she was saying with complete attention. He was like that with everyone—always making you feel as if you were the centre of his universe when you spoke to him. It might have felt affected, I guess, but it didn't. As Rosie had pointed out, Grace was clearly very close to her grandmother. I'd met her parents earlier, and they had seemed so cold and stiff that this wasn't surprising.

Someone else came to speak to Grace's grandmother, so Mark gave her a kiss on the cheek and got to his feet. When his gaze started to roam around the room, I moved quickly—too quickly, as it turned out, because when I launched myself towards the buffet table as if I hadn't eaten anything but a green salad all week, I was so focussed on not making eye contact with Mark that I ended up barging straight into somebody else.

"God, I'm sorry," I said, gazing with horror at the coleslaw which had shunted onto the man's suit from his plate.

"That's all right," he said, putting his plate down on a side table and getting busy with a paper napkin. "It's only my second-best suit."

I looked up to see an attractive man about my age. He had curly light-brown hair and hazel eyes, which were quite twinkly, considering the coleslaw belt.

"You didn't think this wedding warranted the best, then?" I asked, and he shook his head.

"I wore that suit to the divorce courts. It didn't seem right to wear it today."

"Oh."

"Yes," he agreed. "Oh." He stuck his hand out. "I'm Jaimie. Jaimie Faulkner."

I shook his hand. "Beth Bailey. Sorry about just now. I wasn't looking where I was going."

He shrugged. "Don't worry about it. Are you a friend of the bride or the groom?"

"The groom. You?"

"Bride. Grace and I used to teach together."

I couldn't keep the surprise out of my voice. "Grace was a teacher?"

"For a little while. It didn't really suit her."

I could imagine that. Grace and I had met only a couple of times, but she just didn't seem the teacher type.

"What about you? Did teaching suit you?"

"For quite a while, yes. Then I got restless and jacked it in to renovate houses. More money in bricks and mortar than in Shakespeare."

"You were an English teacher?"

"I was. Grace taught business studies. She was a big help when I was setting my business up. What about you? What do you do?"

"When I'm not attacking people with coleslaw? I'm a veterinary nurse."

"Are you? I wouldn't have guessed that."

I considered him. "Why's that? Because I haven't got a litter of puppies poking out of my handbag?"

"No, because you look . . . I don't know, more glamorous than I'd expect a veterinary nurse to look." He pulled a face. "That sounds a bit cringeworthy, doesn't it? I'm out of practise at talking to pretty women, I'm afraid. Sorry, more cringe."

I shrugged. "It's okay. All this vanishes in a puff of smoke at midnight anyway. I'll be out there on the dance floor in my scrubs and latex gloves."

He laughed. "You're funny."

I could have told him I hardly ever got round to wearing makeup. That today I'd had a pressing need to look as amazing as possible. That my makeup was just like my banter and bonhomie—a self-defence. But I didn't. I smiled instead. "I try." I indicated his abandoned plate. "Look, don't let me stop you eating. After all, you nearly died for that coleslaw. I'm just going to grab something myself."

As I loaded up my plate, I risked a glance across the room. Mark was safely ensconced with Grace again. Good. If I could get through the evening without being alone with him, I might be all right.

2

It was Donna Baker who first woke me up to my feelings for Mark.

I was eleven years old, and I'd been in high school for six months. My Aunt Tilda was away for a few weeks, and I was staying with Rosie's family while she was gone. It was winter—a bleak February morning just before half term, and we were in the girls' changing room after hockey. I'd never been into sports and spent the whole time on the hockey pitch chanting inside my head: *Don't pass the ball to me. Don't pass the ball to me.* Fortunately, everyone knew how useless I was, so they rarely did.

If Rosie had been there in that changing room, she'd have alerted me to Donna's approach—a nudge of the elbow, a hissed warning. But Rosie wasn't there, because we hadn't been placed in the same class when we started at the school. So no warning was forthcoming. I'd just looked up from trying to do up the buttons of my school shirt with my frostbitten fingers to find Donna in front of me.

Donna, who had the annoying habit of jumping up and down in front of the changing-room mirror to make her breasts bounce, turning all of us developmentally challenged girls into pools of inadequacy, usually kept to her circle of jeering, loud-talking friends. Together they focussed their attention on rolling up the waistbands of their skirts to see how much leg they could get away with revealing before one of the teachers "had a word" or sent a letter home to their parents. They certainly didn't usually waste their time talking to the likes of me—a relative ant in the arena of their attention, and one Donna would have no qualms about squashing under her borderline regulation shoe if she felt like it.

I looked at her, my face reddening before she'd even said anything, my body as aware as my mind that anything Donna said to me wasn't likely to be pleasant.

So her actual words took me completely by surprise. "Your brother," she said, "is hot."

For about a millisecond, I didn't know who she was talking about. Then it clicked that she meant Mark.

"Mark isn't my brother," I said.

Something flickered across Donna's face—the same expression an adult got when you gave them some backchat. "Adoptive brother, pretend brother, almost brother," she said with a shrug. "Whatever he is, he's hot. And I want you to give this to him."

I'd been so busy dealing with the whole "adoptive, pretend, almost brother" thing that I hadn't spotted the note clutched in Donna's hand, but now she held it out to me.

"And make sure you get a reply."

Her entourage were gathered nearby. One of them said, "Yeah, and make sure it's the kind of reply Donna wants."

"Yes," Donna agreed. "Or else. And no peeking."

The note was a hot ember in my schoolbag all day. I couldn't concentrate on my lessons, not even science, which I usually loved. I kept picturing myself giving the note to Mark, watching him read it, his dark head bent over the words. Seeing a smile spread across his face as he reached the end. Then him looking up at me and saying, "Yes. Tell her the answer's yes. I like her too." And Donna becoming his girlfriend, being invited round for tea.

Or else, if his answer was no, Donna and her mates making my life hell for the rest of my time at school.

"Beth, have you written the homework down?" asked Mr. Dawkins, the biology teacher, and I quickly snapped my attention back to the room.

"Not yet, sir. Sorry, sir."

Rosie had netball practice—unlike me, she wasn't hopeless at sports—so I walked back to her house on my own after school, wondering all the way whether I could lose the note somehow without suffering any consequences. But short of the earth opening up and swallowing both me and my schoolbag with the note inside it, or Rosie's family deciding to relocate overnight to the Costa Brava and taking me with them, I couldn't think of any way at all.

No, the note would have to be given, and I would have to take whatever response I got back to Donna.

Sylvia, bless her, could tell something was wrong as soon as she saw me. "Are you all right, Beth, love?" she asked.

I just nodded, asking, "Is Mark home yet?"

"Yes, he just got back. He's up in his room. I'm making him a hot chocolate. D'you want one?"

"No thank you."

I left her and her concerned glance behind me and went upstairs, my legs like lead.

Music was coming from Mark's room. I hesitated, unsure whether to knock or go straight in. In the end, I knocked and waited.

Mark opened his door, looking puzzled when he saw me. "Beth? Hi. Everything okay?"

I got straight to the point. "Donna Baker gave me this for you."

I held the note out. He took it.

"Donna Baker. She's the tarty girl with the short skirts and the tight jumpers, isn't she?"

I nodded, but Mark was too busy unfolding the note to see. Miserably, I watched him read, waited for the smile I'd imagined would light up his face. It didn't happen.

"She . . . Donna . . . said I had to get a reply from you," I said falteringly.

Mark looked at me, his eyes searching, and it was then, at that precise moment, that I realised Donna was right. Mark was hot, if "hot" meant "attractive." Beautiful, even. His face had changed recently, lost its puppy fat to reveal cheekbones and interesting angles. He was tall and broad shouldered from being on the school swimming team, and his eyes were the green of the moss on the garden wall. He was better than any pop star or actor I'd seen. And he didn't feel like my brother. Why should he? He wasn't. If I'd had a brother, he probably would have been blue eyed and auburn haired like me. Shorter, too, since neither of my parents had been tall.

"I'll give Donna my answer myself tomorrow at school," Mark said, reaching out to put a reassuring hand on my shoulder. "Don't worry, it'll be okay."

Mark was waiting to walk to school with me and Rosie the next morning. We didn't talk much, although Rosie babbled on; I can't remember what about. But it felt good to have him by my side, even though I was bursting to know what he was going to say to Donna.

When we reached the playground, Donna and her friends were waiting for me.

"What do they want?" Rosie asked as I instinctively slowed down.

But when Mark went over to them, I followed.

"Hi, Donna," he said, and he sounded so much like his usual self, I still couldn't tell what he was going to say.

"Hi," Donna managed, and when I looked at her, it was obvious she was nervous. Donna, nervous. Maybe she was human after all.

"Thanks for your note," Mark swept on. "I'm very flattered. The thing is, I'm not actually looking for a girlfriend at the moment. I'm really busy with swimming practise and homework and stuff. But if that changes, I'll let you know, okay? Especially if I hear you've been nice to my sisters."

Donna pouted, glaring in my direction. "Beth says she isn't your sister."

Mark shrugged. "Maybe not, biologically," he said. "But she's my sister in all the ways that count."

Then he turned to smile at me, and right there, right then, the deal was sealed. I was Beth, Mark's sister, and that was the way he would always see me from then on. No matter how I felt about it.

3

At the wedding, I was about to rejoin Jaimie when Grace's two young nieces raced past, almost sending my plate of food flying. Grace had presented them with disposable cameras at the beginning of the reception and told them they were both official wedding photographers. As a distraction technique, it had worked well for about five minutes. Now their cameras were abandoned who knew where, along with their weary parents. I couldn't help but smile at how much fun they were having.

My smile soon faltered, though, wiped out by a pang of longing. I've wanted a family—kids of my own—for almost as long as I've wanted Mark. Well, okay, not quite as long as that. I suppose I was about twenty-three or twenty-four when I first started to feel broody. But now I was thirty-five, and my biological clock was ticking so fast I could hear it in my ears.

"You're eating them up," said Rosie, joining me.

I knew she wasn't referring to the mountain of vol-au-vents stacked on my plate.

"You have to admit they're cute," I said.

Rosie considered the little girls dispassionately. "If you like that sort of thing." She gave me a quick hug. "Never mind. I'm sure you'll find someone to give you babies soon, kiddo," she said. "What about that guy you were just flirting with for ages?"

"Who, Jaimie?" I looked over at him, noticing a look of pain on his face. Obviously, kids and custody had to have been on the agenda at the divorce courts. Poor guy.

I was so busy feeling sorry for Jaimie, I completely missed Mark heading in our direction. By the time I noticed him, it was too late to make my escape.

"Hello, you," said Rosie, kissing his cheek. "How's married life?"

Mark grinned, kissing her back. "So far, I can thoroughly recommend it."

After Rosie, it was my turn for a hug. "Congratulations," I said, hoping he was far too high on endorphins to notice anything stilted about my overbright voice.

He smiled at me. "Thanks, Beth. This is great, isn't it? I'm so glad we didn't opt for a formal sit-down meal. It's much better for everyone to mingle. Hey, Jaimie, have you met my sister, Rosie, and her friend Beth?"

My fellow sufferer pushed his heartbreak aside and rearranged his face to suit the occasion. "I've had the pleasure of meeting Beth but not Rosie," he said, coming over.

I watched Rosie size Jaimie up as she shook his hand. Would she have gone after him if it weren't for Giorgio? Possibly. Although she'd have made a swift exit if I was right about his having children. Rosie had never wanted children, so I didn't suppose she'd be keen on being a stepmother either.

"Jaimie's a property developer," he told Rosie. "You'll have to do a house up for me and Grace someday."

"Willingly. If you ever manage to uproot Grace from her apartment. She does love that place."

"Well," said Mark, "I can see why. It has great views of the city."

"What is this?" Rosie teased. "An estate agents' convention?"

Suddenly, I pictured Mark's flat, a stone's throw from the football stadium. Strange to think I'd never hang out there with him and Rosie on Saturday afternoons again, with the walls practically shaking from the fans' cheers every time the home side scored.

"Well, listen," Mark said, "the band will be starting up again soon. I'd better find my bride for another dance."

Rosie shook her head as he left. "This is the same guy who scribbled on my Barbie Bride doll with his marker pens."

"When was this?" Jaimie asked.

Rosie smirked. "A year or so ago?"

I shook my head at her, telling Jaimie, "He was seven."

Rosie shrugged, as if seven and thirty-seven were much the same thing, hitching her bag onto her shoulder. "I've got to make a phone call. See you kids later."

And then it was just me and Jaimie, alone together as the band started up—loud and relentlessly cheerful. Suddenly I couldn't bear it. I put down my plate of uneaten vol-au-vents.

"Look, d'you fancy going to the other bar to get a drink?"

Relief flooded Jaimie's face. "Yes, let's."

I had a gin and tonic. He had a nonalcoholic beer. "I live in Cambridgeshire," he explained. "I have to drive back tonight. I've got my daughters tomorrow."

Ah, so I was right.

"How old are they?"

"Emily's seven, and Olivia is five."

"Have you got any photos?"

Jaimie smiled, reaching into his breast pocket for his phone. "You know your way to a man's heart, Beth Bailey."

He showed me a photo of two dark-haired girls saying cheese to the camera, the younger one sporting two missing front teeth.

"They look adorable," I said, handing the phone back to him.

Jaimie looked at the image for a long moment. "They are. Well, most of the time. All children are horrors sometimes. But I wouldn't change a thing about them. This is the first year I won't get to see them on Christmas Day. Harriet—that's their mother—and I agreed to take turns. I've got them next year. To be honest, I'm not entirely sure how I'm going to get through it."

I didn't know what to say. I mean, what *can* you say? And I felt exactly the same way he did about Christmas this year, even if it was for different reasons. So I reached out and squeezed his hand.

Jaimie put his phone back into his pocket and curled his fingers through mine. "Hark at me, Mr. Celebration himself."

"It's good you don't feel you have to hide how you feel."

"Is it?"

"Of course."

"You know, I rather like you."

I smiled. "I like you too."

By the time Jaimie left just before eleven o'clock, we'd exchanged numbers and agreed to try and meet again before Christmas. He'd even casually extended an invitation for me to spend Christmas Day with him.

"Only if you haven't any other plans," he said, panicking almost as soon as the words were out of his mouth. "But of course you have. I'm an idiot."

"I have, yes. Sorry."

"No, I'm sorry. We've only known each other for five minutes."

I smiled at him. "They've been a very nice five minutes, though."

He grinned. "They have, haven't they? I'm glad I came today. I almost didn't."

"I'm glad you did too." I was. Talking to Jaimie had made the evening about 100 percent more bearable.

With Jaimie gone, I was more than ready to leave myself. If I hung around here any longer, my mask was bound to slip. But the trouble with having a surrogate family who loves you as if you're their own is that you can't just sidle off without saying goodbye. You have to hug and kiss them all. Make promises to phone soon. Even if the person you've been trying to avoid all night is right in their midst.

"You can't go yet," Mark said, flinging an arm around me. "I've hardly spoken to you. How's work?" He sounded a bit drunk. I wasn't. With Jaimie not drinking, I hadn't drunk much myself.

Mark had always been generous with his hugs. I'd had plenty of practise at not showing how his proximity affected me. That didn't mean it was easy, though, but somehow I did what I'd always done with Mark. Pretended. "You don't want to hear about Sooty's broken leg or Alfie's impacted anal glands on your wedding day."

"Maybe not Alfie's anal glands, I'll grant you that. But I do like to hear about your work, Beth. I do. It's important work. You make a difference to people's lives. To cute little animals' lives. Doesn't she, Dad?"

Richard smiled. "She does, son. You're right, there."

"Your work is a lot more meaningful than my work is," said Mark.

"People would be lost without accountants."

Mark waved his finger at me. "People would be inconvenienced without accountants, not lost. There's a big difference. Anyway, what happened to poor Sooty's leg?"

"He caught it in a wheel."

"Road traffic accident?"

"No, the wheel in his cage. Sooty's a black Syrian hamster."

Mark smiled. "Sorry, I shouldn't laugh."

I did my best to sound stern. "No, you shouldn't."

"Has he got to wear a plaster cast and use crutches?"

I shook my head. "There wasn't much we could do for him, really, except give him painkillers and advise his owner to keep an eye on him."

"To make sure he doesn't get a fever? How do you take a hamster's temperature?"

I had no idea. "No, to make sure he doesn't try to chew his leg off."

Mark reeled back from me, screwing up his face. "Might he really do that?"

I nodded. "Yes, it's quite common with rodents when they injure a leg."

He shuddered. "That's horrid."

Grace and Rosie joined us just then, Grace slipping her arm possessively around Mark's waist.

"What's horrid?" asked Rosie.

"Beth and I were discussing the likelihood of an injured hamster chewing its leg off."

Grace frowned. "Well, I do hope you won't associate our wedding day with such a horrible image, darling."

"Of course not," Mark assured her, kissing her full on the lips.

"Get a room, you two," said Rosie.

Mark smiled. "We have, sis. The honeymoon suite."

It really was time for me to leave.

"Listen, I have to go," I said, ignoring Rosie's frown. "Have a wonderful honeymoon, won't you? Say hello to Paris for me."

Mark bent to kiss my cheek, and I kissed him back. "We will. See you at Christmas."

Grace offered her cheek to me too. "Goodbye, Beth. Thanks so much for your gift."

I wasn't confident Grace would like the dog-themed espresso cups I'd bought from a potter friend. They would probably stay in the back of a cupboard forever. Either that or they'd be used once, then packed off to a charity shop. They'd been a stupid idea.

"See you soon, party pooper," said Rosie.

Richard and Sylvia had gone off somewhere. Suddenly I didn't think I was capable of finding them to say goodbye. "Listen," I said to Rosie, "you couldn't say goodbye to your parents for me, could you? I can feel a headache coming on."

Mark looked concerned. "Will you be all right getting home?"

"Yes," I said. "I'll be fine." Well, I would have to be, wouldn't I? Not just now, but for the rest of my life.

It was good to get home, fictitious headache or not. I loved my flat. My parents had been young when they died, but what money they did have had gone into a trust fund for me. When I'd inherited it at twenty-one, it was enough for me to get a mortgage on a two-bedroom flat in a Victorian terraced house in East London. I'd lived there ever since. It had a large, open room—part kitchen/diner, part sitting room—and, best of all, a garden. And not a concrete yard full of dustbins posing as a garden either. A proper garden with a towering London plane tree, a wild area for the foxes and the hedgehogs, and borders for my herbs and flowers. In the summer, it was filled with the fragrance of evening primroses, lily of the valley, and sweet peas. In the winter, the bare branches of the plane tree were silhouetted against the sky. There was always something to see. It was my oasis, my place for respite. Tending my plants and communing with my wild visitors balanced me.

So I suppose it was no surprise that I kept my coat on and let myself out into the garden when I got back from Mark's wedding. It was too cold to sit down, so I stood instead, holding a mug of coffee it was far too late in the day to sensibly drink, jiggling about to keep warm, sloshing coffee onto the paving stones. I could hear the bass of someone's music on another street. A few passing cars at the front of the house. The clatter of bare branches scraping together in the breeze. I closed my eyes and listened to it all, breathing in deeply, telling myself it was a good thing Mark was married, swiping away the tears that insisted on running down my cheeks. I had to get a grip. Move on with my life. I'd needed to do that for a very long time, and now I had no choice. If I'd done it before, I'd probably be blissfully married with 2.4 kids by now.

I leaned against the doorframe, images of the wedding flitting through my mind. It wasn't the ceremony I'd have chosen for myself— Grace might have opted for a buffet rather than a sit-down meal, but it had still been far too formal and traditional for my taste. If I'd been in her place, I'd have persuaded Mark we didn't need all the rented morning suits and over-the-top hats. The wedding speeches and the hired cars and the photographers. I'd have married Mark in a meadow of wildflowers if I could find a way to make that possible. On a mountaintop or deep in a forest. Somewhere wild and elemental—maybe just the two of us with a couple of unknown witnesses. Either that or at the local register's office with a round of bacon butties for our closest friends afterwards. I wouldn't have made Mark slog for weeks over his vows the way Grace clearly had; I'd have been happy to hear anything that impulsively came from his heart on the day. I would have told him I loved him. That I was a part of him, and he was a part of me.

Except that I wasn't, and he wasn't. And never would be. At least not in the way I wanted.

A tawny owl began to hoot up at the top of the plane tree, and I dried my eyes, enjoying the sound. The owl was a frequent visitor to my tree in the autumn and winter—he felt like a friend. Like someone who knew I was feeling particularly alone tonight.

I stood listening to him, my thoughts moving on to the time I'd spent with Jaimie at the wedding. He'd been nice. Genuine. I liked him. Chatting to him had been fun, interesting. He seemed like a man who was capable of caring for people, if his love for his daughters was anything to go by. Certainly, he'd made being at the wedding just about bearable.

If I was going to have to find someone new in order to forget about Mark for good, then why not him? I was pretty sure he'd call me, but if he didn't, maybe I should call him.

4

Rosie's dad phoned me the next morning. "Hello, love. Hope I didn't wake you up? Only I've got this little shelving unit I knocked up out of some spare wood. Thought it might be good for your bowls and vases and that. You in if I drop it over for you to take a look at it?"

"That's sweet of you. Wouldn't you rather have a lazy day after yesterday, though? You don't want to drag yourself up to Dalston."

"You know me; I don't do lazy. Besides, it doesn't take long to get to yours, does it? Be good to have a run out. Sylvia's resting today. Had a bit too much fizz yesterday, between you and me. Bet she'd appreciate a bit of peace and quiet."

I smiled. "Well, if you're sure, it would be lovely to see you."

When Richard knocked on my door an hour later, I could see right away that the cube unit he had with him had not been knocked up in minutes out of spare wood. It was beautiful, made of pine with tongue and groove joints.

I kissed him. "That looks gorgeous, Richard. Come in, come in. D'you want a hand with it?"

"No, love, I can manage, thanks."

I stepped back to let him go ahead with the unit into the living room. There he stood it in front of the big oak table I'd bought at a furniture auction.

"Now, don't go thinking you have to say yes to it," he said. "I just thought the shelves would look nice on the wall there. You've got so many interesting bits and pieces. I thought maybe you'd be able to see them better up on the wall."

"Richard, I love it. Thank you so much. But you shouldn't have. It must have been so much work."

"I enjoy it. Keeps me out of Sylvia's hair. Think of it as an early Christmas present. Right, then. How about you make me one of those posh coffees of yours while I crack on getting it on the wall? I'll just fetch my toolbox from the car."

Within ten minutes, the shelving unit was fixed to the wall, and Richard and I were sitting side by side on the sofa admiring it with our mugs of coffee in hand. The pinewood cubes looked great with the jade-green paintwork showing through them. I couldn't wait to put some of my precious things on the shelves.

"Looks just like I imagined it would," Richard said with a satisfied smile.

"It's perfect. Thank you." There was so much more I could have said, but I knew I didn't need to. Richard knew how much I loved and appreciated him.

"Your boiler still working okay?"

"Of course. It was fitted by one of the best in the business."

"Good. You need it to be working well. Something tells me we're in for a cold snap."

"I think you're right. Hopefully, it won't be too cold in Paris."

Richard didn't say anything. Just took hold of my hand and squeezed it.

I squeezed his right back, thinking about my own dad, and how it was getting harder and harder to remember him in any detail as the years kept on rolling by. Would we have been close like this if he'd lived? I hoped so.

Sometimes Richard had an uncanny ability to read my mind. "They'd have been very proud of you, your mum and dad," he said.

I wasn't so sure. "Would they? If she was anything like my friends' mums, Mum would probably be wondering why I hadn't got married and given her grandchildren by now."

"Plenty of time for all that. Besides, she'd just want to see you happy." He glanced at his watch. "Speaking of which, I'd better get going. Sylvia will be wanting me to make her happy by bringing in something substantial for lunch, if I know her. That's how her hangovers generally go. Not that she'll admit to having a hangover, of course."

We exchanged smiles, and then I saw him and his toolbox to the door.

"See you at Christmas," he said, kissing my cheek.

"Yes, see you at Christmas. And thank you again for my wonderful shelves."

"You're more than welcome. Bye, love."

"Bye, Richard."

I closed the door behind him and went to decide which of my treasured items to display on my new shelves. It was a difficult choice. I had several pretty bowls and vases, as well as lots of animal sculptures and knickknacks that people—including Mark—had given me as presents over the years. It probably wasn't a good idea to display Mark's gifts. Not just yet. Perhaps I should have a shifting display. Yes, I could be the curator of my own rotating exhibition. And, since it was almost Christmas, I could start with a Christmas theme.

By the time I left for work the next morning, each cube in the shelving unit contained a different tinsel-adorned item. I'd even managed to make an interesting piece of driftwood I'd found on a Cornish beach look festive.

The festive theme didn't stop when I reached the vet's practice where I worked. Clive, my boss, was a total Christmas fanatic who wore a Santa hat constantly from the first of December onwards. The other veterinary nurses and I were charged with the task of festooning the waiting room with glitzy, over-the-top decorations at an indecently early date. Christmas music played in the waiting area, there was a display of festive pet outfits and dog toys, and the air was frequently filled with the smell of heated-up mince pies.

It was only a small veterinary practice—seven staff members worked there, and at the moment we were down one because Naomi, one of the other veterinary nurses, had recently gone on maternity leave, and Clive hadn't got round to replacing her yet. We were a close-knit team, but despite counting each and every one of them as a friend, I'd so far managed to keep my feelings about Mark to myself. Work was a sanctuary—somewhere I could lose myself. I suspected my colleagues had different theories about why I was still single at thirty-five, though, and they were definitely all united by a common desire to change that state of affairs—matchmakers, the lot of them, no matter how much I might protest that I was quite happy as I was.

"Morning, Beth," Tia said in greeting from reception when I arrived. "How was the wedding? Did you meet anyone interesting?"

I put my umbrella in the drip tray by the door. "I might have had an interesting chat with a guy at the wedding reception," I teased. "A long, interesting chat."

Tia's eyes lit up. "Go on," she said. "I want to know everything." But just then the phone began to ring, and the first customer of the day walked in with a cat basket, so the chance for her to quiz me was lost. Not that I was naive enough to think she would forget about it. Tia was like a dog with a bone where romance was concerned, though the interrogation was delayed by Naomi turning up at lunchtime with her newborn. At Dalston Vets, we were all suckers for puppies and kittens, stopping whatever we were doing to ooh and ahh whenever any were brought in. So it was no different with Naomi's baby. Even Clive, who was on his way out to do a house call, stopped to take a look.

"I hope you've given him a suitably festive name?" he said. "Noel, perhaps?"

Naomi looked at her boss, the baby cradled in her arms. "We have, actually. He's called Rudolph."

Clive's face lit up. "Is he?"

"Er, no, Clive," Naomi said. "We wouldn't do that to him. He's called Bembe."

We all laughed, even Clive. "Well, he's a beauty, whatever he's called. Well done." Clive looked at his watch. "Anyway, I've got to go. Is that man of yours looking after Bembe so you can come out ice-skating with us later?"

Naomi shook her head. "I think my ice-skating days are on hold for a while, Clive. But have fun. And happy Christmas."

After he'd gone, she gave a shiver. "If that man thinks I could go ice-skating a week after giving birth, he's lying about having three children," she said.

"Don't forget, he didn't actually give birth to them," Tia said.

Bembe woke up and began to cry. Naomi undid her top, and he latched on straightaway. We stood around watching for a while with smiles on our faces, as if breastfeeding were some kind of weird spectator sport, and then Tia remembered the wedding again.

"Beth met someone on Saturday at the wedding she went to."

"Naomi doesn't want to hear about that," I said quickly, but Naomi looked up from her son.

"I bloomin' well do," she said. "I'm desperate to think about anything other than breastfeeding, poopy nappies, and sleeping patterns, believe me. Go on, who was it? Spill!"

So I told them about Jaimie, but all the while I was talking, I was watching the gorgeousness that was Bembe feeding and remembering Jaimie's face when he'd spoken about his girls.

"He was a nice guy," I finished up. "If he does call me, I'll definitely see him again. We'll have to wait and see, won't we? Anyway, Naomi, how's Tony taking to fatherhood?"

Naomi smiled. "Tony is a man in love," she said. "Totally besotted. He's been great, which is just as well, you know? Because it's all quite . . . well, all-consuming, I suppose, this parenting thing."

There had been just a hint of vulnerability in Naomi's voice, but I wasn't surprised when she quickly hid it with a smile. Naomi wasn't the type to admit weakness of any kind. I was glad she had a diamond like Tony to support her.

Bembe had finished feeding by this time and fallen asleep. Naomi held him out to me. "You wouldn't take him for a moment, would you? While I adjust myself? And I wouldn't say no to a few Christmas chocolates, Tia. I'm still eating for two. And I know for a fact you'll have an open box stashed behind reception."

While Naomi and the other girls ate chocolates and fielded phone calls, I got to cradle Bembe in my arms. I gazed down at his long eyelashes and the dark fuzz of his hair. With his sleeping face; delicate, shell-like ears; and rosebud mouth, he was perfect. Utterly perfect.

"Does this new man of yours want any more children?" Naomi teased as she finished off a strawberry cream chocolate.

I smiled. "I have no idea. And he's not my new man."

"Yet."

"We'll see." I handed Bembe back, instantly missing his weight as she took him from me. "But now I'll have to love you and leave you. Snoopy's anal glands await me."

"Ah," said Naomi. "I do miss the glamour of this job."

I was excited when I met up with everybody later to go ice-skating at the temporary rink outside Somerset House. Everyone was, because we loved this particular Christmas tradition, but I guessed I needed it more than anyone, if only as a means of forgetting the wedding. Anyway, the banter flew thick and fast between us as we queued to get in, and as soon as we were on the ice, we divided naturally into two groups—those of us, like me, who were confident skaters and those who needed to keep to the edge and proceed more cautiously.

As a child, I'd always liked to pretend I was performing in the Olympics whenever I skated. Even now, I felt a bit like a performer as I whizzed happily around the rink. Ice-skating is something I can do, and where better to do it than surrounded by pink-floodlit architecture, the neoclassical stonework transformed into a giant cake, the skaters into flamingos? The graceful ones, anyway.

For half an hour, I forgot about everything else. Even Mark, Grace, and Paris.

Afterwards, there was hot chocolate under a giant Christmas tree decorated with lights and cute miniature Fortnum & Mason hampers, with everyone chattering about their plans for the holidays. And in the middle of it all, my phone rang.

"I bet that's him!" Tia shouted out loudly, high on sugar and endorphins. "The man from the wedding! Go for it, Beth!"

Tia's excitement was catching. I hoped it was Jaimie. Just in case, I took the precaution of walking a little distance away from my colleagues before taking the call. "Hello?"

"Hi. It's Jaimie. From Saturday night? At the wedding?"

I smiled. "Yes, I do remember you."

He laughed. "Sorry, of course you do. How are you?"

"I'm good. How about you? How was your day with your girls?"

"Oh, you know. It flashed past, as usual. I'd planned to take them into Cambridge to see Father Christmas, but Harriet had got in before me on Saturday."

I could hear the disappointment in his voice. "What did you do instead?"

"Well, it will probably sound a bit lame, but I took them to a Christingle service at the cathedral. You know, where the kids all get a candle stuck into an orange? It kept them happy for an hour or so. Then we walked down to the river to feed the ducks."

"I loved feeding the ducks when I was a child."

"Ah, but I bet you didn't have special ducks where you went. We have Muscovy ducks here in Ely."

I laughed. "Are you up-ducking me?"

"Might be." He laughed. "It's good to talk to you, Beth. In fact, I must confess, I haven't stopped thinking about you since Saturday. Well, in the spaces between finding Olivia's missing shoe and making sure the duck bread was divided up absolutely equally, you understand."

"I've thought about you too," I said, because it was true. And it hadn't always been in a comparing-him-to-Mark kind of way either. Jaimie was an attractive guy in his own right.

"I'd really like to meet up with you again."

I felt a glow at the thought of having something to look forward to.

"But I'm not sure it's going to happen before Christmas, sadly. I've got the girls again on Sunday, and I must go Christmas shopping on Saturday. But straight after Christmas if you're free? And can we chat again before that?"

"Sure."

I was grinning when I rejoined my colleagues. Tia cheered and raised her cup of hot chocolate to me. "It was him, wasn't it?" she said. "Shall I start looking for a wedding hat?"

Jaimie was as good as his word. By the time I met up with Rosie to see the Christmas lights along Regent Street a few days before Christmas, I'd heard from him pretty much every day.

Rosie and I always met up in December to see the lights on Regent Street—it was one of our Christmas traditions. They were amazing that year—it looked as if giant luminous snowflakes were falling from the sky. And the snow-scene window display at Harrods on Oxford Street was its usual inspirational self. I was feeling smug about having finished my Christmas shopping too; I was glad I wasn't one of the brow-creased shoppers searching for last-minute inspiration. I was particularly pleased with my gift for Rosie—it was a Giorgio Beverly Hills bear wearing yellow dungarees with *Giorgio* emblazoned across the front. She seemed slightly distant that evening, though—as if she weren't quite present with me. Something was obviously up.

Finally, I nudged her, deciding to find out what was wrong. "Everything okay?"

Rosie pulled a sorrowful face. "I've got something to tell you. Something you won't like."

My heart sped up. Was she ill? Had something happened to Mark in Paris? "What?"

She sighed. "I'm really sorry, but I won't be home for Christmas after all. Giorgio's invited me to spend Christmas with him in Rome. I booked a last-minute flight. I leave tomorrow."

My first response was to be pleased for her. "Wow, Rosie, that's so romantic!" But then I quickly realised exactly what her romantic tryst would mean for me: having to deal with the honeymoon couple on my own. Oh God.

"Weren't you the one who told me your mum needed ten months' notice if we weren't going to be there for Christmas?"

"I know," she said. "But actually, Mum's fine with it. Probably because there's a man involved. She thinks it's romantic too. Look, I really am sorry, Beth. He asked me, and . . . well, I just folded, I suppose. He said it's a perfect time to visit all the sights. And there's this huge Christmas market or something. It sounded fun."

"I won't be able to give you your Christmas present," I wailed, already thinking the Giorgio bear wasn't as great an idea as I'd thought it might be. After all, who wanted a Giorgio bear when you could have the real Giorgio, complete with romantic Rome?

"Keep it till I get back," she said. "It'll make Christmas last longer. And look, if things get too unbearable, you can always accept Jaimie's invitation to spend Christmas with him, can't you? I'm sorry, Beth; I really am. Please don't hate me."

"How could I hate you, you dolt?" I said, giving her a hug.

It was true: I didn't hate her for putting romance before me. How could I? But I did feel let down. And suddenly I wasn't looking forward to Christmas Day at all.

5

Years ago, Sylvia would buy everyone a new pair of festive pyjamas to wear on Christmas Eve as we opened our one permitted present before the big day. Rosie and I would be practically incandescent with excitement, hanging up our Christmas stockings on the special hooks above the fireplace, cutting up carrots for Rudolph, and getting Richard to pour a glass of sherry for Father Christmas—even though we'd stopped believing in him ages ago.

The days of new pyjamas were long gone now. This year, I wasn't expected until Christmas morning.

Richard and Sylvia lived in Middlesex, in London's commuter belt. It took about forty-five minutes to drive there from Dalston. I arrived at their road at nine thirty on Christmas morning dressed in a sparkly black dress and full, festive makeup, smiling as I drove past the light displays in front of everyone's houses. The neighbours competed with each other every year, the displays getting fancier and fancier, but somehow Richard and Sylvia's house always topped the lot. Richard made sure of it.

I parked my car and walked slowly up the garden path, taking it all in. There were lights glowing in the trees and stars twinkling on the front wall, and that was without Santa in his sleigh on the roof and the Christmas trees, snowmen, and elves on the lawn. If that lot didn't get me into the Christmas spirit, nothing would. Maybe the day wasn't going to be as awful as I feared it might be.

Richard let me in. He was wearing a Christmas jumper which sported a picture of two penguins kissing, with the words YULE BE MINE across the middle. I guessed Sylvia had made it for him.

"Happy Christmas, love," he said, giving me a kiss and a hug.

"Happy Christmas, Richard. Amazing lights, as per usual. And I love the jumper."

Richard looked down at his canoodling penguins. "It's class, isn't it?"

"How's Sylvia about Rosie not being here?"

"Somewhere between sobbing her heart out over her empty Christmas stocking and planning what to wear for the wedding. How about you?"

Sylvia bustled out of the kitchen to greet me before I could answer.

"Hello, dear. Happy Christmas! Don't you look lovely!" She hugged me close. "Nice to see there's someone I can rely on, what with Rosie living the high life in Rome and the happy couple still in bed."

Reliable, predictable. Yes, that was me. God, I had to stop feeling sorry for myself.

"Come into the kitchen. I was just getting the turkey on. You can make yourself a cup of coffee and tell me all you know about Giorgio."

Despite my knowledge of Giorgio being minimal in the extreme, I was still in the kitchen helping Sylvia when Mark came down in his dressing gown. His hair was attractively tousled. He looked to be what he no doubt was—a man who'd just made love to his wife of two weeks.

Back when I was a teenager, after my feelings had changed and I suddenly saw Mark as the boy of my dreams rather than my friend's overly bossy older brother, I used to have to prepare myself to see him if I'd been out somewhere and come back to the house. The family still lived in London then—in a town house with the sitting room in the basement. Sometimes I'd have to visit the loo on the ground floor before I went downstairs to greet everyone, just to have time to collect myself.

I could have done with such a space on that Christmas morning, but I didn't get it. One moment I was peeling parsnips ready for roasting, with carols playing on the radio and Sylvia listing all the facts she could think of about Rome, and the next, Mark was saying, "Happy Christmas, Beth," and dropping a kiss on my cheek on his way to kiss his mother.

"Happy Christmas, love," Sylvia said, enveloping him in a big hug. "You two will be getting up soon, won't you? Or it will put out all my timings."

"Your timings are quite safe, Mum. Just making Grace a cup of coffee, and then we'll be down. She doesn't do anything until she's had a cup of coffee."

If Rosie had been there, this would have inspired some banter; I knew it would. But Rosie wasn't here. There was just me, bent over the parsnips with my bruised heart and pretend smile. I could do this. I *could*.

"Did you have a good honeymoon? When did you get back? I bet it was cold, wasn't it?"

I could hear my voice going on and on. When I risked a swift glance up at him, Mark was smiling.

"Yes, thank you. Last night. Yes, I suppose so, but we had our love to keep us warm."

Ha ha. He probably expected me to give him a sisterly shove or something in response to that, but even if I'd wanted to, he was over on the other side of the kitchen making coffee. So I kept my attention on the parsnips.

"Oh, no need to slice them quite so small, Beth love," Sylvia said, whisking them away. "We don't want parsnip chips, do we?"

Now I had nothing to do with my hands and nowhere to hide my face. And to cap it all, Richard came into the room and gave my shoulder an affectionate squeeze.

"Are you okay, Beth?" Mark asked, frowning at me, a cup of coffee in either hand.

"Probably thinking about the time your mum and dad took you to Paris, aren't you, love?" Richard said. "What with Mark and Grace just back from there."

I hadn't been, but now I was.

"I didn't know they'd taken you to Paris," said Mark. "You must have been very young."

"I was seven. Mum wanted to see an art exhibition."

"You arrived on the fourteenth of July, didn't you?" Richard said. "Bastille Day."

I nodded. "Yes. Mum and Dad had no idea about it being any kind of special day. Our hotel was right next to the Eiffel Tower. Quite by accident, we saw all the fireworks being set off to music."

"Cool." Mark waited for a moment to see if I was going to say anything else, but I didn't feel like talking about the magic of those fireworks or the fun of watching it all from my dad's shoulders. How all these years later it was almost as vivid to me as back then.

Mark put the coffee cups down on the table and drew me in for a hug. "Sounds like a very special memory," he said.

I nodded quickly, blinking away sudden tears. "Yes."

He kissed the top of my head and let me go. "I'd better take this coffee upstairs if I want to avoid fireworks here, I suppose. See you all soon."

After Mark had gone, Sylvia frowned at her husband. "What did you want to bring that up for? Beth's upset now."

"I'm not, honestly. I'm fine. Now, what else can I help you with?"

When Mark and Grace finally came down, Sylvia was persuaded out of the kitchen so we could all exchange gifts. I'd bought Sylvia a lovely soft scarf in duck-egg blue, and Richard a new pair of gardening gloves he professed to be delighted with. I normally gave Mark something jokey—the previous year I'd bought him some nylon tattoo "sleeves" which made him look as if he'd spent five weeks at a tattoo parlour when he wore them on his arms. Which he did, all over Christmas.

The jokey presents were a part of my disguise. I was afraid my true feelings would show up in the gifts I chose for him if I didn't keep it light. This year I'd felt stumped. I didn't know Grace well enough to buy her a joke-themed present. I didn't even know what her sense of humour was like. Presumably, she had one, because Mark did. In the end I'd bought them Kitchen King and Kitchen Queen aprons, which was hardly inspired. Judging by their polite reactions, I was reasonably sure they agreed with that assessment.

God, I missed Rosie. I didn't open her gift to me, deciding to keep it until she got back. I missed her even more when she called midmorning and Sylvia put her on speakerphone. She was all ciao this and ciao that, and we could hear Giorgio in the background saying something to make her giggle. Suddenly I felt like the only person on the entire planet who was single at Christmas.

I wasn't the only one who was upset by Rosie's call. After Sylvia hung up, her stiff upper lip went all wobbly. "I'm happy for her, of course," she said. "But she's thirty-five years old. She ought to be here with us with a pack of bouncy grandchildren."

Richard and I both remembered our conversation in my flat when he'd come to fit the shelving unit, and we exchanged glances. *See?* my expression said, and he smiled.

"Do grandchildren come in packs?" Mark asked.

"I'm not sure there is a collective noun for grandchildren," said Grace.

"There is," said Richard, who knew most things. "It's a commotion."

It ought to be a lack, I thought miserably, brooding over my own childless state. *A lack of grandchildren.*

"Come on, love," Richard said to his wife. "Cheer up. It's Christmas."

Sylvia nodded and blew her nose. "You're right. Sorry." She smiled at Mark and Grace. "I'm counting on you two to provide me with a commotion of grandchildren. All right?"

"Give us time, Mum," said Mark. "We've only been married two minutes."

Mark and Grace had given me a five-year diary for my gift. Five years of empty pages—I had no clue what I could fill it with.

"I hope you like your present?" Mark said to me later. "Grace chose it. I wasn't sure at first, but then I thought you could use it to note down some of the more amusing things that happen at work. How's Sooty, by the way?"

I smiled. "The diary was a lovely thought. And Sooty's fine, thank you."

"Still got all four legs?"

"At the last count, yes."

Grace joined us, winding her arm around Mark's waist, as per usual.

"Just catching up on whether Sooty the hamster ate his broken leg off or not," Mark explained.

Grace pulled a face. "Oh yes," she said. "The self-cannibalisation story that threatened to sabotage our wedding. I'm so glad you brought that up again, darling."

She was speaking to Mark, so why did it feel as if her comment were addressed to me?

"We saw a lot of handbag dogs in Paris," Mark told me. "They were like joeys in their pouches. Only their mamas bought their pouches at Dolce & Gabbana."

"That's Italian, sweetheart."

Mark shrugged. "Okay, whatever the French equivalent is, then. Did you know there are so many pictures in the Louvre that if you spent thirty seconds in front of each of them, you'd be there for a total of thirty-five days?"

"How many pictures did you see?" asked Sylvia.

Mark laughed. "Absolutely none."

Sylvia sighed. "It sounds so romantic. Was it romantic, Grace?"

"Of course. It's the City of Love, isn't it? It was perfect."

"And what was it like at the top of the Eiffel Tower?" Sylvia asked. "I've always wanted to go up there."

"We didn't get there either," said Mark.

"You didn't go up the Eiffel Tower?" his mother said, aghast. "I thought that was one of the main things people went to Paris for!"

Grace shrugged, a shrug that said she'd been far too busy making blissful love with her new husband to go sightseeing.

"I was proposed to once, in Paris," I said, desperate to move the conversation on. "On the Eiffel Tower, actually."

Mark stared. "You weren't. Why don't I know about this? Mum, Dad, did you know about Beth being proposed to on the Eiffel Tower?"

"I didn't, love," said Sylvia. "But I certainly want to."

Rosie knew about it—I hadn't minded her hearing my tale of total humiliation. I wasn't quite sure why I'd decided this was a good time to share it with everyone else, but since they were all agog—well, except Grace, who appeared to have developed a sudden fascination for her sparkly red Christmas manicure—I launched into my tale. About how my boyfriend at the time—Danny—and I had decided to climb the 674 steps to the second floor of the Eiffel Tower to avoid the queues for the lifts. How I'd begun to get dizzier and dizzier as the steps wove round and round the structure. How Danny had been so determined to propose in exactly the way he'd planned that he'd underestimated the extent of my vertigo. Just as he had got down on one knee to pop the question, I'd had an overwhelming need to lie down in the middle of all the people. Everything had been spinning round so alarmingly—it was either that or throw up.

"So what did you say when he proposed?" Mark wanted to know.

"That first time? 'Not now, Danny, I think I'm going to be sick,' or something like that."

Mark shuddered. "Not very romantic. Poor guy."

I shook my head, back there on the windswept structure with everyone looking at us. "It got worse."

"How?"

"Well, after I'd recovered a bit, he asked me again, and I had to say no. And because it was only the first day of a four-day holiday, we had to trudge around for days on end with him sulking and barely speaking to me. It was awful."

"But why did you have to say no, dear?" Sylvia asked.

"Because I didn't love him."

Richard nodded. "A sound enough reason, I'd say."

Mark was shaking his head. "I can't believe I don't know about this."

Grace looked up from her fingernail examination. "Well, we can never completely know a person, can we?" she said. "You don't know everything there is to know about Beth, just as you don't know everything there is to know about me."

That hooked him back and had him gazing down into her eyes. "Oh?" he said, stroking a line down her neck with his forefinger. "And what, exactly, is it I don't know about you?"

Grace grinned wickedly. "That's for you to find out, isn't it?"

There was a moment of animal intensity. Then Richard cleared his throat, and Sylvia shuffled off towards the kitchen talking about carrots.

I sprang to my feet and followed her, saying, "Need any help with the brussels sprouts, Sylvia?"

6

Sylvia's cooking was a triumph. Sylvia's cooking was always a triumph. Crispy roast potatoes. Succulent turkey. Perfectly cooked vegetables. A delicious dessert. Yet the actual meal—the event of the meal—was a bit off. Or maybe it was just me who thought the conversation and laughter felt forced, as if everyone were putting on a great big act of bonhomie. It felt like the end of an era—as if Christmas would never be the same again. And after we'd finished eating and Grace and I were in the kitchen clearing up, I received incontrovertible proof of just that.

Traditionally the men did the clearing up on Christmas Day, but Richard said he'd do it after he'd had a ten-minute sit-down and promptly fell asleep, and when Mark got up to do it, Grace stopped him. "No, Beth and I will do it, won't we, Beth? It will give us a chance to get to know each other better."

It wasn't an appealing thought, but I pushed the feeling aside. If Grace was prepared to make an effort, then surely I could too. Life would be a great deal easier if we became friends. Who knew? We might find we had lots in common. We both loved Mark, after all, so obviously we had similar tastes. And anyway, Grace was always going to be present at family gatherings from now on, wasn't she?

But while we rinsed plates and loaded the dishwasher, Grace didn't seem to be in a hurry to ask any "get to know Beth better" questions.

It was all just chitchat about the meal and the best way to stack the crockery for optimum cleaning power.

It wasn't until I had my arms plunged in a bowl of soapy water, ready to tackle the pans and serving dishes, that Grace broached the subject for which she'd obviously brought me into the kitchen.

"I guess if things had turned out differently, you'd be with your real family today?"

On the face of it, it wasn't such a hurtful thing to say. It was true, after all. No doubt I would be round at my mum and dad's house if they'd still been alive. But it was her use of that word *real*—as if I were a complete and utter interloper—that upset me. That and the guilt I hadn't really managed—even now—to shake off.

There had been a lot of guilty feelings when I was a kid, especially at Christmas. Every now and then, in the midst of all the excitement, it would come crashing over me. I'd be tearing the wrapping paper off my presents alongside Rosie, and suddenly I'd remember. My mum and dad were dead. I shouldn't be enjoying myself. Shouldn't be happy like this. It was wrong.

Either Sylvia or Richard was always on hand to give me a cuddle until the bad feelings went away. And as the years passed, the cuddles became a sympathetic smile or a shoulder squeeze, no words ever necessary. They'd always been there for me, those two, constant and reassuring. I loved them to pieces. To label them as anything but my real family felt wrong.

I swiped an arm over my face, realising I still hadn't replied to Grace's question. But perhaps she didn't need me to anyway.

"We never know how life's going to turn out, do we?" she went on. "Though we can make plans, of course. Set ourselves goals. I always said I'd be married before I was thirty, and voilà! Here I am, married at twenty-nine."

I wanted to slap the smug expression off her face so badly that the need made me snap at her. "Was it all a question of timing, then? You marrying Mark? Right place, right time?"

She looked offended. "No, of course not. I love Mark."

Had the woman diarised in when she was going to give birth? Very probably.

"What about you?" she asked. "What have you got planned for your life? Presumably, you don't see yourself turning up here for Christmas every year until Sylvia and Richard pass away?"

My hands stilled in the washing-up bowl. My face had been flushed from the heat of the soapy water, but now I could feel the blood draining from it.

She knew. Grace knew how I felt about Mark. This was her way of dealing with it. Well, fair play to her. But I didn't have to stick around while she twisted the knife.

"Excuse me," I said, abandoning the washing-up brush on the draining board. "I've just got to make a phone call."

Jaimie was surprised—but delighted—to hear from me.

"Is your invitation to spend Christmas Day with you still open? I know there isn't much of the day actually left, but I could be with you in a couple of hours if I leave now."

"God, yes, please come. It would be amazing to see you. As long as you haven't had too much to drink with your Christmas lunch? There aren't any trains running today, what with it being Christmas."

I thought about it and realised I had drunk about as little as I had eaten. Maybe it had been some sort of self-preservation thing or something. "No, I've only had one glass of wine. I'll be fine. Can you text me your address?"

Fifteen minutes later, I was ignoring my guilty conscience and heading out the door. Sylvia was upset and trying to hide it. Richard was gut-wrenchingly understanding. Mark was bemused. And Grace? Grace was smug. Of course she was. By getting rid of me, she'd achieved exactly what she'd set out to achieve. But I didn't care.

"Has Jaimie told you about his hobby yet?" she asked as I swept past her on my way to my car.

"No," I said. "I don't think so. What is it?"

She laughed. "If he hasn't told you, I won't spoil the surprise. Goodbye, Beth."

~

I cried at first. Not shoulder-shudderingly dangerously. Just a steady slide of tears down my cheeks which I kept in check with my coat sleeve.

Mum and Dad were celebrating their tenth wedding anniversary in the Lake District when they died. A fog came down suddenly, and a lorry ploughed straight into them. They both died instantly, and so did my life as I knew it. I went to live with my dad's sister, Aunt Tilda, which meant a new school, and a new routine of going to after-school clubs and childcare during the holidays, since Aunt Tilda worked full-time. I was lonely and grieving, missing both my parents and my friends, especially Rosie. In the end, sensing how miserable I was, Sylvia approached Tilda and offered to have me during the holidays and after school. I often wished I could just stay all the time instead of going home with Tilda when she came to collect me, but she did her best for me, bless her, and we did become closer. I was sad when she died just before my thirteenth birthday.

~

Because it was Christmas, there was very little traffic on the roads, and it was a straightforward journey along the A10 to Ely pretty much all the way. By the time I was halfway there, I was starting to feel resigned, if not quite hopeful. Grace may have been cruel, but she'd also been right. I did need to move on. All my instincts had told me it wasn't a good idea to spend Christmas at Richard and Sylvia's this year, but I'd ignored them because I didn't want to upset anyone. And in the process,

I'd upset myself. God, I was so glad I wasn't still there, pretend smiling over a board game, forcing myself to eat a turkey sandwich I didn't want. It had been fun chatting with Jaimie on the phone these past few weeks, and it would be good to see him in the flesh again.

It was dark by the time I approached Ely. Jaimie had told me to look out for the floodlit cathedral. He'd said when I saw it, I'd be only a few miles away. When it came into view, standing out like a beacon across the dark fields, I couldn't help but gasp out loud. It was so magically pretty with its silver spires stretching up into the night sky—like a fairy castle. Somehow the beauty of it cheered me and gave me hope.

Unmuting the satnav, I followed the directions past a superstore, stopping after I'd turned left at the roundabout to sort out the mess of my makeup with the aid of a wipe and a hand mirror. Then I continued on, turning left down the next street and heading for the end of a close of twenty houses until I reached Jaimie's home.

He must have been listening out for me, as he had the front door open almost before I got out of the car.

"Come in, come in. Did you have a good journey?"

Something about his polite enquiries reminded me we were virtually strangers. Had it been a mistake to rush over here like this? What did I know about Jaimie after all? Not much, really. And here I was, spending what was left of Christmas Day with him. It wasn't the kind of rash thing I normally did.

"Welcome to my humble abode. Can I get you a coffee? Something stronger? I've got wine I can mull somewhere. Or a bottle of cava I can put into the freezer for a fast chill. Or perhaps you want a snack after all that driving?"

Perversely, Jaimie's nervous chatter relaxed me. It wasn't as if I'd driven across three counties to meet an axe murderer. This was Jaimie— Coleslaw Crash Jaimie. And he really was rather sweet with all that curly hair and his little-boy-lost expression.

"A coffee would be lovely," I said, taking my coat off. "But no snack, thanks. I'm not hungry."

"Okay, I'll pop the kettle on. Do make yourself at home while I make it."

He went off to the kitchen, and I wandered through the door he indicated, finding myself in a sitting room dominated by the biggest Christmas tree I'd ever seen in an indoor setting. It was so huge, it must have been an almost impossible task to get it into the house, and I wondered who'd helped him do it. The tree was festooned with decorations. When I went to take a closer look, I saw that many of them had been made by children—presumably, his girls. The fingerprinted paint and clumsily applied glitter were somehow very poignant. My gaze travelled upwards to where a fairy doll with weirdly staring eyes was crammed on the top of the tree, her tiara almost brushing the ceiling. In addition to a wand grasped in her outstretched hand, ready to create magic, there were angel wings, crafted out of what looked like a silver doily, attached to her back.

Beneath the tree, stacks of presents were waiting to be opened—piles and piles of them, all beautifully wrapped in gold-and-silver paper with elaborately tied red bows. No magic the tree fairy could wield would make their intended recipients able to open them until tomorrow, though.

Jaimie came in with the coffee and caught me looking.

I smiled. "Your girls will be so excited when they arrive."

He pulled a face. "Hopefully. Although I guess it could all be a bit of an anticlimax, as they've already done all that today."

"How could it be an anticlimax? Look at all that treasure."

He put the mugs down on the coffee table, smiling ruefully. "I have gone a bit overboard, I suppose. But they took so many of their toys with them to Harriet's new house."

There were dark smudges beneath his hazel eyes. I wondered what the rest of the day must have been like for him, waking up alone in an empty house when he was probably used to his daughters leaping onto his bed at some ungodly hour, desperate to start the day.

"What time are they arriving tomorrow?"

"About nine o'clock." He smiled apologetically. "I'd ask you to stay and meet them, but, well, at the moment they don't know anything about you."

"Oh no, I wouldn't expect that. Don't worry; I'll be out of your hair by then. I can even go home this evening if that's best."

Jaimie smiled, reaching out to stroke my cheek—an intimate gesture which created a ripple of instant reaction through my body. "I'd much rather you stayed and we set the alarm clock," he said, and the next moment we were kissing.

It was ages since I'd kissed anybody properly. Turns out you don't forget how to do it. Within seconds the temperature had risen by about a billion degrees.

"Would you care for a tour of the first floor?" It probably ought to have sounded cheesy, but the tremor in Jaimie's voice was a clue that he hadn't made love to anyone since his split from his wife.

"Yes, please," I said, and he took me by the hand and led me straight upstairs.

The tour started and ended in his bedroom. I laughed as we fell back together onto his bed, but then he was kissing me and stroking my breasts through my dress, and things got intense very quickly. In no time at all, we were tearing at each other's clothing. Five breathless minutes after that, we were both crying out.

"Oh God, I'm sorry," said Jaimie after a moment, sounding mortified. "That was so rushed, I expect your coffee's still warm. Do you want me to go and get it for you?"

I caught his eye, and we both burst out laughing. "It wasn't rushed," I said. "It was hot. And you can make me another coffee later—after we do that all over again."

We got under the covers, and this time we took our time, smoothing, stroking, tasting, exploring. It was all utterly delicious, especially after the exhausting roller coaster of a day I'd had. So I suppose it was no surprise that I fell asleep afterwards.

When I woke up, I was alone. I didn't remember where I was straightaway. The room was completely dark except for a strip of light coming in through the half-open door. Then I became aware of the liquid feeling pervading my entire body and remembered everything. Jaimie. I was at Jaimie's house, in Jaimie's bed. We had just made the most amazing love, despite our slightly unpromising first foray, and now Jaimie must be downstairs, waiting for me to wake up. So why did I feel so sad? This was all good, wasn't it? Good sex? A fresh beginning with a nice man? A break from the Christmas patterns of almost a lifetime?

I wanted it to be good. It was just that Grace's unkind words kept swimming round my brain. *Presumably, you don't see yourself turning up here for Christmas every year until Sylvia and Richard pass away?* And I couldn't stop seeing Mark's arm around Grace's shoulders. The little loving glances they'd given each other as they exchanged gifts.

Oh God.

Quickly, I swung my legs out of bed, looking for a dressing gown or something to slip on. But there was nothing—the peg on the back of the door was empty. I found the light switch and foraged for my torn-off clothes. Then I made my way downstairs and into the sitting room, where I found Jaimie sitting stark naked on the sofa watching *It's a Wonderful Life* on TV.

"Hello, you," he said, sounding completely unembarrassed. "I thought I'd let you sleep. You looked as if you needed it. Are you ready for that snack now? I was just going to make myself a sandwich. And there's a bottle of cava chilling."

Jaimie's penis bobbed up and down as he headed for the kitchen. His complete lack of self-consciousness was somehow alarming, making me feel as if I were the smutty one, wearing clothes. And I couldn't help but stare at him, like a rabbit caught in the proverbial headlights.

"Are you admiring my suntan?" Jaimie asked.

I nodded mutely. His suntan, yes, that was what I was looking at. Not.

"I took the girls to Greece during October half term. We were really lucky with the weather. And, of course, I top it up any chance I get. I expect Grace told you I'm a naturist?"

Grace's parting quip about Jaimie's "hobby" flooded back. No wonder she'd looked as if she wanted to die laughing.

"No," I said. "She didn't think to mention it."

Bloody hell, with a Christmas like this one, what in God's name was the New Year going to bring?

WINTER TWO

❄❄

7

When I saw the Cambridge train approaching, I quickly called to the off-the-leash border collie: "Milo! Here, boy!"

Too late. The train was almost level with us now, and Milo—whose favourite hobby was racing trains—took off, determined to catch up with it, an elusive flash of barking black and white. Dachshunds Toto and Lily, the two other dogs I was walking, were safely on the lead, thank goodness. Oh well. At least I knew Milo would come back after he'd finally accepted defeat, and the railway line was on the other side of the river, so he was quite safe.

The receding train and Milo's barking were the only sounds to be heard. We were alone, me and the dogs. I was used to it now, although I did still miss the buzz of London. Ely was a city—a tiny one, but still a city because of the cathedral. It wasn't exactly bustling. You couldn't jump on a bus to catch the latest play in the West End. And there wasn't the same mixture of different cultures and international restaurants, markets, and clothing stores that you got in Dalston.

It was pretty, though. And besides, Jaimie wasn't in Dalston. He was here, in Ely. Jaimie with his enthusiastic lovemaking. His waggy-tailed approach to life and a smile that lit up his face. Family man Jaimie, full of love for his girls. For Jaimie, I had put my reservations about rural living aside and ignored my longings for my old job and my former work colleagues. After all, wasn't I lucky to have found this dog-walking job when there weren't any veterinary-nurse vacancies going? And it was still working with animals. Worthwhile, too, since without me, these dogs would be shut up all day, living a dull life. The countryside was growing on me too. If you went on the same walks several times a week, you got to notice all the small changes. When Jaimie and I had taken his girls on an organised nature walk, I'd learnt to spot otter runs and the best places to see kingfishers. I hadn't seen an otter yet—the dogs would probably scare them off even if they were around—but it was rare for a week to go by without me seeing a kingfisher, and that flash of brilliant blue always made me gasp with pleasure. You didn't get that in Dalston.

The girls hadn't been that interested in the nature walk, actually. Olivia loved animals, but she'd rather go to a petting zoo than tramp through the countryside. Besides, it hadn't been a good weekend for the girls. Their mother was away visiting her parents on the coast, and the girls probably felt they were missing out. I'd felt for them, I really had, knowing what it is like to long for your mother, and I'd tried my very best to—well, not take her place, exactly, but to make up for her not being there.

The girls. Oh heck. Normally when I did this walk in the afternoons, the Cambridge train didn't pass us until I'd turned back towards the car with all the dogs safe on the lead, which meant that either the train had been early today or I was late. And if I was late, there wouldn't be enough time to return all three dogs to their homes before I had to go and collect the girls from school. And there was a huge black rain cloud heading in our direction.

"Milo!" I called, my voice battling against a wind that had suddenly sprung up. "Milo!"

Lily whimpered, probably sensing it was about to rain. Just as the first fat drops began to fall, Milo reappeared, running towards me with his tongue out, looking thoroughly pleased with himself. Despite everything, I laughed, bending to clip on his lead. It was impossible to stay cross with him, and normally I loved to see him indulge in his favourite hobby. It was just the thought of being late to the school. Again. And the likelihood that I wouldn't be able to find anywhere close by to park, which would mean the girls getting a soaking. And my having to take them with me to drop off Milo.

"Come on," I urged the dachshunds, breaking into a trot. "Let's get you two home, at least."

By the time we reached the van, all four of us were soaked. After giving Milo a cursory wipe down with a towel, I held the door to his travel cage open for him. He jumped straight in, allowing me to spend longer drying and settling Toto and Lily. Milo's owners might have treated him like the child they never had, but he was a farm dog at heart, bred for the wild outdoors. A little bit of rain wouldn't bother him.

Toto and Lily lived together in a house near the cathedral. By the time I'd dropped them off and parked on a side street near the school, it was well over five minutes since the bell marking the end of the school day had rung. As I ran through the rain, my hair plastered to my scalp, everyone—parents, children, toddlers, and babies in buggies—was going in the opposite direction to me.

Either Jaimie or I collected the girls from school two or three times a week. At first, after I'd moved to Ely, Jaimie had always done it. But then the property he'd been restoring had sold, and his next one was farther away. So I'd gladly offered to do it, and now I was mostly the one who collected them when the girls stayed overnight with us. It made practical sense, since my dog-walking work was reasonably flexible, and it was potential bonding time too—just me and the girls. As long as I remembered to look at my watch, that is.

What with the storm clouds, it was almost dark as I hurried across the playground, but not too dark to see that Olivia and Emily were the last children to be collected, sheltering with Olivia's teacher on the porch. The lights in the classrooms behind them were ablaze, illuminating the paraphernalia of Christmas—decorations, Christmas cards, paintings. But there was nothing festive about Emily's expression as I ran across the tarmac, and my heart sank when I saw Olivia was holding a painting. Just how was I supposed to get that safely home through the rain?

"Sorry I'm late," I said to the teacher.

"That's all right," she said. "See you tomorrow, Olivia. Don't forget your costume for the nativity play, will you? Bye, Emily."

"Hi, girls," I said, pretending not to notice Emily's glare. "Sorry, Milo ran off again. Have you done a lovely painting, Olivia? Can I see it?"

Olivia clutched the picture to her chest. "No, it's for Mummy."

Unfortunately, despite my very best efforts and intentions, my bonding efforts hadn't exactly been going to plan.

"Well, you'd better let me put it inside my coat if you don't want it to get spoiled, I think, don't you?"

When Olivia's mouth set into a mutinous line, her sister snapped at her: "Just let her do it so we can get home."

A veritable explosion of glitter erupted in the air between us as Olivia reluctantly passed her painting over to me. "Don't look at it," she commanded. "It's a special painting for Mummy."

"I won't." I unzipped my coat and placed the picture with the painted side against my jumper, silently apologising to it for the glitter coating it was about to receive. Then I picked up the girls' abandoned lunch boxes in one hand and took Olivia's hand in the other.

"Come on, we'll have to run."

"Why did you park so far away?" Emily complained. I didn't answer that, because I knew she knew why. And anyway, with the special surprise I'd got lined up for her, I didn't want us to fall out. I couldn't wait to see her face when I gave it to her.

Finally, we reached the van, and I let go of Olivia's hand to fumble with the door key. As soon as he saw the girls, Milo began to scratch at his cage, whimpering a welcome through the mesh separating the boot from the interior. Olivia strained in her seat to try to pet him, making it impossible to click her seat belt into place. Rain was trickling down my neck from my hair.

"This van stinks," Emily complained as she climbed in and clipped in her own seat belt.

I couldn't deny it. With all the dogs I transported, it always smelled ripe. Today, the smell of wet dog fur had taken the stench to a whole new level.

"I know," I said, trying to ignore the rain percolating between my neck and my coat collar. "It's awful, isn't it? I'll have to take it to be valeted. Olivia, can you turn round please so I can put your seat belt on?"

When she totally ignored me, I tried a different tack. "If I don't get into the car soon, your mummy's special picture's going to get ruined."

That did it. Even though I did feel mean. Olivia turned around and obligingly let me clip her seat belt into place. Finally getting into the van myself, I unzipped my coat, catching a glimpse of the painting as I carefully removed it from my clothing and passed it back to Olivia. It showed a family—a mother, a father, and two little girls—in front of a Christmas tree. Well, what had I expected? A dad and two mothers?

"I bet you're excited about your nativity play tomorrow," I said to Olivia as I drove off towards Milo's house, then wondered if it had been a good idea to mention it. Olivia was to play a shepherd, and at first she'd been a bit distraught not to have been cast as Mary.

But it seemed it was a safe topic now. "Mummy got me a furry lamb to carry," she said. "None of the other shepherds have got a lamb."

Ah. Harriet had saved the day, then. "That's lovely. Have you given the lamb a name?"

"No, he's just Lamb."

The rain was still pouring down when we reached Milo's house. My instinct was to leave the girls in the van while I took Milo inside. After all, it would take me only a matter of minutes. But Jaimie and Harriet had a cardinal rule about not leaving the girls in a car on their own, so I had no choice but to take them—all but kicking and scream-ing—with me.

"Come on, Olivia," I said persuasively. "You can feed Milo for me."

"Can I?" Immediately she began to undo her seat belt and would have dashed out into the rain right away if I hadn't stopped her. And I had to stop her because I still had to convince Emily.

Time to use my trump card. "I bought you a book while I was in town earlier," I said casually. "You can bring it in with you if you like."

Emily's expression was all suspicion. "What is it?"

I couldn't help but smile. "Only the latest Gina Carmichael."

While Olivia needed constant interaction and rarely stopped talking, Emily was at her happiest with her head in a book. I knew for a fact that Gina Carmichael was her favourite author, so I'd dived straight into the bookshop as soon as I'd seen the window display this morning, which, come to think of it, was probably why I'd been running slightly late this afternoon.

Eagerly, I waited for Emily's smile of delight. It didn't arrive.

"Oh," she said dismissively. "Mummy bought that for me yesterday. I've already finished it."

It wasn't the first time Harriet had pipped me to the post. Me—*Hey, girls, I thought we could make some homemade Christmas paper chains for the living room. I've bought lots of different coloured paper.* Olivia—*We did that last weekend with Mummy.* Me—*Girls, d'you want to help me make a Christmas cake?* Emily—*Mum said we're going to do that on Saturday.*

It was hardly surprising, I supposed. But it was disappointing. Time after time I thought of something we could do together, and time after time I was knocked back. But it wasn't the girls' fault their mother kept getting in first. The whole situation was difficult for them, and I of all people ought to understand that. After all, I'd been exactly the same with Aunt Tilda. As Jaimie said, the girls hated the situation, not me. It was just a pity that sometimes that felt like the same thing.

"Oh well," I said. "That's a shame. But I'm afraid you're still going to have to come in with us. You know your dad won't let me leave you in the car."

I got out of the car to take Milo out of his travel cage. Olivia was out as soon as I slid open her door, demanding to hold Milo's lead, which I couldn't let her do, of course, with him being a client's dog.

"Come on, Emily, please. It won't take long."

At last she came, sending Olivia's special picture spiralling to the floor as she did so, and together we sprinted through the rain up Milo's garden path and into the house.

"Don't forget to take your shoes off!" I shouted after Olivia, who was already on her way to the kitchen to find the dog food, and as I bent to unclip Milo from his lead, Emily went ahead and straight into the lounge.

As I put their discarded shoes next to mine on the doormat, I could hear Olivia saying something to Milo in the kitchen.

"I'll show you where the food is and how much to feed him in a moment," I called to her, popping my head round the lounge door to check if Emily was okay on my way past.

She was kneeling on the floor next to the Christmas tree, absorbed in a large book which was lying open on the coffee table. My bonding-potential radar went off, and I went over to take a look, saying, "What have you found?"

Then I reached her and gasped in shock. The book Emily was so absorbed in was an illustrated coffee-table version of the Kama Sutra.

"Er, I don't think you should be looking at that, Emily," I said, lunging for it.

Emily looked at me disdainfully. "It's only about making babies," she said. "I know all about that already."

"Well, I'm not sure the pictures in that book are really suitable for someone of your age. I think Milo's owners must have left it out by accident."

I put the book on a high shelf, out of her reach. "Look, I'll just help Olivia to feed Milo, and then we can go home, okay?"

Emily flopped down onto the sofa as if the boredom of it all might actually kill her, and I made my way to the kitchen, where I found Milo finishing off something that looked suspiciously like sirloin steak.

"Olivia!" I squealed. "Where did you get that from?"

"The fridge," she said, her eyes instantly filling with tears because I'd shouted at her.

The packaging was still on the floor. It *was* sirloin steak. Shit.

Milo was licking his lips ecstatically. Emily came to look. It was the first time she'd smiled since I'd collected her from school.

"Well done, Liv," she said.

A tear dripped down Olivia's cheek. I sighed. "Never mind," I told her wearily. "Just so you know for another time, Milo's food is kept in this cupboard here, okay? Anything in the fridge is for his mum and dad to eat."

"His mum and dad are dogs," Emily informed me scathingly, the smile vanishing from her face.

Quickly I scrawled an apology for Milo's owners and left it with some money on the kitchen table. Then we set off for home.

Jaimie laughed when he heard about it all later.

"It wasn't funny," I told him. "It was awful. There were all these men with impassive faces shafting equally impassive women. And who knows whether they had anything else for their tea?"

"You mean the impassively shafting men and women?"

I gave his arm a whack. "No! Milo's owners. Oh God, it's so embarrassing! I moved the book, so they'll know we were looking at it. I just hope I don't run into them for a while."

"Emily has a point, though, doesn't she?" Jaimie said. "She does already know about making babies. Harriet and I told them both all about it when they were young. And they've been brought up to be relaxed about nudity." He chucked my chin, kissing me on the lips. "She wasn't embarrassed; you were."

58

When I had made the decision to give up my job and move to Ely to be with Jaimie, I had decided to embrace my new life, heart and soul, which meant becoming a vegetarian, since Jaimie and his girls were vegetarian. Well, almost vegetarian. I did indulge in the occasional sneaky bacon sandwich during my lunch breaks and meat fests whenever I went back to London to visit Rosie. My move had also meant embracing naturism, although I didn't really think you could call my approach to naturism an embrace. It was more like one of those awkward greetings when you go in for a kiss on the cheek and the recipient thinks you're going in for a double, but you've already pulled back. Me and naturism were a bit like that. I had got better at it—I didn't feel abject terror at the thought of stripping down in front of strangers the way I had at first. I just still didn't understand the point of it.

Naturism made Jaimie feel liberated. It just made me feel self-conscious. I wasn't entirely sure I wanted to be sitting around having friendly drinks with people I didn't know and may not have anything in common with anyway, let alone without any clothes on. Jaimie said you forgot about the no-clothes issue after a while, but then, if you forgot about it, what was the point? I'd rather have been cosy in a pair of dog-walking trackie bottoms or stylish in a button-through dress with a full, swingy hemline.

The only time I really enjoyed being naked was when we went on holiday to Greece, and that was because of the naked swimming. And despite Jaimie's attempts to make me out as some kind of prude, I had swum naked before I met him. Rosie and I had often done it when we'd been on holiday somewhere hot, slipping down to the sea after dark. Only we'd called it skinny-dipping, and we'd done it for the luxury of the warm water on our bodies, not to parade our nakedness to all and sundry.

Jaimie pulled a fiver from his wallet. "Here," he said. "Here's your five pounds, although I imagine Olivia is the dog's best friend now."

I batted the five-pound note back in his direction, and he laid it down on the table. "Well, I doubt if Milo's owners are. I only hope they had something else to cook for their dinner tonight."

"Maybe they got fish and chips instead of cooking and had more time to try out positions from the Kama Sutra," Jaimie suggested. "What were they doing in the illustrations you saw? This?" So saying, he flipped me over the arm of the chair and pretended to hump me from behind. "Or this?"

Laughing, I turned to see him attempting to balance on one leg with his back arched and an impassive expression on his face as he pretend thrusted.

"Careful," I said. "You'll fall over."

The girls were fast asleep in bed. Very soon, Jaimie and I were making love on the sofa, the floor, and anywhere else we felt like, inventing Kama Sutra positions and giggling until desire took us over and we brought things to a sweaty, passionate conclusion.

"That was fun," Jaimie panted, lying half-on, half-off the sofa. "Thank you, Milo's owners. Come on, let's go to bed."

When we were under the covers, he turned to me, stroking my hair back from my face. "Try not to worry so much about the girls. I keep telling you, they'll come round to you eventually."

I hoped so. I'd thought at first that having the girls as part of my life would satisfy my maternal cravings, but if anything, my desire to have a family of my own had increased since I'd moved here. Jaimie and Harriet were Olivia and Emily's parents, not me.

I'd put off speaking to Jaimie about how I felt so far, but now I said casually, "I can't help thinking everything would work better if the girls had a new brother or sister. You know, if you and I had a child together."

Jaimie's reaction was dramatic, to say the least. His whole body stiffened, and he moved away from me in bed, as if I'd suddenly become radioactive. "Bloody hell," he said. "I should think that would make things more difficult, not less."

My own body felt suddenly hollow—my insides scooped out by his tone of voice. "Why?"

"Because they'd be jealous as hell. Besides, having kids is expensive. And a lot of work. As I thought you'd have realised by now."

A minute ago, I'd been happy and laughing. Now, the bottom of my world had imploded. I should never have brought the subject up. And yet . . . I sort of had to, didn't I? I'd moved here to make a life with Jaimie. I needed to know what that life was going to be. "So are you saying there's no chance of my ever having a baby?"

Jaimie reached out to stroke my hair. "I just think things will get better for you with Emily and Olivia if you give it more time," he said, not answering my question. "You're doing so well."

"Am I? Nothing I do for them is ever right."

"Nothing I do for them is ever right either. They're kids. That's what being a parent is like."

"You didn't answer my question," I said.

He sighed. "Look, it's late, sweetheart. I've got to get up early in the morning. You haven't lived here very long. How about we have this conversation again in six months' time? Okay?" He moved close to kiss me. "Did you know you have glitter on the end of your nose? It looks very cute."

"I'm not surprised," I said, reaching up to wipe it off, remembering Olivia's painting, which was still in the back of my car.

"Oh, by the way, you're reprieved," Jaimie said, settling back against the pillows and yawning widely. "Harriet called me today. She's managed to change that work thing she had, so she can come to Olivia's nativity play after all."

"Oh," I said, disappointed.

"You don't mind not going, do you?" Jaimie said, opening one eye to look at me. "Take it from me, if you've seen one nativity play, you've seen them all."

But I hadn't seen one. Or at least not since I was actually in one myself.

"No," I said bravely. "That's okay. Olivia will be thrilled that Harriet can come."

But I was speaking to myself. Jaimie was already asleep.

8

When we first got together, Jaimie and I saw each other every weekend he didn't have the girls—I went up to Ely once a month, and he came down to London once a month. They were weekends of sex—lots of it—and laughter and talking. I learnt all about Jaimie's childhood on the Kent coast, his time at university in London, his first teaching job in Cambridgeshire, and his meeting of Harriet through a friend of a friend. In turn, I told Jaimie all about myself and my bumpy start in life.

When we weren't in bed, we explored. In Ely, I was awed by the vast magnificence of the cathedral. Entertained by a group of Morris dancers performing with their jingly ankle bells and clashing sticks. Charmed by the reflections of boats as we drank beer outside a waterfront pub, Jaimie's arm firmly around my shoulders.

In London, we saw the crown jewels in the Tower of London and a production of *Macbeth* at Shakespeare's Globe. Went on an adrenaline-charged speedboat ride on the Thames and up in a lift to the very top of the Shard to drink champagne while gazing out at the view of London Bridge. It was like being on holiday, both of us proud to show off what our cities had to offer.

We were on the London Eye in a capsule with twenty or so other people when Jaimie took me in his arms, turning his back on the view of Big Ben and the Houses of Parliament.

"How come you're here?" he asked.

I laughed, unsure what he meant at first. "For the spectacular views? Because it's romantic?"

He shook his head. "I don't mean that. I mean, why hasn't anyone snapped you up before now?"

I shrugged, avoiding his gaze. "I just haven't met the right person yet, that's all. Bad timing, I suppose. Misalignment of the stars."

I'd never mentioned my feelings for Mark to Jaimie, and I had no intention of ever doing so. It was humiliating to think how stupid I'd been to let a crush go on for so long. This was love, wasn't it? This wanting to be with someone to the extent that you neglected your friends and your beloved garden?

Jaimie smoothed a wayward lock of my hair behind my ear. "Well, I'm grateful to the cosmos, then," he said, and when he kissed me, I kissed him back.

The distance between Ely and London made our relationship a kind of courtship, I suppose, and it was exciting to be courting. To get special food in to cook for him. To find out how to give each other pleasure in bed. To talk and laugh together. I hardly saw Rosie, because I was away so much, and I didn't see Sylvia and Richard at all. Or Mark and Grace.

Then, one Monday in late March, when I was getting dressed to catch an early train back to London in time to start work after I'd spent the weekend with Jaimie in Ely, he caught hold of my hand and pressed it to his lips. "I don't want to wait a fortnight to see you," he said. "Come again next weekend."

I frowned. "Haven't you got the girls next weekend?"

He nodded. "Come and meet them," he said.

Because it was still early, the light in the bedroom was dim. But it was light enough for me to see the glow in Jaimie's eyes. To tell how important this was to him. So I smiled.

"All right. I'd love to."

I can't describe how terrified I felt, travelling up by train that Saturday morning. Jaimie's work was important to him. *I* was important to him. But his girls were his everything, and for the puzzle pieces of our lives to fit together, this had to go well. It felt as if I were being invited to enter some sort of weird blend of an interview room and a holy sanctum. Would they like me? Would I like them? I'd bought them gifts to help with the former—Love London snow globes, one containing a mini Tower of London, the other a mini Buckingham Palace, complete with a red-coated, busby-wearing guard. But the latter? Me liking them? What could I do about it if I didn't? When Jaimie adored them?

But then, why wouldn't I like them? They were Jaimie's daughters, and I liked Jaimie. I couldn't exactly say I was in love with him—not yet anyway. But I did like him. A lot.

When the train left Cambridge station for its final run to Ely, I visited the toilets to wash my clammy hands, peering at my reflection in the mirror and trying to dampen down the feeling that, in one way or another, my life was about to change forever. Being dramatic was not going to help anything.

As the train pulled into Ely, I saw the three of them waiting for me on the station platform. Jaimie was holding his girls' hands. It was a warm day in early April, and the sun was shining, turning them into a golden, smiling trio. My spirits lifted. This was going to be all right. More than all right. This was going to be wonderful.

I'd walked right up the platform to the front of the train at King's Cross station, which meant I emerged from it at the far end of the platform at Ely, and Jaimie and the girls were some distance away, near the station exit. We hurried towards each other, the girls both running, pulling on Jaimie's arms in an effort to get to me, and I laughed out loud. What had I been worried about?

"Hello, you," Jaimie greeted me, bending forward to kiss me on the cheek.

"Hi," I said, suddenly shy, smiling down at his daughters. The younger one, who I guessed must be Olivia, was jiggling about on the end of Jaimie's arm as if she couldn't bear to be still, her hair identical to Jaimie's—curly and honey brown. Emily, the older girl, was also smiling, but she was more serious, with dark eyes and dark, straight hair that she must have inherited from her mother. They were both incredibly beautiful children, and something stirred in my belly, looking at them.

"This ragamuffin is Olivia," Jaimie said, lifting Olivia's hand.

"Daddy!" Olivia protested. "I'm not a ragamuffin!"

"And this is Emily. Please excuse their excitement. They love meeting visitors from the train. As it's such a lovely day, I thought we'd go to Payne's Park. It's a children's play area. I hope that's okay?"

I didn't mind where we went, which was just as well, as Olivia was jumping around with excitement at the thought of Payne's Park.

"Just as long as they sell coffee there, that's fine with me," I said.

"They do. And cake."

"And ice creams!" shouted Olivia.

Jaimie laughed. "And ice creams too. But you have to eat the nice healthy sandwiches I've prepared for you first." He twinkled at me. "Do you promise to do that, Beth?"

I laughed. "Yes, I promise."

As we drove into Payne's Park, I could see adventure-play equipment, a rope climbing frame in the shape of a spider's web, and a small animal-petting area. But Olivia and Emily ignored it all, running straight from the car to the indoor area. Before Jaimie had finished paying for the tickets, they had launched themselves into the ball pool.

"Girls, wait," Jaimie called after them, but they were already climbing out of the ball pool and heading for the bouncy castle. "I'd better go and supervise. You couldn't get us some coffees, could you? And a couple of juice cartons for the girls?" He held some money out to me, but I waved it away.

"That's okay. I'll see you in there."

When I took the drinks inside, I saw that Jaimie had used the girls' coats to save a table. I sat down to drink my coffee, looking around for him. At first, I couldn't see him anywhere. Then I spotted him standing with Olivia right at the top of the giant slides. He saw me looking and waved. I waved back. Seconds later he and Olivia whizzed down on adjacent slides, Olivia shrieking her head off in glee.

Jaimie came over. "Sorry, I never mean to go on, but Olivia always says she's scared. Emily's met up with a school friend and left her to it."

I wasn't sure what to say, so I just smiled. I was totally out of my depth, to be honest, never having been to a play area like this before. In any case, Olivia had hold of his hand and was yanking at his arm. "Again, Daddy! Again!"

Jaimie gave a kind of "What can you do?" shrug and allowed himself to be dragged away without so much as a sip of his coffee. I finished mine soon afterwards—it hadn't been that hot to start with—then sat observing the people at the other tables. They were either couples or groups of mums. There was only one other woman on her own, and she had a baby asleep in a car seat next to her. She was bent over a book, one foot rocking the car seat every now and then. I wondered if this was the only chance she got to read and thought longingly of the book I'd bought to read on the train, which was in my travel bag in the car.

I didn't like to be selfish, but sitting on my own at a white plastic table, with children's shrieks reverberating off the walls of a converted barn, hadn't exactly been what I'd anticipated for that morning. I didn't know what I'd expected. Feeding the ducks, maybe? Or a tour of the impressive cathedral?

I scanned the colourful tubes to try and locate Jaimie again but spotted Emily instead.

"Where's Dad?" she asked, coming over.

"Somewhere in there with Olivia," I said, waving my hand at the slides and climbing frames. "Do you want your apple juice?"

I held it out to her, and she took it, using a straw to pierce the carton with well-practised ease, her eyes scanning the apparatus.

"Are you having fun?" I asked, but she was already running away, the empty juice carton abandoned on the table.

"Sorry," said Jaimie when he finally joined me, grimacing at his cold coffee. "I don't suppose you're used to this."

"Not really, no."

He laughed. "Not at all, I'd say."

"My friends who have kids haven't quite reached this stage yet."

"You mean they've got this extreme pleasure in front of them?" he said. "You do get used to it, though. I'm actually jealous this stuff wasn't around when I was a kid."

"Did you have to make do with making mud pies?" I teased, and he laughed.

"We climbed trees and made dens. Probably a whole lot more educational and healthy." He leant across the table to kiss me. "Don't worry, we'll go outside soon."

I didn't feel confident that his idea of "soon" would match my own. "Actually, would you mind if I waited for you out there? I could do with getting some fresh air."

"Sure. We'll be about twenty minutes or so."

"Okay, see you later."

I took myself out to the petting zoo, where there were some very characterful black-and-white pygmy goats who were doing the usual goat thing of wreaking havoc, pressing very close to anyone holding one of the brown paper feed bags you could buy at reception and trying to make a bid for escape whenever anybody opened the gate to their enclosure. This was definitely more me. And I couldn't wait for Emily and Olivia to get tired of the play area so I could share my enthusiasm with them.

When Jaimie and the girls finally arrived, I was sitting down in an enclosed seating area and stroking a copper-brown guinea pig. As soon as she saw me, Olivia ran over. "I want to stroke it. Let me stroke it!"

"Careful," I said quickly. "You'll scare her. Sit down here, that's it. Here, Emily, you sit next to Olivia. Now I'll pass this one to Olivia, and then I'll get one for you, Emily. No, keep it flat on your lap, Olivia. That way, if it should fall or anything, it won't break its back."

"I told you Beth knows about animals, didn't I, girls?" Jaimie said as I found a guinea pig for Emily, but neither Olivia nor Emily answered him. They were too entranced with their charges.

I smiled, watching them. Olivia's curly head was bent over the guinea pig, and she giggled as it twitched its whiskers. "It's trying to tickle me, Daddy!"

I moved on to look at Emily, who was very carefully, thoughtfully stroking the silky black fur of her own guinea pig. "Can we get guinea pigs, Daddy?" she asked, and I worriedly glanced over at Jaimie. Oh dear. What had I started?

But Jaimie only laughed. "We'll see. Maybe next spring. If you're both good, of course."

~

The day got better after that. We ate our healthy picnic, then rewarded ourselves with ice cream. Afterwards, the girls played happily together on the outdoor play equipment. By then, it was time to go home. When we got there, Olivia flopped down in front of the TV, and Emily read her book while I sat and chatted to Jaimie as he cooked pizza and garlic bread for tea.

"Can we go to the station with you when you go home, Beth?" Olivia asked me when we were at the dining room table, her mouth full of pizza. "I like going to the station."

Jaimie answered for me. "Sorry, sweet pea. You'll be back at Mummy's house by the time Beth goes home."

Emily frowned. "We're not going back to Mummy's house till tomorrow," she said.

"That's right," said Jaimie. "Beth's going to stay the night. Well, two nights, actually."

Olivia laughed. "Don't be silly, Daddy," she said. "We don't have enough beds."

Jaimie didn't respond to this statement, meeting my eyes before distracting his daughter with talk of dessert. But Emily went very quiet, and I thought I saw her looking at me very suspiciously. So perhaps it was no great surprise that when Olivia marched into Jaimie's bedroom the next morning and found me lying in bed next to her father, she announced very loudly, "My mummy sleeps there. You can't sleep there! That's my mummy's bed!" And then she ran out to Emily's room to wake her up, shouting at the top of her voice, "Beth's sleeping in Mummy's bed! Beth's sleeping in Mummy's bed!"

Although we did the things I'd imagined we'd do that day—feeding the ducks on the riverside, visiting the cathedral, playing in the garden—the day never completely recovered from that inauspicious start. Olivia seemed tired and cried at the smallest thing, while Emily was icily quiet to the point of rudeness.

"Emily hates me," I whispered to Jaimie later in the kitchen.

He sighed. "She doesn't hate you. She hates the situation she's in, that's all."

It was a relief when it was time for them to return to Harriet's, but it had been such a fraught day that both Jaimie and I felt poleaxed by it, so we sat holding hands in front of the TV like shipwreck victims, neither of us inclined to talk about how things had gone.

9

Who knows? If Jaimie hadn't had to work the next weekend, and if that weekend hadn't happened to coincide with Sylvia and Richard's ruby wedding anniversary, then maybe we wouldn't have repeated the whole me-meeting-the-girls experiment. And maybe, as a result, the course of our relationship would have run differently. But Jaimie did have to work, and I did go to the party.

Jaimie was meant to come with me. Even Giorgio, who was visiting Rosie from Rome for the weekend, was coming. I was meant to be going as Beth and Jaimie, not just Beth. I wasn't meant to be facing Mark and Grace on my own again. But I couldn't invent some excuse and cry off the way I might have for anybody else's party. Because it wasn't anybody else's party. It was Richard and Sylvia's party. So I donned my best red dress in honour of the ruby occasion, secured the peony plant I'd bought as a gift safely in the car so it wouldn't topple over, and set off.

I was last to arrive. It was another warm day, and I could hear them all in the garden when I got out of the car. Laughter and chatter floated to me on the breeze as I made my way round the side of the house clutching the peony and a bottle of red wine, my stupid stomach fizzing with nervousness.

I emerged into the garden and saw Rosie and Giorgio, Mark and Grace, a sprinkling of friends and neighbours with their children, and of course, the happy couple—Richard and Sylvia.

"Beth, darling," Sylvia greeted me, rushing straight over to give me a hug.

"Happy anniversary," I said, kissing her, holding the plant out to one side so it wouldn't get crushed.

"Hello, love," Richard said, also coming over to kiss me.

I kissed him back before presenting them both with the peony. "It's a 'Burma Ruby' peony," I said. "I hope you can find somewhere in the garden for it. I admit, I mainly chose it for the name."

"We love peonies, don't we, Sylv?" said Richard, looking genuinely delighted. "Thank you. Come and let me fix you a drink. You've met Giorgio, haven't you?"

"Just the once," I said, smiling at Giorgio.

Giorgio had his arm looped around Rosie's waist, but he disentangled himself to kiss me. "Ciao, bella," he said. "Your boyfriend, he is not coming?"

I hugged Rosie. "No, sadly he has to work today. He sends his regards to you all."

"What's he doing that's so important?" Rosie asked.

"Supervising the installation of a spiral staircase in the house he's renovating."

"Rather him than me," said Mark, who would be hard-pressed to put up a shelf, let alone make an entire shelving unit, despite Richard's best efforts over the years. I smelt something smooth and spicy on his skin as he bent to kiss me.

Grace was next, with a kiss, kiss on either cheek. "Hello, Beth."

"Hi, Grace. How are you?"

Grace was wearing red too. Great minds think alike, as they say.

"Good, thanks. It sounds as if Jaimie's latest project is going very smoothly, from what he says. Have you been over to see it?"

"Yes, he took me a few weekends ago." It was the garden I remembered from my visit there—hopelessly overgrown but filled with birdsong and flowers. Jaimie had cleared part of it to put down gravel for an extra parking space. All very practical, of course, but I'd felt a bit sad to see so much of that romantic tangle hacked away.

"Everything okay?" Rosie asked me in a moment when we were alone. "You're not cross with Jaimie for not coming?"

"Of course not. This was the only day the stair guy could come. He'd have been here if he could."

It wasn't true, not entirely. I wasn't cross with Jaimie for not being here today—of course I wasn't. But I was disappointed. Here I was, alone again, at Richard and Sylvia's house—the scene of my hopeless, unrecognised love for my friend's brother. If Jaimie had been here with me, I'd have been fine. But as it was . . .

I fixed a smile on my face and took Rosie's arm in mine. "I'm fine, honestly. Aren't your parents lucky with the weather? What a fabulous afternoon."

If Rosie gave me a look because I was talking to her about the weather like some old biddy on a bus, she let it go and led me over to talk to Giorgio. Giorgio, being the charmer he was, soon had me laughing, and I sincerely hoped my friend knew how lucky she was to have found him.

A little while later, I found myself standing next to Grace again.

"How is your family, Grace?" I asked, deciding to try to have a proper conversation with her.

She shrugged. "They're okay. My sister's pregnant with baby number three. Mum and Dad are over the moon, of course."

Had there been a slight edge in Grace's voice as she said that? I looked at her, but there was no clue in her face, so I pressed on.

"That is good news. And how about your grandmother? How's she?"

Now there was a definite change in Grace's expression. She looked quickly away, over at the flower border. "Oh, Nanna had to go into a care home recently," she said, her tone carefully casual. "Everything suddenly got a bit much for her."

I remembered the smile on Grace's grandmother's face as Mark spoke to her at the wedding and was genuinely sorry. She'd seemed like a real sweetheart. "I'm so sorry to hear that."

When Grace looked at me again, her expression was back in neutral. "Well, Mum did choose the best home she could find. More like a hotel than a home, really. I visit her there often."

I nodded, disappointed to be faced with Grace's force field. Again. How she really felt about her grandmother being in a care home was anyone's guess, though surely nobody would be exactly pleased about it, would they? But Grace's stilted sentences were designed to shut me down rather than to invite follow-up questions.

"Well," I said lamely, "just as long as she seems happy."

"She certainly wasn't happy at home. It distressed her—not being able to cope with things. As Mum says, at least at Kenwood Place she has delicious meals cooked for her."

I wondered whether Grace had clashed with her mother about her grandmother going into a home. I also wondered why the name of the care home seemed familiar to me. But then I was distracted by the sound of a child's excited laughter and looked over to see Mark playing with the children of Richard and Sylvia's neighbour—hide-and-seek, by the look of it. The garden was quite large and divided into different sections with lots of shrubs and trees, so it was perfect.

I smiled, remembering umpteen games of hide-and-seek during my childhood.

"Hide-and-seek was one of Mark's favourite games when we were kids," I told Grace and laughed. "I remember one time he hid behind some stacked sheets of wood—it wasn't here, it was in the house in London. Anyway, it took me and Rosie ages to find him. And then, when it was his turn to hide again, he hid in the exact same place." I laughed again. "Rosie and I didn't think to look there because he'd hidden there the last time."

I could still remember Rosie's frustration at not being able to find her brother and our joint disbelief when we discovered him behind the wood sheets for the second time. The smile from the memory was still on my face when I turned to look at Grace. Only Grace wasn't smiling. Not at all. In fact, she looked . . . well, resentful. As if she hated me having a shared history with Mark. Was it possible that I made Grace insecure? Surely not. She always seemed so strong and together.

"It was a very long time ago," I said, but before I could say anything else, Josie, Richard and Sylvia's neighbour—the mother of the boys— joined us and spoke to Grace.

"That husband of yours will make an excellent father one day."

I returned my attention to Mark and saw he was running after the boys now, making them squeal delightedly as they tried to evade capture.

A familiar pang constricted my chest. Josie was right. Mark would make an excellent father. But I'd always known that, hadn't I? He was the sort of man who would read his kids bedtime stories even if he was tired after work. Stand in the rain to watch them play football. Get stuck in with the nighttime feeds and the nappy changes. It was all too easy to imagine Mark carrying a sleepy child up to bed, their arms curled trustingly around his neck. Or giving a child a piggyback ride, galumphing along like a crazed pantomime horse.

As I watched, Sylvia joined Mark and the boys, holding out a box of something to them—sweets or chocolates, judging by the enthusiastic way the boys thrust their hands inside it.

The neighbour shook her head. "Sylvia spoils my boys something rotten. She's longing to be a grandmother herself, I suppose. Anyway, excuse me; I'd better step in before they gorge themselves silly."

When she left, it was just me and Grace again, the atmosphere so brittle it was in danger of snapping. I sneaked a look at her, surprising a complicated expression on her face. She looked . . . well, pretty much how I felt myself. I recognised a fellow child craver when I saw one. Or at least I thought I did. Were she and Mark having trouble conceiving? Surely not. They hadn't been married long. It was far too early for them to be having problems like that. But I knew that even if they were, Grace wouldn't dream of telling me about it. Personal confidences came with friendship, and Grace had made it clear on Christmas Day that she didn't want to be my friend.

But then she surprised me by breaking the silence. "Have you met Jaimie's girls yet?"

I sighed, remembering the debacle of the previous weekend. "Yes. It didn't go very well." I described Emily's sulking and Olivia's clinginess.

Grace frowned. "Emily and Olivia aren't usually like that. They're delightful girls. Actually, Beth, as someone who knows them well, I wonder if I could offer you a bit of advice?"

Her skin was perfect. Her makeup was perfect. Her dress looked as if it had just come from the dry cleaner's instead of straight out of a ragbag like mine did, creased up after the drive here. I badly wanted to leave her to it and go get myself a second glass of wine.

"Of course," I said. "Please do."

"Well, it's nothing much, really. Just that they absolutely adore their mother, so if I were you, I wouldn't try to compete with her, because you'll never win. They'll come round to you. Just give them time."

"After last weekend, I'm not sure I'll be seeing them much again," I said.

Grace's expression grew suddenly intense. "Oh, but of course you will," she said. "Jaimie's crazy about you. You must know that. He told me so just the other day on the phone."

"Did he?" I wasn't sure how I felt about my boyfriend discussing our relationship with Grace. And shouldn't he have told me about his feelings before he told Grace about them?

"He did. In my opinion, it's only a matter of time before he asks you to move to Ely. I mean, neither of you can go on never having any time at weekends to do your chores forever, can you? Something's got to break. And I definitely don't get the feeling Jaimie wants that to be you and him."

I should have been pleased, I suppose. I was. I just didn't like Grace telling me how to feel and what to do. Or the fact that Jaimie had obviously confided in her about not having time to clear his guttering or iron his shirts. "You're obviously going to be a perfect parent one day, Grace," I said somewhat cattily. "You already know so much about it."

There was a brief silence. I felt cruel and wished I could take my words back.

"I don't pretend to be an expert at all," Grace told me coolly. "I just happen to have known those little girls all their lives."

I sighed. "Yes," I said, "of course you have. And thank you for the advice. I appreciate it."

"You're welcome," she said and moved away.

After a moment I moved away too, over to where Sylvia was helping herself to a plate of food from the buffet.

"This all looks delicious, Sylvia," I said. "I hope you haven't been baking for days on end?"

"No, everything's catered. Richard insisted on it. 'Sylv,' he said, 'this party is to celebrate our enduring love, not your ability to bake a sausage roll or a vol-au-vent.'" She giggled. "I didn't put up a fight. Nice for him to think he's spoiling me. Nice to be spoilt too."

"He's a very special person."

"He is. I must admit, I'm really looking forward to us retiring together. Did I tell you we're going to get a camper van?"

"You didn't, but I think it's a great idea. Will you go for a vintage VW or one of those huge Winnebago things?"

"Something between the two, I should think," said Sylvia. "Not too big to drive along country lanes, but large enough to be comfortable. We might get a little dog as well, when we're both around to look after it. It's never felt right before, with us both working." She looked over at Richard, her smile turning into a frown. "Whatever is he doing with that bell?"

I glanced over. Richard had hold of the handbell that lived on the mantelpiece above the fireplace—the one that had belonged to his grandmother and was in the shape of a lady wearing a crinoline gown. Rosie, Mark, and I had often used it in our games as kids, especially hide-and-seek. *Three, two, one, extended bell ring, coming!* Now, hearing the piercing sound it made as Richard rang it, I could appreciate why it had occasionally driven Sylvia crazy.

"Can I have your attention, please, everyone?" Richard called out, and we all stopped talking. "Sylv? Can you come over here for a minute, love?"

Richard held out his hand, and Sylvia went, her cheeks glowing. When she reached her husband, he pulled her close to his side. Rosie and I exchanged a smile.

"Thank you, everyone, for coming today. Sylvia and I really appreciate it. We were just saying this morning—weren't we, love?—that we can't believe it's been forty years since we got married. Only feels like yesterday since I stood at the altar feeling as nervous as one of Beth's skittish puppies."

There was a ripple of laughter. Several people looked round at me with a smile.

"Then I turned round and saw this vision in white standing next to me." He looked into Sylvia's eyes and pressed her hand to his lips. In front of me, I saw Rosie and Giorgio and Mark and Grace move closer together, stirred by the romance of it.

"Every couple has their downs as well as their ups," Richard continued, "but I'm so glad I've been strapped into that roller coaster next to you. Here's to another forty years. Well, thirty, at least."

Everybody laughed. Mark raised his glass. "To Mum and Dad, Richard and Sylvia."

We all raised our glasses.

"Mum and Dad."

"Richard and Sylvia."

Giorgio began to clap, and everyone joined in. Richard kissed Sylvia soundly, a cue for all the other couples to kiss, only me and Gary, Richard's confirmed-bachelor fishing buddy, left on our own with just our wineglasses for company.

"Wasn't that beautiful?" Josie, their neighbour, said to me after she'd disentangled herself from her husband.

"Really beautiful," I agreed. Because it had been beautiful. And my feeling miserable had nothing to do with anything.

But then there was the sound of a car pulling up outside. And a short while later, someone called my name. I turned to behold Jaimie walking towards me with the biggest smile on his face. And I felt as if I'd never been so pleased to see someone in my entire life.

"Jaimie! What are you doing here?"

He caught me in his arms. "Well, it turns out it doesn't take as long to fit a spiral staircase as I thought it did. Also, I've felt wretched all day, wishing I were here with you. So I came."

"Well," I said, grinning, "I'm very glad you did." As I sank into his arms, I saw Grace smiling at us over Mark's shoulder. And for once, I didn't mind her smug expression.

10

One of my favourite things about Jaimie's garden—my garden now too—was the hammock suspended between two trees at the bottom of it. On a sunny day, it was sheer bliss to lie there with the sun filtering through the leaves. If you swung it very gently, you travelled from full sun to dappled shade and back again to the accompaniment of birdsong and softly rustling leaves. Apart from the odd car in the close and the occasional thwack of a golf ball being struck on the golf course next door, there was perfect peace. At least there was on the weekends when the girls were with their mother, anyway.

Jaimie sometimes had to pop over to the property he was renovating or to a DIY emporium for supplies at weekends, and at times like those, I whisked round the house with the Hoover before rewarding myself with half an hour of sheer bliss in the hammock if the weather was sunny. Just me and my dreamy thoughts and the sounds of nature.

This morning the hammock seemed particularly blissful, since we'd eaten out the previous evening and had a bit of a late night, so I soon slipped into a doze, only to be woken by a persistent draft blowing on my neck. Without opening my eyes, I pulled my T-shirt up to cover it. But the persistent draft moved onto my face, and I fidgeted, wondering whether it was about to rain. Then I heard a rumble of laughter close by and opened my eyes to see Jaimie.

"How long have you been there?" I asked, realising he must have been blowing on me.

"Long enough to see what you get up to while I'm gone, lazy lugs."

"I'm only having five minutes before I put a wash on," I said. "I've done the Hoovering."

"Hey, I'm just teasing," he said. "It's the weekend. Why shouldn't you be lazy? Budge up. There's room on there for two."

"Are you sure?" I asked, gingerly trying to move without falling out.

"I'm sure."

Of course he was. He'd probably been in here with Harriet. And the girls.

Seconds later we were lying face-to-face, so close he'd probably be able to count the freckles the spring sunshine had no doubt brought out on my face.

He was smiling, little lines of happiness radiating from the corners of his eyes, and I smiled back, feeling as if I were in a bubble of contentment. Last night, when we'd got back from the restaurant, we'd made sleepy love, as gorgeous and rich as the chocolate sauce that had been drizzled onto my dessert. Now Jaimie's hand was stroking its way down my side to my hip, and the whole tingling cycle was starting up again, flickers of desire prickling my thighs to pool between my legs. I pressed myself into him, stroking his back, and we kissed—lazily at first, then with gathering urgency.

I expected him to speak, to say we should go inside, up to the bedroom, but he didn't. Instead, he swung himself off the hammock and bent to undress me right there in the garden.

"Someone might see us," I said, hiding my bare breasts with my hands.

"Nobody can see," he said, indicating the neighbour's house. "We're not overlooked."

"The postman might bring a parcel round the side gate," I said, but my protests were weakened by the way Jaimie was pulling my shorts down, placing kisses along my thighs as he did so. Besides, the hammock was swinging a bit now, and I needed to concentrate so I wouldn't fall off.

"No one's going to come," he said. "No one, that is, except for you."

And before I knew it, my knickers had gone too, and Jaimie was doing incredible things to me with his mouth.

A while later, we were both sated and lying side by side in the hammock again.

"God," I said. "That was good."

"Wasn't it?" Jaimie said, swinging the hammock.

My body felt like liquid—as if it could easily pour through the strings of the hammock onto the grass. But if I'd thought Jaimie might fall asleep, I was mistaken.

"Come on," he said after a few minutes. "Get up. I thought we could go into Cambridge and go punting."

"Punting?"

"Yeah, you know, one of those flat-bottomed boats you propel along with a pole?"

I whacked him on the arm, knowing he was being sarcastic. "I know what a punt is, silly. You just took me by surprise, that's all."

He laughed. "Well, anyway, I thought we could punt to Grantchester to have tea. There's a tea shop with tables in the old orchard. You'll love it."

It sounded wonderful. But did we have to go today? Right now?

Apparently, we did, because Jaimie was soon in full waggy-tailed golden retriever mode, tipping me out of the hammock, chasing me indoors, and booking both the punt and the tea on the internet while I showered and got changed.

It was a glorious afternoon, and as Jaimie punted us along the river, plunging the pole confidently into the water to propel us past the magnificent architecture of the famous colleges, I admired his muscular arms, watched the ducks and swans, and smiled at the antics of the punts filled with university students. One young lad, clearly trying to impress his girlfriend, pushed his pole into the riverbed a little too hard and almost left himself dangling from it when it wouldn't immediately come free. "Take care, Freddie," his girlfriend laughed. "I don't want to have to rescue you."

I smiled, struck by a chord of memory. Hadn't Mark fallen into the river when he was punting once? Yes, he had. I could distinctly remember his girlfriend at the time—had it been Sue? Mary?—telling us about it over dinner at Richard and Sylvia's. How Mark had had to climb out onto the bank because he couldn't get back into the punt, and had emerged covered in slimy green duckweed.

"What's funny?" Jaimie asked me.

"Nothing," I said. "I'm just having a good time, that's all."

"Another ten minutes and we'll be eating strawberries and cream in the orchard at the tearooms."

"Sounds utterly blissful," I said, tucking the memory about Mark and his slimy duckweed away and settling down to enjoy the view.

I didn't see Mark until early June, when he came up—with Grace, of course—for the Ely Folk Festival. The Folk Festival was an annual event held in the field where Milo liked to chase the trains. Apparently, Grace was a big folk fan and had been coming to the festival for years. I wasn't so keen on folk music myself, but Jaimie liked it, so I didn't mind.

"Jaimie!" said Grace as she got out of the car at ten o'clock on the dot, arms spread wide.

"Hello, Grace," Jaimie said, beaming, giving her a hug. "Hi, Mark. Great to see you."

When he emerged, he had Grace's red lipstick on his cheek, and she made a show of wiping it off for him before she turned my way.

She looked me up and down. "Hi, Beth," she said, with a kiss, kiss on both cheeks. "Look at you in your folksy dress. You don't see many like that in East London."

Grace herself was wearing skintight white jeans I would never in a million years have had the courage to wear and a skimpy red vest top. She looked amazing.

"Well," I said, probably sounding defensive, "I live here now, not East London."

"So you do," she said, patting my arm and walking past me as if she owned the place. "And it's good to see you here. Jaimie, I'd murder a cup of coffee before we set off. Is that all right? I didn't want to stop in case we got caught up in the traffic. And I'm desperate for the loo."

I turned from following her progress, and there was Mark.

"Hi, Beth."

"Hi."

He was wearing a crumpled blue shirt that made his eyes look sea green. I'd always liked him in forget-me-not blue. But I could have done without the gaping, tonsil-revealing yawn he was currently subjecting me to.

"Sorry," he said. "I slept nearly all the way here. Grace was listening to some work thing. You look lovely, by the way."

"Folksy, Grace just said." I wasn't even sure what that meant. Little old ladyish? Like a milkmaid?

He considered me, head tilted. "No, not folksy. Pretty. You look pretty."

I had never known how to take compliments from Mark, so I turned my back on him and led the way into the house. "Well, er, thank you. Shall we go in?"

"Better had. Grace and her coffee. She needs to get a main line set up. I'm going to hold out for a beer myself. There will be a beer tent at the festival, I assume?"

"I think so."

"D'you remember Paul and Rosemary, who ran the Student Union bar?" Grace asked Jaimie when we were sitting round the kitchen table and she was sipping her precious coffee.

"Once met, never forgotten," Jaimie said.

It was curious, watching him interact with Grace. I'd seen him talk to her at Richard and Sylvia's party, of course, but it was different here in his home. *Our* home. He was all smiles and bounce, the host with the most. But then we hadn't had any other chances to socialise with guests, so maybe this was just how he was. It was kind of cute.

"They were the oddest couple," he told me and Mark. "Both body-builders. Paul raced pigeons too. Gave them all strange names."

"What sort of names?" asked Mark.

"I don't know—ridiculous things, like Hercules."

"Don't forget Cleopatra," said Grace.

Jaimie laughed. "Oh yes. There was a Cleopatra, wasn't there? Didn't she go missing?"

"I think she did, yes."

"Maybe she ran off with Mark Antony," said Mark.

When I sniggered, he grinned at me.

Grace lifted her eyebrows. "Very funny, darling," she said, sweeping on with her tale. "Anyway, I ran into Paul and Rosemary the other month when I was giving a business advice session. They've just opened a pub outside Cambridge. Wanted advice about employing staff."

"Goodness," said Jaimie. "Fancy that. I can't imagine them running a business." He laughed, looking at me. "If she'd had a few drinks, Rosemary used to stand on a table and do all these muscle-rippling moves to make her tattoos come to life."

"What, like this?" asked Mark, striking a pose.

"Yes," said Grace. "But with more muscle."

"Hey," said Mark, pretending to be offended.

She stroked his face. "Don't worry, I never have found overly muscular men attractive."

"That's just as well," Mark said. "Because I have an accountant's muscles."

"Remember that bodybuilding competition Paul and Rosemary organised?" asked Jaimie, continuing the conversation as we set off on foot for the festival, and he and Grace were off down memory lane, walking in front, with Mark and I behind.

It was a perfect late-spring day, and the gardens were full of frothy lilacs and silky magnolias. When a tabby cat came out of someone's drive to weave around my legs, I stopped to stroke it.

"Still charming the animals, I see," said Mark.

"I try," I said, giving the tabby a final stroke before moving on. "How is everyone? Have you seen your parents lately?"

"Not for a few weeks. Mum sent you her love."

"That's nice. I must phone her."

"I'm quite surprised about today," he said.

I looked at him. "Surprised about what?"

"I didn't think you liked folk music."

I shrugged. "It's quiet in Ely. You have to make the most of any events that come up."

"The Folk Festival is a wonderful event," Grace chipped in. "Isn't it, Jaimie?"

"That's what I keep telling Beth," Jaimie said.

"I can't imagine why you think you don't like folk music, anyway. It's so beautiful. And some of it's very lively. You can certainly dance to it."

I can dislike folk music if I want to, I wanted to retort, but I kept on smiling, wondering whether Grace was this bossy with Mark. But of course she was.

"Are there too many milkmaids and wandering rovers in folk music for you?" Mark asked me, laughter in his voice.

Grace swept on, not giving me the chance to reply. "Folk music has so much history and depth. And passion. Maybe you've just been unlucky with what you've heard up until now. We'll have to educate her, won't we, Jaimie?"

"Sounds like she's in for a fun day," said Mark.

"Er, I am here, you know," I said, and Jaimie dropped back to give my hand a quick squeeze.

"We're only teasing you."

"Yeah, don't kick your milk pail over," said Mark. "We'll soon be roving around the beer tent."

"Very funny." I gave him the kind of shove Rosie would have given him had she been there and burst out laughing when he pretended to stagger. God, it was good to see him. I'd been a bit nervous about it, to be honest, but the familiarity of our banter was a warm rush I'd really missed. Even at the height of my teenage crush, he'd managed to make me laugh.

Grace and Jaimie had walked on a bit, still talking about old times, no doubt, so a space had opened up between them and us.

Enough space for Mark to be able to say, "I haven't seen Jaimie this happy for ages," without Jaimie hearing.

I looked at him. "Really?"

He nodded. "God, yes. He's a man transformed. Grace was so worried about him when he split from Harriet. One time she came over, and he was just lying on the floor sobbing his heart out. She said it was dreadful."

God, poor Jaimie. No wonder he didn't want to talk about it.

"Has Grace ever said why they split up? Jaimie's never told me." A part of me felt a bit bad, asking the question, but another part of me really wanted to know. When he wasn't missing the girls, Jaimie always seemed so sure of himself. In fact, he'd been at his most vulnerable the night we'd met, at the wedding reception.

Mark sighed. "I think Harriet just fell out of love with him. Wanted more from life than they had. Something like that. It's meant the world to him, you coming into his life."

I was glad.

"Did Grace visit him a lot?" I asked.

"After the split? Yes. Loads of times. We'd only just met, so I wasn't sure what I thought about it at first. But they're mates, aren't they? They've known each other forever." His mouth lifted at one corner. "Though obviously knowing someone ever since you watched a barmaid body popping in the Student Union is nothing compared to knowing someone ever since you chased them around the garden with a packet of itching powder."

A clap of laughter burst from me. "Oh, your bloody practical-joke phase! You were such a complete pain in the backside."

"You loved it."

I shook my head at him. "Your poor dad was always getting plastic fried eggs shoved onto his breakfast plate."

He grinned. "The dog went through a terrible phase of pooing on his favourite armchair as well."

I snorted. "That fake dog poop was about as realistic as the finger with a nail through it."

He laughed. "I'll have you know, that finger had Mum running to call for an ambulance several times!"

"Only in your imagination."

"You two, honestly," Grace said as she and Jaimie waited for us to catch up.

We were still in high spirits by the time we reached the festival field, and when Jaimie said, "Now, now, kiddies, best behaviour while we pay the nice man," I started laughing all over again, linking my arm in his.

He smiled down at me, pleased by his own humour, but then something caught his eye, and his smile amped up about 200 percent.

"Emily!" he called. "Olivia!" And I turned to see the girls racing towards us.

"Daddy!" Olivia cried, running full pelt at him. Both she and Emily were dressed in what were clearly their best dresses, their hair so elaborately plaited and entwined with flowers they looked as if they were dressed more for a wedding than a music festival.

Jaimie scooped Olivia up in his arms for a kiss, then put her down to kiss Emily. "Hello, you two!" he said, face alight. "Fancy seeing you here! And don't you both look lovely? Don't they look lovely, Beth?"

But anything I might have said was wiped out because the girls had noticed Grace.

"Auntie Grace! Auntie Grace! I've got a new dress!"

"It's beautiful, Olivia. You look just like a princess. You too, Emily. Oh, come here and get hugged, both of you."

It was the first time I'd seen Grace with the girls. Jaimie had told me how fond she was of them, and they of her, but this was the first time I'd witnessed it. I wasn't sure how I felt, to be honest. More inadequate than ever, probably.

The girls weren't on their own, of course. A tall, slim woman with long, dark hair was hard on their heels. She, too, was wearing a fancy summer dress, much fancier than my "folksy" bargain from Cambridge Market. Harriet—it had to be. Even if she hadn't been the spitting image of Emily, I'd have guessed it was her by the sudden tension wafting from Jaimie, inspired, no doubt, by the man at Harriet's side—a man as tall and slim as Harriet was, with dark eyes and jet-black hair. A man, moreover, who was casually holding Olivia's and Emily's abandoned cardigans over his arm.

"Harriet," Grace said, moving in to kiss her. "How good to see you."

Harriet kissed her back. "You too, Grace. It's been ages."

"It has. Far too long."

As they pulled apart, I saw Grace's gaze move on to the man by Harriet's side.

"Sorry," said Harriet. "This is Calum. Calum, this is my ex-husband, Jaimie, and his friend Grace." She cast a glance over at me and Mark.

"Hello, Calum," said Grace, drawing Mark forward. "This is my husband, Mark."

Mark shook Harriet's and Calum's hands. "Pleased to meet you."

"Likewise," said Calum, looking as if he wasn't sure whether to put his hand out to shake Jaimie's or not, but judging by Jaimie's thundercloud expression, he made the right choice when he decided not to.

All eyes were suddenly on me. Jaimie pulled himself together to introduce me. "This is Beth."

"She's Daddy's girlfriend," Olivia said helpfully.

"Yes, thank you, Olivia," Harriet said. "I guessed she must be."

"Hello, Harriet. Calum."

We shook hands. For a moment, nobody seemed to know what to say. Then Grace began to chatter on about the festival until Harriet looked at her watch. "Well, anyway, we're booked for a craft workshop to make teddy bear clothes, so we'd better go. I'm sure we'll run into you all again later. Hurry up, girls. Lovely to see you again, Grace."

The girls ran off with hardly a *Bye, Daddy* for Jaimie, and when I looked at him, I could tell he was totally devastated.

"I didn't even know Harriet was sodding well seeing anyone, and there he is, helping my daughters to make clothes for their teddy bears," he said.

"Oh, love," I said and was going to go comfort him, but Grace got there before me, taking his arm and sweeping him on towards the beer tent.

"You do know those girls will never love anyone as much as they love you, don't you, Jaimie?" I heard her telling him. "You're the perfect dad."

Which was exactly what I'd been going to say.

"I suppose so."

"Of course you are. Anyone else will always pale into insignificance. Now, come on; let's get a beer and track down some inspiring music."

Some girlfriend I was, letting someone else comfort my boyfriend when he was obviously distressed.

"He's bound to find it tough, seeing another man with his girls, I guess," Mark said as we followed.

I nodded, wondering whether Calum found the whole stepparenting thing as difficult as I did. It was a shame the two of us couldn't get together to share notes. Discuss tactics. "Yes."

In the music tent, we sat in a row, with Mark and me at either end and Jaimie and Grace in the middle.

"Are you okay?" I asked Jaimie, reaching for his hand.

He gave a brave smile. "I'll have to be, won't I? I can't stop Harriet seeing someone. It's just another thing to get used to, isn't it?"

"Grace is right, you know. Nobody will ever replace you in their eyes."

He sighed. "I know."

The band began to play its set, one song following another and sounding—to my ears, at least—remarkably similar to the one that had preceded it. I kept hold of Jaimie's hand, hoping the music would cheer him up. That sometime in the future he'd be able to accept Calum, if only because he loved his girls and their happiness was the most important thing.

And then I tried to imagine Emily and Olivia having fun with practical jokes. Would they like them? Probably. Didn't all kids like them? I'd liked it when Mark sometimes roped me and Rosie in, persuading us to join him in jumping out from behind the fridge to spray poor Richard with our water pistols. Or to slide whoopee cushions into place on the sofa as somebody sat down.

Poor Richard and Sylvia. They must have been saints. Either that or very good at hiding their true feelings.

Mark may have moved on from practical jokes when he discovered football, girls, and cars, but I knew he'd still laugh his head off if anyone tried to trick him with fake dog poop. Some things never changed.

At the interval, Mark and I headed for the bar together to get more drinks, leaving Grace and Jaimie chatting animatedly about Jaimie's latest renovation project.

"Why d'you think Jaimie and Grace didn't get together when they were at uni?" I asked Mark as we waited to get served.

"Didn't Jaimie meet Harriet very early on?" he said. "I think they were just all in the same group of friends. Besides, Grace was fated to meet me, wasn't she?"

I knew that, as a mathematician who frequently got his mind blown about the origins of the universe, Mark would never really believe in such a thing as fate. But I was slightly fuzzy headed from drinking beer before lunchtime. Enjoying being in Mark's company. So I teased, "Did an astrology expert see your meeting with Grace in the stars, then?"

He nodded. "Yep, that's right. By the way, talking of stars, did you know there are two hundred billion trillion of them in the universe?"

I considered his question. "I think you've told me that before once. Only I'm pretty sure last time you said it was two hundred billion trillion and one."

He laughed. "You're right. I apologise. God, it's so good to see you. You can't imagine."

I bloody well could.

"Rosie asked me to check up on you. Make sure you're happy here. So are you?"

The question sobered me up instantly. It ought to have been straightforward to answer. After all, Mark had just told me how much happier Jaimie was since I'd moved here. But somehow I couldn't help thinking of the day I'd actually moved away from Dalston. My churned-up feelings as Jaimie drove the hired van away from my flat. The way I'd craned my neck out the window to try and catch a last glimpse of my plane tree. It was still hard to accept I would never enjoy that garden again, not properly.

But then, what good was a garden on your own, really?

"Yes, I am," I said. "The girls can be a bit hard work sometimes. But we're getting there, slowly. I do miss some of the things I left behind, though. You lot, for one."

I'd had every intention of saying that casually, but my voice went and cracked. And as we hadn't been served yet, I didn't even have a glass of beer to hide behind.

Mark was staring at me. "We miss you too," he said, pulling me in for a hug. "But nothing's changed really, has it? Not really. We're still family. We still love you."

Bloody hell. I was going to start crying in a minute.

I tried another smile—more successfully this time—and put some space between us. "I know you do. And I am all right, honestly. Tell Rosie that."

"All right. But if you ever need to talk . . ."

God, I couldn't smile again. "Thanks. I appreciate that. Look, you couldn't bring my beer for me when you get served, could you? I've just thought of something I need to tell Jaimie."

Sweet, waggy-tailed Jaimie, who didn't deserve to have been discarded by Harriet for no good reason at all.

"Sure."

I found him on his own in the music tent, Grace having popped to the loo. He looked a bit forlorn, and I guessed he'd probably been thinking about his girls.

I sat down next to him and gave him a big kiss.

"What was that for?" he asked, holding me.

I smiled back, shrugging. "No reason. Just because," I said, and kissed him again.

Then I settled down to give folk music a better try than I'd done before. And sometime during the afternoon, a man with the most beautiful voice I'd ever heard sang a song called "Carrickfergus."

"Oh," I said, after it was over. "That was so beautiful. The words, the tune, the voice—everything."

"Are you crying, Beth Bailey?" Mark teased me, and I gave him a watery grin.

"Might be," I said, and Jaimie laughed.

"We have a convert, Grace!" he said.

"There you are, you see, Beth," she said. "I told you so, didn't I?"

With the magic of the song still upon me, not even smug Grace could kill my mood. "You did indeed, Grace. You did indeed."

11

The folk festival was a distant memory on the Saturday before Christmas, as Jaimie and I got ready to take the girls to see Father Christmas. Both of them were beside themselves with excitement—even Emily, who usually liked to play it cool—and it was catching. I was really looking forward to it as we donned our coats and hats in the hallway, and I'm not actually a Father Christmas fan.

I hadn't got anything against him personally, you understand, or I wouldn't have had if he were real. But he wasn't real, and I'd always loathed the whole spinning-an-elaborate-web-of-lies-to-children aspect of Father Christmas. All that magical-sleigh, flying-reindeer, and coming-down-the-chimney crap. It seemed so wrong to spend all year encouraging children to be honest only to totally deceive them. If I had a child of my own, I just didn't think I could do it. But when I'd said that to Rosie once, she had pointed out that everyone else would tell them about it. That I'd take my son or daughter to the school Christmas fair, and there would be Santa, giving out presents and ho-ho-hoing, and if I didn't let my little one join the queue, they'd be left out and devastated. It was a total dilemma.

Anyway, Olivia and Emily had been well and truly hoodwinked by the big FC scam long before I came onto the scene, so there was no point in me trying to exert my principles or stand on any moral high horse. A trip to see the bearded man was a highly anticipated event on the pre-Christmas agenda, so I might as well get into it. And if nothing else, it was another potential bonding opportunity. The girls were bound to be in a good mood, and if they were in a good mood, maybe I'd have more luck getting close to them.

As we set off in the car, Olivia was so excited she could hardly keep still in her seat. Or at least she was excited until Jaimie drove right past the turnoff for Cambridge and headed in the opposite direction.

"Daddy," cried Olivia. "We missed it!"

"No, we didn't," said Jaimie. "We're going to see Father Christmas somewhere different this year."

"But Mummy always takes us to Cambridge," she said tremulously.

"We like Cambridge," Emily added.

Jaimie's smile stiffened. "Well, you'll like seeing him at Thursford too," he said. "I promise. There's a magical wonderland to walk through on the way to see him, with dancing penguins and everything."

In the side-view mirror, I could see Olivia's worried expression as she weighed whether seeing a dancing penguin was worth it.

"How far is Fursford?" she asked.

"Not far. Just over an hour or so. It's in Norfolk."

The girls hated travelling any distance. When we'd gone on holiday to Greece, they'd moaned and complained all the way to Stansted Airport, and that was twenty minutes closer to Ely than Thursford.

I knew why Jaimie was doing this, of course. Because he wanted to outdo Harriet. To put all Harriet's trips to see Father Christmas into the shade, so the only way she could outdo him next year was to fly the girls to Lapland. And I had a sneaking feeling that if she didn't fly them to Lapland, then Jaimie would do so when his turn came round again. Even though Emily would be ten then and surely sceptical about Father Christmas at that age, if she wasn't now.

I felt a bit like an alien from another planet when we reached Thursford. An alien who'd been suddenly sucked up into a giant, shaken-up snow globe. I hadn't been anywhere like this since I was Emily's age. No, I had *never* been anywhere like this. Because places like this hadn't even existed when I was a kid.

If they had, I had no doubt I'd have been as excited as Olivia obviously was, standing there with her mittened hands clenched into fists, open mouthed at all the amazing illuminated creatures and palm trees as far as she could see. This part of the Thursford experience was billed as an "Enchanted Journey of Light," and it was certainly living up to its name.

Maybe I hadn't been anywhere like this before. Maybe I didn't have much experience with children. But I had been a child once. I had experienced the magic and anticipation of Christmas. And Thursford was magic and anticipation by the dumper truckload. All I had to do was dive in.

"Olivia," I said, pointing. "Look at that giraffe! Shall we go and see it?"

She took off at a run, and I laughed, running after her. But by the time I reached the giraffe, she was already running on towards a lion. "Wait for me!" I cried, laughing.

"Don't go off on your own, Olivia," Jaimie called after us. "We need to keep together."

When I joined the lion, Olivia was still there. She pointed. "Look, Beth, the mummy lion's got a baby," she told me.

I crouched down next to her. "So she has. Isn't it adorable? D'you think it's a boy or a girl?"

"A girl. She's called . . . Lexie."

"Is she? What a lovely name."

As we gazed at Lexie together, somehow Olivia's hand crept up into mine, giving me a start. It was the first time she had ever held my hand because she wanted to. Without being forced to because we were crossing a road.

Hardly daring to believe it, I froze, the lion cub blurring in front of my eyes, my entire attention focussed on not blowing the precious moment by punching the air or jumping up and down with joy. Any hint of crazy, over-the-top hand-clinger behaviour was likely to cause Olivia to bolt. And having her willingly hold my hand was such a bloody hard-won achievement that I wanted it to last forever.

It didn't, of course. Olivia dropped my hand and took off as soon as her fascination with the lion cub came to an abrupt end. But as I followed her to join Emily and Jaimie, it didn't matter. Olivia had held my hand once, so she would do it again.

All I had to do now was win over her sister.

The joy stayed with me right the way through the Enchanted Journey of Light, and on inside to the automated displays on either side of the pathway that wove through the Magical Journey leading to Father Christmas's grotto.

There were snowmen and giant teddy bears, elves with banging hammers busy making toys for Santa. The famous dancing penguins. Just as she had done outside, Olivia kept running on ahead to see what was next, and Jaimie kept calling her back to point out some unnoticed detail, keen to make the experience last.

Emily made slower progress, examining each display carefully. It was a perfect opportunity to spend some quality time with her.

I went over to join her in front of a display of animated polar bears. Her long dark hair was lying silkily against her red coat, her dark eyes taking everything in. She really was the most beautiful child. Or she would be if only she smiled more often. I so wanted to connect with her, to find a way to stop her viewing me as some kind of threat. I just needed to find some common link, that was all. Animals were the obvious answer.

"The polar bears are so sweet, aren't they?" I said.

Emily nodded but didn't answer.

I tried again. "Look, that one's carrying a basket. I wonder what she's got in it?"

"If it were real life, she wouldn't have a basket," Emily said.

She wasn't wrong. "That's true," I said. Then, desperate to keep the conversation going: "What d'you think a polar bear would put in a basket if it did have one?"

The look Emily gave me could only be described as pitying. I wasn't at all surprised when she moved on to the next display without answering, leaving me there on my own, feeling utterly foolish and despondent. *Good one, Beth.* How had I expected her to reply to such a ridiculous question? *I think a polar bear would put seal guts in their basket, Beth.*

And just like that, much of the happiness and confidence from Olivia holding my hand evaporated. I joined Emily at the next display anyway, telling myself sternly that today was about the girls, not me. That there would be other times to connect with Emily, once she'd got over thinking I was a prize idiot who speculated about the contents of a fictional polar bear's basket.

Maybe all my attempts at positive thinking paid off, because suddenly Emily said, "Fish pie."

I looked at her, ridiculously pleased she had spoken but not having the faintest idea what she was on about. "Fish pie?"

"I think the polar bear would have fish pie in her basket."

I smiled, feeling as if I'd won the lottery. "Excellent suggestion."

As you'd expect, there were children everywhere in the Magical Journey. Children older than Olivia and Emily, as well as younger children too. All gazing in wonderment at the displays. Or gaping boggle eyed from their buggies or their fathers' arms or charging along in their all-in-one zip-up suits to stop and point at something. "Mumma, look!"

Thursford was definitely the very last place on earth for a person with a rampaging biological clock.

I might not have found being a sort-of stepmother easy, but that didn't mean I'd be a bad mother. If I had a baby, we'd learn together, I knew we would. There wouldn't be anyone else's shoes to fill except my own, for one thing. No ghost of Harriet.

But I couldn't have a baby by myself, could I? Jaimie had promised we would revisit the subject of having children in six months' time. By then I would be thirty-six. And that was old to start thinking of having a baby. My chances of conceiving would be even slimmer than they were now.

Just then my hungry gaze was caught by a particularly gorgeous baby girl with a mop of bright red hair. She was staring at me over her father's shoulder. When I waved to her, she gurgled, bashing her father with the toy she was holding, and her dad looked round to see what had caught her attention. I looked away quickly, moving on, remembering Mark's wedding, when Rosie had chided me for devouring the children.

Finally, we reached the end of the displays, and it was time to meet Father Christmas. A teenage boy who was dressed as an elf ushered us through a doorway, and there he was in his glittering grotto, complete with a long white beard, a red suit, and a bulging sack of presents at his side.

The costume department had made an effort, I'd give it that. The beard looked real, not like some of the cotton wool held on by elastic confections you sometimes saw. But I still didn't like him much. Not that it was anything personal. I'd just associated Father Christmas with disappointment since I was four years old, that was all. And Mark was entirely to blame.

Rosie and I were four, and Mark was seven. It was a sunny day in late October, and we were all out in the park at London Fields. I can't remember what Rosie and I were playing—one of our "let's pretend" games, probably. Anyway, our mums were sitting on a picnic blanket in their coats, and us kids were a short distance away from them but clearly within sight. Mark had pedalled off on his bike to see some friends.

Then, suddenly, he came pedalling quickly back, his face bright red and his legs pumping up and down. When he got close, I saw he was trying desperately not to cry.

"Father Christmas's not real!" he shouted. "It's all a big fat lie. Stephen Thomas just told me. He says it's just our dads. He saw his dad put the presents under the Christmas tree last year."

Message delivered, he pedalled away again, leaving Rosie and me to stare at each other in dumb shock. Father Christmas not real? Could it really be true? By a sort of silent mutual consent, we didn't discuss it, just traipsed back to our mothers with quiet, miserable faces. We refused to answer when Sylvia asked, "What on earth's up with you two?"

When Mark pedalled up shortly afterwards in the same sorry state, our mums shook their heads at the unpredictability of children and took us home. But one afternoon, just before Christmas, I was at Rosie's house, and Mark presented us with proof of what I'd instinctively known was true ever since that day in the park.

"Come and see what I've found," he said, whispering so Sylvia— who was downstairs in the kitchen dealing with the weekly wash— wouldn't hear.

We followed Mark into Sylvia and Richard's bedroom, where we found their huge, dark wooden wardrobe standing open. Mark half climbed inside, lifting up an old blanket. "Look," he said to his sister. "You asked Father Christmas for a My Little Pony, didn't you? Well, there it is!"

I watched as Rosie lifted the box from beneath the blanket and peered through the plastic at the gloriously maned pony inside. She was smiling at first, happy she was going to get the toy she had asked for.

"If Mum and Dad wrap this up and say it's from Father Christmas, that's proof it's all a lie," Mark said.

Just then, Sylvia called up to us from downstairs. "Are you kids all right up there? You're being awfully quiet."

Mark snatched the My Little Pony toy from his sister's hands and shoved it back under the blanket. Leaving him to close the wardrobe, Rosie and I trailed out of the bedroom, Rosie sucking her thumb—something she hadn't done in ages.

It wasn't Mark's fault. He'd just been so devastated to find out the truth that he'd needed to share the misery to feel better. And on Christmas morning, when Rosie opened her My Little Pony toy from Father Christmas, she didn't say anything about anything. But she never did love that horse as much as she'd expected to, and somehow Christmas lost some of its sparkle.

But Olivia and Emily's sparkle about Christmas and Father Christmas was still fully intact, and I watched as they quietly answered Father Christmas's questions about what they wanted for Christmas. Noticed the polite way they smiled as they accepted their gifts. They were awed by him—even cynical, too-old-for-her-age Emily.

Jaimie, of course, was beaming, snapping away on his phone while the girls and FC smiled dutifully for him, confident his girls would remember this moment forever.

But then it was time to leave, and I watched any awe Emily and Olivia had felt dissolve as soon as the wrapping paper was ripped off and cast aside, the presents approved of but quickly forgotten.

It was a relief when it was time to get back in the car for the drive back to Ely and I was free to stop smiling my fake smile.

"All right?" Jaimie asked, placing his hand on my knee after the girls had fallen asleep in the back.

I covered his hand with mine. "Mm-hmm."

"I think they liked it, don't you?"

"How could they not? It was magical, as billed."

"The elves were a bit grumpy, though, I thought."

I assumed he meant the teenagers dressed up in elf outfits with ridiculous fake pointed ears, not the mechanical toy-making elves.

"You would have been grumpy, too, at their age."

"I'd have been glad to have been earning some cash."

"It was all fine. The girls didn't notice any teenage angst. Honestly. They loved every minute of it." I thought about confiding in him regarding my faux pas with Emily at the polar bear display, then thought better of it. Emily might not be as sound asleep as she appeared to be. Besides, I knew what Jaimie would say. *Try not to take it so personally. Hang in there; she'll come round eventually.*

"What time's everyone arriving tomorrow?" Jaimie asked.

"About twelve."

Mark, Grace, and Rosie were all arriving the next afternoon—Rosie to stay for a few days, and Mark and Grace en route to Norwich to see her sister again. I was really looking forward to seeing Rosie. I still hadn't got used to not seeing her two or three times a week like I used to. But Mark and Grace? Not so much. I'd felt unsettled after their last visit. But that had been months ago. Surely things would be easier this time.

"I was thinking of asking Grace if she wants to take a look at my property after lunch. She could come with me when I drop the girls off. Then we could go straight on to Fordham. If that's all right with you?"

It actually sounded like heaven. With Grace and the girls gone, it would be like the old days round at Mark's flat—just me, Rosie, and Mark. Though without the sounds of the crowd from the football ground next door.

"Of course that's fine. It will be good for you to get her opinion."

"I hope she'll like what I've done."

"Of course she will. You made a big success of the last place, after all. You know what you're doing."

"I do seem to, don't I? It was always a risk, quitting teaching. But thanks to Grace, it was a considered risk. You have to go for your dreams, don't you?"

What I really felt like doing was falling asleep like the girls. To fill the distance between Thursford and home with oblivion. Clearly it was not to be. Jaimie wanted to talk, which was fair enough, since he was the driver. But I wished he didn't want to talk about this. It was depressing. My dream had always been to be a veterinary nurse. In fact, my role at Dalston Vets had pretty much been my dream job. Perhaps it was time to ring round all the local veterinary surgeries again to see if any vacancies had come up.

"Thanks for coming along today," Jaimie said. "It meant a lot to me. You mean a lot to me. I hope you know that."

I smiled, shoving aside my miserable thoughts. "Thank you. You mean a lot to me too."

That evening, Jaimie presented me with an early Christmas gift in a sparkly silver bag.

"Here," he said. "I got you this."

"I can't open this," I said. "It's not Christmas yet."

"I've bought you something else for Christmas. This is just a little something extra."

"You spoil me."

He shrugged. "You deserve to be spoiled. Go on, open it."

Intrigued, I opened the package. Inside it was a dress—a sophisti-cated-looking black one. And, in a smaller packet, a bright red lipstick.

"They're lovely," I said, baffled.

"I thought you could wear them tomorrow."

I frowned. "Tomorrow?"

"Yes. You're not dog walking, are you? And we're going out for a meal later on. Grace always looks so glamorous, doesn't she? I thought you'd like to too. Go on, try it on."

"What, now?"

"Yes, why not?"

I was still wearing the jeans and jumper I'd been wearing all day. If the girls hadn't used up all the hot water for their baths, I'd have been in my pyjamas and dressing gown after a good old soak myself. I was feeling a bit sleepy after our day out and not in the mood to put on glamorous clothes. But, of course, I went upstairs to get changed. It would have been churlish not to. I had to wriggle a bit to get the dress over my head—it was quite tight fitting—but as I pulled it down over my hips, I knew that was the way it was supposed to be.

I stood in front of the mirror, gazing at my reflection. I'd lost a few pounds since moving to Ely, maybe in part due to the vegetarian diet. Anyway, for whatever reason, there were fewer bulges for the tight-fitting jersey material to emphasise, and I suspected Jaimie would approve. But did he really mean for me to wear it all day the next day? Not just for our meal out?

Jaimie joined me at the mirror. "You look fabulous," he said. "Like the woman I met at the wedding reception last Christmas."

I frowned, meeting his gaze in the mirror. "Is that who you want me to be?" I asked. "Do I disappoint you?"

"Of course not!" He turned me round to face him, planting a kiss on my lips. "I just think you look even more gorgeous than ever when you make a bit of an effort. Now, let's get this off, shall we?"

"I only just put it on."

"So?" he said, kissing me again.

12

I wore the dress the next day, as Jaimie had requested. And the lipstick. I even painted my nails red to match. The girls loved it and asked me to paint their nails too.

"What's this colour called, Beth?" Olivia asked.

I tilted the bottle of nail polish to take a look. "Cherry Kisses."

"Strawberry Kisses would be better," Emily said. "I don't like cherries."

"No," agreed Olivia. "They're yucky."

"It's a nice red, though, don't you think?" I said. "Well, I hope you do, because it's the only colour I've got."

"It's okay," said Emily, holding out her hand.

"Me first!" said Olivia, trying to barge her sister away.

"I tell you what, I'll do one of Emily's hands, and then I'll do one of yours, Olivia."

"But we need both our hands done," protested Olivia.

I pretended to be surprised. "Do you? Are you sure?"

"Yes, silly."

"Okay, then. Both hands it is."

Then, when I was painting the nails on her left hand, Olivia smiled cheekily and said, "Poo-poo brown is a good colour for nail varnish."

She erupted into giggles, watching my face. I wasn't sure whether I ought to have been rebuking her, especially as I badly wanted to smile.

"Dog Dirt Damson," suggested Emily, impressing me with her knowledge of fruit.

"I tell you what," I said. "Next time I go shopping, I'll be sure to keep a lookout for both those shades."

But Olivia hadn't finished. "Dog Wee White!" she said, giggling.

"Dog wee isn't white—it's yellow!" Emily corrected her.

"Thank you, girls. I think that's enough, don't you?" I said, finally stepping in. "If you like dogs so much, you can help out at the dog show my company is running next spring."

Their eyes grew wide with excitement. "Can we, Beth? Really and truly?"

"Yes, of course. You can help to judge the waggiest-tail competition." I looked at them, mock stern. "Of course, you'll have to promise to be sensible. No being cheeky. No being rude."

"We promise. Don't we, Emily?"

"Good," I said. "I'm glad to hear it. Now, we'd better paint the nails on your other hands, hadn't we?"

My heart lifted as I got busy with the nail polish again. For five minutes or so, the girls and I had actually had fun together. Maybe Jaimie was right. Maybe it was just a question of time. Perhaps being more girlie or joking around was the way to break down some of the barriers between me and Jaimie's daughters.

But before I could start pencilling in a spa break or stand-up comedy gig, the girls ran off to play Pop-Up Pirate!, smearing their nail varnish in the process and forcing Jaimie out to the superstore for nail polish remover when I discovered I hadn't got any. "Harriet will go crazy when she sees them in that state," he muttered as he left the house.

While he was gone, the Pop-Up Pirate! game deteriorated into a row, Emily announced she was bored, and Olivia kept rushing to the window to ask when "Auntie Grace" was going to arrive.

Partly to escape, I ventured outside to the woodpile in my unsuitably glamorous dress for logs to keep the wood burner going. It was drizzling, the sky like a wet grey flannel stretched out behind the spindly branches of the grey poplar trees beyond the property. Ghastly Grey, Olivia might have called it. Miserable Murk.

As I stood there, I could hear nothing—absolutely nothing at all. No birdsong, no golfers on the golf course. The idyllic hammock-slumbering days of summer were a distant memory. And suddenly I was overwhelmed with nostalgia for my old neighbourhood. For my garden and my old flat. Had my tenants taken good care of it? They'd promised to do so, but that didn't mean they had. Their tenancy had just ended, so I would need to go and check the place over before I let it anyway, so I'd soon see.

Staring out at the spindly trees, I pictured myself going down my steps, letting myself in. Would it still feel like home? Or would I feel a bit displaced, the way I did here sometimes?

The sound of Jaimie's car pulling into the drive reached me, and I shook my head at myself, turning my back on the garden and going into the house.

Jaimie was in the kitchen. He held up a bottle of nail varnish remover and a bag of chocolate chip cookies to show me. "Peace offering," he said. "Sorry I snapped."

I shrugged. "No, it's all right. I should have thought. They're too young for nail varnish just yet."

He gave me a little squeeze and moved past me to put the kettle on. "Maybe just a little," he agreed.

And somehow, hug or not, shared laughter with the girls or not, I felt as if I'd failed. Again.

Mark, Grace, and Rosie arrived promptly at twelve o'clock. Of course they did—Grace was driving. If it had been Rosie behind the wheel, we'd have been given a two-hour window for their arrival, the exact time being determined by when Rosie got up. She was notoriously late for everything, which made it constantly surprising that she had such a high-powered job involving lots of travel. Rosie was to catch a train back to London on Tuesday, just in time for Christmas with her parents at Enfield. She'd already called me a traitor because I wasn't going there this year, but I could hardly leave Jaimie, as this was his big Christmas with his girls. And besides, after abandoning me for Giorgio the previous year, she didn't have a leg to stand on anyway.

The girls rushed out the front door the second the car pulled into the drive.

"Auntie Grace! Auntie Grace! Our Christmas tree is even bigger than the one we had last year!"

"Is it really? Good job I've brought you lots of presents to put under it. Come here and let me hug you."

Rosie was emerging from the car, stretching and yawning like a sleepy squirrel. I walked past the girls to hug her.

"Hello, you," she said, hugging me back.

"Hello, you back. Hi, Mark."

He bent to kiss me. "Hi, Beth."

Rosie yawned. "Sorry, I only woke up when we got to Cambridge."

"She had a bit of a late night last night," Mark explained. "Wasn't even dressed when we arrived to pick her up."

"Well, it is nearly Christmas," Rosie said. "Some of us like to go out and have a good time at this time of year instead of staying in with Netflix."

I grinned. God, it was good to hear them bickering.

"I've missed this," I said. "Did you have a good journey?"

"Yes, all fine. Except for when I woke up. I thought there must have been a nuclear disaster or something."

"She means all the black fields," Mark explained. "Or at least I think she does."

"It's only because they've been ploughed," I said. "They looked a bit better before that."

"The soil in the Fens is some of the most fertile in England," added Jaimie, sounding put out.

Actually, I thought Rosie's description was pretty accurate. The vast black fields stretching as far as the eye could see were a bit depressing.

At first, when I'd moved here, the emptiness of the place scared me. In London, if you wanted to see a long view, you had to go to Hampstead Heath or pay a small fortune to go to the top of the Shard. In the Fens, there was nothing but long views—the fields stretched away into the distance, unrelentingly flat. And the skies were huge. Beautiful sometimes, but huge.

"Don't listen to my sister, mate," said Mark, stepping forward to shake Jaimie's hand. "She'd be lost without sugar in her coffee."

"Actually, potatoes are the main crop these days, not sugar beet," Jaimie explained as he and Mark went indoors. Grace followed with the girls, who were still clinging to her like monkeys and bombarding her with compliments and questions. Her coat was open, allowing me to see that she was dressed in jeans. Expensive designer jeans, but jeans nevertheless. So much for the glamour Jaimie had been on about.

Rosie and I stood with our arms still around each other, watching them.

"Popular, isn't she?" said Rosie.

I shrugged. "She's glamorous and stylish. A link to their past too."

"They still casting you as the Wicked Witch of the East, then?"

"Not all the time. Sometimes, I suppose. I think we're starting to get somewhere, though."

Rosie shook her head, considering me. "Good. Because you'd never cut it as a wicked witch. Witches use too many frog toes and newt eyes in their potions. How's the dog walking going?"

I shrugged. "It's fine."

"As good as that, eh?"

"It'll do for now. How about you? Where's the gorgeous Giorgio this Christmas?"

It was her turn to shrug. "Gone to see his family."

I looked at her. "You haven't broken up again?"

She shrugged. "I don't know. Possibly. D'you mind if we don't talk about it? Anyway, why are you done up like a dog's dinner? Is there a party I wasn't told about or something?"

I smiled ruefully. "D'you mind if we don't talk about it?"

We joined the others in the sitting room. Mark was reaching forward, apparently to get something from Olivia's hair. "You've got something behind your ear, Olivia."

She squealed. "What is it, what is it?"

"It appears to be . . ." Mark drew his hand back and held up a chocolate wrapped in golden foil. "A chocolate. Whatever is it doing behind your ear?"

Olivia jumped up and down, trying to reach it. "Give it to me! Give it to me!"

"Not too many, Olivia," said Jaimie, but he was smiling. "It's almost lunchtime. Beth's made some lovely soup."

"I want one!" said Emily.

"Well," said Mark, examining the side of her head, "let's have a look, shall we? Yes, you're in luck. There's one behind your ear too." He drew it out and threw it to her. She caught it, grinning all over her face.

"Has he been practising that?" I asked Rosie, but it was Grace who answered.

"Practising what? It's magic."

I think it was the first time she'd ever made me laugh. Maybe there was hope of us becoming friends after all.

The soup was lentil and vegetable—a recipe I'd perfected since my switch to vegetarianism, and we ate it with the freshly baked bread Jaimie had brought back from the superstore when he'd bought the nail polish remover.

"How's your latest project coming along, Jaimie?" Grace asked between sips.

Jaimie nodded enthusiastically. "Really well, thanks. I'll be ready to put it on the market in the New Year. I thought you might like to come over and see it this afternoon, actually, if Mark doesn't mind? If you'd like to, that is."

"I'd love to."

"No problem, mate," said Mark. "Go for it."

"Thank you," said Grace.

I wasn't sure whether she was being sarcastic or not at the idea she had to get Mark's approval before agreeing. In any case, she was talking to the girls now.

"I've got early Christmas presents for you both if Daddy doesn't mind? There's just time for you to open them before you go back to your mum's. You don't mind, do you, Jaimie?"

He could hardly say he did, with Grace's hand already in her bag and Olivia jumping up and down in front of him.

"Of course not; it's fine."

Jaimie's benign expression didn't even change when Grace's impromptu presents turned out to be makeup sets, albeit without the controversial nail polish. Honestly, I despaired, I really did.

It was a distinct relief when they all headed off, leaving me, Rosie, and Mark on our own, and silence descended on the house. I made coffee, and the three of us sat lined up in a row on the sofa in front of the wood burner, Rosie in the middle and Mark and I on either side of her. Together we watched the flickering flames, each holding a mug, content for a while to be silent.

It was Rosie who broke the silence. No surprise there. It was always Rosie who broke a silence. "So," she said to Mark, "what's all this I hear about you resigning from your job?"

"You're resigning?" I sat forward in my seat to look at him.

"Yes, that's the plan. In the New Year. I'm going to go it alone." He smiled. "Become a wealthy, hot-shot entrepreneur. That type of thing."

I looked at him, carefully examining that smile. It didn't convince me, somehow. "How does that feel?"

The smile fell away. "It terrifies the life out of me, to be honest."

"Grace's idea, I presume?" Rosie said.

"Yes, I suppose so. But she does have a point, doesn't she? I am stuck in a rut. Have been for years."

"A cosy, fur-lined rut," said Rosie. "You like your job."

"I guess. But it's time for a change. I've been there for years."

I wanted to ask more questions, to try and find out what he really thought about the changes he was about to make. But he got in first, diverting the conversation to me.

"Anyway, how about you, Beth? How's it going with renting your flat out?"

I pulled a face. "My tenants just moved out, actually, so I've got to find someone new."

"That shouldn't be hard, though, should it?"

"Hopefully not."

Mark's gaze travelled around the living room, taking in the chintz sofa, the floral curtains, and the bowl of potpourri on the coffee table. Jaimie still lived in his marital home—he'd remortgaged in order to buy Harriet out, and I suspected he'd kept the fluffy, floral things around for the girls' sake. "I loved your old flat. It was so completely you. If you don't mind me saying, it doesn't look as if you've had the chance to leave your mark on this place yet."

"Says the man who put all his things in storage when he got married," scoffed Rosie.

"Not all my things."

"Oh yeah, sorry, I forgot. You were allowed your gaming chair, just so long as it stayed in the spare bedroom."

Mark shrugged. "Well, that is where I go to play computer games."

"Still allowed to do that, then, are you?"

I saw a flicker of irritation cross Mark's face.

"Put your claws back in, sis. Please. As you said, it's nearly Christmas."

Rosie shrugged. "I'm just saying . . ."

"Well, don't."

"Just looking out for my favourite brother."

"Your *only* brother can look out for himself, thank you."

It was sort of like Saturday afternoons in Mark's flat, brother and sister sparring, me acting as the audience, only the subject matter was different. Back then, we'd all been single.

"Maybe, but I still think you've both changed yourselves to suit your partners. I mean, would you really have tried naturism if you hadn't met Jaimie, Beth?"

"Probably not," I had to admit. "But then maybe I'd have been missing out."

Rosie laughed. "Oh, come on! The only thing naturism's given you is a nasty head cold."

Sometimes I wished I didn't confide so comprehensively in Rosie. "I was probably coming down with one anyway. And anyway, naturism has given me more than that. A sense of freedom. Confidence about my body . . ."

Rosie ignored me, which was sensible. I didn't really believe what I was saying, and Rosie, knowing me as she did, could no doubt detect that.

"Honestly, Mark, if you can believe it, Beth and Jaimie's local naturist club organised a country walk without any clothes on. Totally starkers. In *October*. And she and Jaimie went on it."

Mark was trying not to laugh. "Is that really true?"

"Well," I said, "we did wear walking boots, so I suppose we weren't totally naked."

That tipped him over the edge. He began to howl, clutching his stomach.

"And it wasn't a very long walk. Only a mile or so."

I'd been terrified when we first set off along that track through the woods. Every rustle of autumn leaves sounded like a crowd of people approaching us. Jaimie and the others just chatted casually about the autumn colours or pointed out birds and squirrels while I kept on high alert, expecting total humiliation at any second. Agreeing to go on a naked walk had been a real test of my feelings for Jaimie.

"You'll love it, Beth," he'd said when he was trying to persuade me. "It's wonderful to feel the breeze on your skin. It really puts you in touch with nature. I can't explain it. You have to experience it for yourself."

"Weren't you cold?" Mark asked after he'd recovered himself enough to speak.

"A bit, I suppose, but not really. If you get naked regularly, your body becomes used to having fewer clothes on."

"So you don't normally have the wood burner going, then, you and Jaimie?" Rosie asked. "You just sit here in the buff?"

We had done that at first, when we were alone. I'd become used to being in the house without any clothes on. Then, when winter came round and Jaimie was working until late, I'd gone back to my jeans and jumpers.

"God only knows why you agreed to it in the first place," Rosie said. "Just because naturism's Jaimie's hobby doesn't mean you have to take it up."

I couldn't explain, not with Mark there, and Rosie probably wouldn't have understood anyway. I'd just felt so grateful to Jaimie when I'd moved to Ely. So aware that if it wasn't for him, I'd probably still be moping about my flat, longing hopelessly for something I could never have. Jaimie had brought me back to life. I'd wanted to please him.

"I didn't start my naturism journey with the naked walk. I eased myself into it at first by taking my clothes off when we were in the garden."

"The garden isn't overlooked, then?" Mark asked.

"No. It's very private. Anyway, I got used to that. Liked it, actually. It was freeing. And then the next step was going for a drink at the club bar."

I hadn't liked to refuse when Jaimie had suggested that either. Deep down, I hadn't wanted to go at all. Well, not even deep down, I suppose. But just as he'd done later on with the naked walk, Jaimie had somehow managed to persuade me it would be a life-affirming experience.

"What was that like?" Mark asked.

I shrugged. "It turns out a glass of chardonnay tastes the same whether you're wearing clothes or not. And pub bores are pretty much the same whether they're naked or dressed. Except, if they're naked, you have to make eye contact with them a bit more than you probably would do normally."

Once again Mark laughed, then sat there, staring into the flames, shaking his head. Probably imagining me naked. God.

"To get back to my original point," persisted Rosie, "in my opinion, both of you have sold out. You've changed yourselves to try and suit your partners, and I'm not sure that's a good thing. They ought to love you just as you are."

I looked down at my dress, suddenly feeling a bit bleak, then noticed Mark sit up a little straighter in his seat.

"Relationships are all about compromise, though, aren't they? Perhaps your inability to accept that is the reason you and Giorgio keep splitting up."

There was silence for a moment. Because I knew why she and Giorgio had split up, I felt really bad for Rosie.

"You know nothing about it."

"You don't know anything about my and Beth's relationships, but that doesn't stop you voicing an opinion, does it?"

"Actually, Giorgio and I keep splitting up, as you put it, because he wants to get married and have babies."

She sounded quite upset, but Mark, brother-like, didn't seem to notice. "Well, what's so wrong with that? You're good together. He's a great guy . . ."

Rosie stood up, her hands clenched at her sides. "Nothing's wrong with it if being a parent happens to be what you want," she shouted. "I just don't happen to want that. And he does. Okay? Now, excuse me, I'm going to the loo."

She strode off, and then it was just me and Mark.

"Oh dear," he said. "I've upset her, haven't I?"

"Yes," I said sadly. "She's hurting at the moment. But you weren't to know."

He sighed. "Giorgio's a really nice guy. It's such a shame."

"I know."

He looked at me. "I'm right about compromise, though, aren't I? I mean, Grace compromises. She does. I'm allowed to eat Pot Noodles for my lunch on Saturdays now."

We exchanged glances. Smiled. I noticed the planes of his face in the firelight. Jaimie's face was all curves, but with Mark it was the jaw-line and cheekbones you noticed.

"I suppose there's no way to compromise about having kids, though, is there?" he went on. "You either want them or you don't."

Oh God. I looked away, focussing my gaze on the flames in the wood burner. "Men often say they don't want children. But then their partner gets pregnant, and the man ends up thinking it's the best thing that ever happened to them." It was what I secretly hoped would happen with me and Jaimie.

Mark nodded. "Yes, I know a few guys like that. But then I suppose men don't actually have to carry the kid for nine months, do they? Or give birth to them. Rosie never has been the maternal type. I'm an idiot."

I reached across the space between us to squeeze his hand. "She'll be all right."

He took my hand in his, and we smiled at each other. Then, just as I was afraid he might ask something about me and Jaimie and children, Rosie returned, her slightly pink eyes a giveaway to the fact that she'd been crying.

Mark let go of my hand to pull her in for a hug. "Sorry, sis. I'm a complete idiot. Grace is always telling me so."

"You've finally managed to find something Grace and I actually agree on, then," Rosie said with a sniff. "For your information, just because I don't want to do all that grown-up stuff, it doesn't mean I don't care. I do. It's Giorgio who's changed, not me. I told him right from the get-go that I wanted to keep it light."

"Things change, though, don't they?" Mark said, but he spoke softly, still hugging her close. "People fall in love."

"They do," she agreed, crying a little more.

I got up and joined in with their hug so the three of us were in one giant embrace. And all the while, the conversations we'd just had about compromise and children swirled round and round in my head until I felt as if I were going crazy. Was I compromising what I wanted most in life for Jaimie? If I were to accidentally fall pregnant, would he be like one of those men I'd described who don't want children—in Jaimie's case, more children—and then turn out to be delighted, devoted fathers?

"Anyway," Mark said at last, "this is all very maudlin, isn't it? Tell us one of your funny animal stories, Beth, to cheer us up. You must have some, from the dog walking."

So we sat back down on the sofa, Rosie dried her eyes, and I told them about Milo, the Kama Sutra, and the sirloin steak. Rosie had heard it all before, of course, but that didn't stop her laughing. Soon we were all laughing our heads off, including me.

"Oh, that's so funny," said Mark. "What did the old gang at Dalston Vets say when you told them about it? I imagine Clive was in hysterics."

That sobered me up. Although I kept on smiling, my thoughts were suddenly on Clive and all my other friends at Dalston Vets. Beyond sending them a Christmas card, I hadn't been in touch with them lately. It was the whole Christmas thing, I think. All the ice-skating and decorations and tacky jokes I knew they'd be enjoying. I didn't even know who was on Christmas duty this year. Angela, who'd replaced me, maybe? Or Naomi, perhaps, now that she was back from maternity leave?

Mark was laughing again, his eyes screwed up. "I can't stop thinking about it. D'you think the dog helps them to choose which position to try?" He put on a different voice. "What d'you think about page forty-seven, Milo? One bark for yes, two barks for no."

I couldn't help laughing at that. Neither could Rosie.

So we were all laughing when Mark's mobile began to ring, and there was laughter in his voice as he answered it.

"Oh, hi, Mum. Beth's just told us the funniest story . . ." he began, but as Sylvia started to speak, his expression changed in an instant. When he got to his feet, Rosie and I exchanged glances, stricken by a dreadful sense of foreboding. Instinctively, I reached for her hand.

"Oh God. Yes, of course. We'll come right away. Yes, as soon as possible. I'll text you when we're near. All right. Try not to worry, Mum."

"What is it?" Rosie asked. "What's happened?"

Mark's face was grey. "It's Dad. He's had a heart attack. He's in Chase Farm Hospital."

Rosie's hand went up to her mouth.

"Is he all right?" I asked.

"I'm not sure. We need to get there right away. Oh Jesus, Grace has got the car, hasn't she? How far is Jaimie's property from here?"

"I'll drive us," I said, because of course I was going too. It was *Richard*. "They'll be ages yet. Come on. We can call them from the road to let them know what's happened."

We reached the hospital an hour and a half later. Sylvia was in the family room in the coronary unit. I caught a glimpse of her through the window as we approached—her eyes glazed and shocked, staring into space, her handbag clutched on her lap. Lost. The minute she saw us, she leapt to her feet to gather us in for a hug.

"Oh, my loves. Thank God you're here. I've needed you all so badly."

Rosie pressed her face into her mother's shoulder, sobbing. "Oh, Mum."

Sylvia stroked her hair. "Shh, sweetheart. Shh. It's all right. Dad's still with us."

"How is he?" Both Mark and I spoke at the same time, standing shoulder to shoulder, staring into Sylvia's worry-ravaged face.

"He's . . . they're operating on him right now. They said . . . well, they didn't say very much, actually. Only that the next few hours would be critical. I think we should get some news soon. We ought to. It's been ages. You can't imagine how . . ."

Her voice broke, and Mark ushered her to her seat again. "Sit down, Ma." I hadn't heard him call his mother Ma for years and years.

She sat, Rosie and I taking the seats on either side of her and Mark kneeling on the floor.

"I found him out in the garden," she told us. "The lunch was ready, so I called him to come in. I was running a bit late, you see, because Josie wanted me to look after her kids while she nipped out. Anyway, I called to him to say lunch was on the table. Only he didn't come. And I was mad because I didn't want the dinner to go cold. It was a bit of best beef, you see, a treat. And the Yorkshire puddings had turned out just right. Anyway, I went out there, all irritable, saying, 'Richard? Where are you?' Only I turn the corner and there he is, lying on the ground, out cold." She looked up at us with big, agonised eyes, caught up in the memory. "I thought . . . I thought, at first, he was dead. I think I must have cried out, because Josie heard me and came straight round. She called for the ambulance."

I put my hand on Sylvia's shoulder, unable to imagine the terror she must have felt while she waited for the ambulance to come.

"Did Dad regain consciousness at all?" Mark asked.

Sylvia gave a jerky nod. "Only briefly. He said . . . he said, 'Oh, Sylv.' That's all. Then he . . . went back to sleep. And I've been sitting here thinking about all the things I've cooked him that I shouldn't have. All the cakes and the fried breakfasts. You know your dad. Always has thought salad is . . . for . . . rabbits."

He did. I could even hear him saying it. *If I was meant to eat lettuce, I'd have a twitchy nose and a white tail on my backside.*

"But I should have made him eat it, shouldn't I?" Sylvia was saying, hands up to her face as she sobbed. "I shouldn't have listened to him. Stupid sod."

"You can't blame yourself, Mum," Mark said.

"No," I agreed. "Richard is his own person." His own lovable, dependable, funny, loyal person. God, he had to come through this. He had to come through this and moan about the sudden lack of cooked breakfasts. I imagined one of us presenting him with a fake rabbit's tail as a gag Christmas gift.

"They're right, Mum," said Rosie. "It's not your fault."

But Sylvia only shook her head, swiping her tears away with the backs of her hands. "I've been sitting here racking my brain, trying to think whether there've been any signs of anything wrong. There would be, wouldn't there, if he's got a bad heart? But the only thing I can think is he's been tired lately. More tired than usual. I put it down to his age. But sixty-eight isn't old, is it? Not these days."

"Shh, Mum," Mark said. "This isn't doing anyone any good. Dad wouldn't want you to be saying these things, thinking these things. You know he wouldn't."

Sylvia's voice came out on a wail. "I know. I just don't know how to stop."

She had her hands over her face now, openly sobbing, and my throat was closed up, clogged by a dam of tears. I'd never seen Sylvia like this. She was always so in control in a crisis. So practical. Saying things like, *The sun will come up in the morning, you'll see.* Like the time Mark wrote off his first car, or Rosie fell out with a boyfriend and thought the world had ended. But when I thought of her saying it, I saw Richard standing right beside her, one hand resting on her shoulder, telling us, *Your mother's right, you know.* They were a team. They always had been.

"Do you want a cup of coffee, Mum?" Mark was asking, probably feeling as helpless as I did, casting about for something, anything, he could do to help. "Or a glass of water?"

Sylvia pulled herself together with a supreme effort. "Thanks, love. There's a jug of water over there. The nice nurse brought it. You can get me some if you like."

She rummaged in her bag for a packet of tissues, but it was a new pack, the tissues tightly jammed inside, and her fingers were shaking too much to be of much use.

"Here, let me." I took the packet from her, sliding a tissue out.

"Thanks, love," she said, giving my arm a squeeze, then blowing her nose.

After Mark had brought Sylvia a cup of water, he strode to the door to look out along the corridor, shoulders hunched, spine stiff with anxiety. My hands ached with a need to go over and smooth the planes of his back. To massage the tension from his muscles. I so wanted to nuzzle into his side and whisper, "It will be all right. He'll come through this."

But I couldn't do any of those things, not the way I wanted to, so instead I sat next to Sylvia and thought of the three of us back at Ely—me, Mark, and Rosie laughing our heads off about Milo and the Kama Sutra. Me being so bloody entertaining. Enjoying the peace and quiet without the girls.

And all the time, Richard had been fighting for his life on the cold, hard earth in his garden, and Sylvia had been dealing with it all.

It wasn't right. Shouldn't even have been possible. You ought to have known if someone you loved so much was in such grave danger. Got a sign or something. Felt the pain like a javelin in your own chest.

My phone began to ring suddenly—a jaunty jingle of a ringtone that seemed wildly inappropriate for the occasion. Michael Bublé's "It's Beginning to Look a Lot Like Christmas," downloaded in a dull moment to try to entertain Jaimie's girls.

"I'm so sorry," I said, getting to my feet.

"It's all right, love," Sylvia said. "It'll be your Jaimie, checking up on you. You answer it."

But I didn't want to speak the words I would have to speak in front of Sylvia and the others. And I certainly couldn't bear to leave the three people I loved most in the world to go up the corridor to talk to Jaimie in private. So I rejected the call and switched my phone off. Mumbled something about speaking to him later.

And in any case, just then Mark said, "Someone's coming," and stepped back from the door.

It was the surgeon, still dressed in his scrubs, and I knew what he was going to tell us straightaway, even before he opened his mouth, because it was there in his eyes. In the terrible fatigued droop of his body.

Every particle of moisture left my mouth. My hands began to tingle. Sylvia was shaking her head. "No," she said. "No."

When the surgeon began to speak, Sylvia covered her ears so she wouldn't hear his words. But the rest of us heard them. Every agonising one of them.

"I'm so very sorry, Mrs. Groves. Your husband had another heart attack on the operating table. We did our very best to revive him, but I'm afraid . . . we weren't successful."

Richard was gone. It wasn't possible. Couldn't be possible. Except that it was, wasn't it? Because it had happened.

After the surgeon left, we held each other, the four of us, sobbing brokenly, utterly stunned and heartbroken.

Finally, Sylvia pulled away, voicing what we were all thinking. "However will we do life without him?"

I didn't know. I couldn't imagine. As I leant against the warm support of Mark's shoulder, I only knew that I didn't want to.

13

We couldn't bury Richard until the New Year because everything but grief stops for Christmas. I stayed at Sylvia's house for a couple of nights—so did Mark and Rosie. None of us really tried to sleep, not that first night, anyway. I spoke to Jaimie on the phone, but afterwards I couldn't remember what we'd said to each other. I felt frozen, I think. Numb. Nothing made sense. I knew he asked me when I'd be coming home, but I couldn't tell him because I didn't know, not exactly.

"Don't worry," I promised. "I'll be back for Christmas Day." Although it seemed the most unlikely thing in the world to be saying.

The day Mark went with Sylvia to register the death, I left my car at Sylvia's house and took the train into London. Rosie was taking compassionate leave from work but had to go in to see to a few things, so it seemed as good a day as any for me to go to my flat to see what sort of a state my tenants had left it in.

Dalston is twenty minutes by bus from Liverpool Street Station. I sat on the top deck and looked out at the passing streets—at the bustle of the last-minute Christmas shoppers; a man dressed as Santa ringing a bell as he collected for charity; an optimistic display of sleds outside a shop, waiting for the snow we hadn't had for years in the UK. As we got closer to my stop, I spotted Dalston Vets. What was going on in there right at this moment? Had any puppies uncovered hoards of Christmas chocolate and made themselves ill on it? Or eaten a Christmas orna-ment or a strand of tinsel? Very probably. There had always been some Christmas emergencies to deal with when I worked there.

Then it was almost my stop, and I stood up and rang the bell. As I got off the bus, a woman was approaching me, pushing a buggy. She was wrapped up against the cold—a heavy coat, a huge multicoloured scarf, a hat pulled right down over her ears—but I still recognised her.

"Naomi!"

"Beth!" Naomi's face lit up, and we hugged each other in the mid-dle of the busy street as if our lives depended on it. "It's so good to see you! It's been ages."

"I know. I haven't been back here in ages. How's this little guy?" I bent over the buggy to take a look at Bembe. He was sitting up, wrapped up in warm clothing, his feet kicking at the toasty-looking blanket covering his legs. "Wow, you're not so little now, are you, little man?"

Naomi laughed. "No, definitely not. He's doing well. We all are. How about you? What brings you here?"

I straightened, the sadness descending all over again. "My tenants left. I came to check the flat over. But I was here anyway. Well, in Enfield. Because . . . because . . . well, Richard died. You know, Rosie's dad?"

"Oh, Beth, baby. I'm so sorry. I never met him, but you spoke about him so often, I feel as if I did. He was a good 'un."

"He was. It was a heart attack. On Sunday. All very sudden."

"I'm so sorry."

"Me too." A tear ran down my cheek. I wiped it away.

"Listen," Naomi said. "We were just on our way home. Why don't you come back for a coffee? Tony's out."

I looked down the street in the direction of my flat. I hadn't been there for more than six months. I wasn't looking forward to finding out what sort of state it was in.

"All right," I said, smiling at Bembe because you couldn't help but smile at Bembe, even when you felt sad as sad could be.

Naomi's house was like an explosion at a Christmas factory, the way it was every year. Fairy lights twinkled over mirrors and pictures. A giant Father Christmas figure stood proud in the hallway. Candles waited to be lit. There were no fewer than three red-leafed poinsettias on the windowsill. And there was, of course, a Christmas tree. Slightly smaller than usual probably, so that it could be set up high, out of Bembe's reach. But it was extravagantly decorated nonetheless, with tinsel and baubles and chocolate treats.

I walked past it all, trying not to let it all exhaust me, while Naomi popped Bembe into his high chair and gave me rice cakes to feed him while she made coffee. The little boy's dark eyes were huge and lively, examining every facet of my unmade-up face—a face suffering from neglect and pinched by the cold of endless winter dog walks—then the next minute dropping to focus on the very important task of dismantling his rice cakes on his high-chair tray.

"He's just so adorable, Naomi," I told my friend, taking my mug of coffee from her.

"He is, isn't he? Which is just as well, isn't it, mate? Since you're such a lot of hard work for Mummy?" She chucked her son under the chin, speaking in a funny, high-pitched voice that made him giggle. "Yes, you are, aren't you?"

I smiled. "He likes that."

"Oh yes, he laps up anything fun. You should see him with his dad. Tony throws him up in the air and catches him. I can't watch sometimes. But Bembe loves all that rough stuff." She sat next to me at the table. "I don't suppose you'll be able to have the funeral for a while, what with Christmas coming?"

"No, not until the New Year. The undertaker's coming tomorrow to discuss the arrangements with Sylvia."

"How's she taking it? Silly question, I suppose. She must be devastated."

"She is. But she's all right, I think. I mean, she's still functioning in a stunned sort of way. Still thinking about everyone else. I guess it will really hit her after the funeral, when it's all over, and it's just her in the house."

"God, yes."

"It's just so hard to take in, Naomi. That we won't see him again. He was always there, you know? Even when I didn't see him very often. And I hadn't seen him very often lately, what with living in Ely."

Naomi took my free hand in hers. "Listen, sweets, don't be feeling guilty about that. He wouldn't want you to. You had your life to lead."

I sighed. "I know that, but I just think if I'd seen him more often, maybe I'd have noticed something. I don't know, some clue he had a heart condition."

"Sylvia saw him every day, though, didn't she? And presumably she didn't notice anything."

"She says not, apart from him being a bit tired. But nothing too much, not really."

"Well then."

Across the room, Bembe was sitting up, shouting, and banging a toy train with a toy brick.

"Guilt is all wrapped up in grief, and you're grieving, mate."

Tears began to run down my cheeks all over again. I put my coffee down and fumbled for a tissue. "How did you get to be so wise?"

"Some of us are just born that way, I guess."

I smiled. "I guess." It was good to speak to her. Very good. I'd spoken to Mark and Rosie, of course, but that was different somehow because they felt every bit as bad as I did.

"How's everything going, anyway, in Ely?" Naomi asked, and I sighed.

"All right." I wasn't at all sure that was true, to be honest. But I was completely sure I didn't have the strength to talk about it just now. "How about you? How's it working out for you, being back at work part-time?"

"Ah," Naomi said with a strange expression on her face. "About that. I might not be back at work for much longer."

"Oh?" I said. "Is it too much for you?"

"It is, if I'm honest. Dashing about, getting Bembe ready to leave for the childminder on time. Feeling guilty because he's playing with something and doesn't want to go. Not being able to concentrate because I'm so damn tired. But I'd probably be able to cope with all of that if it weren't for the other thing."

I frowned. "What other thing?"

Bembe crawled over, having abandoned his bashing game, and Naomi pulled him up onto her knee. She was grinning all over her face as she looked at me, and suddenly I knew what she was going to say.

"You're not pregnant again?"

"I am. Four months. Talk about timing, eh?"

I thought of lucky Bembe, having a sibling close to his age. "It's not bad timing—it's perfect. Oh, congratulations! I'm so pleased for you."

"Thanks. I'm not sure Clive agrees with you about it being good timing, though. I think he's shell shocked. Especially as the girl they got in to replace you hasn't worked out very well. Not sure she'll be sticking around for much longer. Kind of hope not, to be honest. She's never fit in."

She looked down at her son and was suddenly very absorbed in pulling up his left sock, which was hanging off his foot. I knew my Naomi. Knew how hard it must be to stop herself from saying anything else. So hard it would take her until lunchtime to get Bembe dressed in the mornings if she put as much attention into his other clothes as she was putting into adjusting his sock. *You can go back to your old job if you want to.* That's what she wanted me to know, but she wasn't going to push it. She was going to leave me to draw that conclusion myself, even if it drove her crazy to stay silent.

Suddenly Bembe began to cry. Lustily.

"Sorry," Naomi said. "He probably wants a nap."

I got up. "I'll leave you to it."

"You don't have to. He usually goes down quite quickly."

"I'm going to have to face the flat at some point," I said, zipping up my coat. "But it was wonderful to see you. Thanks for listening."

She hugged me. "Oh, sweetheart, anytime. You're always welcome here. You hear me?"

"I hear you. Thank you."

As my feet took themselves along the familiar roads to my flat, I noticed some changes—apart from the Christmas trees and decorations on display in people's windows. A new pair of yellow curtains in the window of the big house on the corner, some spray-painted graffiti on the postbox. But some things were the same. The plastic flowers in the window box at number fifty-eight. The pride-and-joy BMW that rarely left its parking spot outside number sixty. And then I was there at number seventy-six, going down the stone steps to the basement. Putting my key in the lock and turning it.

I'd known it would be cold—the tenants had been gone three weeks, and it had been bitter this December. There had even been ice in the fountains at Trafalgar Square—I'd seen it on the national news. But though I'd expected it to be cold, the icy air still hit me like a wall as I went in. Walking along the hallway, I could see my breath. I switched on the light—this part of the flat had always been dark—and immediately frowned. The large mirror was askew, as if someone had knocked into it. And when I straightened it, I noticed a long scuff mark along the wall, as if something large had been dragged past it. With my heart sinking at these signs of a lack of care, I walked on towards the main room and pushed the door open. And immediately gasped in horror and despair.

Someone had covered Richard's beautiful pinewood shelving unit with black gloss paint. It would never be the same again.

"Oh, Richard . . ." Dropping my bag on the sofa, I went over to touch the shelves, sobbing as I remembered Richard putting them up. How we'd sat together on the sofa afterwards and I'd known the shelves were Richard's way of saying, "You'll be all right, love."

But I wasn't. I wasn't all right at all.

14

When I turned my key in the lock at Jaimie's on Christmas Eve, Olivia ran down the hall to meet me.

"Beth! It's Christmas Day tomorrow!" she cried, practically jumping up and down in her excitement.

I hadn't forgotten the way she'd held my hand at Thursford, and the enthusiastic greeting instantly warmed my heart. I was going to bend down to Olivia's level to respond to her, but Jaimie intervened.

"Don't crowd Beth, sweetheart. She's had a long journey. She's tired."

I had, and I was. But I still wished he'd given me time to say, "I know! Isn't it exciting?"

Now Olivia was regarding me warily, her thumb sliding thoughtfully into her mouth.

"My friend Katie's daddy is called Terry," she said. "He's quite nice. If he died, I wouldn't be very sad, though. But I would be if my daddy died. Very, very sad."

Obviously, Jaimie had mentioned something to her about Richard. I swallowed. "Well, you see—" I began, but once again Jaimie cut in.

"D'you know what? I think it's time to prepare the carrots for Rudolph and his friends. Want to help, Olivia? Or shall I ask Emily?"

"Me, me, me!" shouted Olivia, taking off at a run and dragging Jaimie with her, instantly forgetting me.

I hung up my coat, then put my nose into the living room. Emily was absorbed in a book. "Hi, Emily."

She didn't look up. "Hello."

"Your dad and Olivia are preparing carrots to leave for Santa's reindeer, if you want to help."

Still, she didn't look up. "That's babyish."

"Okay, just thought I'd tell you."

I could have turned away and left her to it. Accepted that we still seemed to be taking part in a one-step-forward, two-steps-backwards sort of bonding dance. Certainly, that was my instinct. But if Olivia knew about Richard, then surely Emily did too? Maybe she just didn't know how to talk to me about it. So I sat down on the arm of her chair, hoping to connect with her. Emily's eyes moved sideways fleetingly, the only acknowledgment of my presence. A bit like you might acknowledge an annoying fly that had settled nearby.

"What are you reading?"

A shrug. "Just a book Mummy got me from the library."

"Who's it by?"

She turned the book towards me so I could see the cover.

"It looks good. Is it?"

"Mm-hmm."

"Have you read any of that author's books before?"

Emily shook her head.

"When I was a child, I had about ten favourite books I never got tired of. After I'd read them all, I started over and read them all again. Somehow, I liked knowing exactly what was going to happen."

Silence. Emily's eyes were fixed on her book. When she turned the page, I felt like she was swatting me—the annoying fly—off the arm of the sofa.

And yet I still persisted. "Do you ever feel like that?"

Emily shrugged. "I guess. Sometimes."

She carried on reading. I could think of nothing else to say. It was time to give up. For now. "Well," I said, getting up, "see you later then. Enjoy your reading."

Collecting my bag from the hall, I trudged upstairs to the bedroom, where I sat on the edge of the bed, staring into space. After a while, Jaimie came to find me. "How are you feeling?" he asked, stroking my neck beneath my hair.

I leant back into his hand, enjoying his caress. "Still a bit raw. Don't think you need to protect me from the kids, though. I don't mind answering any questions they might have."

"I know, but you know what Olivia's like. She'll go on and on. And it is Christmas Eve."

With a pang, I realised he hadn't been protecting me at all. He'd been protecting Olivia, cutting short the conversation in case I talked about anything miserable and spoiled the buildup to Christmas.

"Listen, after they've both gone to bed and I've wrapped their presents up, we can snuggle up together on the sofa, okay?"

But the girls weren't in bed until gone eight, and then the present-wrapping extravaganza seemed to last forever. In the end, I left Jaimie to it and went to run myself a bath. So it was a surprise when I went downstairs afterwards in my dressing gown to find the world's biggest present beneath the Christmas tree.

"Bloody hell, Jaimie. Whatever is that?"

Jaimie grinned. "A drum kit for Olivia. There are five different drums, a set of hi-hat cymbals, and even a little stool. I can't wait to see her face when she opens it. She's going to flip."

I couldn't look away from the massive gift-wrapped box, my mind vividly picturing Olivia pounding away with the drumsticks.

Finally, Jaimie seemed to notice something was wrong. "What?"

"Well, it's going to be incredibly noisy, isn't it? Where are you going to put it?"

He shrugged. "I hadn't thought. Just in the dining room, I suppose." He studied my face. "You don't object to me buying her a drum kit, do you?"

I could have said the prospect felt like sheer torture, but what I actually said was, "Well, it's just that it's noisy enough here sometimes as it is."

Jaimie turned his back on me to gather together the wrapping paper and Sellotape, then pulled another toy from the bag of toys waiting to be wrapped. "They're just children, Beth. Children make noise. It's quiet enough when they aren't here, isn't it? Too quiet."

They were his girls. This was his house. His business. I'd never disputed that, because I knew how much it hurt him when he didn't see his girls for days on end. But now, at a time when I just felt like curling up somewhere to lick my wounds, didn't I deserve a bit of consideration?

"I think I'll go to bed," I said.

"Okay. I shouldn't be too much longer here."

I was like a ghost all through Christmas Day—there and not there, going through the motions. I didn't know where Mark was spending Christmas, whether he and Grace had gone to Enfield to be with Sylvia and Rosie, but I felt so guilty about not being there myself. But then, if I'd decided to spend Christmas with them, I'd probably have felt guilty about not being with Jaimie.

The truth was, I didn't want to celebrate Christmas. Why would I? Richard had been a part of my Christmases for more than twenty-five years. And now he was gone. No house lit up with extravagant, over-the-top lights. No proudly worn but ridiculous Christmas jumper. No Richard to say, "So were you good this year? Good enough for Santa to come calling?" Or to hold his stomach as if he were Santa and say, "Ho, ho, ho!"

It was almost an out-of-body experience, opening my presents early on Christmas morning. Like I was looking down on the room as Olivia, incandescent with excitement, tore the wrapping paper off her drum kit. At myself playing the part of Beth opening her gifts—another dress and some lingerie from Jaimie—*Thank you, how lovely.* Watching Jaimie and the girls open theirs—*I didn't think you'd read that book yet, Emily? I just saw the colour and thought of you, Jaimie.*

And then, after the wrapping paper was cleared away, I helped Jaimie cook Christmas dinner to the accompaniment of Olivia's drumming. Gamely pulled Christmas crackers. I felt like an outsider, like an interloper. But it wasn't only my grief that made me feel that way. I'd probably have felt a bit like that anyway, even if Richard hadn't died.

At some point during the afternoon, I remembered what Mark had told me about Jaimie's desperation following his split from Harriet and imagined him lying distraught on the dining room floor, the way Grace had found him. Six months before the two of us had met at Mark's wedding, that was all. Was I some sort of rebound romance for Jaimie? Had he been drawn to me because he didn't want to be alone? The tight black dress, the lingerie, and the makeup—all of Jaimie's Christmas gifts seemed to say that he wanted me to be someone else. The woman he'd thought I was at the wedding, maybe, when I'd gone over the top with my appearance to help myself get through the day. If I was right, then Jaimie must have been disappointed in me every day when I put on my trusty old walking boots and cagoule to go to work. But what woman would put on full makeup to walk dogs in all weathers? Grace, probably. Not that Grace would ever work as a dog walker.

I had tried so hard to be a part of this family. To be an accepted and valued part of Olivia's and Emily's lives. I'd dreamed up ideas for activities, told them stories, talked about the animals they liked. I'd learnt to make birthday cakes. Done my best to construct last-minute fancy dress costumes. Bought them sunflower seeds to plant in the garden. But the truth was, if I walked out the door today and never came back, neither of them would probably miss me very much. Not even Olivia. Their adoration of Harriet had always been a solid steel barrier to our closeness.

Pretending to be okay when I wasn't probably would have given me a headache anyway, but with Olivia's drumming, my head felt as if

I'd come out the loser in a boxing ring by teatime. So I took myself off to bed early. And when I woke up the next morning, I knew I wasn't capable of a repeat performance.

"Jaimie," I said before Olivia could come into our bedroom or go downstairs to pick up her drumsticks again, "I'm sorry, but I think I'm going to go and see Sylvia and Rosie."

Jaimie frowned at me in the half light. "Are you sure they'll want you there? I don't imagine they're doing anything very Christmassy."

"I don't want to do anything Christmassy."

He sighed. "I know. But what I mean is, don't you think they'll want to be left alone with their grief rather than have to think about a guest?"

Would they? I entertained the idea for maybe ten seconds, everything in me reeling at what it implied. Jaimie thought Sylvia and Rosie wouldn't feel they could grieve if I was there. But that was precisely why *I* needed to be with *them*. So I wouldn't have to pretend to be okay. Wouldn't have to fix a smile on my face. I wanted—and needed—to be with my fellow sufferers. People who understood what I was going through because they were going through it themselves.

"I think they'll be fine with it."

"Well, you know best," he said in a tone of voice that suggested that was very far from being the case.

I didn't ring ahead to say I was coming. I just turned up on the doorstep. Sylvia's face was grey with fatigue when she opened the door, but her eyes lit up as soon as she saw me. And it wasn't just the illuminated reindeers Richard must have set up in the front garden in the week before he died.

"Beth, love," she said. "Oh, how lovely to see you. But you're meant to be spending Christmas with Jaimie and his girls. You didn't need to come."

I took her into my arms for a deep hug, inhaling the commingled smell of mince pie, coal fire, and the coconut bath oil I'd given her for Christmas. "Yes," I said, my voice wobbling a bit, "I did. I really did."

"Well," she said, sniffing, "I can't tell you how good it is to see you. Come on, come in. Rosie? Beth's here. She's come home to be with us. Isn't that wonderful?"

You see, that was what Jaimie didn't seem to understand. Rosie, Sylvia, and Mark were my *family*. Or as close to a family as I was ever going to get. Much closer than the borrowed family I'd been trying to fit into with him for the past eight months, anyway.

Jaimie and I definitely needed to talk. And soon. But not now, not when I was so sad and vulnerable and still had Richard's funeral to face.

"Hello, you," said Rosie, taking me into her arms for a hug. She was dressed in a pair of red brushed-cotton Christmas pyjamas, and I had never been so glad to see anyone in my life.

"Mum and I just broke open a box of chocolates. Come and gorge yourself."

"And a bottle of sherry," added Sylvia.

"Fabulous."

A fire was blazing in the hearth—somebody had done a good job, considering Richard had always been chief fire maker in the household. The three of us settled down in front of it, and Sylvia charged our glasses.

"To Dad," Rosie said, and we clinked our glasses together.

"To Dad."

"To Richard."

As we sipped our sherry and smiled at each other, tears glittered in our eyes, and I thought of myself this time last December, oblivious to anything the year would bring. Surely next year would be kinder? Hard as it was to believe right then, the hurt and loss of Richard's passing would start to mellow just a little bit. Olivia would tire of her drum kit. Jaimie and I would have a good talk and sort our problems out. And maybe, just maybe, he would even agree to having a baby with me.

Well, I could only hope, couldn't I?

WINTER THREE

❄❄❄

15

"I'm a bit scared, to be honest," I said on the phone to Rosie.

"I'm not surprised," she said. "I'd be absolutely terrified. Not that I'd be in your position in a million, trillion years, of course. But look, just because you've put your application to adopt in, it doesn't mean you have to go through with it. You never know, you might come to your senses."

The idea of adopting a child had come to me six or seven months after my breakup with Jaimie. I'd seen a TV programme about children in the care system—all these tragic kids shifted about from pillar to post, desperate for a new mum and dad. It made me cry, it really did. Then I got hooked on a podcast that followed parents who were applying to adopt. Their stories really moved me too—all that yearning and soul-searching as they talked about how much having a family would mean to them.

After that, I seemed to see adverts for foster carers everywhere I went. And then one Sunday morning in the bath, I had a light-bulb moment. *I could do that,* I thought. *I could adopt.* As soon as the idea popped into my head, I wondered why I hadn't thought about it before. It seemed like an obvious solution.

Rosie hadn't shared my enthusiasm about it when I told her, though. She never came out and said it, but even so, I knew she thought I'd lost my mind.

"I do want to adopt," I told her now. "But wanting something doesn't make it any less scary, that's all."

"Oh, well, I expect everybody else will feel the same way you do."

"Probably. Though no doubt they'll all be getting a confidence boost from their partners. Let's face it, I'm bound to be the only single person there."

"Probably, yes. But then, if you weren't single—if you were still with Jaimie, say—you wouldn't be doing this, would you?"

"I suppose not."

Staring out into the garden, I imagined how it might be if I were still with Jaimie—him not committing to having a baby with me, me still trying to get his girls to like me. "You don't think I should have stayed with him, do you?"

I heard Rosie sigh. "We haven't got time to debate that, darling, have we? Not if you want to get to your session on time. You did say it started at seven?"

I looked at the clock. "Oh God, yes. Thanks. See you on Monday for the lights?"

"You bet. Six o'clock under the Christmas tree in Trafalgar Square."

"Six o'clock."

"Go and sock it to them!"

"I'll do my best."

"Oh, and for the record, no, I definitely don't think you should have stayed with him."

I smiled. "Thanks."

The Introduction to Adoption Information Session run by Adoption East London was a bus ride away. As I hurried towards the bus stop at the end of my road, I wondered why I'd made myself potentially late by calling Rosie. And why I'd asked her about Jaimie. Why was I even thinking about Jaimie right now? God, if he knew I was doing this, he'd laugh out loud. He wouldn't be able to believe it. But so what? It had been eleven months since our split. What Jaimie thought and didn't think about anything connected to my life was completely irrelevant. Thank goodness.

~

My departure from Jaimie's life had been a messy affair. Let's just say he didn't take the news that I wanted to break up with him at all well. In fact, it took a while to convince him I really meant it. And after I had, he wanted me gone as soon as possible.

"I'm going to work," he'd said. "I'll be back by four. I want you and your belongings gone by the time I get back. Understood?"

But it wasn't as simple as that, because even though I'd let out my flat furnished, I still had all my other belongings in Ely—most of them crammed into Jaimie's attic. He'd hired a van when I moved in, but obviously I couldn't expect him to do that this time. So I decided there was nothing for it but to have a ruthless cull of my belongings. That way, everything would fit into my ancient car.

Only, on the way to the dump, my car died.

Ely isn't exactly a thriving metropolis, but my car happened to choose a roundabout for its final demise, and a queue soon built up behind me. As I tried fruitlessly to turn the engine over, wishing I hadn't ignored the knocking sound that had started up the previous week, people started sounding their horns angrily.

Finally, I got out, and a man helped me to push my car to the side of the road. Then I rang roadside assistance.

As I stood at the side of the road, waiting, I stared bleakly through the car windows at the belongings I'd been going to dump—boxes of books I'd wanted to read again, my old college folders, a little armchair in need of renovation that had belonged to my grandmother. I didn't really want to throw any of it out. At least, not hastily like this.

Tears filled my eyes—stupid tears that soon had doubt and panic raging inside me. The next few weeks were going to be so bloody hard. Why had I done this to myself? Jaimie was a perfectly good man. Decent. Attractive. Good in bed. Okay, so he always put his girls before me, but that made him a good father, not a bad partner. And he hadn't definitely said no to us having a baby together. I hadn't given him the chance to, had I? The six months weren't up yet. God, what if I never met anyone as nice as him ever again?

Craving comfort, I phoned Rosie.

"Ah, kid," she said after I'd explained the situation. "I'm so sorry. But it was the right thing to do if you weren't happy, wasn't it? And the important thing now is to sort out how to get your stuff back here. Look, Mark's just popped round for a cup of tea. I'll put him on, shall I? He can help you out."

"Oh, no," I said hastily, but too late—Rosie had gone, and I could hear a rumble of voices as she spoke to him.

Then Mark was on the line. "Beth? Jeez, I'm so sorry. Look, where exactly are you? I'll hire a van and come straight over. But it'll take me three hours or so to get there, at a guess."

Hearing his calm, concerned voice made me promptly burst into tears. He'd sounded like Richard—kind and practical. And I knew that, had he still been alive, Richard would have been the first person I'd have called to get me out of this dilemma.

As I swiped the tears away, the flashing lights of the recovery vehicle headed towards me along the road. Suddenly I wanted Mark and his hired van more than I could say.

"Thanks, Mark. Thanks so much. The recovery services are just arriving."

"Have them tow the car to a garage, then let me know where you are. I'll come straight to the garage to get the stuff from the car, and then we can go on to Jaimie's for the rest, okay? And try not to worry, okay? Everything will be all right."

The garage people were lovely to me, making me a cup of coffee and offering several more, letting me wait in their cosy reception area. Even so, I had never been so glad to see anyone as I was to see Mark when he finally turned up.

"Sorry it's taken so long. I got here as fast as I could."

I hadn't seen Mark since the funeral a few weeks previously. His eyes were dark shadowed, tired looking. It didn't look as if he'd slept much since then either. Now, here he was, having to drive up to Ely to rescue me.

"I'm sure this is the very last thing you wanted to do today. Thanks so much."

"I don't imagine it's the best day of your life either," he said. "Come on, let's just get it over with. Everything'll seem better when you're back in Dalston."

"Think so?"

"I know so."

We got on with transferring everything from my poor broken car. Mark frowned when he saw my grandmother's chair.

"Your gran's chair," he said, loading it up. "You weren't going to take that to the dump?"

"I was in a panic."

"Understandable. But I'm glad the chair escaped. Maybe I could help restore it? There must be some YouTube videos on chair restoration."

Somehow I was pretty sure Grace wouldn't be impressed with that idea. Come to think of it, she probably wouldn't be keen on Mark helping me out like this at all, being that she and Jaimie were such close friends.

"I hope this won't get you in trouble," I said as we drove towards Jaimie's house.

Mark shrugged. "It's not a problem," he said, and I hoped that was true.

I wanted to offer Mark a cup of tea at Jaimie's, but I didn't, because it didn't feel like my house any longer. If it ever really had. So we just got straight down to it. And when Jaimie turned up—hours earlier than expected—I was very glad we had.

"Mark," he said, getting out of his car. "I didn't expect to see you."

"Hi, Jaimie. We're almost done. Want to go and have a final check around, Beth?"

Jaimie called after me nastily, "Make sure you haven't taken anything of mine."

"Hey, Beth's not going to take anything of yours, mate," I heard Mark say in my defence. "She wouldn't do that. Let's try to make this as pain-free as possible, shall we?"

I toured the house, checking for anything I'd forgotten, mentally saying goodbye as I went, peeping into the girls' bedrooms as if they'd be there—Olivia with her dolls, Emily with a book. And suddenly, with a jolt, I realised I'd probably never see them again. That, despite everything, I would miss them. Our relationship may not have been easy to negotiate at times, but they'd still featured heavily in my life for the past year. Would I even find out what they ended up doing with their lives? Possibly, secondhand via Grace. Whatever it was, I hoped it would bring them joy. That they would both come to accept their parents' divorce and learn to thrive.

I moved on, continuing my search for anything I might have left. There was nothing. No trace that I'd ever lived there. Except for the blue-handled cutlery set I'd bought before Christmas, distributed between the cutlery drawers and the dishwasher. Should I take it? No, I didn't need to scrabble about for knives and forks. No need to be petty. I had a perfectly good cutlery set at the flat already. And I didn't need any reminders.

It was time to go.

"Beth's not as perfect as you all seem to want to make her out to be," Jaimie was saying to Mark as I came out of the house. "None of you has a clue what she's like really."

"Look, lay off, mate, okay?" Mark said. "Things haven't exactly been easy for us lately." He looked in my direction. "All done, Beth?"

I nodded, glancing over at Jaimie, thinking about the time Grace had discovered him lying distraught and broken on the dining room floor. Somehow I didn't get the impression he was going to do anything like that this time. He was angry—very angry—but not desperate. He would be all right.

"Yes," I said. "I'm ready."

Mark held the passenger door open for me. I spoke over my shoulder as I got in. "Bye, Jaimie."

He didn't answer.

"Okay?" Mark asked as we left Ely behind us.

I shrugged. "Not really. As you say, it'll be good to be back in Dalston."

"Of course it will. I never did think Ely felt right for you."

A lorry stopped suddenly up ahead. When Mark braked sharply, a box tipped up, sending an avalanche of books cascading onto the van floor.

"Sorry there's so much," I said after a quick glance to check everything was okay.

"This is nothing. If Mum ever decides to sell her house, her attic is full of my stuff. She's even got my old model aeroplanes up there. Remember helping me to fly them?"

"Of course."

The memory was welcome. Anything to stop me thinking about Jaimie and agonising about whether I'd done the right thing.

I'd been about twelve years old when I'd helped Mark to fly his planes. I was chief launcher, which involved standing for long hours in the cold while Mark tinkered with the planes, waiting for the exact moment to throw them into the air so he could take over with his controller. Watching him hunt for thermals, his face lighting up when he found them, the carefully constructed balsa-wood-and-tissue-paper planes circling ever higher in the sky.

I'd loved every second of our time together, and it was devastating when Mark switched his allegiance from model planes to girls, and the contraptions got stowed in the attic to gather dust.

"You were quite obsessed for a while."

He smiled. "Sorry about that."

"No, I enjoyed it. Well, except for the time I accidentally stood on that model you'd just finished making. I didn't enjoy that."

He laughed. "Me neither. But it mended." He lifted his hand from the steering wheel to cover mine briefly. "Just as this will too."

Oh God. Only yesterday, Jaimie had loved me. Now he hated me, and I was alone again, sitting in a van with my worldly belongings and a man I'd borrowed from his wife.

"You're so strong, Beth," the borrowed man said to comfort me.

"I'm really not," I said.

"You are. You decide what you want, and you go for it. I've seen you do it time and time again. You'll bounce back from this, you'll see."

I thought about the accuracy of that statement now as I waited at the bus stop to catch a bus to the Introduction to Adoption meeting. I hadn't exactly bounced back. Not at first, anyway. I'd been more like an overcultivated field, lying fallow for a while to regenerate, tending my garden and redecorating my flat. Easing myself back into my work and my friendships. And now, here I was, doing what Mark said I did. Deciding what I wanted and going for it.

Or I would be if the bloody bus came along and ever managed to get me to the meeting.

16

I wasn't late for the meeting, but I was the last to arrive. And the second I walked into the crowded room with the social workers lined up at the front ready to start, I saw someone I knew: Mrs. Bateson, one of our clients at Dalston Vets—the one with Nugget, the corgi.

Oh God. I hadn't expected to see anybody I knew here. Maybe I could go across the room to sit in one of the spare seats by the window before she spotted me?

But before I could make my move, one of the social workers came over with her clipboard, and while I was giving my name, Mrs. Bateson looked over and saw me. The next minute she was waving enthusiastically and gesturing towards the free seat next to her, giving me no choice but to go and take it.

"Hi, Beth. Fancy seeing you here! I had no idea you were planning to adopt. This is my husband, Karl. Karl, this is Beth, one of the nurses at the vet. She was so good with Nugget after he had that tooth out."

Karl held his hand out for me to shake, but there was no time for further conversation because the session started.

By coffee break we had dealt with the adoption process and learned how our applications would proceed. We'd also watched a couple of videos with adopters speaking about their experience of the adoption process. After the break we were going to learn more about why children end up in care and look at some case studies. I knew this would make me feel emotional, because I already felt emotional from watching the videos we'd seen. People just like me, desperate to have children, baring their deepest feelings and frustrations to the camera. I wasn't sure I'd have been brave enough to agree to be filmed.

Already there was so much to take in. I'd have liked to have sat quietly with my coffee and biscuit to sift through it all. But Mrs. Bateson—Tina, I'd discovered—wanted to chat.

"If I were single like you, I'd just shag a stranger to get pregnant rather than going down this whole adoption route. I mean, don't get me wrong, Karl and I are totally committed to adopting, but this whole application process is a complete chore, isn't it?"

God, I hoped my application wouldn't become an open topic of conversation whenever Tina came in for Nugget's worming tablets. And I certainly hoped she wouldn't dish her shag-a-stranger advice out to me in reception.

"Well," I said, "they have to be thorough, I suppose, don't they? These children have already been through such a lot."

"I know, and like I said, I'm not complaining. We'll jump through any flippin' hoop they want to throw at us to get our family. I was just surprised to see you here, to be honest. I said to Karl, 'An attractive girl like Beth, she ought to be married with a couple of kids by now.'"

"Ah, well," I said, longing for Karl to return from the toilet, "life doesn't always turn out the way we expect it to, does it? Excuse me, I just want to take a look at the book table before coffee break's over."

I smiled and got to my feet, hoping against hope she wouldn't join me. Fortunately, Karl returned just then, so the moment of danger passed. Though I supposed I'd better get used to being the focus of talk, hadn't I? If my application was successful, everyone would have to know about it. Otherwise, if I mysteriously acquired a baby or a toddler overnight, they might assume I was a child snatcher.

I picked a book up from the table, pretending to browse but really using it as an excuse to check out my fellow applicants. With London being as multicultural as it was, it was no surprise the participants reflected this—an Asian couple, a Black couple, two white couples, and a same-sex, mixed-race couple. And me, a single white woman. I'd expected to be the only single applicant, but I hadn't expected to feel so awkward about it. Or for anyone to blatantly tell me that sleeping around with strangers was a better option for me to become a mother. Perhaps I should have said what I was thinking instead of being polite. *What about STDs? What about morals?*

But really, Tina and her opinions were mind clutter compared to the important message of this evening, weren't they? The message had already come across loud and clear, and we were only halfway through. Adoption was going to be hard. Very hard. But for those of us who could stick it out through the application and matching processes, it might also be extremely rewarding.

"If you could make your way back to your seats, please, everyone?" The three social workers running the session were at the front again. The one on the left—Jenny—was tiny, with long dreadlocks and glasses. Sallyanne, standing in the middle, was young and eager looking with her apple-cheeked smile. And then there was Clare, on the right. Older than the other two, she was very neat looking with her precisely cut dark bob. Like Sallyanne, she was smiling but in a very different way. Clare's smile was . . . assessing—if a smile can be called assessing. There was confidence about the way she held herself, her weight evenly distributed on both feet, her hands clasped in front of her. I guessed she'd probably done about a hundred of these sessions before, but I also guessed she hadn't become blasé about it. Her gaze—with that relentless smile— passed over each of us in turn as she spoke. Registering us. Sorting us, maybe. Into definites, maybes, and impossibles.

I shuddered.

"Someone walk over your grave?" whispered Tina, but I just smiled.

"Okay," said Clare. "In the first part of tonight's session, you found out all about the adoption process. In this second part, we're going to look at some case studies as a first step towards familiarising you with the types of children waiting to be adopted. So if you can work with the couple nearest to you? There should be two groups of four and one group of three. We'll hand out the case studies for you to read, and then one of us will join you to help you discuss it."

People shuffled about, moving chairs into semicircles, exchanging pleasantries as they waited for the social workers to hand out the case studies. And then it went quiet as heads bowed and everyone began to read.

Our case study was about a two-year-old boy with alcohol-dependent parents. His half sister lived with him, and his grandfather tried to see him as much as possible but had health issues that often made that difficult.

I was soon totally absorbed, the little boy gaining my sympathy and empathy even before I'd reached the part about the domestic abuse and his mother ending up in hospital. How his half sister's father took her away to live with him, leaving the little boy alone.

"It's awful, isn't it?" said Tina when I let out a sound of distress.

But I just nodded, reading on about how the little boy had spent some time in foster care before being returned to his mother when she split up with his father.

"Don't tell me they got back together," said Tina, and sure enough, in the next paragraph, I discovered it was true.

The little boy's parents had recontinued their destructive relationship. Then, one night, the boy was injured during a fight. A neighbour rang the police, and the boy was placed in emergency foster care, only to be moved to another foster family a week later. Not surprisingly, with all the upheaval and all he had witnessed, the little boy was withdrawn and unresponsive at first.

"Poor little mite," said Tina.

"Don't worry," said Karl, who'd read on. "He came round after a bit. It says he got fond of them."

I was already reading about the monthly contact the boy had with his mother and sister—when his mum turned up, which she didn't always do. How both these contacts stopped when he was adopted. The case study finished by saying the boy had now reached many of his developmental targets and, despite being a handful at times, was happy in his new home, generally responding to clear, firm boundaries.

"Ah, he came good in the end," Tina said with satisfaction.

Clare, the social worker, had joined us while we were reading. "What do you think the issues were for this little boy?" she asked now. "The things that might have affected what the adopters had to deal with?"

"Well, he can't have known whether he was coming or going, can he?" said Tina. "It's awful how some people can stay in situations that are harmful to their children."

"Did the brother and sister really have to be separated?" I asked. "And the grandfather—couldn't he keep seeing him? It seems very harsh for them all to be separated like that."

"None of these situations are straightforward," said Clare. "There are always difficult decisions to be made where adoption is concerned. I'm not personally familiar with this case, so I can't give you any more details. But it's possible that making a complete break in this way was felt to be the best way for both children to settle into their new families. And I'm sure that annual letterbox contact will have been in place."

"It's being cruel to be kind," said Karl.

"I'm sure social services would never knowingly be cruel, Karl," said Tina.

Clare said something in response. I don't know what. I'd pretty much tuned them out by then. I couldn't stop imagining the boy and his sister hiding somewhere together to try to escape the shouting, maybe seeing the father hit the mother. Hugging each other for comfort. How it must have been for the little boy after his sister had gone and he was all on his own. The bewilderment of suddenly being uprooted from everything familiar.

In a way it reminded me of myself, after I'd moved to Ely, having been used to the bustle of cosmopolitan London. Which was ridiculous, of course. Me relocating to Cambridgeshire was nothing like a child being removed from his family.

"What's going on in your mind, Beth?" Clare asked.

I blinked when she spoke, so caught up in my thoughts I had to wipe my eyes on the back of my hand. "I was just imagining all that little boy must have gone through. Thinking how it must have stopped him trusting people."

"Yes, indeed," Clare said. "And that lack of trust has a knock-on effect on a child's behaviour and development."

"Trust can grow back, though, can't it?" asked Tina.

"Sometimes, yes," said Clare, but she said it in a way that made me supply the rest of the sentence: *But sometimes it doesn't.*

And then I thought of myself at nine years old, both of my parents suddenly gone. What would have happened to me if Aunt Tilda, Sylvia, and Richard hadn't been around? Would my story have ended up as a case study for potential adopters?

17

On the Saturday after the session, I went to Enfield to help Sylvia do some jobs in the garden. Richard had always done the majority of the gardening, but occasionally he and Sylvia did it together. Now it was all left to Sylvia. Mark had suggested she employ a gardener, but Sylvia didn't want to, and I didn't blame her. A stranger being there would have emphasised Richard's absence. Besides, I was more than happy to help out. Working on the borders Richard had dug and fertilised so carefully was like paying tribute to him. And anyway, it was good to see Sylvia.

We worked together companionably for an hour or so, talking about this and that, our conversation occasionally dwindling into a relaxed silence, the way it can when you're with those you're closest to. A tame robin made us smile when it hopped onto the garden fence, completely undaunted by our presence. And when we heard the tinkling music of an ice-cream van driving down the road, we both laughed out loud.

"He's hopeful in December," Sylvia said, laughing.

"Mark and Rosie would have been up for it," I said, and she laughed again.

"They would. You, not so much. They always had a sweeter tooth than you."

I pictured the three of us on hot summer days—seated in a line on Sylvia and Richard's front garden wall, Rosie and Mark finishing their ice creams in record time and me making mine last until it dripped down my arm.

"What was I like after Mum and Dad died?" I asked, my thoughts drifting back to the little boy in the case study and forward to my first social worker home visit, due to take place on Tuesday evening.

Sylvia straightened, pushing her blonde hair back from her face, leaving a smudge of dirt on her cheek. "Oh, darling, you were lost. A little lost soul. You'd be playing with Rosie one minute, all smiles, laughing about something together—you remember how you two used to get the giggles? You only had to look at each other, and you'd be off. But after your parents died, you'd suddenly go all quiet and creep up on the sofa next to me for a cuddle. You never wanted to speak about it. You just needed a cuddle. We did a lot of baking together, remember?"

"Chocolate muffins."

"Chocolate muffins, ginger biscuits, cheese straws . . . Richard used to say he had his own private baker's shop right in his own home."

We shared a smile. I remembered those days, Sylvia letting me scrape out the mixing bowl. Chocolate all around my face, a measure of comfort in my heart from the deliciousness of the smells in the kitchen and the magic of having created something so wonderful from such unpromising ingredients.

"Yum!" Richard would exclaim when he came into the kitchen, making me laugh when he closed his eyes in exaggerated rapture.

"How are you doing now?" I asked Sylvia, drawing her in for a hug.

"Oh, you know, jogging along," she said, hugging me back. "Sometimes I'm just like you were back then—I get absorbed in whatever I'm doing and think to myself, *That'll make Richard howl when I tell him*, and then I have to remember he's gone all over again."

"I know," I said. "I do that too."

We gave each other a final squeeze and got on with our weeding.

Sylvia sighed. "I do worry about Mark, you know. Rosie's okay, I think. Have you seen her lately?"

"We're meeting up on Monday night to go and see the Christmas lights."

"Oh, that's nice. Anyway, as I say, she's all right, I think. She's been letting her grief out. But I get the feeling Mark's been bottling his up, what with getting his business up and running."

"How's that going, d'you know?"

"I'm not sure. He and Grace aren't likely to tell me if anything's wrong, are they? Wouldn't want to worry me. And he has got Grace to talk to. The thing is, he'd probably have spoken to his father, too, if he'd been here, what with Richard being self-employed for most of his career." She sighed. "I don't know, love. I'm probably worrying for nothing. You do when you're a mum. You'll find that out yourself soon enough."

"I guess I will."

"I think it's a wonderful thing you're doing."

"Do you? Not crazy?"

"Not at all. I think it will be hard, yes, but really worthwhile. I'll give you all the support I possibly can."

"You always have."

"Oh, darling, how could I not? We always loved you, Richard and me. And Tilda . . . She meant well, bless her, but well, let's just say she was sometimes out of her depth."

"Was I that bad?"

"Of course not. You were grieving, that's all. You just needed a haven. It'll be the same for any child you adopt. That's what they'll need too."

"That's what you still are to me, you know, a haven. Richard was too."

"Yes, I know he was. Bless him. I can't believe it's been almost a year since he went, I really can't."

I thought about the cruise Sylvia was going on over the holiday period. "Where will the ship be on the actual anniversary?"

Sylvia dug her garden fork hard into the soil so it stood up by itself, and then she reached for her secateurs to start cutting the ivy back. "We'll be in Bridgetown, Barbados. It's a day's stopover. I shall do a bit of shopping—you know how bored Richard always got when I dragged him round any shops—and then I'm going to go on a trip to Harrison's Cave. Richard would have liked that, wouldn't he? It's got lots of stalagmites and stalactites."

I smiled. "I can hear him talking about it," I said, "explaining which is which. *The 'mites go up, and the 'tites come down.*"

Sylvia laughed. "Yes, he would say that, wouldn't he? Anyway, yes, so I'm going to do that—something for me, and something for him, just as we would have done if he were still here."

"And what about Christmas Day?"

Sylvia pulled hard at the ivy, and a long strand came away from the wall. "We're at sea on Christmas Day. No doubt there'll be heaps of things organised. But to be honest, I'll probably just lie low in my cabin all day. Send out for room service." She reached out to squeeze my arm. "But I shall be quite all right. Don't you worry about me. What about you? Are you still on sick-animal duty over Christmas?"

"Yes, if there are any sick animals to look after."

Sylvia shoved the ivy strand into the garden waste bin, pressing the leaves down to make room for more. "Next year we'll have a Christmas to remember. Richard would want us to do that. But I like to think he'd understand us not feeling up to it this year."

She straightened to look at me, her hands rubbing the small of her back. "Did Jaimie understand what Richard was to you, darling?"

My eyes instantly filled. "No," I said. "Not at all."

"I'm so sorry," she said. "That must have been very lonely for you. Richard was your dad. Your second dad."

"He was," I said. "He really was." The tears slid down my face.

"Come here." Sylvia reached for me, and as we held each other to have a good old cry, the robin popped onto the fence to watch us.

18

On Monday, Rosie and I met each other as planned at the foot of the Christmas tree in Trafalgar Square. Starting our Christmas light spotting beneath the tree had become one of our traditions—the tree was always so impressive, and this year's was no exception. The people of Oslo donated it every year to thank the UK for helping them during the Second World War, and the tree was at least twenty metres tall and decorated in the Norwegian style with vertical strings of lights. Towering between the Trafalgar Square fountains, floodlit in violet, the tree was a symbol of hope, which, after the twelve months Rosie and I had had, was something we both definitely needed.

After we'd admired the tree for a while, we went to a nearby café for a cup of coffee before setting off for Regent Street. Rosie was wearing an incredibly cute leopard-print bobble hat and matching scarf. I doubted whether I looked quite so cute myself. My own hat and scarf were bright red, and as my nose felt pinched by the cold, I suspected it was the same colour. But I didn't care. This was Rosie—the girl who'd held my hair back from my face as I vomited from food poisoning one ill-fated Spanish holiday. The girl who'd seen me red eyed with stinking colds and with a spot-covered face during our teenage years. We knew each other, warts and all, Rosie and me.

"I saw your mum last weekend. We did some gardening together."

Rosie stirred sugar into her coffee. "She wasn't too busy ironing her bikinis, then?"

"I'm not sure whether she's packing a bikini."

"You can't go on a Caribbean holiday without a bikini."

"I wanted to give her a really nice sun hat for her Christmas present, but there weren't any in the shops, with it being Christmas."

"She can buy one out there. It'll give her something to do."

Something about Rosie's tone caused me to frown. "Do you mind about her going? You sound as if you do."

She shrugged, frowning herself. "Dad would have hated a cruise. All those smug people crammed in together and overindulging. Like a floating housing estate."

I spooned some of the chocolate-sprinkled froth from the top of my cappuccino into my mouth. "Your mum will love chatting to people, though, won't she? She's so sociable. And think of all the sights she'll get to see."

Rosie wasn't convinced. "Sunburnt beer bellies? Women parading their breast implants?"

"I'm sure it won't be like that."

She sighed. "Oh, don't listen to me. I'm just worried about her, that's all. I think she'll get out there and be lonely as hell."

"Well, let's hope you're wrong. Or, if you're not, let's hope the tropical seas and the dolphin sightings help a little."

"I'm going to miss her."

Now it was my turn to sigh. I could certainly empathise with that. "I know."

"You too. I can't believe you've managed to get out of Christmas with Mark and Grace."

"I'm sure it won't be that bad."

"D'you reckon? You do know her parents will be there? And her sister and her husband. And their *baby*."

The way she said the word *baby* with such horror made her sound like a heartless monster. "Not exactly a baby now," I soothed. "She's one."

"Well, she won't be able to talk to me about the latest fashions or laugh at Christmas cracker jokes, will she?"

"Will Grace even have Christmas crackers?" I wondered out loud.

Rosie's eyebrows shot up cynically. "If she does, they'll probably be the super-posh sort, I suppose. You know, the sort containing a fully functioning corkscrew or a spanner set instead of a fortune-telling fish."

I smiled at that, remembering an occasion a few years back when we'd all tried out the red cellophane fortune-telling fish Rosie had got in her Christmas cracker. One by one, we laid it on our palms, as directed by the instructions, and one by one, we laughed as the fish curled right up to indicate we were "passionate." But then when Mark had passed it to his dad for his turn, it had fallen into Richard's full wineglass.

"Oh dear," Richard said. "That's a passion killer." And we all fell about laughing.

I sighed. "You'll be all right," I told my friend. "Perhaps it's best to think of Christmas as just another day. That's what I'm going to do."

"Well, it is, isn't it?" said Rosie. "Another day Dad isn't here with us."

Straightaway, my eyes filled with tears. "I know."

We gripped each other's hands for a while, then Rosie got a packet of tissues from her bag and offered me one, and we both blew our noses, the stereo trumpeting sounds making us laugh.

"Your mum was reminding me about our giggling fits the other day."

"God, yes. They were crazy, weren't they? Sometimes my stomach hurt so much from laughing I couldn't stand it. We didn't even always know why we were laughing, did we?"

I shook my head. "It didn't seem to matter."

"I haven't had a good laugh like that for ages. Perhaps we should go to a comedy club or something."

But we both knew we wouldn't, and the acknowledgment took the smiles from our faces.

I drank some of my cappuccino, licking the froth from my upper lip. Rosie drank her black coffee.

"How was the introduction session last week? I thought you'd call to tell me about it."

I had thought about calling Rosie. But I couldn't shake off the feeling she didn't quite approve of what I was doing. So in the end, I hadn't.

"It was all right. Quite a lot to take in. Emotional at times. But then, I think the whole application process will be emotional."

"I wrote my reference and sent it off."

I squeezed her hand. "Thank you."

"I hope it's all right."

"Why wouldn't it be?"

Rosie shrugged. "I don't know. I'm out of my depth with anything to do with kiddos. You know that."

"You know me, though. You know what I'm like."

"Yes, but not as a potential parent, not really."

"You saw me with Olivia and Emily."

"Not that much. And besides . . ."

"What?"

"Well, that wasn't exactly an ideal situation, was it?"

"You mean they hated me?"

It was her turn to squeeze my hand. "They didn't hate you. It was just that the whole time they were with you, they wished you were their mother."

She'd hit the nail right on the head. "Did you say that in your reference?"

"Don't be daft. Of course not. I went on about you being a very caring, thoughtful person. Nurturing, that sort of thing. I steered well clear of your overcompetitiveness at board games and your annoying habit of still having Easter eggs left to eat five weeks after Easter."

I smiled, knowing she was remembering the Easter she'd stolen half of my Easter egg and tried to rewrap it so the theft wouldn't be discovered. Stupid, really. I'd have given it to her if she'd asked for it.

"What about my foray into naturism?" I asked.

"Oh, I spoke about that at great length."

We smiled at each other. "Thank you for doing it, though. She's coming to see me tomorrow evening, the social worker."

"To interrogate you?"

"That's probably how it will feel. I've been trying to prepare for it, but it's difficult when you don't know exactly what they'll be asking."

Rosie put her coffee cup down in its saucer. "Come on," she said. "Let's hit the Christmas lights. I'm told there's an angel theme along Regent Street this year."

There was. Right along the length of the glamorous shopping street—from Piccadilly Circus to Oxford Street—winged figures reached towards the sky in reverse dives, their arms extended vertically, their wings stretched out to their sides, the drapery of their clothing swinging out below like butterfly plumes.

"Wow," I breathed, squinting to get the full effect of the silver-blue dazzle of the lights.

"The wings look as if they're moving, with the way the lights are programmed," said Rosie.

"It's very effective," I agreed, and as we slowly walked along from angel to angel, the thrill of that sparkle seemed to infiltrate my bones, adding to the gleam of optimism from the Trafalgar Square Christmas tree. As I gazed up at the angels, everything seemed possible. They didn't predict a lonely, miserable Christmas and an unfulfilled New Year. Quite the opposite.

"I love doing this with you," Rosie said, linking her arm in mine. "I missed it last year."

I thought of the previous year and shuddered. "Me too. Let's never miss it again."

Rosie glanced my way. "Well, all right," she said. "But you do realise this is the last time it will be quite like this, don't you? If you adopt a kiddo, we won't be strolling along all relaxed like this. We won't be en route to a swanky cocktail bar for mojitos either."

"Well, no," I conceded, "I suppose not. But it will be even more magical with a child with us, won't it? Children adore Christmas lights."

"They'll like it for about two minutes. Then they'll be cold or hungry or bored, and you'll be trying to distract them instead of listening to me tell you what I got up to at the office party. You'll be wiping their disgusting snotty noses or backtracking five hundred metres to find their lost glove. I do have other friends with children, you know. Hell, all my friends have children apart from you. And now you're about to join the club too."

I shook my head at her. "How did you get to be so cynical about children?"

Rosie shrugged. "You've got me all wrong," she said. "I love children. I just can't eat a whole one."

"Very funny."

"Sorry. Look, don't listen to me."

"I'm not. I won't."

"Good. You've got to do what feels right for you. And if that means taking on a wrecked little life and trying to turn it around, then so be it."

"Maybe the hardest things are the most worthwhile," I said, hoping it was true.

Rosie sighed. "Maybe. Anyway, like I say, don't listen to me. Let's go and get our mojitos. Next year we'll just have to bring our own supplies. You can turn the bottom of the buggy into a cocktail bar."

"Promise me something," I said. "If my social worker follows up your reference by phone, don't mention that plan to her."

She laughed. "All right."

When we arrived at the cocktail bar, the barman was receiving some instruction from his supervisor. Clearly new to the job, he looked nervous after the supervisor left and he came over to take our order. "What can I get you, ladies?"

I watched a wicked smile form on Rosie's face and instantly pitied him. I'd seen that smile before. Many times. "I think I'll have a No Commitment, please," she said, settling herself down on a barstool. "And my friend here will have a Full-On Responsibility."

Memories of Olivia and Emily inventing names for nail varnishes resurfaced, but I pushed them gently away. "No," I contradicted my friend. "I'll have a Brimming Over Cup, and she'll have a Bitter Cow."

Rosie grinned. The barman looked as if he were contemplating quitting.

"Actually," Rosie said, "my friend's wrong. I'm so over Bitter Cows. I'm all about Sowing Wild Oats now. It's utterly delicious, Beth. You should definitely try it." She smiled at the barman. "Yes, I'll have a Sowing Wild Oats, please. With extra oats."

I burst out laughing. The barman glanced nervously over his shoulder for his supervisor, who was nowhere in sight. "Er, I'm very sorry, madam," he said, "but I'm afraid I'm not familiar with any of those cocktails."

"Well," I said, "in that case, we'll both have mojitos, thanks."

"Spoilsport," said Rosie after the barman had scurried off to make them. "I can just taste that No Commitment now. Passion fruit, peaches, and vodka with a dash of champagne."

"It sounds absolutely disgusting."

"Don't knock it until you've tried it."

"I have tried it. It gave me a hangover."

We smiled at each other, both aware we weren't talking about cocktails.

"You'll be all right, kid," she said. "We both will."

But later, as I tried to get to sleep, I realised what Rosie had said was true. Our friendship would never be quite the same once I had a child. But that didn't mean it wouldn't continue, did it? We'd been friends forever. We always would be.

19

"What makes you want to adopt a child now, Beth?"

Clare Carter was seated at my dining room table, next to my shelving unit. I'd liked Clare the least out of the three social workers at the introductory session. I'd respected her—she'd seemed experienced and very good at her job. But I hadn't wanted her to be allocated to my case, because I sensed that the other two social workers—Jenny and Sallyanne—might give me an easier ride. But of course, I'd been teamed up with Clare. Of course.

Clare struck me as a woman of strong opinions. For example, I saw her notice the colour I'd painted the shelving unit—flamingo pink—the minute I'd shown her into the living room. While she didn't quite shudder, it was a very close-run thing. She certainly *thought* a shudder.

I supposed the shelves were quite bright against the jade-green walls, especially with all the tinsel and Christmas decorations adorning the items on display, but after the paint stripper didn't work, I went to the DIY shop, and that pink just called to me. It was as if Richard were looking over my shoulder. I could almost hear him laughing. *If that's the colour you want, you go for it, girl. But make sure to do two coats. Pink can come out a bit streaky.*

I invited Clare to sit on the sofa—I thought soft furnishings might be a bit less formal and more relaxing. But she opted for a wooden dining chair at the table, so I guessed she wanted it to feel formal and unrelaxed. But perhaps I'd have felt tense on the sofa.

As I sat down opposite her, I wished my chair were facing the garden instead of the door to the spare bedroom. A view of the garden and the odd friendly sparrow or blackbird might have helped me feel less like I was facing a firing squad.

But this was no good. No good. I had to focus. Put any negative thoughts behind me. This woman had the power to make or break my dreams. Besides, it was hardly a controversial question, was it? *What makes you want to adopt a child now?*

"Well, I've always wanted to have children, and I'm thirty-seven now. Mentally and financially, I'm ready for it. I don't have any debts, and my job is secure . . ."

God, I sounded as if I were speaking in support of a bank loan application. I'd put all this across much better in the written application I'd agonised over for a week—the one I'd read snippets of to friends, tweaking the tone, triple-checking spellings and grammar.

I sighed. Dried up.

Clare Carter smiled. "Take your time."

"I suppose I thought I'd have a family by now, but for one reason or another, that hasn't happened, so I thought . . . Well, I'm sure you've read about my situation. My childhood. I was practically adopted myself after my parents died—my Aunt Tilda and my friend's parents shared care of me. So I thought . . . well, you're always hearing about children needing families, aren't you? I thought maybe I could put my experience to good use. To help a child."

It sounded frustratingly lame to my ears. Certainly, I'd done little to convey the exciting light-bulb moment I'd had in the bath one Sunday night, lying in the bubbles contemplating my childless state. *Why not adopt? Christ on a bike! I could try to adopt!*

"Thank you," said Clare, jotting a note down on her pad. "There's a lot to unpack there. Why don't we start by discussing that distressing time in your life when you lost your parents? How did you find out about their accident?"

My stomach clenched. I wasn't sure what to do with my hands. I generally play with my hair when I have to talk about this kind of heavy stuff, but I was trying really hard not to fidget like a nervous wreck.

"I was at school. In a science lesson. We were doing an experiment to learn about electric currents. The school secretary came to fetch me out of class. When I got to reception, there was Aunt Tilda, standing with the head teacher. They took me into the office, and then . . . well, they told me."

I hadn't wanted to leave that experiment. Mrs. Hounslow, my teacher, had put me in charge of my group, and we were about to be the first group to connect up the light at the top of a model lighthouse. No doubt my expression had been surly as hell as I followed the school secretary out to reception. I had no idea why I'd been called out of class. Mum and Dad were still away, so it wouldn't be my mum waiting to take me to the dentist or some other forgotten appointment. It was Aunt Tilda. And Aunt Tilda as I'd never seen her before, her smart black jacket done up on the wrong buttons, her eyes red rimmed as if she'd been crying.

"So you went to live with your aunt?"

I nodded. "Yes." If it had been anybody else, I'd probably have changed the subject at this point. Offered them another cup of tea or a biscuit. Asked them a question about themselves. Anything so they'd take the hint and drop it. I'd been a very miserable young girl for quite a long time after my parents died, and I didn't like to dwell on it.

But if I wanted this application to work, I didn't have a choice, did I? If Clare Carter wanted me to talk about the day I lost my virginity or my first experience of smoking, I would have to talk about it, wouldn't I? She called all the shots.

"And what was Tilda like?"

I thought about it for a moment. "'Worried' probably describes it best. Stressed. But that's hardly surprising, is it? She was a single woman with a high-powered job in the city, without much experience with children, and suddenly she had complete responsibility for the well-being of a nine-year-old child. It was no wonder she was worried and stressed . . ."

Clare's pen was writing, writing, her bobbed hair swinging as she bent over her pad of paper, and it suddenly occurred to me that—leaving the high-powered City of London job aside—I had, in fact, pretty much described my own situation. Single. Little experience with children. Worried. Well done, Beth. Well done.

"And how, in your view, do you think your aunt coped with this situation?"

"She did her very best. Aunt Tilda was like that—thorough in everything. With hindsight, I can see she probably had to make a lot of sacrifices for me. Cut down on her social life and her holidays, that sort of thing. She was interested in archaeology, but she couldn't drag a young child along on digs. We went a few times when I was a bit older, but . . ."

I had a sudden flashback to a holiday in Scotland volunteering on a dig when I was twelve. How utterly bored I'd been. How sulky, stomping about the place in my Doc Martens while the rain slashed down outside all week long. I doubted whether Tilda would have repeated the experiment had she lived to do so, but in fact, it proved to be the last holiday we had together. Because she died the following year, and I went to live with Richard and Sylvia permanently.

"Tilda sold her house in Hampstead so I could go back to my school in Enfield and my friend's mum and dad could look after me sometimes."

Tilda sold her house in Hampstead so I could go back to my school in Enfield . . . The short sentence made it sound so easy. As if Aunt Tilda had put her house on the market right away. But it hadn't quite happened like that. Well, not at all like that, in fact. At first, Tilda had tried to make things work by moving me in with her in Hampstead, uprooting me from everything familiar and everyone I loved who I hadn't actually lost. She had her spare bedroom decorated in a way she thought I'd flip out about and enrolled me at her local primary school.

I hated that bedroom because it was so beautiful. It was everything I'd ever wanted in a bedroom. And I felt as if I'd swapped my parents for it. As if maybe, if I destroyed it, they'd come back. I didn't suppose I really thought they would. After all, I'd been to their funeral, so I'd seen their coffins side by side in front of the altar, and I'd seen Sylvia, Aunt Tilda, and all my parents' friends crying at the sheer waste and tragedy of their passing. I hadn't cried myself. I was still frozen, I guess. Numb. The sight of that beautiful, freshly decorated bedroom almost undid me, but not quite. I managed to hang on.

Aunt Tilda took the morning off work to take me to school that first morning. After that I was destined to attend a breakfast club and an after-school club while Tilda travelled to and fro from work. But that first morning, Tilda took the morning off work and laid out my school uniform for me. Then she attempted to tackle my hair. Even though I was nine, my mum had always brushed it. It was long and thick—difficult hair. Reddish auburn, like my dad's. Aunt Tilda didn't have a clue what to do with it, so in the end she left it to me to sort out myself, and I tied it back like a horse's mane.

My feet dragged as we left the house. I did not want to go to any new school, and I kept thinking of my mother's capable fingers flying over my head as she put my hair in a neat french pleat. Kissing me before I ran across the playground to join my friends.

Aunt Tilda and I were awkward about kissing. It was different when my parents were alive, and we didn't see Tilda very often. Then, it felt natural for my aunt to kiss me hello and goodbye when she came for a visit. But now I was with her all the time, and there were more opportunities for kissing, but I think we were both painfully aware it would feel as if she were trying to replace my mother if she kissed me good night or, in this case, goodbye. So when we got to the school, Tilda settled for giving me a pat on the shoulder and shot a big false smile in my direction which didn't quite hide the worry in her eyes.

"Have a good day, Beth. I'll be here to collect you at three o'clock."

But she had to collect me well before that because a girl called me Carrot Head at the midmorning break, and I punched her so hard in the face that her nose bled right down her school uniform.

After that, I pretty much refused to go to school, let alone to the after-school club Tilda had arranged for me. And if Tilda ever did manage to get me to school, I caused trouble. I hated them all, the kids in my class, even those brave enough to try to befriend me. They didn't have a hope in hell of becoming my friend, because they weren't Rosie.

Aunt Tilda stuck it out for a bit more than a week before I made her cry. The tipping point came when she discovered a great big tear in my bedroom wallpaper. I'd found a minute loose corner and picked at it with my fingernails until I'd managed to free enough from the wall to pull it. The sound as it ripped upwards was so satisfying it made me smile for the first time in a month.

But I didn't smile as I watched Aunt Tilda cry. I'd expected her to be angry—I'd have been able to cope with that. But she wasn't angry, just heartbroken. "Oh, Beth," she said, holding her arms out to me, and when I went into them, it was somehow the permission I needed to cry myself.

That was when Tilda made her big decision to put her house on the market—after I'd put us both through sheer hell. Tilda completely changed her life for me, but the truth was, despite everything she did, I was always happier when I was round at Sylvia and Richard's house. So no, nothing about that situation was easy enough to describe in one sentence.

But I could hardly spew all that out to Clare Carter, could I? Not without sounding violent or deranged. I hadn't punched anybody before that day on the Hampstead playground, and I haven't punched anybody since. But she'd know I was capable of it.

Or would it be a good thing to tell her? So she could see I had empathy for children going through difficult times? I couldn't tell quite yet. I wasn't familiar enough with the adoption application game we were playing. Because it did feel like a game—a game of adoption application chess—and a dangerous one at that.

"That must have been very hard for you," Clare said. "Nowadays a child in the position you found yourself in would probably receive counselling, but I suspect that was in short supply in the 1990s."

I had absolutely no idea. But I was pretty sure I wouldn't have been receptive to it if it had been offered.

"You say in your application that your aunt died when you were nearly thirteen?"

"Yes, she had lung cancer."

"Coming only four years after the death of your parents, that must have been very hard."

I nodded. "It was, yes."

"And then I see you went to live permanently with Richard and Sylvia Groves?"

"Yes. Their daughter, Rosie, is my best friend."

"And how did that work out for you?"

I thought about those years. Richard and Sylvia being their full-on supportive selves. Rosie and I sharing a bedroom and staying awake until late, giggling and gossiping. Me, in mega-crush-on-Mark mode, encountering him on the landing when one of us was on the way to the bathroom. Raucous family meals which everyone did their loving best to make me feel a part of.

"It was fine," I told Clare inadequately. "I missed Tilda, but I was happy. Richard and Sylvia treated me like a second daughter."

"And are you still close to them? Will they form part of your support group?"

I swallowed. "I'm still very close to Sylvia, but sadly Richard . . . passed away this time last year."

Even after twelve months I was incapable of speaking those words without tears pricking my eyes, and when I saw Clare notice them, I pushed my chair back and got to my feet.

"I'm so sorry," I said. "I didn't offer you a cup of tea or coffee."

"Not for me, thank you," Clare responded. "We have a great deal to get through today."

Which didn't give me permission to make a hot drink for myself.

"Well, I'll just get myself a glass of water, if that's all right. Can I get one for you?"

"No, thank you."

If I'd sought to distract Clare from my grief about Richard, then my attempt was a dismal failure. When I sat back down again, she was right there, with her direct gaze and her poised pen.

"Your reaction shows me you felt Richard's death very keenly. Would it be correct to say you're still grieving?"

Just for a moment, I paused, trying to second-guess what the best answer would be. Did grieving show empathy or weakness? But then I realised it didn't really matter. I was incapable of pretending not to still be grieving for Richard. And besides, I'd already given myself away.

"Yes, I suppose I am. He meant a great deal to me."

"I imagine his death also served as a reminder to you of all your other losses. To lose three significant family members by the age of thirteen is quite something, is it not?"

I nodded, taking a sip of my water.

"I'm not talking about these things to make you miserable, you understand," said Clare, and inside my head I could hear Rosie's voice saying, *Oh yeah?*

"Only to acknowledge the emotions you're very likely experiencing at the moment. My first duty must always be towards the children we seek to help. Adoption is far from being an easy ride. For anyone. The children we're looking to place need adopters with resilience and strong emotional resources."

"Yes," I said, pulling myself together. "I appreciate that. And actually, apart from when I attended the funeral, I didn't take any time off work because of Richard's death. I am a strong, resilient person. In fact, my job regularly requires me to deal with death. Obviously, as a veterinary nurse, it's the death of pets I encounter on a weekly basis, not people. But they're usually very much-loved pets, and you have to be compassionate towards their owners while at the same time building up your personal resilience in order to deal with it."

Even though I'd sounded as if I were at a job interview, it felt as if I'd scored a point when Clare nodded and made a note on her pad. But if I'd thought the difficult questions were over, I was wrong.

"I couldn't help noticing several guidebooks on your bookshelves. Have you done a lot of travelling?"

This time, I noticed the potential trap. Not that there was a lot I could do about it, barring telling her a pack of lies about collecting guidebooks as part of a fantasy tourism habit.

"Yes, quite a lot. Especially in my student days."

"When was the last time you went abroad?"

"A year and a half ago. For a family holiday to Greece."

Clare consulted her notes. "Was that while you were in a relationship with Mr. Faulkner?"

I flushed. I wasn't sure why. I saw Clare notice. "Yes, that's right."

"We'll need to discuss that relationship in some detail, since Mr. Faulkner has children. I thought we could do that in our next session. We have time to meet once more before Christmas."

The need to talk about Jaimie didn't come as a surprise to me. I'd guessed I'd have to at some point. But that didn't mean I was looking forward to it.

"How do you feel about not being able to travel or go on holiday easily if you adopt a child?" Clare asked now, slightly leaning forward in her seat towards me.

I answered honestly. "I feel fine about it, actually. I'm glad I travelled when I did, but now I'm content to stay put. And the UK has so much to offer, doesn't it?"

Clare looked doubtful. "Many of our children have never been on holiday at all—not even in the UK. They've lived very uncertain lives. They may have lived with several different foster carers before they come to you, for instance. It's important they have stability so they can start to trust and start to believe their new situation is permanent. Holidays of any description probably wouldn't be a good idea for several years."

I nodded. I could understand that. "That's fine. There are parks nearby. And the garden, of course."

"Yes, about the garden." Clare moved a little so she could see out the window. "From what I can see, it looks very pretty. But perhaps not very child friendly? Would you be prepared to make over some of your flower borders to grass, do you think?"

I blinked, hoping she wouldn't go on to suggest I get the plane tree chopped down. "Yes, of course," I said. Because although it would pain me to pull up my flower borders, I sincerely believed having a child enjoy the garden was likely to give me a great deal more pleasure.

Clare scrutinised my expression, as if to gauge my sincerity, then gave a satisfied nod. "We have to be quite certain of an adopter's commitment," she said. "I'm sure you understand that. Were you to have pets, I'd be asking you whether you'd be prepared to rehome the animal should your child be afraid of it, or if, indeed, your child demonstrated cruelty towards it."

A child who was cruel to animals? Was that really likely?

Clare seemed to read my thoughts. "It can sometimes happen, unfortunately. A child may come from a home where the parents habitually mistreated animals. Or sometimes, a child may behave towards an animal in the way an adult has behaved towards him or her."

God, it was so very sad.

"But you don't have any pets, so we don't need to worry about that. Unless you ever bring any animals back here as part of your work?"

"I do occasionally, but only on a voluntary basis. I'm not required to."

Clare nodded and made a note. "Good." She closed her notebook. "I think that's sufficient for today. I'll leave you some worksheets to complete before we meet again. And perhaps you could do some research about any local schools or groups that might accept you as a volunteer? You really need to get as much experience with children as you can to support your application. I realise this isn't the best time to approach anyone, with Christmas fast approaching, but if you make enquiries now, you'd be able to start in the New Year."

"Of course," I said, and Clare took her leave, having arranged another appointment for the following week.

After she'd gone, I felt a bit bleak. Instinctively, I reached for my phone to call Rosie. But once again, I changed my mind. Rosie already thought I was crazy, trying to adopt. If I told her about grassing over my garden and potentially having to deal with cruelty towards animals, she'd only advise me to withdraw my application.

I wandered over to the bookshelf which had given away my love of travel, running my hand across the book spines. Australia, Thailand, Colorado, Cuba . . . So many places, so many memories. Most years, somewhere different. Had I spoken the truth when I'd said those days were over? Yes, I thought so. At least for now. All that travel had been a hunger for discovery—not only about places but also about myself. For years, I'd been searching for something. I still was, I supposed. It was just that now I was searching closer to home.

My hand came to rest on a guidebook to Belize. I pulled it out. The cover image was of a woman swimming in crystal-clear water with a palm-tree-festooned island on the horizon. I smiled, opening the book to read the inscription. *For Beth. Happy holidays! Smithy.*

Smithy. God, it had been a long time since I'd thought about him. He was the one who'd first given me the travel bug. Without Smithy, I might never have travelled to all those other countries. Where was he now? The last time I'd mentioned him to Mark, he'd said they'd lost touch. Which was sad, since they'd been such good friends at university. But probably inevitable given the circumstances. Poor Smithy.

20

I was meant to be driving myself to uni on my first day—the car Richard had picked out for me was parked on the forecourt, taking up precious space. A red Mini, which Mark immediately nicknamed the Ladybird. But I'd failed my driving test, so for now, I couldn't drive it.

"Mark can give you a lift in, can't you, Mark?" suggested Sylvia.

"'Course I can," said Mark.

So it was all settled.

I hadn't deliberately applied to the same university as Mark. It just happened to be the closest university to Sylvia and Richard's where I could study veterinary nursing. I could have studied somewhere else in the country, but I didn't want to. Why would I when I knew I wanted to settle down in London eventually? At least, that's what I told myself.

I was excited to be starting my course and pleased to be free of the petty rules and regulations of school. And now here I was, getting into Mark's Vauxhall Astra for the thirty-minute journey to my future.

Despite the fact that we lived in the same house, Mark and I rarely spent any time alone together. We kept different hours—Mark often out late with his uni friends or round at a girlfriend's house. Rosie and I had been knuckling down to get through our final school exams all year, so after we'd finished them, we spent most of the long summer lolling about idly in hammocks strung between trees at the bottom of the garden.

But Rosie had started a new job at the end of August, so the day I started university, she'd already left the house in her smart office clothes. As Mark drove away from the house, I had the sense that nothing was ever going to be the same again. Having experienced more than my fair share of change and upheaval in my life, I suppose it wasn't surprising I felt suddenly scared and overwhelmed. Certainly, I could have done with Rosie's moral support.

Mark somehow seemed to sense how I felt. Or maybe it was just blindingly obvious.

"It will be all right, you know," he said. "For about five minutes, everything will seem a bit strange, but then you'll make friends and you'll be fine."

"I hope so."

"I know so. Your driving test too. Don't worry about that. You're bound to pass next time. Anybody can clip a kerb when they're reversing. I do it all the time."

I knew Mark would have ribbed Rosie something rotten if she'd been the one to clip a kerb during her driving test, and yet here he was, being really nice to me. Sylvia must have had a word with him. But I wished she hadn't, because I wasn't sure what to say to this nice, reassuring Mark. Teasing Mark—the Mark I was used to—would have been much easier to deal with.

Silence fell—the kind of total silence you get when you wake up one winter morning and it's been snowing. A blanket of silence where nothing feels the same as usual.

Mark switched the radio on. The sound of Bryan Adams singing a song from *Robin Hood: Prince of Thieves* filled the car.

He groaned. "I can't believe this is still number one," he said, switching the radio off.

"Rosie and I loved that film," I said.

"Only because you've both got a crush on Kevin Costner," Mark retorted. "No idea why. He didn't even try to do a proper accent."

"You're only jealous because he's such a heartthrob," I said.

"Jealous? Of that blow-dry fanatic? I'm surprised he even did all that high-action stuff when it could have messed up his hair."

I grinned. Good. We were back in familiar territory.

Mark was right. I did make friends quickly with the people on my course. We were the same age, all crazy about animals and their welfare, sharing the same frustrations and successes. It was easy. I was happy. I even passed my driving test the second time around, as Mark had predicted. I still saw him after I started driving myself to uni, though. He and his friends hung out in the same cafeteria and student bar as we did, and sometimes my friends and I joined them, or they joined us. And that's how I met Smithy.

My course was a practical one—half my time was taken up by academic study, but for the other half I was based at various veterinary practices to gain hands-on experience. The first time I witnessed an animal death as part of my work—a much-loved cat we had tried and failed to save on the operating table after a road traffic accident—I came home feeling tearful. The cat's owners, including five-year-old twin girls, had been waiting for news in the waiting room. I hadn't had to break the bad news to them myself, but I had witnessed their heartbreak, and it had cut me to the quick.

When I got home and realised Mark had a few friends round, I tried to sneak upstairs without anybody seeing me. But Sylvia's distress radar was fully active, and after I'd told her what was wrong and received a sympathetic hug, I was urged to join everyone in the kitchen for pizza. Everyone sympathised with me, and Smithy tried to distract me with talk of a trip he was planning on taking to Belize in the summer.

"There's a coral reef, so we're hoping to do some snorkelling. And we're going on a boat trip to try to see a manatee."

"What's a manatee?" I asked, never having heard of one.

"It's a sort of sea cow," he said. "They have flippers and a flat tail. They've become quite rare now, but I really hope we see one."

"It sounds like a wonderful trip."

"Why don't you see if there are any places left, if you like the sound of it?" Smithy surprised me by saying. "Mind you, it's quite expensive. I can only afford it because my parents gave me some money for my twenty-first birthday to top up my savings."

Money wasn't really an issue for me. At the age of eighteen, I'd inherited the money left to me by my parents, as well as some money from Aunt Tilda. I was going to use it to buy a flat in London, but it wouldn't hurt to spend a bit of it for a holiday.

"What about the friend you're going with? Won't he mind if I tag along?"

"Kevin?" said Smithy. "He won't mind."

I never did get to find out whether Kevin minded me going or not, because almost as soon as we arrived in Belize, he hooked up with the only other single girl on the trip, and the two of them quickly became inseparable, leaving me and Smithy alone for the majority of the time. We visited Mayan ruins and caught glimpses of crocodiles laid up on riverbanks when we went on a boat trip through the jungle. We saw butterflies as big as our hands and tiny, jewel-bright hummingbirds. Rays and multicoloured fish swam past as we snorkelled, and dolphins arced out of the sea. We ate local food, drank local beer. It was fabulous. Apart from Smithy developing a crush on me.

On our final night, everyone danced on the sand to the music of a local band. When the music turned romantic, Smithy grabbed me.

"I'm sorry we didn't get to see any manatees," he said, holding me close.

I tried a joke. "It's not your fault they're shy."

But Smithy's face was suddenly serious, and I knew he was going to kiss me.

"It's been a fantastic trip," I said, trying to keep things light.

"It wouldn't have been nearly as good without you," he said, lowering his head.

For a fraction of a second, I thought about letting him kiss me. About kissing him back. Smithy was a really nice guy, and it wasn't as if Mark returned my feelings. In fact, he was totally oblivious to them. Why not go out with Smithy?

But then I tried to picture us back home, Smithy's arm around me as we sat in the pub with our friends, and I just couldn't do it. So I pulled back.

Smithy's hands tightened on my shoulders. He looked down at me. "It's Mark, isn't it?" he said. "You're in love with Mark."

I thought about denying it. But in the end, I just said, "Don't say anything, will you?"

And he sighed and let me go. "You should tell him," he advised me.

I shook my head. "He doesn't see me that way. Never has."

"So, what? You're going to spend your whole life pining for the guy?"

"Of course not. Eventually my feelings for him will go away. I'll meet someone and be able to move on."

"Just not me, eh? I get it."

~

I put the guidebook to Belize back on the bookshelf. Smithy worked abroad somewhere now, and as far as I knew, he was still unmarried. As for Mark, well . . . It had been a while since I'd heard from him. Grace still hadn't forgiven me for breaking up with Jaimie, which must have made it difficult for Mark to get in touch. Plus, he was busy with his fledgling business. Was Sylvia right about him keeping his grief unhealthily bottled up? I hoped he was okay.

Perhaps I should take my travel guides to a charity shop so someone else could make use of them. Make space in the bookcase for children's books.

21

"Who do we have here?" Clive, my boss, asked. "Blazer, is it?"

I stroked the blaze of white on the collie cross's neck, which had no doubt inspired his name. "Yes, that's right, poor boy."

Clive removed his Santa hat and finished scrubbing his hands. "I think he should be all right. I'm fairly confident I can completely remove that tumour. So long as the cancer hasn't spread to any other organs, he'll soon be chasing balls around the park again. Won't you, boy? Yes, you will."

I smiled as Blazer's tail thumped. All animals adored Clive, even when he did dreadful things to them, like administer the kennel cough vaccine up their nostrils or manipulate their sore legs to find out which movements caused them the most pain.

The tumour on Blazer's hindquarters was standing out in its full glory because I'd already shaved the fur around it for surgery, and now, while Clive checked the instruments I'd laid out for him, I inserted the cannula that would take the anaesthetic into a vein in the dog's shaved leg.

"Is she hurting you, you poor boy?" joked Clive. "She can be like that, you know. She has a vicious side to her. But don't worry, I'll protect you."

Blazer's tail thumped again as Clive spoke in a silly tone of voice, then stilled as the anaesthetic took effect. Clive placed a surgical drape over the patient, leaving the tumour site exposed.

"You look a bit tired today, if you don't mind my saying so," he said to me.

"I didn't sleep very well. Too much churning around in my head."

"Adoption stuff?"

"Mostly."

Clive nodded and picked up his scalpel. "Okay, vital signs still all right?"

"Yes, all good."

"Right. Blazer, old boy, we're going in."

We didn't speak after that, apart from about what we were doing. Clive always gave his patients his complete attention, and I was busy too, monitoring Blazer's vital signs, watching Clive's skilled hands in action. I always enjoyed assisting with surgery, being an important part of a team. I'd missed the work so much while I'd been away in Ely.

In less than fifteen minutes, the procedure to remove the tumour was complete. "Okay, we'll get that sent off to the lab, though I've no doubt in my mind they'll say it's malignant. I still think he'll pull through okay, though—I couldn't detect any sign it had spread at all. Yes, I predict another sparkling success story, if I do say so myself."

Accustomed as I was to Clive's lighthearted blowing of his own trumpet, I smiled, glad Blazer was going to be all right.

"What about you?" Clive went on, preparing to suture the wound. "Have you got the feeling your adoption application is going to be a sparkling success story too?"

I pulled a face. "It's too early to say. She—the social worker—wants me to get more experience with children. I've got to look for volunteering opportunities."

"You can borrow my kids whenever you like," Clive offered. "Or better still, I could put you in touch with Jake."

"Who's Jake?"

"How can you not know Jake? He's the patron saint of young people in these parts. He runs local youth projects. My kids love him. I'll give you his contact details."

"Thanks, although I guess as I'm looking to adopt a younger child, I need to approach some nurseries and primary schools too."

"Sure. The head teacher at the infant school is Mr. Khan. Siamese cat with a broken tail. Had to do an amputation. Nice guy."

"You know everybody."

"You'd know him yourself if you'd been around last year. It was during the dark reign of She We Never Speak Of."

"Awful Angela?"

"That's the one." Clive finished suturing Blazer's flank. "There you are, old boy," he said. "All done."

Then, as we got Blazer ready to carry to the kennels to recuperate: "I do hope you won't be leaving us when you adopt? We couldn't manage without you again."

"Don't worry, I'll need the salary as a single parent. I might need to jiggle my hours around if I'm going to volunteer at a school, though."

"That's all right. Jiggle away. Just don't leave me again. Ever. All right?"

I smiled. "I'll do my best."

Together we carried Blazer to the kennels, where I'd be able to keep an eye on him for the next couple of hours and feed him a small meal once he was fully awake.

"I'll text you Jake's details in case you don't have any luck with the school, shall I?" Clive asked on his way out again.

"Yes, please, that would be great. Thanks so much, Clive. I owe you."

"Well, actually," he said, "you could do me a favour on Saturday if you're free? Jasper and I are meant to be visiting a care home to do some therapy duty, but Cara's coming home from university, and she's begged me to go and fetch her. I could cancel, but I hate to let them down this close to Christmas."

Jasper was Clive's three-year-old cocker spaniel. With Clive's help, he regularly volunteered as a therapy dog, spreading joy to elderly residents of care homes, many of whom had had to give up their pets when they moved in. Giving Jasper a good fuss was the next best thing for them.

"Of course I will. Just give me the details, and I'll be there."

"See?" Clive said to the sleeping Blazer. "She's an absolute treasure."

I phoned the school Clive had mentioned during my lunch break, but as I'd suspected, they asked me to call back in January, after the Christmas holidays. So without much hope, I phoned the number Clive had texted to me along with a name—Jake Jackson.

He answered straightaway, and after I'd introduced myself and explained why I was calling, he said, "Come round this evening, if you like. We've got a session straight after school—three thirty to six thirty."

"I'm at work at the moment, but I could get to you by five thirty?"

"Sure," he said. "That's fine."

"But I'll be in my uniform—I won't have time to go home and change first."

"What uniform's that?" he asked. "Firefighter? Astronaut? Nurse?"

I smiled. "Close. I'm a veterinary nurse."

"Cool. See you later then, Beth."

Nerves kicked in when I approached the youth centre at five thirty. What would Jake have told the kids about me? Perhaps I ought to have arranged to meet him for a chat first rather than diving straight in. Still, it was too late now. I was here. And Clare would be impressed if I could give her some evidence that I'd taken steps towards increasing my experience with children when we met next week.

A teenage boy drew alongside me at that moment and pushed the entrance door open.

"You coming in?" he asked, holding it for me.

"Yes, thanks." I followed him inside and was about to ask where I might find Jake, when Jake himself appeared in front of me.

"You must be Beth, right?"

"Yes," I said. "Jake?"

"That's me." He was tall and slim, with dark eyes and a shaved head, the tattoos on his arms clearly inspired by street art, and when he put his hand out to shake mine, I felt a flicker of attraction I hadn't felt since I'd split up with Jaimie.

"I'll give you the grand tour, and then I'll make you a coffee."

"Thank you. I really appreciate this."

"It's no problem."

Jake showed me a chill-out lounge with leather sofas, a TV, and a ping-pong table where a frenetic match was in progress.

"Are you any good at table tennis?"

"No, really lousy, sorry."

He grinned. "That's okay. Too much to expect our volunteers to be animal whisperers and ping-pong champions."

He led the way from the lounge and flicked on a light in a slightly more formally set-out room so I could see inside. "This is our meeting room, where we hold information and advice sessions—drug misuse, well-being sessions, mentoring, that sort of thing."

He closed the door and moved on. "And this is our art room for anything messy. In fact, if you're up for it, you could get stuck in now. Some of the kids are painting lanterns with glass paint at the moment—you know, like the ones at the Festival of Light?" He looked at my face. "Eastern Curve Garden?"

I'd seen the posters for it. "I haven't managed to get down there yet."

"You should. It's great, isn't it, guys?"

Five young people were seated around a table—three boys and two girls. Some of them nodded. Most looked at me curiously.

"Here," said Jake. "Take a seat. I'll make you a coffee. How d'you like it?"

"White, no sugar, please."

Jake nodded and went on his way, and I smiled round at everybody like an idiot, anxious to hide my sudden nervousness.

"These look great, guys," I said, shrugging my coat off onto the back of the chair. "I'll have a go myself if that's okay?"

One of the girls shrugged. Nobody else said anything.

"I love your designs," I tried again, helping myself to a jam jar and a paintbrush from the centre of the table. "They're really imaginative."

"You can't do a Christmas tree," one of the boys told me. "We've run out of green paint."

"Right," I said, disappointed because that was exactly what I'd been going to do. "No Christmas trees."

"Or Father Christmas," said another boy. "Because there's no red left."

"Okay," I said, my smile starting to feel strained. "I'll do some coloured stars. Or Christmas baubles. They're all sorts of colours, aren't they?" Nobody replied.

Warily, I dipped my paintbrush into the paint. I hadn't painted anything at all since I'd painted the shelving unit flamingo pink, but how hard could it be? And it didn't matter how it turned out anyway. I'd come here to interact, not to create great art.

"So how long have you guys been coming to the centre? Do you like it?"

Well done, Beth. Two questions at once.

"Two years."

"A year."

"It's all right."

"Jake's great."

"He seems like he'd be fun," I said.

"He is. This is a bit lame, though," said an older-looking boy, looking at his lantern in disgust. The picture he was painting was of a spider's web. It looked as if it might be more suited to Halloween than Christmas.

One of the girls was looking at the embroidered logo on my uniform. "Do you work at the vet's?"

"I do. I'm a veterinary nurse."

"Do you, like, take animals' temperatures and stuff?"

"Sometimes, yes. And I do blood tests and generally help the vet out and look after the animals if they're in for surgery."

"Our dog had puppies last week," said one of the younger-looking boys. "Mum says we can keep one."

I smiled at him. "That's nice. What sort of dogs are they?"

He shrugged. "Black ones and brown ones."

The older-looking boy pushed his lantern away and stuffed his paintbrush into a jam jar of water. "Our dog had puppies too, but my dad drowned them."

"Oh, that's . . ." I broke off, unsure how to continue. If I said it was awful, it would seem like a criticism of the boy's father, and while I felt criticism would be very well justified, it wasn't my place to give it.

Thankfully, Jake returned with my coffee at that point.

"Is Logan telling you gruesome stories?" he asked.

"Well, unhappy ones, perhaps," I said.

He nodded. "Maybe we save the sad animal stories for Beth's second visit?" he suggested.

Jake's presence inspired the kids to ask me questions about their pets, and before I knew it, it was time for the session to end, and my glass jar was covered with depictions of Christmas baubles, which, if you looked closely, did *not* look more like balloons.

"Not bad for a first attempt," said Jake, holding it up to the light. "What d'you think, guys?"

"It's cool, miss."

"Thanks. It's not half as good as all of yours, though."

"Stick around, Beth," said Jake. "I'll just let this lot out."

When Jake returned, he was shrugging on a leather jacket. "Fancy coming to the Curve Garden to see the lights? We could get a beer, and I could tell you more about the centre. They serve food there if you're hungry."

It was the first time since my split with Jaimie that a man I didn't really know had invited me to anything. And Jake seemed like a really nice guy. I smiled. "Thanks. I'd like that."

"Great," said Jake, smiling back at me. "Let's go."

22

Dalston East Curve Garden was a community garden established in a space that had once been derelict railway land. Now it was an oasis of peace with trees and flowers, and a space for picnics, games, and creative workshops. I'd forgotten about it when I'd been talking to Clare the other day, but now, as I walked towards it with Jake, I thought what a bonus the garden would be for me with a young child to entertain. Sure, I had my own garden, but the Curve Garden would be a place my child and I could go to socialise with others.

My child and I . . . It was becoming increasingly real to me that sometime next year I might be a mother. That it wouldn't just be me in the flat. Not just me I had to think about when I was doing a food shop.

Jake's voice startled me out of my musings. "I hope Logan didn't upset you with all his talk of puppy drownings."

"Well," I said, "I can't say it was the highlight of my visit. Mostly, I felt sorry for him, though. And the puppies, of course."

Jake nodded. "He's all right, really, Logan. Just has some difficult issues to deal with at home. He was in bits about those puppies, actually. Sobbing outside the centre. Wouldn't come in because he didn't want the other kids to see him like that."

Jake sighed. "Kids like Logan have to act tough to get by. Trouble is, the tough act can end up sticking. We do what we can for young people, but it can be difficult watching the fallout when that's not enough. Kids can end up blaming you, holding you responsible."

I thought about Olivia and Emily—of the walls they'd put up against me. Had I tried as hard as I could to break their barriers down? I'd thought so at the time, but maybe my own vulnerability and unhappiness had held me back when the going had got tough. Maybe I ought to have kept on pushing, been more determined to forge a relationship with them. Shown them I wasn't trying to replace their mother.

Sometimes, in the middle of the night, I imagined the three of us walking somewhere hand in hand, laughing together—me, Olivia, and Emily. Me offering them something different. Something good they could love me for. But the fantasy never included Jaimie—good old beloved Daddy Jaimie swooping in and taking over, needing to be the centre of his girls' attention, needing to be needed.

"Looks as if that's struck a chord," Jake said.

I nodded. "This time last year I was a stepmother to two girls. It was really hard."

"Being a stepparent *is* hard. And unfortunately, it's an increasingly likely scenario in new relationships as you get older, isn't it? I've been on both sides of the equation—coparented kids that weren't mine and suffered the pain of a stranger coparenting my kids. It's a minefield either way. But anyway, enough of the doom and gloom. We're here."

We entered the garden and walked together around the paths, admiring the lanterns hanging in the trees and lined up on the walls, Jake pointing out those made at the centre. It was so pretty with all the different colours and the strings of fairy lights. The air was filled with the smell of a bonfire, of burgers and something sweet. I could hear laughter and children's excited cries. I was really glad I'd come.

Of course, because I worked in the community as I did, it wasn't long before I was recognised.

"Hello, Beth. What d'you think of the lights?"

"Hello, Mrs. Riches. They're very pretty, aren't they? How's Patch?"

"Sulking 'cause you lot won't let him have any mince pies, but all right apart from that. We're sticking to his diet!"

"I'm glad to hear it. See you later."

"Do you get a lot of that when you come to community events?" Jake asked.

"Yes. You must too, don't you?"

"Sometimes. Speaking of which, hello, Francis; hi, Ben."

I recognised two of the kids from the lantern-making activity at the centre.

"Is Beth your girlfriend now, Jake?" Francis asked.

"No, Francis, we only just met. As you well know. See you guys later."

Jake and I moved on, exchanging a smile.

"Sorry about that."

"It's okay. Just kids being kids."

"Shall we get some food?"

"Great idea."

We joined the queue and took our spoils to a couple of free chairs beneath the trees.

"Mmm," I said, biting into my burger hungrily.

Jake smiled. "You look as if you're enjoying that."

I smiled back, taking a sip of my beer. "I am. It's really good."

"So," he said. "Adoption, huh? That's a noble thing to do."

Was it? I hadn't thought of it like that.

"Especially adopting an older child. They're the ones that need it the most."

I didn't like to tell him my heart was set on adopting a younger child. That my call to the centre had been a reserve option.

"It can take some of our more troubled kids a while to trust, but when they do, they repay you in spades."

"How many children have you got yourself?" I asked, thinking of what he'd said about having experienced a stranger being a stepparent to his children.

"Two. A boy of seventeen and a girl of fifteen. They live with their mum. We split up ages ago. Totally my fault. I've grown up since then. Or at least, I like to think so."

"My boss was singing your praises," I said. "That's how I heard about you. His kids have been to some of your events. Clive, from Dalston Vets?"

"Oh, Clive. Sure, I know Clive. Always ready with a joke."

"That's him."

"He must be fun to work for."

"He is."

Music started up somewhere in the garden. I listened to it while I ate, still enjoying the sight of the coloured lanterns. Then someone called my name, and I looked up to see Naomi holding Bembe's hand and pushing a buggy containing her new daughter, Precious, with the other.

"Naomi! Hi."

Bembe broke free from his mother and rushed towards me, hands in the air, demanding to be picked up. "Up, Beth. Up, up, up!"

I pulled him up onto my hip, where he instantly started pointing at the different lights. "Red! Blue!"

"That's right," I said. "They're so pretty, aren't they?"

"I'd be careful if I were you," warned Naomi. "He badly needs a nappy change. Actually, since you're here, d'you mind watching Precious for me while I take him to the toilet?"

"Of course," I said, turning to her, noticing she was looking at Jake. "Oh, sorry, this is Jake from the East London Youth Centre. Jake, this is my friend Naomi, and this is Bembe and Precious."

"Nice to meet you, Jake," said Naomi, the twinkle in her eye telling me she approved of what she saw.

"Hey, Bembe," Jake said to Bembe, holding his hand up to be high-fived.

Bembe obliged, putting all his strength into it, laughing as Jake pretended to stagger backwards. He was having so much fun he protested when Naomi took him off for his nappy change, his cries causing Precious to stir in her buggy.

"Shh," I said, rocking the buggy until she settled again.

Looking up, I noticed Jake's eyes on me. "You look like a natural," he said.

"I'm going to be her godmother," I told him. "Naomi and her husband asked me last week."

He smiled. "Cool."

Something about his expression made me think he might start quizzing me about whether I really wanted to adopt an older child, so partly to distract him, I asked him about the centre. "How d'you think I'll best be able to help out when I start volunteering?"

When Naomi returned with a still-protesting Bembe, Jake was talking about possible sessions on small-animal care and helping out with whatever was going on by being a "listening ear," and I was nodding along, taking it all in, because whether I was interested in adopting an older child or not, I was interested in helping out at the centre. While I could, at least.

"Somebody's tired," Naomi said, bending to strap a wriggling Bembe into the buggy next to his sister. "We'll have to head off. Good to meet you, Jake."

"You too."

"See you soon, Beth." Naomi's gaze was fierce as she drew close to kiss me. I knew exactly what message she was communicating. She wanted me to come round ASAP to give her the lowdown on Jake.

"See you soon."

"Nice family," Jake said as we watched them leave.

"The best."

Silence fell—the first silence between us since we'd arrived at the garden. I sensed it was either time to say goodbye and go our separate ways or . . . well, not.

"I might get another beer," Jake said. "D'you fancy another?"

I looked at him. He had a nice face. The face of someone who's lived a lot of life and emerged all the better from it.

"Yes," I said. "I think I would, thanks."

He returned with not only more beer but also a hot water bottle for me to tuck into my coat, and we sat and chatted—not just about the project but about ourselves too.

"So what's it like, the adoption process?"

I pulled a face. "It's tough, as you'd expect. And I think it's about to get tougher. We're going to discuss my relationships at my next home visit."

"I'm guessing you're not looking forward to that?"

I looked away from him into the trees. "Let's just say my last relationship ended a bit . . . messily," I said.

"Ah," he said. "Still, it's rare for relationships to end smoothly, I guess. She won't judge you on that."

I wasn't so sure, but I was grateful when he didn't ask any more questions about it.

When my hot water bottle had cooled down, we took another tour around the gardens, and then, as if by silent agreement, we headed for the exit and stood there grinning at each other.

"This has been fun," Jake said. "Thanks for coming."

"Thanks for inviting me. I've really enjoyed it."

"You're okay to get home?"

"Yes, I'm just a couple of streets away."

He fumbled in his pocket and pulled out a card. "Here. My mobile number in case you need to speak to me before we see you at the centre in the New Year."

My gloved fingers touched his as I took the card from him. "Thanks."

"Bye, Beth."

"Bye, Jake."

It was gone ten o'clock when I got back to the flat. When I took my phone out of my bag, I had a voice-mail message.

"Hi, it's Mark. Listen, I need your advice about something. It's important. But don't call back now. Grace'll be home soon. I'll try you again soon. Okay, bye for now."

I sat down at the table, some of the pleasure of the evening draining away, Mark's face in my mind now instead of Jake's. Whatever could he want me to advise him about? And why was it so secret?

23

On Saturday morning I went round to collect Jasper from Clive's house. Jasper was all decked out in his Therapy Dogs harness and a pair of clip-on antlers—antlers he divested himself of the minute he got into my car—and we set off. I was wearing the Santa hat Clive had insisted I wear, but it was almost Christmas, so I didn't really mind. Besides, the elderly residents wouldn't be looking at me; they'd be looking at Jasper. And Jasper, with his shiny, newly brushed copper-and-white coat, looked an absolute treat.

We arrived at the care home without incident, and I gave Jasper a quick tour of the front gardens to relieve himself. When we went in, we both had smiles on our faces, anticipating the pleasure our visit would bring. Well, to be fair, Jasper was panting and wagging his tail rather than actually smiling, but he was doing these things with a great deal of enthusiasm, and it was as close to smiling as a dog can get. Clive had always told me how much Jasper enjoyed his work, and now I could see it was true.

"Hello," I said to the woman at reception. "We've come to—"

But she cut me off, coming swiftly round the desk to greet Jasper. "Jasper! There you are! We've missed you!"

Clearly, no introductions were needed, then.

"I'm Beth, one of Clive's colleagues. Clive couldn't make it today, unfortunately."

"Yes, he rang to let us know to expect you. Thanks so much for stepping into the breach. D'you want to follow me?"

She led the way, and I followed—with Jasper straining on the leash. Hopefully, he would calm down when we actually got to meet the residents. I certainly didn't want him jumping up and knocking anyone over, giving someone a broken limb for the festive season.

The lounge was a large room decorated with tinsel and holly and smelling not of cabbage, as I'd imagined it would, but of freshly warmed mince pies. Around twenty residents were seated in comfortable-looking wingback chairs. All of them looked up as Jasper and I made our entrance.

Including, of all people, Grace.

Grace was sitting over by the Christmas tree with a familiar-looking elderly lady. Kenwood Place. Of course, Grace had told me ages ago that her grandmother was a resident here. Now I knew why Kenwood Place had sounded familiar when Clive had given me the details.

I waved in Grace's direction, unsure how I felt about seeing her. My feelings about her were so complicated; they always had been. Our paths had barely crossed since my split with Jaimie, and judging from Grace's expression, she was about as pleased to see me as I was to see her.

The whole time Jasper and I were making our smiling, tail-wagging, yes-his-coat-is-so-soft-isn't-it rounds, I felt as if Grace were watching me. She probably wasn't watching me at all—it just felt like it.

Then, suddenly, there we were, Jasper and I, in front of Grace and her grandmother.

"Hello, Beth," Grace said. "I'm not sure Nanna's very keen on dogs."

"I bloomin' well am," countered her grandmother, who proceeded to prove it by leaning forward to pet the ever-receptive Jasper.

"He likes that. It's good to see you again, Mrs., er . . ." I trailed off, realising I didn't actually know her name.

"Call me Iris, love. And you can come again, you can. This little chap is gorgeous."

A care worker turned up with a cup of tea for me. I reluctantly took the spare seat next to Grace to drink it.

"How are you, Grace?" I asked, lifting the teacup to my lips.

"I'm well, thank you. How are you?"

"Very well, thank you."

Silence descended. Hell, I wished the tea weren't quite so hot. I thought about Mark's voice-mail message. Wondered again what advice Mark wanted from me and why it was such a big secret.

Then Grace said, "I went to see Jaimie last week."

My heart plummeted still further. "Did you? How is he?" I didn't really want to know, to be honest. Not because I wished him ill, of course not. The very opposite, in fact. I could just do without having him on my conscience more than he already was, that was all.

"He's all right. Still a bit angry with you, I think."

I flushed, wondering whether Grace was angry with me too. Probably.

"I'm sorry to hear that." Then I lifted my chin. "But I had to do what I thought was right, didn't I? And I'm sure Jaimie will meet someone new soon. Someone much better suited to him than I ever was."

Grace looked at me consideringly. "Perhaps you're one of those people who's happiest on their own," she said.

I wasn't sure whether she'd wanted to hurt me or not. But she flipping well had. *And* made me feel lonely. But I wouldn't let her upset me. I wouldn't. Or at least, I wouldn't show her she had. "Maybe I am." It was a blatant lie, but at least it would end the conversation.

When I returned my attention to Jasper and Iris, I found they both appeared to have fallen asleep—Iris in her chair and Jasper on his back with his legs in the air.

"Looks like they've worn each other out," I said to Grace. But even as I spoke, Iris's eyes flicked open, button-like and alert.

"Who's asleep? I'm not asleep." She looked at me. "I know you, don't I?"

"This is Beth, Nanna," Grace said. "Rosie's friend. You remember Rosie, don't you? Mark's sister?"

Iris shook her head. "So many people, so many names," she said.

"We've only met once," I reassured her. "At the wedding."

"Wedding?" she said. "I don't remember any wedding." Her attention moved on from me to Grace. "Go and fetch my knitting bag from my room, will you, dear? I've got something for you."

Grace looked reluctant to leave me alone with her nanna—did she think I would poison her or something?—but Iris reached out to give her a gentle shove. "Go on. It's something special. Been working on it for weeks, I have, and finally finished it last night."

"All right."

After Grace had departed to fulfil her mission, Iris turned to me, her eyes sparkling. Speaking in a loud whisper, she said, "It's one of those baby jacket things. A you-know-what. A matinee jacket."

I froze. No, surely not. Sylvia would have told me if Grace was pregnant, wouldn't she? She wouldn't have been able to help herself. But perhaps she didn't know?

One thing was certain, though: if Grace was pregnant, then I had a whole new level of pain rocking right in my direction.

"And matching booties," Iris continued proudly. "Really tricky pattern, it was. Wasn't sure I'd get it done before the baby came. But I managed it, just. Lovely soft wool. Pink, since it's a girl. Another girl. Shame, really, since she's already got two. I imagine they wanted a boy this time."

A tidal wave of relief washed over me. Iris wasn't talking about Grace at all; she'd got confused.

"It's Louise who's having the baby, I think," I told her. "Grace's sister." I was going to add something along the lines of, *She seems to go in for Christmas babies*, but Iris frowned, her expression indignant.

"That *is* Louise," she said. "Her that's just gone to get my knitting bag. That's Louise."

Before I had the chance to reply, Grace was back, carrying a rose-patterned knitting bag. Iris took it from her and reached inside to pull out a soft, pink matinee jacket, handing it over to Grace triumphantly.

"There you are, Louise. Knitted specially for your little one when she comes. Love in every stitch there is."

Shit.

I couldn't look at Grace. Couldn't stop myself from looking at Grace.

Her expression gave away nothing. But the way she swallowed, the way her fingers gently stroked the lovingly knitted baby jacket, said absolutely everything there was to say.

Eventually, with great composure, she smiled. "Thank you, Nanna. It's really beautiful."

Iris beamed, patting Grace's hand. "You're welcome, pet."

Soon afterwards, Iris said she was tired and asked Grace to take her back to her room, so we said our goodbyes. After I'd watched Grace wheel her grandmother away, Jasper and I did a few more tours around the residents. But even as I chatted and smiled, agreeing that Jasper was indeed very cute, I could still see Grace's fingers moving over the soft wool. If I'd ever wondered whether Grace yearned to have a child or not, now I had my answer. Difficult as it was to imagine, Grace was just like me.

I'd left Kenwood Place and was clipping on Jasper's seat belt when Grace emerged. For a moment, I thought she was going to just call out a goodbye and take off, but to my surprise, she came over.

"I hear you're trying to adopt."

I wondered who'd told her. Sylvia, perhaps. "Yes."

"I hope that works out for you."

"Thank you."

"Though, presumably, you do know it's going to be incredibly difficult? One of my clients adopted a child a few years ago. The little girl turned out to have foetal alcohol syndrome. It's affected her development in so many ways. It's been very tough for Helen and her husband. But worthwhile too, obviously. She wanted so much to be a mother."

As soon as I'd stopped reeling from Grace's sad tale, I nodded. "It is a very strong impulse."

"Yes," Grace agreed, "it is."

There was silence for a moment. Then she looked at me. "I expect you know Mark and I have been having trouble conceiving?"

"I did wonder. But I wasn't sure, no."

She gave a little shrug. "We've had the tests. Apparently, there's no reason for it. Nothing physically wrong with either of us."

"Well, then, perhaps it will happen in time?"

"Perhaps."

Suddenly I wondered if I'd ever seen who Grace really was. She'd always spoken to me with such self-assurance. Bossiness, even. As if I were the younger one, not her, and she needed to bestow her superior wisdom and advice on me. Yet here she was, just as vulnerable as I was. Of course she was. Everyone was vulnerable beneath the surface. Some people just hid it better than others.

She was fiddling with her car keys. "But getting back to your situation, I do think it's a shame."

I frowned. "What d'you mean?"

"Well, the girls. If you'd stayed with Jaimie, you'd have had two perfectly good stepdaughters to fill the void with."

I flushed.

"They were upset, you know, when you left so suddenly. Oh, they didn't say as much, but I could tell. I know them so well, you see, and I think, in some ways, to them, it was like losing their mother all over again when you went."

What? "But they haven't lost their mother. Harriet's alive and well. Very much so."

She shook her head. "Maybe that's why it didn't work out for you with them, then," she said. "You not understanding that. The girls might see Harriet, spend plenty of time with Harriet, but what about when they need her when it's Jaimie's weekend to have them? Sometimes only a mother will do."

I could feel the blood drain from my face. The familiar sick feeling in my stomach that came with a chasm of memories opening up. A chasm it sometimes felt as if I'd spent my whole life tiptoeing around.

Grace reached out a hand, not quite making contact with my arm. "I'm so sorry, Beth. That was extremely tactless of me. Of course you of all people must understand that."

"Oh, yes."

For about a millisecond, we'd been within touching distance, Grace and I. And now we weren't. There didn't seem to be anything else to say.

"Well, look, I'd better go. But good luck with your application, okay? I hope it works out for you."

"Thanks. And I hope . . ." But I wasn't sure how to finish that sentence, so my voice trailed off.

"Thank you. Goodbye, Beth."

"Bye, Grace."

She began to walk away, then turned round for one last parting shot.

"And I do hope you won't wake up one day and regret everything you could have had with Jaimie."

24

"So I'm seeing a pattern of relatively short-term serial monogamy in your relationship history. Would that be an accurate assessment?"

"Yes, I suppose it would."

Maybe there was a hint of defensiveness in my tone, because Clare said, "You understand, this is not intended to be in any way critical of you. I'm simply recording the facts."

I forced myself to smile. "Of course."

"But just to be clear, you've never had a relationship that has lasted more than a year?"

It sounded so awful. Especially if you added my age to the equation. *You're thirty-seven years old, and you've never had a relationship that's lasted longer than a year . . .*

"Yes," I said. "That's correct." It was. It just wasn't the whole picture. But I couldn't give her the whole picture, could I? Being in love with someone who doesn't view you romantically for more than half your life was hardly going to impress, was it?

"And your relationship with Mr. Faulkner, which ended"—Clare consulted her notes—"last January, was the most serious of your relationships to date?"

I nodded. "Yes."

"And you moved to live with Mr. Faulkner in Ely?"

"I did."

"How long had you known each other before you moved there?"

"About five months."

Clare tilted her head slightly. "So that was a big commitment on your behalf after a relatively short amount of time."

"I suppose it was."

She looked at me, waiting, making me realise how monosyllabic my responses were.

I dredged my mind for more. "The fact that we lived some distance from each other probably sped things up a bit."

"Could you tell me a bit about that relationship, please? It's important, obviously, because Mr. Faulkner has children, and you had regular contact with those children."

I hesitated, speed-trawling through memories of my time in Ely, trying to decide how to portray those months in a positive light. It shouldn't have been too difficult. After all, it hadn't been all bad. Far from it. But Clare wasn't interested in hearing about great sex, and sometimes when I thought back to those months, it was one of the few truly positive things I could remember. Reluctant naturism, missing my work as a veterinary nurse, missing my home city, almost taking up a folk-dancing hobby out of sheer boredom—none of these were either positive or relevant to my decision to adopt. The pushing-a-stone-up-a-mountain reality of my relationship with Jaimie's girls was definitely relevant, but equally definitely, it would fail to impress Clare if I described it with complete honesty.

"Is this a difficult topic for you, Beth?" Clare asked after the silence had stretched on a bit too long.

"No, it's fine. I'm just trying to decide where to start."

"How about describing your relationship with Mr. Faulkner's daughters?"

I sighed. I couldn't help it. Clare's eyebrows immediately lifted. She sat there waiting, pen poised.

"Emily and Olivia are both very sweet girls. But they do have strong personalities, and they didn't want their parents to split up. Which is only natural, of course. I think it's fair to say they still hadn't accepted this state of affairs when I moved to Ely. That they secretly hoped Jaimie and their mother would get back together."

Clare wasn't writing very much. Oh God. The stillness of that pen! Obviously, she thought I hadn't got to the juicy nitty-gritty yet. My head was starting to ache.

"They didn't react well when I first moved to Ely. They seemed to resent my being there."

"And how did that make you feel?"

How did she think it had made me feel? Rejected. Frustrated. Lonely. Inadequate.

"Well, it was very difficult, of course. But I kept on trying to . . . bond with them."

"And how did you do that? What kinds of things did you try to bring that about?"

"Well, Emily was very interested in reading, as I am myself. So I had conversations with her about books. Bought her books sometimes. And Olivia was very interested in animals, and of course, I work with animals myself, so . . ."

My voice petered out. I wasn't impressing myself, let alone Clare, and I was also painfully aware of how pitiful my attempts to start those conversations had been. That this was like a job interview where you exaggerated your experience to try and make it sound like a strength.

My greatest weakness is that I sometimes take on more than I can handle, but I've installed a project management app and find that really helpful . . .

That kind of thing.

My greatest weakness with Jaimie's girls was that I was, frankly, terrified of them. Because Jaimie cared for them so much, they had shedloads of power over me. Now that I don't see them anymore, I realise I should have expected more support from Jaimie to help us to bond better.

"Was Mr. Faulkner supportive of the relationship between yourself and his daughters?"

Ah, right on cue.

Vividly I recalled the way Jaimie had brushed my insecurities aside. *They'll come round. These things take time.* It didn't take much of a stretch of imagination to conjure up an older version of the two of us at either Emily's or Olivia's wedding—me sitting next to Jaimie but still very much on the fringes of family life—had we stayed together.

"It could be . . . difficult. Time was often at a premium because every moment with the girls was so precious to him. He found it so hard not seeing them every day. Also, he was very busy with his home-renovation business, so sometimes, even when it was his turn to have the girls, he couldn't always meet them from school."

"And did that duty then fall to you?"

Duty. That didn't sound like a very nice word, even if it was an accurate one.

"Well, yes, but obviously I didn't mind. I had the more flexible job, and Jaimie was often working some distance away . . ."

"How did Emily and Olivia take it when you and their father split up?"

But I had absolutely no idea how they'd taken it, did I? Because after Jaimie and I had our final conversation, I never saw Olivia and Emily again.

I licked my lips. "Well, I'm not entirely sure, to be honest. Jaimie decided . . . Well, it all ended quite suddenly, you see."

Clare frowned. "Are you saying you didn't actually have the chance to say goodbye to Emily and Olivia?"

Numbly, I shook my head. "No. I wanted to, but Jaimie said . . . Well, it was his decision. I didn't have any say in it."

It had haunted me, though, sometimes, even before my recent encounter with Grace. I'd often pictured Jaimie breaking the news to them—taking them down to the river to feed the ducks, maybe, while he did it. Had they minded? Shed a few tears, maybe? Even though I didn't want to think of them being unhappy, a part of me had wanted them to miss me. Because I missed them. Things hadn't always been easy between us, but we'd been a part of each other's lives for almost a year.

But maybe they hadn't been sad about me leaving at all. Maybe they'd been glad. There was no way for me to know.

Now Clare was making notes. Copious notes. I waited for her to finish.

Finally, she looked up. I already knew what her next question was going to be. "And can you tell me why your relationship with Mr. Faulkner ended?"

25

At Richard's funeral, Jaimie and I sat in the second pew from the front. The pews were only big enough for five, and Grace was with Mark, so there wasn't room for me and Jaimie too. It shouldn't have mattered, I suppose, but it really did. I wanted to clasp Rosie's hand, feel Sylvia's shoulder pressed against mine. Not just passively witness their bowed heads.

We'd planned to meet at Sylvia's house an hour before the funeral to set off together, but an overturned lorry on the A10 had put paid to that plan, and I was just grateful we'd managed to get there at all.

"Beth," Sylvia greeted me as Jaimie and I hurried through the grave-yard to the church entrance at the last minute. The way she took me into her arms and held me was almost my undoing before the funeral had even begun.

"Hello, you," said Rosie, when I hugged her next, and we kissed and cried a little as we held each other.

Then it was on to Mark—a silent, warm hug, a pat on the back with minimal eye contact. And finally, Grace—polite, restrained, her face expertly made up.

"I'm so sorry for your loss, Beth."

While Jaimie greeted everyone, speaking a few words about the traffic, I put my arm back around Rosie and watched Mark. He looked pale and gaunt, stiff from holding his feelings in, his hair sticking out to one side as if he'd washed it and then forgotten about it. I watched as Grace reached out in a vain attempt to flatten it, and Mark closed his eyes, suffering her attentions like a small boy whose mother cleans his face with spit on her handkerchief.

The congregation—Richard's friends, workmates, ex-customers, neighbours—was already gathered inside the church. We, the family group, were waiting, speaking in hushed voices, to follow the coffin inside. As the pallbearers began to carry the coffin from the hearse through the churchyard, I heard Mark swear under his breath and looked to see what had caught his attention.

"Jeez. Couldn't they have found men of a similar height?"

I didn't blame him for being annoyed. The scene was fairly ridiculous. One of the men was almost twelve inches shorter than the others, which meant Richard's coffin was slanted at an odd—and frankly unsafe-looking—angle. Rosie's hand went to her mouth. I heard her swift intake of breath. But worse was to come. The church was ancient, with a low entrance door, and as the pallbearers entered with the coffin, the front of it scraped the keystone, almost dislodging the wreath of cream-coloured lilies resting on top. All but the shorter pallbearer quickly bent to accommodate the dimensions of the entrance, their sudden movement causing the coffin to list slightly. Mark quickly reached a hand up to steady it, and the six men collected themselves and proceeded into the church.

With disaster averted, we followed—Sylvia with Rosie, Mark with Grace, and me and Jaimie at the rear—walking to the accompaniment of sombre organ music. I clutched Jaimie's arm hard, staring straight ahead to avoid making eye contact with anyone, my throat closed off, my breathing shallow.

"Are you all right?" Jaimie whispered when we were seated in the pew.

I jerked my head in a nod, although actually I was far from all right. In that moment, I felt that I would never be all right again. I knew that Sylvia, Rosie, and Mark felt the same.

The organ music ended. The vicar began to speak. "Dearly beloved, we are gathered here today to say farewell to Richard Anthony Groves and to commit him into the hands of God. We shall now sing hymn number sixteen, 'The Day Thou Gavest.'"

The organ started up again, launching into the tune. I remembered the miserable-sounding hymn from my school days. How bored I'd been in the stuffy school hall singing the old-fashioned-sounding words. Now, each word felt like shrapnel to my heart.

The day Thou gavest, Lord, is ended; The darkness falls at Thy behest . . .

Jaimie was singing beside me in a deep, melodious voice I realised I had never heard before. Why not? We'd been together for a year. Why the hell hadn't I ever heard him sing? And why was I even thinking about that now?

I couldn't sing myself; the razor blades in my throat wouldn't allow it. And I could mostly only hear Grace's high-pitched voice coming from the pew in front of me. Sylvia pitched in every now and then. Faltered. Regrouped. Tried again. Stop, start; stop, start.

The hymn came to an end. The vicar spoke a few words. I heard none of them. I was remembering Richard's arm around my shoulders as we watched TV one evening shortly after I'd gone to live with the family for good. A game show was on, and the four contestants were attempting to dance the flamenco, the women swishing their bright, frilly skirts and shuffling and stamping their feet, the men wearing fedoras and holding their hands aloft. All of them looking outrageously foolish.

I had no idea why that particular memory surfaced out of all the memories stored up in my brain, but it did. I could feel Richard's body shaking with laughter next to mine, could see his head thrown back as he guffawed without restraint.

And suddenly I wasn't thinking about Richard any longer; I was thinking about my own father, who had so loved to dance. I was thinking about him and Mum dancing the tango, their backs ramrod straight, their faces appropriately brooding. They'd competed in dance competitions together, my parents, taking it seriously, leaving me with Tilda if they'd had to travel away from home.

When the competition was more local, Tilda and I dressed in our best dresses and went to watch. My dad always looked so handsome in his dress suit, a number pinned to his back, his auburn hair gleaming beneath the spotlight, and my mother was glamorous in her jewel-coloured satin dresses. I loved being a part of the audience, even though when I was younger, I always cried when they were eliminated from the competition.

By the time they were killed in a car crash on their way back from a long weekend in the Lake District to celebrate their anniversary, I'd stopped that crying. Maybe someone, somewhere, knew I'd need my tears for the long years I'd be without them.

I was sobbing brokenly now. Jaimie's arm was around me, holding me tight. Rosie looked at me over her shoulder, her own eyes rimmed in red. Then the vicar finished speaking, and Mark stood to go to the front to give his eulogy. I blew my nose, trying to pull myself together for him.

He waited for a moment, looking down at his piece of paper, gathering his courage. Then he cleared his throat and began.

"My father was very skilled with his hands. He could make furniture. He could mend clocks. Fix cars. Construct complicated spaceships out of Lego. You name it. He tried—unsuccessfully—to pass some of those practical skills on to me. Stood patiently as, time after time, I bungled the things he found effortless. Yet he never once gave me the impression he was anything but proud of me.

"As a heating engineer, Dad had the magic touch. Could coax old boilers back from the dead. Diagnose what was wrong just by listening to them. He took me with him sometimes, when I was growing up. I never did learn how to fix a boiler. But I did learn the importance of setting aside time for a cup of tea and a chat with some of his older customers.

"My dad wasn't a fix-and-go sort of a man. If he had been, we might have had a new car. More expensive holidays. But we wouldn't have had Dad. The world just lost a nugget of kindness. It will be a far colder, bleaker place as a result."

Mark's voice faltered to a stop. He folded up his piece of paper. Then he looked up at us, the tears spilling down his cheeks. "I shall miss him more than I can say."

As he returned to his place, more tears leached from me, Mark's misery piling up on top of mine. By the time the service was over, I was a dried husk of a person who couldn't imagine speaking normally about ordinary things to anyone ever again. Yet as we followed the coffin down the aisle and turned towards the exit, I caught a glimpse of the hollow-eyed determination on Sylvia's face. It was as if she were telling herself, *I will get through this. I will get through this.* And suddenly I wanted to find some strength so that Sylvia wouldn't feel she had to shore me up as well as deal with her own grief.

As we emerged into the unforgiving January day, I took in some gulps of cold air. One. Two. Then another. And another. And when Jaimie asked me again, "Are you all right?" and I answered, "Yes," it was less of a lie than it had been before. Richard wasn't here to support Sylvia any longer, so we had to do it. It was as simple as that.

At the graveside, I disentangled myself from Jaimie to go and stand between Mark and Rosie. Sylvia was on the other side, next to the vicar. When he began to speak, she closed her eyes.

"Almighty God, as you once called our brother Richard into this life, so now you have called him into life everlasting."

Next to me, Mark shook his head, as if to reject the vicar's words.

"We therefore commit his body to the ground, earth to earth, ashes to ashes, dust to dust."

Tears were sliding down Mark's face now. I reached to clasp his hand.

"In the hope of resurrection unto eternal life, through the promise of Our Lord Jesus Christ, we faithfully and victoriously give him over to your blessed care. Amen."

"Amen."

"Amen."

Suddenly Mark began to cry—loudly, shockingly, his whole body shuddering as his self-imposed restraint failed him. Sylvia—who was sobbing herself—reached out to him across the grave. Rosie placed a comforting hand on his arm. I sensed Grace stepping forward from her place next to Jaimie, but I was there first, opening my arms to hold Mark close. He clung to me, sobbing, and I clung back, feeling every shudder of his body against my own, sobbing right along with him.

"Oh, Beth," he said.

"I know," I soothed. "I know."

"Those guys," he said brokenly into my hair. "Those ridiculous guys. I thought . . . they were going to drop him."

"Your dad would have laughed," I said, because it was true. Richard would have thought it was absolutely hilarious.

Mark drew back slightly and nodded, though he didn't smile. "He would."

He drew back fully then, wiping his face on his suit sleeve. Grace joined him, squeezing his arm. Jaimie joined us and did the same to me. And then it was time to take a handful of soil to throw into the grave.

While I waited for my turn, I felt as if I were outside the scene, looking in. As if I weren't quite part of what was happening. My mind, however, was totally clear. The thunderbolt I'd experienced when I'd held Mark in my arms had completely lifted the fog I'd been living in all year, causing me to see everything in the sharpest focus. Everything

I'd done in the past twelve months—giving up my job, my friends, the city I loved—had been an elaborate distraction. A displacement activity. I wasn't in love with Jaimie. I had never been in love with Jaimie. Because I was still head over heels in love with Mark.

My handful of earth fell onto the polished wood of Richard's coffin with a soft thud. As I passed the box on to Rosie, Jaimie stepped forward to take my arm—there for me. But I had never really been there for him, and I was so sorry I was going to have to hurt him.

~

Back in Dalston, Clare was still waiting for me to answer her question. If I didn't do it soon, she would think I was trying to hide something. I *was* trying to hide something.

My mind flitted through the list of reasons for my split with Jaimie, deciding which one to select. For although the realisation that I was still in love with Mark came firmly at the top of the list, there had been many other things I hadn't been happy with in our relationship. Although without my graveside epiphany, Jaimie and I probably would have stumbled along together for a while longer.

Could I tell Clare how tired I'd felt of having to constantly struggle to fit in? How displaced and overlooked I'd felt, living in Ely? That I couldn't really be me living there with Jaimie?

"Richard's death made me realise how much I missed my family and friends in London. I'm not a country girl, not really. I tried to be, but . . . My tenants had recently left, so the flat was vacant, and then my old job at Dalston Vets became available again. I don't know, everything seemed to be working to make me move back here. It was sad to break up with Jaimie, but I suppose I just realised Ely and our relationship weren't right for me."

Clare looked up from writing in her notebook. My heart began to pound as I waited for her to say, *What if you realise adoption isn't right for you after a child has come to live with you?* Or something like that.

But she didn't. Instead, to my absolute horror, she said, "I'll need to speak to Mr. Faulkner, if that's all right? We always speak to ex-partners where there are children involved."

Holy shit.

"Is that a problem for you?"

I did my very best to keep the dismay and blind panic from my face. She wanted to speak to Jaimie. Which meant she'd very likely discover I hadn't been completely honest with her.

"No," I said, "I'm sure that will be fine. When do you want to speak to him?"

"As soon as possible. Although, obviously, I know it might be difficult, as it's almost Christmas. Perhaps you could let me know when you've had the chance to speak to Mr. Faulkner about it so I know when to call?"

I fiddled with the corner of the table. "What if . . . what if he doesn't want to speak to you?"

"Is that likely?"

I thought back to that final conversation and the way Jaimie had humiliated himself, trying to get me to change my mind.

~

"I'll speak to the girls, make sure they're nicer to you. We can do the things you want to do instead of what the girls want to do all the time. We can drop the naturism. Whatever it takes, Beth. Please. Don't do this. I know I could have tried harder. I will try harder. I promise. I love you; we've got something good together. We've had some happy times, haven't we?"

We had, along the way. Just not consistently enough of them. Certainly not enough for me to feel my life away from the places and people I loved—from Mark—was enough.

"I know how much you miss London. We'll make sure we go there more often. And I'll do all I can to help you to find another vet nurse job. Limit the amount of time Olivia does her drumming."

He sounded so desperate to make me stay. Yet in my heart I knew he didn't love me. Not really. We had used each other, Jaimie and I. I wasn't completely to blame. I may have plunged myself into our relationship to try to get over Mark, but Jaimie had done exactly the same thing to get over his split from Harriet. It hadn't worked for either of us. One day Jaimie would probably see that, but right now, he wasn't going to be convinced unless I told him the truth. So I did. Or part of it, at least.

"It's not just those things. I do miss London. And my job. And I do find it hard sometimes with the girls, and not having my own space. But . . . there's something else. Someone else."

Jaimie froze. "You're seeing someone else?"

I shook my head. "No, but . . . I do have feelings for someone else."

"Who?" He fired the word at me like a bullet.

I lied. I had to. "It's no one you know. And . . . and nothing has happened."

"Yet."

The short word dripped with venom. Before my eyes, Jaimie had transformed from someone desperate to change my decision into someone who hated me.

"Well," he said, "you'd better fuck off, then, hadn't you?"

"What about the girls?" I asked.

"What about them?"

"Well, will I . . ." I was going to ask whether I'd ever see them again, but of course I wouldn't. "Can I say goodbye to them?"

"No fucking way. Forget it, Beth. Just fucking forget it."

∼

"I'm not sure whether he'll be prepared to speak to you or not, to be honest," I said to Clare.

She looked at her watch and closed her notebook. "Well, as I say, if you could let me know as soon as possible?"

26

I knew I should call Jaimie straightaway. Get it over with. If I brooded about it, the terror would only increase.

But before I could, Mark rang me.

"Beth. Hi. Sorry not to have called you back before. How are you?"

"I'm okay."

"Sure? You don't sound it."

I closed my eyes. Talking to Mark was always wonderful and terrible mixed up together in a cocktail shaker. Bliss and torture on the rocks. And all I seemed to do lately was pretend. Capable Beth. Happy Beth. In-Control Beth.

"I've just had a session with my social worker. You know, about the adoption? I've got to phone Jaimie to see if he'll agree to speak to her. I was just going to do it."

"God, that's tough. Good luck."

Mark had been there with me in Ely when Jaimie's eyes were lasering hatred, so I knew he really did appreciate how bad the phone call was likely to be. "Thanks."

"Why does your social worker want to speak to him?"

"To get an idea of how I interacted with his girls."

I heard him sigh. "It's not supposed to be this difficult, is it? Having children."

Had Grace told him about seeing me at Kenwood Place? I couldn't tell. So I just said, "Still no joy for you and Grace?"

"No. It's really getting us both down. I feel like a failure, you know? And Grace . . ." He sighed again. "Well, Grace seems determined to take it out on me. All we do is row these days. It's hardly a recipe for making a baby, is it?"

"Not really, no."

"She's always out somewhere these days too. Home late, weekend appointments. And then, when she is home, nothing I do is right. Or enough. *Did you make that phone call? Get that new contract? Haven't you contacted so-and-so yet?*" He sighed. "To be honest, some days I just want to stay in bed in the morning, not sit at my desk in a shirt and tie to have video conferences with clients."

"You're probably still grieving."

"Yes. But how long's that going to go on for, Beth?"

"I don't know. As long as it takes, I suppose. I don't think there's an exact time span for grief, is there?"

Another sigh. "I suppose not. But anyway, I've decided to do something positive about it." His voice sounded suddenly more positive. "So I'm getting us a puppy."

I hadn't expected that. "A puppy? Wow."

"Yes, I know. I'm not stupid. I don't think a puppy's going to magically solve all our problems. But it will be a little being to care for together, won't it, until we get pregnant? Something to practise on? I think . . . I hope that will bring us closer again. And if nothing else, it will get me out of this flat, because I'll have to take it for walks. That's got to be good."

He sounded so excited. Like a little boy who's found out he's getting a new bike for Christmas.

"So anyway, the reason I called the other night was to ask your advice about the best breed to get. But it doesn't matter anymore because I've chosen now. One of my old work colleagues has some pups at the moment, so I've reserved one of those."

"What is it?"

"A border collie. You should see him, Beth. He's so cute—a little black-and-white fluff ball. I know Grace is going to melt when she sees him."

A border collie. God. Milo and his train chasing. His incessant ball fetching. So gorgeous but so . . . *relentless* with his constant, inexhaustible energy. Of all the breeds Mark could have chosen, a border collie was the very last one I would have advised him to get if we had spoken.

"You do know border collies need lots of exercise, don't you?"

"Of course. Like I say, that's no problem with me working from home."

I tried to think of something positive. "The two of you can both take him to puppy socialisation classes. Let him meet other dogs."

"We can, can't we? It'll be fun. It feels like eons since Grace and I had fun." The bitterness was back in his voice.

"Well," I said, "I can't wait to meet him. What's his name?"

"That's for Grace to decide. He's her present. Anyway, you're waiting to make your call, aren't you? Don't let Jaimie give you any grief. You did so much for those girls. And I hope it works out for you, the adoption thing. Let me know if Jaimie gives you a hard time, and I'll go round and hit him."

I had to smile at that. "I bet you've never hit anyone in your life."

He laughed. "True. But I do a great line in terrorising people with fake dog poo and itching powder."

"I'll bear that in mind if things get nasty."

"You do that. 'Night, Beth. Love you. We'll miss you at Christmas."

"I'll miss you too."

Of course I would. But I certainly wouldn't miss watching him give Grace a puppy as a surprise gift. I could imagine every detail of it in Technicolor. Mark's secretive smile as he left the room. Him saying,

Close your eyes. No peeking! A telltale yip that had Grace's eyes springing open before Mark could place the wriggling ball of fluff into her outstretched hands. His wall-to-wall grin as she reached out for the puppy. *Oh, Mark, he's gorgeous!*

No, thank you.

"Bye, Mark."

"Bye, Beth."

I got up to refill my glass of water, then sat back down and waited for my churned-up emotions to settle. It took a while. First, I had to do quite a lot of fantasising about relocating to somewhere on the other side of the planet. Somewhere remote, without phone reception. No way for me to see or speak to Mark until I'd got him out of my system once and for all.

But then, in a sense, that was exactly what I'd tried to do when I'd moved to Ely, wasn't it? And look how well that had turned out.

Sighing, I returned my attention to the one thing I could do something about: my adoption application and the dreaded phone call to Jaimie.

When we'd split, I'd thought I'd never have to speak to him ever again. And now here I was, voluntarily ringing him. If anything could be called a test of my commitment to the adoption process, this was it. And it was one thing I couldn't afford to stuff up.

"Beth?"

"Hi, Jaimie."

"What do you want?"

I'd intended to start off by asking after the girls, but nothing about Jaimie's stark question invited conversation. But then, I should hardly have been surprised, should I?

"I'm sorry to bother you, but I need to ask a favour."

"You need a favour from me? Ha! That's a bit rich, isn't it?"

He sounded so cross. What would I do if he hung up?

Haltingly, I explained. To say he was incredulous was something of an understatement.

"You're applying to adopt a child? You? Miss Unmaternal of the Year?"

Heat swept through me. How bloody dare he? I'd tried—over and over again—to make headway with his girls. To judge me unmaternal because they hadn't really been interested in getting close to me was completely unjust. But I couldn't get mad at Jaimie, not when I needed him on my side. So for about the five hundredth time in a fortnight, I bit my lip. "That's not really fair, is it?" I said as mildly as I could manage. "I did my best with your girls. The fact is, they didn't want me to be maternal towards them."

"Is that what you're going to say to the social worker?" he said scathingly. "'I did my best'?"

"Isn't that all anyone can say?"

I heard his impatient sigh. "Look, I was just on my way out to pick them up from Harriet's."

"Would you like me to call back?"

"No, it's all right. I'll do it."

"You'll speak to the social worker?"

"I said so, didn't I?"

"Thank you, Jaimie, I—"

"But it's a lot more than you deserve, okay? I just want you to know that. And I'm not lying for you."

"I don't expect you to. Of course not. Is there any time that's best for you for her to—"

But I was speaking to myself. Jaimie had gone.

27

Two days before Christmas, Rosie called me after work to say she wasn't going to Mark and Grace's for Christmas Day after all. She was flying to Rome to see Giorgio instead.

"I know, I'm stupid. I'll probably get off the plane and want to get straight back on it again."

"You won't. You love Giorgio."

"Yeah, but what good's that? Nothing's changed. I still don't want kids, and he still does. It's crazy."

"Maybe you should just enjoy this time together."

"Well, I will, won't I? God, I can't wait to see him. But in a few days, the heartache will start all over again. God, listen to me. Prebooking heartache."

I gazed at a strip of photos of me and Rosie displayed on the shelves Richard had made me. They'd been taken in a photo booth on a day trip to the coast years ago. Both of us were smiling like idiots, neither of us with a care in the world. "Oh, Rosie, I don't know what to say."

"Of course you don't. You're too nice to say what his family probably thinks—what he probably thinks himself—that I'm unnatural because I don't want kids."

We'd had this discussion so many times before, Rosie and I. As much as we adored each other, we were wired up totally differently when it came to having children. For me, it was a fundamental need—I couldn't imagine living my life without having a family. For Rosie, it was the exact opposite.

"It's like people think you're shallow and selfish if you don't want children," she often said. "Or somehow deficient as a person. I say, if only more women really faced their doubts about being a mother, we wouldn't have so many badly treated kids in the world, destined to become needy adults. Motherhood's a club. If you're not a member, you're looked down on. What's wrong with only having life goals of doing well at work and having fun? And why should I constantly have to justify my choices?"

Rosie didn't have to justify herself to me, of course. In my view, she contributed enough to the world by simply being her. But maybe because of my friend's strong opinions about motherhood, I'd examined my own more than I might have done otherwise. Why did I have this compelling need to be a mother? Why wasn't the life I currently led enough for me the way Rosie's was for her? I loved my job and felt I was good at it. Moreover, it was work that had value, both for animals and for people. I had a great home, lots of friends, and the freedom to travel should I want to. Why this insistent need for a small being to care for, to wake me up at night, to be totally dependent on me?

Sometimes I wondered if my deep craving for a family was connected to having lost my parents so young. Maybe, without knowing it, I'd been deeply lonely—was still deeply lonely—despite being on the receiving end of Richard and Sylvia's love. If that was the case, how could I be sure that bringing a child into my life—by whatever means I managed it—would be the answer? What if I still felt lonely when I had a child who needed me?

Whenever I thought about these things, my mind went round and round in circles, just the way Rosie's did. But just like Rosie, I always came back to my original starting point—the one connected to my gut. For whatever reason, I wanted children so much it hurt. And if I hadn't been so hopelessly in love with Mark for most of my life, I'd probably have them by now. You couldn't will yourself to love people, just as—apparently—you couldn't will yourself to stop loving them.

"Is anything anybody says going to stop you catching that plane?" I asked Rosie.

"Not a chance."

"Well, then, go. Have a fabulous time. And if you start to doubt you did the right thing, think about the strain of living up to Grace's perfect Christmas."

"God, yes. And her sister's baby! Thanks, pal. See you when I get back."

"I'll have the tissues handy."

"I'll need them."

I was still thinking about Rosie's dilemma as I left the flat and walked up to the supermarket. She and Giorgio had been an on-off item for more than three years now. They'd both tried dating other people, but their hearts hadn't been in it, and I could see why not. Apart from the baby issue, they were just so perfect for each other. It was sad.

"Beth?"

A voice plucked me from my thoughts. I focussed and saw it was Jake.

"Oh, hi," I said, registering how good it was to see him. "How are you? I'm just heading up to Tesco. I'm on duty over Christmas—well, if we get any emergencies, that is. I'm hoping they'll have some tempting microwave dinners to get me through the festive period."

He raised one dark eyebrow. "In case you get a call out? Or in case you can't be bothered to cook?"

"Either-or."

He laughed. Then we stood there smiling at each other for a while before he asked, "Any movement on the adoption application?"

I pulled a face. "Well, I phoned my ex, and he agreed to speak to the social worker, so it's just a question of waiting to see if he decides to stuff things up for me or not."

"Surely he won't. Not unless he's a total bastard."

Thinking of the scathing tone of Jaimie's voice made me feel depressed all over again. "Well, let's just say he wasn't very friendly when I rang."

We were in the way where we were standing—shoppers were having to make a detour around us like a peloton splitting at a roundabout in the Tour de France. It was cold too—a wicked wind was diligently seeking out every minuscule crevice between my coat collar and my scarf.

"Well, listen," said Jake. "I'm around over Christmas if you fancy meeting up sometime? My kids are going away with my ex-wife and her husband."

For just a moment my thoughts stuck with Jaimie, as I realised this was Harriet's year to have the girls. Then I forgot about him and focussed on the way Jake was looking me straight in the eye. I remembered the spark of attraction I'd felt for him when we first met, the ease with which we'd chatted together at the light festival.

"That would be nice," I said. "Though it might be difficult for me to plan anything very much in advance. It depends what animals I'm looking after, if any."

"That's okay. I haven't made any plans, so I can be flexible. And I'm happy to come round to yours if that's easier. Just give me a call."

He was looking at my mouth now. God, he was looking at my mouth. The flicker of desire I'd felt before was back again, only now it felt more like a flame. For some reason I started thinking about his tattoos. I'd never dated a guy with tattoos before, but on Jake they seemed right. Did he have any more elsewhere on his body? On his chest, maybe, or his back? What would it be like to run my hands over them, to explore them? There was no rule against having red-hot sex on Christmas Day if you were single and planning to adopt, was there? Presumably, Clare hadn't sneakily installed CCTV cameras around my flat.

Jake and I were still smiling at each other like a pair of lovesick teenagers. He could probably read my mind. It was definitely time to go.

"Well," I said, "I'd better get to Tesco."

"Before they run out of lasagnes?"

"Exactly. Because everyone knows zappable lasagnes are a popular Christmas dinner choice."

He smiled. "Bye, Beth. I'll wait to hear from you. I hope no puppies or kittens get sick in the next few days."

~

Right up until Christmas Eve, it actually appeared as if I wouldn't have any pets to look after. But then a tabby cat called Tiger was run over by a taxicab, and Clive had to perform an emergency splenectomy and leg amputation.

"Sorry, Beth," he said. "He's a young cat, so he should be fine to go home tomorrow afternoon, but I think we ought to keep him in overnight. I'll come in myself to check on him later this evening and first thing tomorrow morning, but if you could pop in at lunchtime tomorrow for the family to collect him if he seems okay? Run through what they need to do for him?"

"Of course."

"Call me if you have any doubts at all. I'll stay off the wine until I hear all's well."

"Okay. No problem."

I was actually quite glad to have an animal to take care of over Christmas, since I hadn't made any plans. Though of course I wouldn't have wished an accident on poor Tiger. The taxi driver had been really apologetic when he'd brought him into the surgery, even though he hadn't been at fault—Tiger had run straight out in front of his cab.

After Tiger had been settled into his recovery cage and Clive and I had wished each other a happy Christmas, I popped round to Naomi and Tony's with my Christmas gifts to find Naomi stressed out because Bembe had a cold and Precious was teething. Tony, who worked shifts at a local hospital, wasn't home yet, although he had got Christmas off this year.

"Poor man," said my friend as she opened the door to me. "His first Christmas off for two years and both the children are ill and cranky."

Naomi herself looked flushed and tired, holding a bawling Precious in her arms. Bembe was crying somewhere in the background. It was literally Rosie's idea of hell.

I reached out to take Precious from her. "Go and see to Bembe. I'll hold the baby for a bit."

Naomi looked doubtful. "Are you sure? I don't want to give you a headache on Christmas Eve."

I could hardly hear her over the screaming. "Don't worry about it," I said. "My Christmas is cancelled anyway."

"I almost wish mine was," Naomi said wryly, heading off to see to her son.

Precious's screaming didn't faze me too much, though it probably would have done if she'd been my daughter and I'd been listening to it all day long.

I improvised, walking her around the living room, chatting to her about the Christmas decorations, and showing her the coloured lights on the Christmas tree and the twinkling fairy lights Naomi had arranged around the mirror. Then I sang to her—Christmas carols and Christmas songs, whatever popped into my mind—rocking her in my arms, listening to the distant sound of Naomi reading Bembe stories when her cries began to fade a little. Finally, she stopped screaming and fell asleep, and suddenly all was quiet in the flat.

I stopped singing and hummed instead, rocking the baby gently while I gazed down into her face. Naomi and Tony had chosen the perfect name for her. She was precious. So very precious.

Sometimes I thought that if only Rosie would let herself do this— hold a sleeping baby, gaze down at the perfect curl of her eyelashes, touch the silken down of her head, be the focus of a sudden, unexpected smile—she would change her opinion about having children. I couldn't, in all honesty, imagine how anybody could be immune.

"Thank you," Naomi said softly, coming back into the room. "Want me to take her and put her in her Moses basket?"

"I'll hold her for just a little while longer to make sure she's properly asleep," I said, and Naomi gave me a knowing smile.

"Bembe's absolutely sparko. When you can bear to let her go, we can have a little pre-Christmas drink."

"Only a small one," I said. "I'm officially on duty."

Naomi stretched wearily. "You and me both," she said. Then she looked at me, still cradling her sleeping daughter. "Are you really sure adopting a child is what you want?"

I kept my gaze on Precious's face, taking my time to reply. "Honestly?" I said. "I really don't know."

~

The next day, Tiger was doing as well as could be expected, and after his owners had driven away with him to carry on with their Christmas and I'd texted Clive and locked up the surgery, the holiday stretched emptily before me. I walked home, wondering how things were going for Rosie and Giorgio. Whether Sylvia was happy on her Caribbean cruise. How Mark was getting on with Grace's family.

For a moment, as I turned my coat collar up against the drizzle, I felt a little sorry for myself. Then I remembered Jake and felt a twitch of excitement instead. I hadn't told Rosie I might be seeing him. I hadn't told anybody about it because I didn't want to feel under pressure. I wanted to be able to make a decision based purely on my instincts. Now here I was, alone with those instincts, and they were telling me to go for it. That spending time with Jake on Christmas Day would be fun, whether we ended up in bed together or playing a competitive game of Scrabble. And after the last two Christmases and my recent stresses, fun was exactly what I needed.

My phone was already in my hand, ready to call Jake, when I reached my flat.

But I never got to make the call. Because someone was sitting on my steps waiting for me—someone with a hat pulled down over his ears against the cold.

Mark.

28

"Merry Christmas," Mark wished me, but his face looked broken, and it was all too obvious there was nothing merry about the Christmas he was having.

"Mark. What's happened? Why are you here?"

He got up from the steps and looked down inside his coat. When I heard a whimper, I guessed immediately what was wrong—even before a furry black-and-white head peeped out at me from his coat collar.

"Grace didn't want him. Can you believe that? Wouldn't even entertain the idea of having him. Wanted him gone right away. We rowed. It was awful, Beth. I didn't know where to go or what to do. So I came here."

The puppy was wriggling, trying to break free from the confines of Mark's coat.

I pulled myself together. "Come in, come in."

"Sure you don't mind?"

"Don't be daft."

I led the way inside, setting my phone down on the table and heading straight over to fill the kettle, my mind in an absolute whirl.

"We're not disrupting your plans or anything?"

Any thoughts of hot sex with Jake on Christmas Day afternoon had immediately evaporated at the sight of Mark's defeated expression.

I couldn't remember ever seeing him look like this—as if he'd had a good kicking. Apologising for taking up space.

"I just finished work," I told him. "I had to wait for an injured cat to be collected. But let me meet this little guy."

I went closer, and the puppy wriggled into my hands, a bundle of squirmy black-and-white fluff with a black patch over one eye. Totally delicious. "Hey, buddy. Nice to meet you." I glanced over at Mark. "Still no name?"

He shook his head. "We didn't get that far. Like I said, Grace wanted nothing to do with him. It was as if I'd offered her a pet garter snake or something."

The puppy was licking me all over my face. It was impossible not to smile. He was turning me into goo, the way all puppies did.

"How can I have been married to her for two years and not have any idea she'd react like this? It's crazy."

I sat down on the sofa with the puppy wriggling against my chest. "Didn't she explain why she didn't want him?"

Mark shrugged out of his coat and tossed it onto a chair. "She said something about not having the lifestyle for a dog, and me needing to get it out of the house before she bonded with it. But it wasn't just what she said, Beth. It was the way she said it. So cold."

I thought back to Kenwood Place, when I'd taken Jasper over to Grace and Iris. Grace hadn't tried to stroke him once, come to think of it.

"Is she at home on her own now?"

"Her family will have arrived by now, I suppose."

He sat down on the chair Clare usually chose, elbows resting on his knees, the mix of emotions on his face reminding me of the little boy who'd pedalled like fury across London Fields to tell me and Rosie there was no such thing as Father Christmas.

"You can leave him here with me if you like," I said. "You'll be all right here with me, won't you, buddy?"

The puppy licked my face to seal the deal, using my shoulder blade as a launchpad to leap onto the sofa.

"I'm not sure I even want to go back," Mark said.

I didn't say anything about the significance of such a decision—that leaving your partner in the lurch on Christmas Day was a big thing. Because it was absolutely none of my business. And besides, at that moment, the puppy squatted in the middle of the sofa to have a wee.

"God, I'm sorry." Mark made a grab for him, sending a stream of wee spreading right across the sofa cushion.

"Don't worry about it," I said, getting up for some paper towels and thinking about Grace and Mark's oyster-grey sofa. Unlike mine, which was battered and comfortable and covered with a throw to conceal the worst of the wear, theirs was like new after two years of use. Grace's sister probably wouldn't dare to sit on it to feed her baby, given the risk of projectile vomit.

As I dabbed with the kitchen towel, Mark watched me, an utterly miserable expression on his face. Meanwhile, the puppy leapt to the floor and began trying to wiggle his way beneath the sofa.

"You'd better not let him go under there," I said. "He'll get stuck. How about distracting him with some food?" I looked at Mark. "You did bring some with you, didn't you?"

Mark put his head in his hands. I dropped the kitchen towel to grab the back end of the puppy before he could disappear altogether.

"I left it behind when I stormed out. God, I'm an idiot."

I didn't wholly disagree with him, to be honest. But not so much because he hadn't thought the whole get-a-puppy-for-Christmas surprise through properly. More because he'd thought it a good idea to marry puppy-immune Grace in the first place.

"No, you aren't. You were just upset. Anyway, we have everything we need at the surgery. I'll just pop up there and get it."

I phoned Jake on the way to the surgery. His voice was chipper when he answered, and I was sorry I was going to have to disappoint him.

"Hi, Beth. Happy Christmas!"

"Happy Christmas, Jake."

"So shall I come over? Got the microwave plugged in and ready?"

"Well, the thing is . . . Look, d'you mind very much if we make it tomorrow instead? I'm sorry to let you down, but a friend's just turned up out of the blue. He's in a bit of a state, to be honest, because . . . well, let's just say he needs a listening ear."

"You're swapping sick dogs for depressed friends, then, is that it?"

The lightness in his voice came as a relief. "Something like that. D'you mind?"

"Of course not. That's fine. We didn't have any definite plans, did we? What time tomorrow? If you're sure you still want me to come, that is?"

"Yes, I'm sure. About twelve?"

"Twelve it is. I'll look forward to it."

"Me too."

"Happy Christmas, Beth."

"Happy Christmas, Jake."

When I returned to the flat with supplies, Mark was sitting on the floor with his back against the sofa. The puppy had hold of his Christmas jumper and was tugging at it for all he was worth. Mark was letting him do it.

"Grace's aunt knitted it for me," he said. "She never has liked me."

The jumper was far too big for him, with a knitted picture of Rudolph on the front, his nose so red it looked as if he had an extremely vicious head cold.

"I brought a few toys for him. Clive always stocks a few things at Christmas." I put the puppy food on the table and tore off the packaging from a rubber dog bone. "Here," I said, holding it out to Mark. "Try and tempt him with this while I get his food ready."

Mark waggled the bone about, his face lighting up when the puppy took the bait. "Good boy! That's it, get it. Get it! Oh, what a fierce boy he is!"

I laughed—amused as much by Mark's daft tone of voice as the comic way the puppy was growling, his bottom stuck in the air so he could use all his strength to tug at the bone.

The game lasted until I placed a bowl of dog food down on the floor, and then the puppy flew over to gobble it up.

"I guess he was hungry," said Mark.

"Yes. You know they need to eat four meals a day at his age, right?"

"I do now." The overwhelmed tone was back in his voice.

"Look," I said. "You'd better call Grace, hadn't you? I'm having a microwave curry for my Christmas dinner. If you decide you're not going home, there's a spare. Or I can eat them both if you decide to leave the pup here."

"You'd do that?" he said.

"What?"

"Eat two curries?"

I smiled at his attempt at humour. "It's Christmas. Everyone deserves a blowout at Christmas."

He hauled himself off the floor and headed for the spare bedroom, his shoulders slumped again. The puppy's bowl clunked on the kitchen floor as the bedroom door closed, and I turned to see the little guy standing on the edge of the bowl to tip it up. "There's nothing under it, buddy," I said, switching the radio on to muffle the rumble of Mark's voice and turning the oven on high to cook the samosas and onion bhajis to go with the curry.

While I was doing all this, the puppy suddenly began to sniff the floor. Acting on instinct, I quickly grabbed a newspaper and put it down. When I placed the puppy on it, he immediately relieved himself. "Good boy!" I said, disposing of the newspaper. I was still smiling at how clever the puppy was when Mark emerged from the bedroom.

"Is your spare curry a korma or a madras?" he asked.

"Went as well as that, did it?" I asked, although I really didn't need to because I could tell from his face.

"I've been ordered home. I mean, literally ordered. 'Dinner will be ready in an hour. I told Mum and Dad you had to go out and do a favour for a friend. I suggest you get back here ASAP.'"

"Cooking Christmas dinner can be quite stressful." Or so I believed, not ever having actually done it. Wasn't even doing it now, unless microwaving curries counted.

Mark sat on the dry part of the sofa. The puppy immediately tried to scramble up. Mark lifted him onto his lap, where he promptly fell asleep.

"It just made me think about our whole marriage, you know? Her ordering me about like that. That's what she always does—says how something's going to be. Expects me to just toe the line. And generally, I do."

I watched him stroke the puppy's silken fur, aware he was making a decision about much more than where he was going to eat Christmas dinner. It was difficult to stay silent, but somehow I managed it.

Finally, he looked up. "That curry smells very good," he said.

"I haven't started cooking it yet."

His smile was wan. "It still smells good. I'd like to share it with you, if that's all right?"

I nodded and pierced the film covers on the curries with a knife. Stab, stab, stab.

Within ten minutes our Christmas meal was on our plates, the bhajis and samosas arranged on a platter in the centre of the table. I hadn't bought any Christmas crackers because I hadn't expected company, so we didn't have any paper crowns to wear, but I'd improvised by giving Mark a stripey bobble hat and myself a straw boater, so we looked appropriately ridiculous.

Mark poured wine from the bottle I'd had chilling in the fridge and raised his glass.

As I lifted mine, I wondered what he would toast to, given the circumstances. But in the end, he just said, "Happy Christmas, Beth."

"Happy Christmas."

The curry was surprisingly good. It was as if it knew it was being served for a special occasion and had presented its most fragrant, spicy self.

"Mmm, this is delicious. Maybe we need to change our traditional Christmas fare in this country."

"Well," I said, "it would certainly be a lot cheaper."

I couldn't help but think of the probable waste at Grace's house— Mark's empty place, appetites likely dwindled due to the atmosphere.

Before sitting down to eat, Mark had sent Grace a text message— presumably to tell her he wouldn't be back for dinner—then turned his phone off. I felt sorry for Grace, to be honest, having to cope with her family on her own, all her efforts to make a perfect Christmas ruined, but I did think a large part of the situation was her fault. Even if she hadn't wanted the puppy, couldn't she have been kinder to Mark? She must have realised how disappointed he was by her rejection of his surprise. He'd only done it to try and cheer her up about them not having a baby yet.

"What d'you think Dad would think about all this?" Mark asked, the bobble on his hat quivering as he cut up a large chunk of chicken.

I thought Richard would have advised Mark to go home. *Leave the pup with us, son. We'll take care of it. Go and sort your marriage out.* But I didn't want to say that. "I'm not sure."

"He'd probably have thought I was a complete prick."

"He wouldn't have said that."

"Maybe not, but he'd have thought it. And it's true. I am a prick."

"You just wanted to give Grace a nice surprise," I started, but he shook his head.

237

"No, not for getting Buddy."

I looked over at the sleeping bundle of fluff. "Is that what you're going to call him?"

Mark grinned. "Why not?"

I nodded, grinning back. "Good choice."

"No, I meant for marrying Grace to begin with. God knows what I thought we had in common. Rosie was right last Christmas—what she said about Grace trying to change me."

"She said that about us both," I reminded him.

He pointed his fork at me. "Yes, but you got out, didn't you? You ended it with Jaimie, whereas I stuck around for another helping of bludgeoning and criticism."

There was a slight tremor in his voice as he finished, a brightness about his eyes which made me shudder at the thought of where I might be myself if I'd just dragged through another year of never quite measuring up to what Jaimie and his girls wanted me to be.

Mark swiped a hand across his eyes and smiled across the table. "Sorry. This is all very maudlin for Christmas lunch."

"It's all right," I said, although in truth, I didn't know quite what to feel. I couldn't risk thinking about the possibility of Mark's marriage being over, in case I accidentally let a chink of hope into my heart. Which would be a ridiculous thing to do. Time after time I'd been forced to accept that just because Mark was single, it didn't mean he would look at me as anything other than a sister or a friend. Why should anything have changed?

"I tell you what," he suggested. "Let's not talk about it anymore. Or even think about it." He reached for the wine bottle and topped up our wineglasses. "Agreed?"

"Agreed," I said, but that lasted only until we were halfway through our dessert—a tin of sliced peaches I'd found right at the back of my store cupboard—because my phone rang. It was Grace, ringing me because Mark's phone was off.

"Could I speak to my husband, please, Beth?" she said, cold as you like, as if it were my fault he was here eating curry and tinned peaches.

"Yes, of course," I said, holding my phone out to Mark. "It's for you."

This time, he didn't go into the bedroom to speak to her. So I left the room instead, shutting myself in the bathroom and sitting on the closed lid of the toilet. Even in there, I could hear his raised voice.

When he knocked ten minutes or so later to tell me he'd finished, I grabbed some towels to cover the wet patch on the sofa until I could clean it properly.

Buddy was still asleep, oblivious to the drama he'd caused. There was no sign of Mark. His coat had gone. Had he left while I was collecting the towels? Then I saw him through the french doors, outside on the patio, so I got my own coat and went out to join him.

"Just needed a bit of air," he said.

I nodded, folding my arms around my body to keep warm, looking up into the bare branches of the plane tree.

"Remember those baby owls in the trees in the back garden when we were kids?" Mark said suddenly.

I did. Mark had seen them from his bedroom window and had come down to get a better view from the garden. I'd been the only one around to share his excitement. Sylvia, Richard, and Rosie had all been out for the evening—Sylvia and Richard for a meal, Rosie at the cinema with her boyfriend at the time.

"They were so soft looking, weren't they? So . . ."

"Snuggly?"

He smiled. "Yes."

We stood side by side, watching and listening, but there were no owls today, baby or otherwise. Just a dog barking somewhere and the sound of an occasional car passing in the street.

When Mark began to talk, it was almost as if he were speaking to himself, trying to work things out in his mind.

"Grace was just so beautiful. So perfect. She knocked me off my feet when we met, you know? But it wasn't just her looks. I loved her self-confidence, the way she knew exactly what she wanted."

"And what she wanted was you?"

"Yes, at the time. It was dazzling. We were both dazzled, I think. But it didn't last. God, even on our honeymoon, if I'd bothered to look, things weren't right. She didn't want to go to the Eiffel Tower, can you believe that? Insisted we go to see the architecture in the financial district instead. I mean, sure, it was impressive. But better than the Eiffel Tower? I don't think so. Even then, that early on, I was giving way to what *she* wanted, letting what I wanted slide."

I wondered if really, Buddy—poor little Buddy—had been an act of rebellion. A way of Mark asserting, *Here, this is me. This is something I want. Time for you to compromise and give way to me for a change.*

"You know, at his age, Buddy would soon be snapped up from a rescue centre. You wouldn't need to worry about him finding a good home."

"What? So I could go back and carry on as before?"

"Does it have to be like before? Couldn't you go to couples therapy or something?"

He sighed. "I doubt Grace would. Why would she, when she thinks she's perfect and everything that's wrong is all my fault?"

He had a point.

"I'm not sure love can be trusted anyway. Well, not love, but the whole being-in-love thing. Not if it means you can't really see a person. Because you need to be able to really see a person, don't you? To judge whether you've got a good future together or not?"

I looked at him. Saw a grown-up version of the boy I'd first met at the age of four. Even the way he was plucking restlessly at his jumper with his fingers made me think of a mealtime when he hadn't wanted to eat something—I forgot what, but I did vividly remember the way his bottom lip had stuck out and his fingers had plucked at his T-shirt.

"Maybe people in successful relationships love each other warts and all," I suggested.

"Or maybe they don't have warts."

"Everyone has warts. Metaphorical ones, at least."

"Doctor, doctor," he joked. "I've got metaphorical warts."

I wanted to be able to think of a clever punch line to create a moment of light relief, but nothing came to mind. Instead, I just started shivering, because it was seriously cold out there, and the cold had got through my coat.

"Come on," Mark said. "Let's go back inside. I don't want your catching pneumonia to be on my conscience along with everything else."

Inside, I laid the towels on the sofa so we could sit down. Buddy was still fast asleep in one corner of the room—a tiny, tucked-up ball of fluff.

Mark poured more wine. "No, much better to accept it's over, I think. Even if I went back, I'd never be able to forget the way she looked at Buddy. She recoiled, Beth. From a *puppy*."

Since this was also incomprehensible to me, I didn't know what to say. So I just said, "D'you want a cup of coffee? I'm going to make one for myself."

"Let me make you one. It's only fair, since you did all the cooking."

"It is very hard working, zapping things," I agreed.

Mark smiled. "You always have managed to cheer me up," he said, reaching out to tuck a stray strand of hair behind my ear. "How do you do that?"

My mouth was suddenly dry. When I tried to speak, no sound came out until I cleared my throat. "We've . . . just known each other for a long time, that's all."

Mark's hand was stroking its way down my neck now. He had never, ever touched me in that intimate way before. And he hadn't looked at my mouth like that before either—in the sexually charged way Jake had looked at it when we'd run into each other in the street.

"We have, haven't we?" he said. "For years and years."

It's not that a brother doesn't touch you. He does. A brother pretend bashes your arm or gives you a playful shove. Hugs you when you meet. Tickles you when you're kids. But he doesn't hold you like this, not even when your heart is broken.

When Mark had driven that hired van to fetch me and my belongings from Jaimie's, we'd hugged for a very long time at the garage. But we hadn't melted into each other like this. My breasts hadn't found a home against his chest. A lick of heat hadn't flared down my body like a flame catching on kindling.

For me, the potential of it had always been there, desire coursing beneath my surface like magma. I'd had to train myself to not acknowledge it. To get on with my life like a person who lives at the foot of an active volcano gets on with their life.

But now Mark was holding me, looking at me with total focus. Examining my face as if he'd never seen it before. And in a way, he hadn't, had he? Because I'd never allowed him to see this me. Never let myself respond the way I wanted to. But how could I not respond now, when his hand was beneath my hair, deliciously caressing my scalp and the nape of my neck? When every plane, curve, and jut of his body was imprinted onto mine and his mouth was steadily descending to make contact?

The kiss was every bit as intoxicating as I'd ever imagined it would be—sweet and soft and firm, demanding all at the same time, the core of me lava hot as my lips parted to let in his tongue. I reached for him with shaking hands, pulling his body hard against mine.

But then Mark moved back to put space between us, and it was over as quickly as it had begun. I watched him rub his hands together as if to wipe the touch of me away. And I felt disgusting. Repulsive. Utterly betrayed and rejected.

"God," he said, his voice shaking. "I shouldn't have done that."

Just for a second, a window had opened, showing me a glimpse of the paradise I'd craved for so long. But now that window was boarded back up with a thousand nails, leaving me in ice-cold darkness.

"I'm so sorry, Beth."

I couldn't look at him. Wanted very much to throw myself onto my bed and cry for the rest of the century. But I couldn't—wouldn't—do that with him here. Wouldn't suffer his pity.

"You should go," I said. "You can leave Buddy here with me, but you should just go."

"You want me to?" Without looking, I could imagine his big-eyed, sorrowful expression.

"Yes."

He got up. "Right. All right. Well, I'll . . . I'll be in touch about picking up Buddy."

"Okay."

"Look, Beth, I . . ."

I didn't want to have to yell at him to get out, but I would if I had to.

"Goodbye, Mark."

After he'd gone, I lay on my bed and cried and cried and cried. There were around twenty-five years' worth of tears to cry, after all. Buddy licked my face for a bit, but after he got bored of that, he dived for my fingers or tugged painfully at my hair instead.

Finally, he went to sleep in the crook of my neck, and I let him stay there, completely against all the rules of dog training. He wasn't mine to keep, so I didn't have to be the bad guy who shut him away in another room overnight to get used to being away from his siblings. Let somebody else do it. Let bloody Mark do it.

We could so easily have ended up in bed together, Mark and I. But the horror on his face when he'd pulled away told me he would have been using me for comfort. Because he was upset about Grace. Which showed just how much he cared about me and my feelings.

We were never going to be unselfconscious with each other again. This was always going to be a snagging thorn between us. In a few short seconds, I had lost everything—my secrets, my brother, the man I loved.

"Oh, Buddy," I said, sobbing into his soft fur. But Buddy was oblivious, gone wherever puppies go when they zonk out.

"Happy Christmas, Beth," I told myself. "Happy bloody Christmas."

~

Buddy was still with me the next day when Jake came round at twelve o'clock.

"Who's this little guy?" he asked, reaching out to stroke him.

"This is Buddy. He's my friend's pup. I'm looking after him while he sorts things out."

"Your depressed friend?"

"Yep."

Jake stroked Buddy's ears. Buddy promptly wriggled adorably onto his back in my arms and began to savage Jake's hand with his needle-sharp teeth.

"Hmm. I can see how you'd be depressed when you have this little guy in your life. Ouch!"

"Like I said yesterday, it's a long story," I said, prising Buddy's teeth from Jake's finger. "Anyway, come in. I'll fix you a drink. Did you have a nice day yesterday?"

Jake shrugged, taking off his leather jacket. "I ate too much, drank too much, overdosed on crap TV. It was fine. How about you? Did you get to do any of those traditional things, or was it all counselling and doom and gloom?"

"No, I . . . it . . ." To my horror and embarrassment, tears suddenly swamped my eyes. "Oh God," I said, "I'm sorry." But there was absolutely nothing I could do to stem the flow.

"Hey, hey," said Jake, concerned. "*I'm* sorry. I was being flippant. Yesterday must have been really hard for you."

"It . . . it was," I sobbed, and Jake drew me into his arms for a hug.

"Hey," he said. "It's all right. Shh."

It was good to be held. Comforting. Or it would have been if a wriggling mass of puppy weren't jammed between us.

Suddenly Jake was pulling back. "Oh, I think Buddy may have . . . leaked on me," he said, and when I looked, I saw a dark stain on the front of his freshly ironed shirt.

"Oh God, I'm sorry," I said.

"No, don't worry, that's okay. But I think I'll have to take it off, if you don't mind?"

"Of course. I'll see if I can find you a T-shirt or something. The bathroom's just on the right, if you want to have a wash."

"Thanks."

"Jesus, Buddy," I said to the unrepentant pup, taking him with me into the bedroom while I searched for a T-shirt large enough for Jake to wear.

The only thing I could find was a joke T-shirt Rosie had given me years ago with the slogan I'M NOT RUDE, I JUST HAVE THE BALLS TO SAY WHAT EVERYONE ELSE IS THINKING emblazoned across the front. Needless to say, I hadn't worn it much. Still, it looked as if it would fit Jake okay.

I was just emerging from the bedroom with it when there was a knock at the door. I went to open it, still carrying Buddy.

It was Mark, complete with a stubbly, unshaven chin and a chastened expression.

"Hi," he said. "Sorry to just turn up. I thought I'd better . . ."

Buddy had begun to yap and wriggle the second he saw him, so I thrust him into Mark's arms.

"Right. Here he is, then. Come in for a moment while I get his stuff together for you. He's had his breakfast."

"Thanks. Look, Beth, about yesterday . . ."

But I did *not* want to talk about that. Fortunately, at that moment, the bathroom door opened, and Jake emerged, naked from the waist up, displaying an extremely buff chest with a tattoo of an eagle inked right across it.

"Hi," he said, stretching out a hand towards Mark. "I'm Jake."

Moving like an automaton, Mark took his outstretched hand. "Mark."

I gave the T-shirt to Jake. "Here," I said. "This should fit you. I'll just get Buddy's bits and pieces, Mark."

"Little Buddy peed on me," I left Jake explaining as I hurried into the living room, snatching up puppy pads, dog toys, and the few cans of food that were left.

"Here," I said, returning to present Mark with a carrier bag.

He took it from me, his green eyes boring into mine, saying, *Can we talk?*

"Bye, then," I said, refusing to acknowledge any cues. "Have fun with Buddy. I'd ask you to stay, but Jake and I have plans."

"Do we?" Jake asked when Mark had left and I'd shut the door after him.

Jake still hadn't put the T-shirt on, which meant his toned chest was still very much on display. I guessed that if I wanted to, I could lead him straight into the bedroom and set about doing things with him that were guaranteed to put Mark and this whole debacle of a Christmas right out of my mind for a while.

Except that this was Jake. And even though I didn't know him well, I sensed he was kind and considerate—a thoroughly decent human being. Besides, it probably wouldn't work anyway. Not for long. After a pleasant interlude, I'd still emerge with the horror of yesterday etched as firmly on my mind as the eagle on Jake's chest.

So I said, "I'll put the kettle on," and led the way back into the living room. Jake covered up his gorgeous chest with the ridiculous T-shirt, and after I'd made the tea, I told him everything. The whole painful history of me loving Mark. And it turned out Jake knew exactly what it was like to yearn for someone you can't have, because he'd once fallen for his best friend's wife and had to distance himself from his friend in order to cope with it.

And sometime during that day—which started off with confessions and sympathy and ended with haphazard picnic food and several hilarious games of Pictionary—Jake Jackson and I became friends instead of potential lovers.

WINTER FOUR

❄❄❄❄❄

29

Logan and I were working in the garden at the centre. It had been Jake's idea to develop the area at the back of the building into a garden, and over the past year, we'd transformed it from a dumping ground to a tranquil haven. It had flower and vegetable borders, as well as a seating area for chilling out, all against the backdrop of an ever-changing graffiti wall.

Logan had a natural flair for gardening—green fingered, Richard would have called him. As we worked together, raking up fallen leaves and wrapping terra-cotta pots in Bubble Wrap to stop them from cracking in the frost, I could see the tension he'd arrived at the centre with falling away. I had no idea what was worrying him. Sometimes he spoke to me about his problems, but not often. I did know Logan's homelife was difficult. That his mother was a single parent to four children and money was tight. And that he didn't get on with his stepfather and was always in trouble at school for something or other. But being in the garden seemed to help him—tending to the plants, seeing them bloom, nurturing them, and being creative.

I knew the feeling.

"You're a miracle worker," Jake liked to tell me, but he was wrong. It wasn't me; it was the act of gardening itself. Volunteering at the centre helped me too. It had been a good decision to keep at it after I'd decided not to adopt after all. Making a difference to young people's lives, even in a small way, gave me a deep sense of fulfilment. Now, in December, floodlighting meant we could garden even after it got dark, though the cold temperatures limited the amount of time we wanted to be outdoors.

"I've just put the kettle on, if you want a hot drink, guys," Jake told us from the doorway, and as if by silent mutual consent, Logan and I stowed our gardening tools away in the shed and headed inside.

Once we left the garden, Logan rarely spoke to me. If ever it was raining and we couldn't work outside, I was lucky if I got more than a grunt out of him. But I didn't mind. I understood. Logan had to be a lot of different people in his life, but just as long as he could be the Logan he was in the garden, I thought he would be okay.

In the kitchen, Jake handed me a cup of coffee. I took it gratefully. "Thanks. You don't realise how cold you are until you stop."

We sat together for a moment, sipping our drinks. Then he asked, "Done all the dreaded Christmas shopping?"

"Most of it. Just the difficult ones left."

"I bet they're for men."

I smiled at him. "They are, actually. How did you guess?" Mark and Gary, Sylvia's boyfriend. Man friend. Gentleman caller. I hadn't made up my mind how to refer to him yet.

"We're difficult buggers," Jake joked.

"What about you? Have you done yours?"

He nodded. "I've been a good boy. Got it done early. Though the kids only wanting money made it easier."

"What have you got for Tish?"

Jake's face lit up. Clearly, he was very pleased with whatever he'd bought for his girlfriend. "Ah, well, I'm not sure I ought to say. It's a surprise, and she did say she might pop over this evening."

Right on cue, the door opened, and Tish came in.

"Speak of the devil," Jake said, opening his arms to give her a kiss.

"Who are you calling a devil?" Tish asked, wrapping her arms around him and kissing him back. "Hi, Beth. You all right?"

"Hi, Tish. Yes, I'm fine, thank you. Just thawing out."

"Tell me about it. It's almost too cold for the bike."

Like Jake, Tish rode a motorbike. Also like Jake, she wore a leather jacket and had several tattoos, only hers were mainly of Disney characters and inspirational quotes.

Tish and Jake had met at a motorbike club in the spring and clicked straightaway. I was really happy for them. Jake was a good friend. I was glad nothing had happened between us—I'd have been using him if it had. Using sex to try to make myself feel better after the debacle with Mark. If Jake and I had gone to bed, we'd have been awkward with each other afterwards. Too awkward for me to volunteer at the centre. And that would have been a great shame.

I went over to the sink to wash my mug up. "Mind if I get off a bit early? I'm meeting up with Rosie to see the Regent Street lights."

"Sure," said Jake. "No problem. Tell her hi from me. And you have a great Christmas, yeah?"

I went over to give both him and Tish a peck on the cheek. "Thanks. And a very happy Christmas to you too."

"See you in the New Year."

I nodded, a tingle of excitement stirring in my belly at the thought of New Year. I hadn't told Jake anything about my plans, in case they didn't work out. I hadn't told anyone about them except for Naomi and Rosie. And even they didn't know I'd got an official date through, because I'd received the letter only today. I was going to tell Rosie tonight.

Rosie herself called me when I was waiting for the bus.

"You're not ringing to cancel on me, are you?"

"Of course not. I'm ringing to tell you . . ."

"Hello, Bethy," came a familiar voice in the background.

"Giorgio?"

"Yes," said Rosie. "This one turned up out of the blue. Mind if he tags along with us?"

"Of course I don't. It will be lovely to see him."

"You see, *cara*," I heard Giorgio say. "I told you this."

I laughed. "The bus is coming. I'll see you both under the Christmas tree."

"Under the tree."

"Ciao, Bethy."

I was still smiling as I got on the bus and swiped my Oyster card. Giorgio coming along might mean I wouldn't be able to tell Rosie my news, but it made me so happy to see my friend with her love. Last Christmas, Giorgio had surprised Rosie by declaring that he wanted a relationship with her more than he wanted to be a father, and ever since then, they'd spent every possible minute they could with each other, flying back and forth between London and Rome. Which meant I hadn't seen her as much as I usually did, obviously, so the first hour of any meetup we managed to organise was always a sort of breathless catch-up. Especially after I joined Tinder.

Rosie loved hearing about my dating escapades. Though there hadn't been any of those to talk about since July, not since Tom.

Just as I thought of Tom, my phone rang, and his name appeared on the caller display. I was tempted to reject the call, but experience told me my ex-boyfriend would only keep calling until I answered if I did that.

"Hi, Tom. I can't speak just now; I'm on my way somewhere."

"Oh. I hoped I could pop round with your Christmas present."

I couldn't hide my dismay. "Tom, we agreed we wouldn't buy each other presents."

"I know, but I didn't think you really meant it. And I saw something perfect for you. I had to get it."

"Well, that's very kind, but I haven't got anything for you because we agreed not to buy anything for each other."

"That's all right. I don't expect anything."

But that wasn't true. Tom did expect something—me to relent about my decision and start dating him again if he only wore me down enough. It was never going to work. I'd told him so. Over and over again.

I really wished I hadn't been persuaded to start dating. But January and February had been particularly bleak months, which was probably why I'd been receptive to Naomi's suggestion.

~

When Clare's home visits had started up again in the New Year, I'd been feeling low after my disastrous Christmas. And one look at her grim expression told me she'd spoken to Jaimie and that his report on my mothering skills hadn't been favourable.

"What did he say about me?" I asked her.

"I can't tell you that. It's confidential."

I stared at the floor, so frustrated I could have screamed. I wanted to try to explain to her how difficult and unresponsive the girls had been. How very hard I'd tried. That being a stepmother was one of the most challenging things I'd ever done.

But then she said it herself: "Look, I know how challenging it can be to be a stepparent, especially in a situation where the children still hope their parents will get back together."

"Yes," I said with feeling, but Clare swept on.

"But being an adoptive parent can be much more challenging than that. No matter how inadequate a child's parents have been, they are still that child's parents, and the child is still likely to long for them. Miss them. Illogical as it is, they may even blame you for their being taken away from them. This is unlikely to last forever, of course, but it could last long enough for you to start to wonder whether you've done the right thing."

"My relationship with Jaimie's daughters wasn't part of the reason Jaimie and I split up," I said, not wanting Clare to think I didn't have sticking power. "If it hadn't been for . . . other circumstances, I would have persisted with them. They may never have viewed me like a second mother, but I don't think they'd have gone on resenting me."

But Clare latched on to the earlier part of what I'd said.

"Yes, as to those circumstances you mention, Mr. Faulkner intimated that one of the reasons your relationship ended was because you told him you had feelings for somebody else. And yet, when we spoke about this before Christmas, I don't think you mentioned that?"

Blast Jaimie to hell. Obviously, he'd used the conversation with Clare as an opportunity to get his own back. But I wasn't going to let him and his girls—or anybody else, for that matter—destroy my chances of adopting. I could be a good mother if I got the chance. I just needed to be given that chance.

So I leant forward in my chair, holding Clare's gaze. "It's true, I did tell Jaimie that. And it's true that I do—did—have feelings for somebody else. But nothing came of it. Will ever come of it. And . . . everything else I told you about why Jaimie and I split up was true. We wanted different things from life. I didn't love him as much as he deserved to be loved. Look, right now, my focus isn't on a relationship. It's 100 percent on becoming an adoptive parent. I'll do whatever I need to do to make that happen. I've already arranged to volunteer at the youth centre, and I'll ask my boss if I can change my shifts so I can volunteer at a school too. I want to get as much experience with children as possible."

Clare looked at me. I thought I saw a gleam of approval in her eyes at my fighting spirit. "That sounds very helpful," she said. "And if you like, I can put you in touch with another single adopter so you can have a frank conversation about the challenges she's faced." She smiled. "And the joys, of course."

I smiled back, feeling suddenly hopeful that Jaimie's negativity hadn't blown my chances of adopting after all. "Yes, please, that would be great."

Clare was as good as her word, emailing the contact details of a single adopter—Marie—to me the very next day.

When I first called Marie, she asked me to call back because she was dealing with an all-out tantrum. Actually, she didn't need to tell me that, because I could hear the screaming over the phone. When I tried again, Marie told me these tantrums were fairly frequent. That they came out of the blue and probably amounted to her little boy testing her to see if she would stick around, even when he was naughty.

"The social workers say it's a phase, and you have to believe that, don't you? Otherwise, you'd go crazy. And he's a little cuddly bunny most of the time. Except for when he's not."

Then she added, "I can't deny all this would be easier if I had a partner. Someone to share my woes and my triumphs with. But then, I suppose all single parents might say the same thing."

Marie's adoptive son was six years old—she'd adopted him when he was five. When I asked her if she'd have liked to have adopted a younger child, she said, "Yes, of course. But it was always made clear to me that since the demand for babies and toddlers is high, younger children almost always go to a couple. Hasn't your social worker told you that?"

My heart sank. "No," I said, "she hasn't. Not in so many words, anyway."

"Well," advised Marie, "I would mention it next time you see her, if I were you."

I did.

And after I'd asked the question, Clare gave me one of her full-on piercing stares. "While it's not written down in black and white that couples should have priority where babies and toddlers are concerned, in reality, it does often turn out that way, yes. We have far more older children waiting to be adopted, and it's much easier to look after a baby or a toddler if there are two of you."

I nodded, trying not to be sucked down into a despondent vortex at the thought of never having a baby to care for.

"Is that a problem for you, Beth?"

"No," I said, sick with disappointment. "It's not a problem." What else could I say? If I said it was, if I told her that the thought of not caring for a baby or a young child was totally gutting, then I was pretty much drawing a line under my application, wasn't I?

So I told myself I would get over my disappointment. That it was an adjustment I had to make, that was all. That adopting an older child was such a worthwhile thing to do, I would come round to the idea in no time. Better an older child than no child, right?

And I threw myself into my volunteer work at a local school after I had made this pact with myself. I pictured the things I would do with my child—reading, making dens, going to local parks, baking. It would be rewarding, it really would.

Only then Naomi signed Bembe up for a toddler gym class on Saturday mornings. Tony worked weekend shifts sometimes, so I offered to take care of Precious when he was working. That way, Bembe wouldn't miss out. However, as soon as I started taking care of Precious, my attempts to convince myself I'd be fulfilled by adopting an older child were blown right out of the water.

Precious was at the age where she was crawling everywhere at a hundred miles an hour and laughing her cheeky little laugh when she wasn't smiling. I would build towers with her large plastic building blocks for her to knock over. Help her complete her wooden puzzles. Once, I even set up a huge sheet of plastic on the kitchen floor and "painted" with her. In short, the two hours Naomi and Bembe were away were an absolute frenetic joy.

Around eleven thirty, I'd put Precious in her high chair, wipe her hands, and give her a snack and a drink. Afterwards, we would sit in the squashy armchair together, and I would read to her. Normally, Precious bashed the book with her chubby hands and made sounds along with me, her face filled with delight when she heard the sound of her mother and her big brother arriving home. But occasionally, when our play had been particularly full on, she fell asleep against my chest, the way she sometimes had when she was a young baby.

And I held her close to my heart, a feeling of complete bliss sinking right into my bones.

Naomi came home and found us that way one day. Bembe had fallen asleep in his buggy, so she left him there in the hallway and crept in to find her daughter asleep in my arms. And me with tears running down my face.

"Hey," she said, concerned. "What is it? What's wrong?"

I smiled a watery smile, swiping at my eyes with my free hand. "Nothing," I said. "Everything's perfect."

Naomi unbuttoned her coat, taking it all in. "You were born to look after babies," she told me. "You know that, don't you?"

"Don't," I begged her, the tears starting up all over again. "Please don't."

She lifted her hands. "Look, all I'm saying is, you could pause your adoption application for a while. For all you know, your perfect man might be living two streets away, and you just haven't met him yet. This time next year, you could be married with a baby on the way."

"What's Clare going to think about me as a potential adopter if she finds out I've paused my application to shag around? She's hardly going to be impressed, is she?"

Naomi shrugged. "You don't have to shag around. Just go on some dates. You don't even need to tell her about it. Say you're going to take four or five months to get lots of experience with children. She'll approve of that, won't she? Go on, mate, give it a chance. What have you got to lose? If it doesn't work out, you can always restart the adoption process."

Naomi had planted a seed in my head that morning—a seed which germinated after I'd spoken to Marie again to hear that her little boy was in trouble at school for constantly hitting other children. Coinciding as this did with Jake having to temporarily ban Logan and another boy from attending the centre for a while after they got into a fight, I began to wonder whether Naomi was right. Try as I might to convince myself that adopting an older child would be right for me, I couldn't seem to shake off my longing to have a baby.

Had I been too hasty? I was thirty-eight now. There was still time for me to conceive. Just.

So I spoke to Clare, as Naomi had suggested. And just as Naomi had told me she would, Clare approved of my plans. We put my application on hold for six months.

Then I got busy creating a Tinder profile.

30

My foray into the world of internet dating wasn't exactly success-ful. At least my string of disastrous dates kept Rosie entertained for hours on end when we met up—the no-shows, the guys who'd posted outdated profile photos, the guys who couldn't stop speaking about their exes.

But then I met Tom, who was normal in comparison, with a regular job for an engineering company and reasonably good looks. Not much of a sense of humour, but maybe he just needed to get used to what made me laugh?

Just sleep with him, I could hear Tina Bateson saying in my ear. *What are you waiting for?*

I did sleep with Tom, not because of Tina Bateson's imagined whis-pers but because I wanted to. But when I did, somehow it didn't feel quite right—Tom's overconscientious attempts to give me pleasure, the little glances to see if he was doing a good job or not. I began to feel self-conscious, which is never a recipe for sexual satisfaction. I had a creeping suspicion I might be fooling myself. Again. Trying to convince myself I felt something I really didn't.

And then the questions started up: Did I really want to conceive a child like this? To be shackled to Tom or someone like him for the rest of my life because of joint parenthood? And I knew I was probably going to have to end our relationship, and that wasn't going to be pleasant, because Tom appeared to adore me. Worst luck.

I still hadn't done anything about it by the time of Sylvia's memorial dinner at the end of July, on what would have been Richard's birthday.

Tom had stayed over the night before—I hadn't planned for him to, but we'd gone to see a local band and had a few drinks, so one thing had led to another. Now I needed him to leave, but Tom didn't seem to be in any hurry to go anywhere. After I finished showering and returned to the bedroom to get dressed, he was still in bed.

"I was thinking," he said, propping himself up on one elbow to watch me put on my underwear. "I've got a cousin who lives in Enfield. Kate. I haven't seen her for ages. I could drive you if you like. That way you could have a few glasses of wine with your lunch."

On the face of it, it was a nice offer. But with doubts starting to creep in about Tom and me, I was wary of offering him false encouragement.

"Thanks, but I'm not planning to drink today, so I'll be fine. My car could do with a drive out."

I slipped my dress over my head. When I emerged, Tom was right there, ready to zip it up. How had he managed to get out of bed so fast? It was kind of creepy.

"Okay, whatever you think. I'll go and see my cousin anyway, though, now I've thought of it. I might go on the train if you don't need a lift. Kate lives right near Enfield Town station, so it's handy. Is that anywhere near your family?"

"Not really," I said, brushing my hair in front of the mirror, my back to him. "They're at Enfield Lock, near the river."

"Nice."

"It is."

I turned, trying to ignore the fact that he was totally naked. Well, after Jaimie, I was used to naturism. "Anyway, I'd better get going. I said I'd arrive early to give Sylvia a hand, so . . ."

Finally, he took the hint. "Oh, sure. I'll get dressed. Silly me."

～

I wasn't actually looking forward to the meal. It was bound to be emotional. Even after all this time, we all still missed Richard like crazy. And apart from that, this would be the first occasion I'd spent any amount of time with Mark since last Christmas. It was going to be tough, seeing him, reliving that hurt and humiliation.

But it had to be done. Unless I was planning on turning my back on Groves family gatherings forevermore.

Mark and Buddy had been living at Sylvia's ever since his split with Grace, so I expected to have to deal with seeing him almost as soon as I got there. But he was out.

"Mark's taken Buddy for a walk," Sylvia told me after we'd kissed. "I expect they've popped into the pub on their way home. They often do on Sundays."

"How is Mark?" I asked, following her to the kitchen.

Sylvia sighed. "Not great, to be honest. I always thought Grace was such a nice girl, but she's really had her claws unsheathed while they've been trying to sort a settlement out. Honestly, she didn't put her flat on the market when they got together, did she? She's still got somewhere to live, whereas Mark has to put up with living with his old mum."

She forced a smile. "Anyway, how are you, darling? We don't seem to have seen very much of you lately. Rosie says you have a boyfriend?"

I sighed, then told her about Tom and how it wasn't really working out for me. "I thought I should at least give dating a try before I went down the adoption route, but it's been a complete disaster. I should have stuck with my application. I might have had a child by now if I had."

It was good to talk about it all. I'd really missed seeing Sylvia so much, what with avoiding Mark.

"Adoption isn't something to rush into, though, is it?" Sylvia said now. "Not when there's another life at stake. Playing devil's advocate, perhaps if you'd been totally sure about adopting, you wouldn't have paused the process? Just a thought." She took my hand and squeezed it.

I squeezed hers right back. Sylvia was right. As usual. God, I loved her.

"How about you?" I asked. "How are things with you?"

"Well," she said, and something about her expression made me look more closely at her. Was she blushing? "Things are all right. Good, actually. That was partly why I wanted you all to—"

But just then the front door opened, and Rosie called out to us, so Sylvia broke off, calling, "We're in the kitchen, love."

"Hi, both," said Rosie, coming in. "Goodness, the traffic was bad. What? No rapturous border-collie welcome? Don't tell me, my dear brother's popped out for a swift half or three."

I frowned at that. Was Mark drinking too much? The way Rosie had spoken suggested as much. But there wasn't time to ask about it—or, indeed, even to get back to the intriguing thing Sylvia had just been about to tell me—because the front door opened again, and the scrabble of frantic paws on the laminate flooring signalled Buddy's—and presumably Mark's—return.

"Hi, Buddy," I greeted the dog, smiling at his enthusiastic welcome as he entered the kitchen—his entire rear half wagging along with his tail before he shot off to fetch me his favourite ball.

"That dog is besotted with you," Rosie said.

There was no chance to quip that Buddy had good taste because there was a rumble of male voices in the hallway, and then Mark was there. And he wasn't alone.

"Look who I found in the pub, everyone," he said.

"Smithy!" I cried, jumping to my feet, causing Buddy to start barking with excitement.

Smithy smiled at me, for Smithy it was, and I saw that the years since I'd last seen him had treated him well. He was slim and deeply suntanned, his hair bleached a light blond. I'd heard he'd been working in Dubai for several years now, and he looked good.

"Hi, Beth. Hi, everybody. It's good to see you all. Hope you don't mind me crashing your family lunch, Sylvia?"

"I said you'd have cooked plenty, Mum," said Mark.

Sylvia came over to kiss Smithy's cheek. "I have. And of course it's all right. Of course. It's lovely to see you after all this time."

"I was so sorry to hear about Richard."

Sylvia patted Smithy's hand. "Thank you, dear. Yes, it was . . . well, you know, I'm sure. But, Mark, fix Smithy a drink, will you? I just need to get the vegetables on."

"How are you, Beth?" Smithy asked me while Mark searched out a beer and Rosie helped her mother to peel potatoes.

I couldn't stop smiling at him. It was so good to see him again. As far as I knew, this was the first time he'd been back to this country in years. "I'm fine," I said. "How about you? You look great."

Smithy smiled, a slightly lopsided smile that took me right back to our time in Belize together. "I'm okay, thanks. Just back to visit family. Still working overseas. Mark says you're volunteering at a youth centre?"

Curious that Mark had picked that particular fact about me to mention to his friend. "Yes, it's in Dalston, near where I live. I really enjoy it."

In the distance, we could hear Mark speaking to Sylvia, asking about a bottle opener.

"You're still single, then?" Smithy asked me softly.

"Well," I said, "I have a boyfriend at the moment, but it's nothing serious. So yes, I'm still single."

"You never . . ." Smithy gestured towards the kitchen door—and Mark—with his head.

I shook mine. "No."

"You do know you might have saved him a broken marriage if you'd said something. I didn't get to meet Grace, but she sounds like a right piece of work."

I pulled a face. "Let's just say I never really warmed to her."

"Why would you?" Smithy began to say, but I could see Mark coming from the kitchen, so I shushed him.

He joined us, handing Smithy a bottle of beer. "Here you go, mate." He put his arm round Smithy's shoulders and looked at me. "So what d'you make of my big surprise, Beth? Good, eh? You two always did get on well, didn't you? Belize buddies and all that."

"It's a fantastic surprise," I said, meaning it, looking in Smithy's direction. "I'm looking forward to hearing all about your life in Dubai."

"Why don't you come over and experience it for yourself instead of me telling you about it?" Smithy said.

I stared at him. "What?"

"I'll give you my contact details. You can come and visit whenever you like."

"Whoa!" said Mark. "Beth's got a boyfriend." He looked at me, his expression unreadable. "Or so I'm led to believe?"

Rosie chose that moment to join us. "A boyfriend she badly needs to dump," she said. Then, to me: "Haven't you done it yet?"

I sighed. "No. But I do really have to."

"Just tell him straight," said Mark. "That's my advice. *This isn't working.* What's his name?"

"Tom."

"*This isn't working, Tom. I suggest we split.* Oh, and while you're at it, throw in a puppy gift rejection if you can. In my experience, that really helps to underline a person's true feelings."

"Not that you're bitter or anything, mate," said Smithy.

"Me? Bitter? Whatever gives you that idea?"

We all stared at him. He sighed, shaking his head at himself, looking in my direction. "Sorry, Beth. That was insensitive of me. I know you'll be gentle with the poor guy when the time comes."

It was distressing to see him like that, hollow eyed, pale, obviously a bit drunk. If there hadn't still been that awkward post-kiss hangover between us, I'd have hugged him.

Either that or given him a good shaking.

"I'll do my best to be gentle," I said, looking straight at him. "But rejection is never easy, is it?"

Our gazes connected for a charged moment. Mine fell first, and I stood there, trying to pull myself together, wondering whether things would ever be right between us again. Possibly not.

"Well, this is all very cheerful," Rosie said into the tension.

"Isn't it?" said Smithy. "How's your love life going, Rosie?"

Mark answered for her. "My sister has been swept off her feet by a tall, dark Italian."

"I wouldn't say he's particularly tall," said Rosie. "More medium height."

"But totally gorgeous," I said, and she nodded.

"Oh yes, he's definitely that. What about you, Smithy? Not married yet?"

"I'm married to my job," he said, looking happy about it. "Hence my ability to invite gorgeous women to come and stay with me whenever they care to." He glanced in my direction, and although he was smiling, beneath it, his expression was every bit as intense as it had been on the beach in Belize two decades ago. I blushed. I couldn't help it.

Mark was scowling. "A job's the best thing to be married to, in my opinion. Though you'd have to like what you do for a living for it to work, I suppose."

"Are you not happy with your work, then, mate?"

"Oh please, don't get him started on the woes of self-employment, Smithy," groaned Rosie. "Grace made him give up his job to become an entrepreneur."

"Nobody can make you do anything," said Smithy. "Not unless you let them."

Mark knocked back more of his beer. He looked as if he were formulating how to respond to this, but before he could, there was a knock at the door.

"Could someone get that, please?" called Sylvia. "I'm just checking the casserole."

"I'll go," I volunteered, keen for some respite.

When I opened the door, Gary, Richard's fishing friend, was on the doorstep. Dressed up in smart trousers and a freshly ironed shirt, he was holding a bouquet of flowers and a bottle of wine. Obviously invited by Sylvia.

"Hi, Gary, how lovely to see you," I said.

"Hi, Beth."

Sylvia was suddenly there at my side. "Hello, Gary," she said, kissing his cheek. "Come in, come in. Are those for me? How sweet of you."

Rosie and I exchanged glances as Sylvia ushered Gary down the hallway and into the kitchen.

"Is that what I think it is?" Rosie whispered.

"Depends what you think it is," I said.

"A date?"

"I'm not sure," I said, speaking vaguely because I was also listening to what Smithy was saying to Mark.

"Sometimes what's best for us is staring us right in the face, and we can't see it."

Oh God. Smithy's hints were so unsubtle. If only I could sink into the floor. Vanish in a puff of smoke. Turn back time so I'd stayed in bed this morning instead of coming to Enfield.

"Why do I feel as if I'm on the receiving end of some weird cross between a pep talk and a bollocking?" Mark complained.

"Because you are, mate," said Smithy kindly. "Look, I'm buggering off back to Dubai on Tuesday, so I can say what I like. Don't let life happen to you. Have a long, hard think about what you want and a long, hard look at what you've got, and see what syncs. Okay?"

"I'm beginning to wish I'd left you at the pub," said Mark, but he was smiling as he said it, and Smithy laughed.

"Only looking out for you, mate," he said, but he glanced over at me as he spoke, and what was more, I saw Rosie noticing.

All in all, I was very glad when Sylvia announced lunch was ready and it was time to troop into the dining room.

The casserole was delicious. Sylvia's meals were always delicious. After we'd finished eating it, she tapped her wineglass with her spoon, and we stopped talking to look at her.

"As you all know," she said, her eyes glittering with tears, "if he hadn't been so cruelly taken from us, today would have been Richard's seventieth birthday. Thank you for coming to remember him with me. He was the best husband and the best father anyone could hope to have. I think about him every day, and I know you all do too. Well, perhaps not you, Smithy."

She smiled in Smithy's direction, and there was a ripple of laughter around the table.

"He was a top bloke," said Smithy.

"He was," agreed Gary.

"To Dad," said Mark, raising his wineglass.

"To Dad."

"To Richard."

We clinked our glasses together and drank.

But it seemed Sylvia hadn't finished yet. She cleared her throat. "There's something else," she said.

"I'm hoping it's one of your trifles, Mum," said Mark.

"Or lemon meringue pie?" said Rosie.

"Actually, I've made a trifle *and* a lemon meringue pie," Sylvia said with a quick smile. "I'll fetch them in a moment. But first of all, I wanted to tell you that—"

But whatever Sylvia wanted to say would have to wait, because at that moment there was another knock at the front door.

Mark was closest. "I'll go," he said, getting up from the table.

We waited, silent, listening to a rumble of voices. Then Mark came back. And Tom was with him.

31

I wasn't going crazy, was I? I hadn't given Tom the address without realising it? How the fuck had he found me? And even more to the point, why?

"Tom," I said. "What are you doing here?"

He came over to kiss me—to kiss me!—as if turning up here like this were the most natural thing in the world. "Kate wasn't home, so I thought, *Why not try to find Beth so I haven't had a wasted journey?* And it was literally so easy. You said this place was at Enfield Lock, near the river, so I just walked about until I saw your car parked outside."

That was *how* he was here, not *why* he was here—he'd answered a different flipping question.

Despite the absolute nerve of the guy, kind, lovely Sylvia's hostess instincts had switched on, and she was asking Mark to find Tom a chair and offering him a drink. In no time at all, Tom was squeezed in beside me at the table, his hand clamped to my knee, gawping round at everybody with a vacant grin on his face.

"Well," he said. "Hi, everyone."

Somehow I pulled myself together enough to do the introductions. "This is Tom, everyone. Tom, this is Sylvia and her son, Mark. You already know Rosie. And this is Smithy, Mark's friend, and Gary, a friend of the family."

"Very pleased to meet you all," said Tom, still with that inane grin. "Cheers, everyone."

"Cheers," everyone said with varying levels of enthusiasm.

Tom's possessive hand felt like it was branding my leg. I shifted in my seat but didn't manage to dislodge it. It was like a giant billboard pronouncing SHE'S MINE! ALL MINE! I wanted to flick it off the way you'd flick off an uninvited spider. Or a snake. Why had I ever experienced any confusion about whether Tom was right for me or not? He absolutely was not, and the sooner I told him so, the better.

"Well," said Sylvia into the uncomfortable silence, "who's for dessert?"

"Yes, please," said Tom loudly, sticking his hand up for good measure.

To my left, I could sense Smithy doing his best not to explode with laughter. Across the table, I could see Mark and Rosie glowering, while Gary just looked uncomfortable, and Sylvia still had her polite smile on.

"Whoops!" said Tom, clamping his free hand over his mouth. "I'm a bit of a dessert freak, aren't I, Beth Beth?"

Beth Beth? Oh God, get me out of here.

Hearing Smithy begin to splutter, I spoke quickly to divert attention. "You were about to tell us something, weren't you, Sylvia? Before Tom arrived?"

"Oh," said Sylvia as if she'd forgotten. "That's right, I was." She cleared her throat and smiled, looking suddenly beautiful. Then she reached out to take Gary's hand. "I wanted to tell you all that . . . well, Gary and I have been . . . are . . . seeing each other. We didn't set out to, did we, Gary? It was only that we both missed Richard so much. In a way, it was our shared grief that brought us together."

"Indeed it was," agreed Gary, beaming.

"I hope you all won't mind too much," continued Sylvia, looking round at us all. "I've been so very lonely without Richard. And I do feel"—she smiled at Gary, and he nodded, smiling back at her—"*we* do feel he would have approved."

I could feel tears prickling my eyes. Looking across the table at Rosie, I could see she was in the same state.

"Of course we don't mind, Mum," she said.

Just at the exact same time, Tom said, "Out with the old and in with the new, eh?"

There was a frozen silence. If only the desserts had already been on the table, I'd have upended them both on Tom—the trifle over his head and the lemon meringue pie right in his stupid face. Instead, I got to my feet, finally dislodging his hand, and walked round the table to hug Sylvia.

"Sylvia, Gary, I'm so very happy for you," I said, giving them both a resounding kiss.

"Thank you, darling."

"Thanks, Beth."

"But now I've got to leave, I'm afraid. There's something very pressing I need to do. Come on, Tom."

With a chorus of goodbyes trailing after me, I left to drive Tom home. Not my home but *his*, where I proceeded to tell him in no uncertain terms that we were through.

That is, I thought I'd said it in words that were impossible to misinterpret. But here he was, still ringing me up nearly five months later, so perhaps I'd been subtler than I thought I had.

"Where are you going?" Tom asked me now. "Will you be home for me to pop in with your present later?"

"I'm meeting Rosie to see the Regent Street lights. I don't know when I'll be home. We'll probably go for a drink afterwards, as we usually do. You could always drop it at work for me if you're passing by? Or leave it until the New Year? Anyway, I've got to go now. Bye, Tom."

Giorgio and Rosie were kissing when I got to the Christmas tree in Trafalgar Square—a full-on, unrestrained, no-holds-barred snog. I put two fingers in my mouth and wolf-whistled at them. They drew apart, grinning at me.

"Hello, *cara* Bethy," said Giorgio. "You look even more beautiful every time I see you."

I kissed him. "I doubt it. I'm wearing my gardening clothes. Sorry, guys."

Rosie kissed me on the cheek. "Just so long as you're warm. Is it me, or does it get colder each year we do this?"

"It's just you," I said, gazing up at the Christmas tree, taking in the strands of silver lights stretching from top to bottom and the crowning star. Every year, the tree looked magical. Hopeful. Maybe this coming year, some of that magic and hope would spread in my direction.

"So beautiful." I sighed.

Rosie linked her arm in mine, resting her head on my shoulder to gaze at the tree with me. "Isn't it?"

Giorgio smiled, patiently waiting for us to complete our vigil. But he was stamping his feet to keep warm, his gloved hands thrust into his coat pockets. He was used to the milder temperatures of winter in Rome, so eventually we took pity on him and got moving.

We were about halfway along Regent Street, admiring the dazzling angels, when I saw a tall man with light-blond hair approaching me. *Tom.* And not just Tom but Tom carrying a large gift-wrapped box.

Hell. How had he managed to find me? I shouldn't have let it slip where I was going this evening.

"Beth! I found you."

"Tom," I said. "What are you doing here?"

"I came to give you your present, of course. Here."

When he thrust the box in my direction, my arms moved reflexively to take it. It was heavy. As I struggled to hold it, something clicked into place inside my mind—something that absolved me. Enough of the guilt. I hadn't really treated Tom that badly. I'd decided we weren't right for each other, that was all, and I had a right to do that. It was time to put an end to this once and for all.

"I'll just be a minute or two," I told Rosie, and she nodded.

"We'll be over here if you need us."

"Okay."

"Look, Tom," I said, after she and Giorgio had moved off to stand beneath the next set of Christmas lights. "I can't accept this."

"It's heavy, isn't it? I'll carry it for you if you like. I'm not doing anything this evening. I can tag along with you and help you home with it."

"Tom, you're not listening to me. I can't accept this gift from you because we're not together anymore. If I take it, you'll start hoping we'll get back together. And we won't. Look, you're a good man. I'm sure you'll meet someone right for you soon. But that person just isn't me. I'm really sorry, but I think it's best if you don't phone me or try to see me again."

Suddenly I realised Tom wasn't listening to me. Wasn't even looking at me. He was looking over at Giorgio and Rosie instead.

"Your friend's just gone down on one knee," he said. "I think he's proposing."

I looked over and saw he wasn't making it up. Giorgio was indeed down on one knee, holding something out to Rosie. Rosie had her hand up to her mouth. She was nodding. Oh my God! I wanted to scream and jump up and down.

But then Tom spoke, drawing my attention back to him. "How romantic."

"Please take the gift back."

But he just shook his head mulishly, stuffing his hands into his jacket pockets. So I put the box down on the pavement in front of him. "Goodbye, Tom. Please don't try to contact me again."

When I started to walk away towards my friends, Tom called after me: "Why did you even join a dating site in the first place?"

It was a fair question. I glanced back briefly, the rejection on his face reminding me of the way I'd felt last Christmas, when Mark had so obviously regretted his kiss.

"I shouldn't have," I said. "I'm so sorry."

"Are you all right?" Rosie asked when I reached her.

I nodded vigorously, determined not to cry. "Yes, of course. Did I just see what I thought I saw?"

Rosie flashed her engagement ring at me, a smile splitting her face in two.

Giorgio's smile was a carbon copy. "She say yes!" he said, lifting his arms up to the sky like one of the sparkling angels strung above him.

"Well, of course she did. Oh, congratulations, both of you. I'm so thrilled. Your mum will be over the moon, Rosie."

I kissed and hugged them both, and then we carried on up Regent Street, admiring the lights, though to be honest, I think Rosie and Giorgio shone brighter than they did. And when we reached Oxford Street and Rosie began talking about which cocktail bar we should go to, I held back.

"I'm going to call it a night. It's been a long day. And besides, you two need to celebrate together."

"I am sorry, Bethy," said Giorgio. "I did not mean to take over your evening. I just ask the question before my courage run away from me."

"It's fine," I told him. "More than fine. It's totally fantastic."

We hugged, but before she drew away, Rosie asked, "Will you be in on Saturday morning? It's not one of your Precious mornings, is it?"

"No, term's finished for Bembe's class."

"Good. Okay if I pop round then?"

"Of course."

"Great. See you then."

They headed off hand in hand, completely wrapped up in each other, as they should have been. I hadn't been able to tell Rosie my big news after all, but that didn't matter. I'd tell her on Saturday.

One way or another, next year was going to be an exciting year for both of us. I couldn't wait.

32

Rosie hadn't said what time she'd be coming round on Saturday morning, but I was back from popping out to the shop for milk and biscuits by nine. Then I settled down to a spot of cleaning—not because Rosie was coming over but because I'd totally neglected the flat lately, what with work and looking after Precious.

I had my rubber gloves on and was in the middle of scrubbing out the kitchen bin when the knock on the front door came. I went to the door like that, intending to finish off the job before I made Rosie a cup of coffee.

Only it wasn't Rosie. It was Mark.

"Oh," I said. "Hello."

"Hi," he said, smiling at me. "Sorry to surprise you like this. Nice gloves, by the way."

I peeled them off. In the old days, I might have made a quip about them being Stella McCartney or something, but not now.

When I didn't say anything, Mark pressed on. "So anyway, I'm on my way to the Museum of the Home. They've got a special Christmas exhibition on."

"It's on every year." I'd been several times. Enjoyed it every time.

"Yes. Well, do you want to come with me?"

I'd barely seen Mark since Sylvia's lunch party, and while a part of my mind registered that he was looking better—a lot better—than he had then, I was still glad to have a ready excuse not to spend time with him now.

"Sorry, I can't. Rosie's coming round this morning. I'm expecting her any minute, actually."

Mark's face fell. Despite everything, I had a sudden, almost overwhelming impulse to phone Rosie to put her off. To make myself available to Mark so he wouldn't be disappointed.

Old habits die hard, I guess.

"Well, can I come in for a minute? Grab a cup of coffee, perhaps? I promise to scamper when Rosie gets here."

I stepped back reluctantly. "Sure."

I left him taking his desert boots off and went to put the kettle on.

"Did you enjoy the snow the other week?" he asked.

That great conversation fallback—the weather. Ugh.

"It was pretty," I said, spooning coffee into a french press. "I was working, though, so I didn't get the chance to go sledging or make any snowmen."

"D'you remember that giant one we made one winter, the three of us? With the carrot nose and the pieces of coal for eyes?"

Of course I bloody well did. "Yes, I remember."

We'd been out for hours—so long our hands had turned blue and we couldn't feel our feet in our wellies—rolling giant snowballs and balancing them on top of each other, hunting out sticks for the snowman's arms.

"I never did find out what happened to the scarf we used on him. Mum went bananas about it."

"Someone somewhere is still carrying that guilty secret," I said, because it was just too damn hard not to slip into banter with Mark, even when I really, really didn't want to.

"Think they'll take it to their grave?"

"Very probably."

He took off his coat and slung it over a chair. Just like he'd done last Christmas. *Exactly* like he'd done last Christmas.

"I suppose you've heard the good news about Rosie and Giorgio?"

"I was there when he proposed. Or nearby, anyway. It's fantastic news, isn't it?"

"Hopefully, yes. I mean, I really like Giorgio. Who wouldn't? And I can see he makes Rosie very happy. It's just . . ."

The kettle boiled. I turned away to pour water onto the coffee grounds, not wanting to talk about why Mark might be cynical about Rosie and Giorgio's marriage working out. Not wanting to talk about anything, really. I had shut and bolted the door labelled MARK in my mind a year ago. Maybe one day I'd be able to leave it ajar, but not yet. No matter how much it felt as if invisible fists were pummelling on it, clamouring to get it open.

"But obviously I hope they'll be very happy together."

I finished preparing the coffee and brought Mark's over to him. I resolutely didn't ask whether there'd been any progress on his divorce.

"How's Buddy?"

"Buddy's good, thanks. Mum and Gary have been taking him to agility classes."

I was surprised. "Have they?"

He nodded. "It was Mum's idea. We take Buddy for regular walks, of course, but he has so much energy. And what with him being a working dog, she thought he'd enjoy it."

"And does he?"

He smiled. "Loves it. He's a natural, apparently. Mum and Gary are already talking about aiming for Crufts."

"Really?" My eyes widened at the mention of one of the world's biggest dog shows.

"Certainly are. Got their sights on a trophy, and Buddy's only been to five or six sessions. Apparently, he's got star quality."

"Didn't you want to take him to the classes yourself?"

"I haven't got the time. Or I won't have, not if Buddy really becomes a superstar." He paused. "I'm applying to do a teacher training course in September. To become a maths teacher." His head was down, and he looked suddenly shy.

A maths teacher. Yes! That was so right for him. "That's fantastic, Mark."

He looked at me hopefully. "Do you really think so?"

"Of course I do. You'll be brilliant at it."

He smiled. "Thanks. I'm pleased, I must admit. Finally—finally I know what I want to do. I'm looking forward to spreading the joy of maths to the world, you know? Anyway, as I won't be working from home anymore, Mum and I have agreed to share care of Buddy. He'll be with her during the week and with me at weekends. A bit like the child of divorced parents but without the need to shunt a suitcase back and forth."

"Won't he need a suitcase for all his dog toys and trophies?"

Mark smiled. "They can go in the boot of his chauffeur-driven limousine if he gets really famous."

Damn. Despite all my efforts, we were back to our normal bantering selves. This could easily act as a gateway to a serious chat—which I was determined not to have—about how strained things had been between us lately. Where the hell was Rosie?

Right on cue, my phone bleeped with a message.

Sorry, can't make it today after all. Last-minute Christmas shopping. See you next week. R. XXX

"Bad news?"

"Yes. Rosie can't make it today after all."

"Sorry to hear that." He raised his eyebrows hopefully. "Though I suppose that does mean you're free to come with me to the Museum of the Home after all?"

Five minutes later we were on our way. It was a quiet walk, what with me simmering like a pot about to come to a boil, resenting the fact that Mark thought he could just turn up and decide what I was going to do on the Saturday before Christmas. Furious with myself for relapsing and just going along with what he wanted.

Not that I didn't want to go to the Museum of the Home. I always enjoyed going there, especially at Christmas. I just didn't want to want to go with Mark. Yet, despite everything, it seemed that I did. And I really shouldn't.

"Do you know about the history of the museum?" Mark asked, breaking the silence. Well, I supposed somebody had to break it. The Museum of the Home was two miles away from my flat. "It was originally built as an almshouse for the poor by this guy Geffrye. People were very altruistic in those days if they could afford to be, weren't they?"

"It was probably an attempt to salve his conscience," I sniped. "Geffrye was connected to the slave trade. That's how he got the money to be altruistic. Didn't you know?"

Mark's face fell. "Was he? No, I didn't know that."

"Not a lot of people do."

This time, when silence fell, Mark didn't try to break it. Not at first, anyway.

Then he said, "Look, Beth . . ."

And I just couldn't bear whatever he was going to launch into. Couldn't bear to think about the days after Christmas when I'd ignored his calls. The uncomfortable atmosphere between us over the dinner table at Sylvia's—Mark hollow eyed from the fallout of splitting with Grace, Buddy acting as an effective buffer for our awkwardness.

"Where d'you think Rosie and Giorgio will get married?" I asked. "Enfield or Rome?"

When Mark smiled sadly, I knew he was only too aware I'd spoken to shut him up. But he responded gamely anyway. "I'd have thought you'd know that better than me. Presumably, you're going to be a flower girl or a matron of honour or whatever they call it?"

"The word *matron* conjures up images of starched nurses' outfits," I joked, casting desperately around for a scrap—no matter how small—of humour and feeling sadder than I'd felt since last Christmas as I did so. "I'm not sure that's the look Rosie will want to go for with her bridesmaid outfits."

"You'll have to go down the flower-girl route then."

"A frothy party dress, becoming braids, and a woven basket of posies?"

He pretended to appraise me, then nodded. "I reckon you could pull it off."

Oh God, we were here at the museum. Thank God we were at the museum. At least now we could talk about the exhibits.

The Museum of the Home's main exhibits—which were all decorated for Christmas at this time of the year—were sitting rooms from across the ages, decked out with original furniture and paintings for their period, with well-researched place settings on the tables and artificial representations of food of the day.

Visitors weren't allowed in the rooms—you had to stand behind a silken rope and gaze into the interiors, staring back into the past. The first room dated from 1600 and had a table groaning with food, which I knew, since I'd been here several times before, was mainly sweet, sugar having been so expensive at the time that it was an expression of wealth. A sort of sweet-tasting version of keeping up with the Joneses.

As I looked at it now, it was all too easy to imagine images of the mock eggs and bacon made entirely of sugar paste being posted on Instagram, had Instagram existed back then.

As we moved on, Mark had his head in the information leaflet and read aloud about the elaborate cake which formed the centrepiece of the table in the Regency Room.

"Did you know that green food colouring had arsenic in it in those days? Fancy dying because you had a slice of cake."

I couldn't think of an answer to that, witty or otherwise. By the time we reached the Victorian Room, my head was throbbing. Why the bloody hell had I come here with him today? Apart from the awkwardness between us, everything about the bloody Victorian Room screamed children—the china doll reclining on the armchair. The building blocks. The wooden Noah's Ark and the carved animals coming out of it two by two. And the 1950s room was no better, with wrapping paper strewn everywhere, almost as if the family had just stepped out for a moment.

I stood there, looking at it all, my arms wrapped around myself for comfort, trying to cling to my belief that one day soon I would have a family like this one. But all I could think about were the ghosts of Christmases past—Christmases I'd spent with my parents and Christmases I'd spent with Sylvia and Richard, Mark and Rosie. So much lost joy.

Mark still had the information leaflet in his hand, but suddenly I realised he'd stopped reading from it.

"I have two things to tell you," he said. "A big thing and a small thing."

I swiped my eyes with my sleeve. "Don't tell me," I said harshly. "The toy soldiers on display contain harmful lead? The paper chains are somehow radioactive?"

"No, nothing like that."

"What, then?"

He looked at me. Took a deep breath.

I began to feel worried. "What is it?"

"It's Grace and Jaimie."

I frowned. "Grace and Jaimie?"

He nodded. "Let's just say they aren't going to be alone this Christmas. And I'm not talking about Jaimie's girls being with them."

I gaped, realising exactly what he meant. "Grace and Jaimie are seeing each other?"

"Seeing quite a lot of each other, I imagine. If Jaimie's kept up his naturism tendencies."

"I don't believe it," I said, but even as I spoke, I realised I absolutely did. Jaimie and Grace were perfect for each other. Jaimie wouldn't have to buy Grace dresses and lipsticks to try and improve her; she was always so well turned out. Hell, Olivia and Emily even already liked her, the jammy cow.

Then I remembered Mark telling me last Christmas that Grace was barely at home. That she had often had weekend clients. And my thoughts took a leap further. "D'you think they were seeing each other when you two were still together?"

"Yes, I do. Definitely. But I don't care. Good luck to them, I say. What about you? Does it bother you?"

Considering I'd lived with Jaimie for almost a year, and that I'd spent most of that time making our relationship my priority, bending over backwards to make his girls like me, the extent to which I didn't care was shocking.

"Not in the least."

Mark smiled. "Well, that's good, then, isn't it?" he said.

Silently we walked on to the 1990s room, a bright, cheerful interior with coloured plastic chairs arranged around a table adorned with gaudy foil Christmas crackers.

"So," I said, "what's the small thing? You said you had two things to tell me. Something big and something small. What's the small thing?"

Mark shook his head. Something about his expression set my heart racing.

"That was the small thing—Grace and Jaimie getting together."

"It was?"

"Yes."

A family joined us at the display, their voices loud and intrusive.

"Look, can we go outside?" asked Mark. "Would you mind?"

Numbly, I shook my head, following him past the remainder of the exhibits and out the exit doors. He led me round a corner, out of the wind, and reached out to turn my collar up, keeping his hands there afterwards.

"The big thing is"—he stopped to sigh and took hold of my coat lapels—"I've realised I'm a complete idiot. Well, actually, I realised it last Christmas, only the timing was . . . well, crap, if we're being honest about it. And then you would barely speak to me, and who could blame you after I'd behaved like a total dick? Certainly not me."

Oh God. I wasn't up to hearing this. To raking it all up again. Unfortunately, I wasn't up to saying something bright and corny like, *Never mind. It's all water under the bridge. It's all in the past. Let bygones be bygones.* I was too busy trying not to cry and not having much luck at it.

And besides, his hands had moved from my coat lapels to my shoulders.

"Christ, when I saw you with that idiot Tom, I was so jealous. And what Smithy said really got to me too. Look, last Christmas, when we kissed, when I kissed you, I realised something. Something I've spent the last twelve months coming to terms with." He sighed. "I don't need to tell you it's been a tough year for me, what with splitting with Grace, sorting everything out. Trying to keep my head above water with work. And then there was the whole Mum-getting-together-with-Gary thing. I mean, it's cool; I really like Gary, and Mum's right—Dad would have approved, wouldn't he? He'd be egging her on. And it is great—really great—to see her happy. Only somehow, seeing her happy with Gary meant grieving Dad all over again. So I suppose I've been a bit depressed, what with one thing and another.

"Look, the point is, it was all excuses. Because I was just so bloody terrified. I mean, it's a big thing, isn't it, when you've loved somebody for as long as I've loved you? To try and change the terms of that love?"

Tears began to run down my cheeks. It was happening. At long last, it was happening. And I wasn't quite sure whether I wanted to hold him close or give him a good shaking for making me suffer so much while he worked things out.

Mark reached out to wipe my tears away, bringing his face close to mine.

"But then I'd sort of lost you already anyway, really, hadn't I, by being such a dick? So when Gary told me straight out it was time I did something about it if I didn't want to lose you altogether, I—"

I managed to spit some words out. "Gary said that?"

He nodded. "Yes. Apparently, he and Dad had several conversations over the years about it. About you and I . . . well, being made for each other and—"

"Richard thought that? That we were made for each other?"

Another tear ran down my cheek. Once again Mark stroked it away. "Apparently so, yes."

Dear Richard. Dear, dear Richard.

"Don't cry. I can't bear to see you cry."

"I can't help it. I miss him so much."

"I know."

Of course he did.

"I still hear him in my head all the time. Do you?"

"Yes." I did hear Richard—giving me encouragement, sometimes even advice—but his voice was absent now. Maybe because he thought this was up to me and Mark. Well, it was, wasn't it?

"Rosie was there when Gary said what he said," Mark continued, "so of course she started on at me as well, and . . ."

I opened my eyes, realising the truth. "She was never going to pop round to see me this morning, was she? It was all a fix to get me alone with you."

He nodded. "Do you mind?"

I gave a little hiccupping laugh. "What? Mind my oldest friend tricking me, or . . . ?"

"Or me telling you I love you. Want to be with you. Can't imagine my life without you."

Tears again. Lots of them. I closed my eyes to try and stem the flow. It didn't work. "Do you know how long I've wanted to hear you say that?" I asked, still feeling like hitting him, my words coming out in tearful spatters. "Do you?"

"Tell me."

"Ever since bloody Donna Baker gave me that note for you when I was eleven years old, that's how long."

"What, when I had all those spots? When I was a New Order fanatic?"

"Yes!"

He frowned, remembering. "I had George Michael hair. I wore double denim."

I laughed through my tears, remembering him looking exactly like that. "I thought you were gorgeous."

He smiled. "I probably thought so myself at the time."

"You did."

His smile faded. "I wish you'd told me how you felt. Why didn't you?"

I sighed in frustration. "Because you never gave me any hint you felt the same way. And you didn't, did you? I was like your *sister*. I had to watch you work your way through all those girlfriends. Every time you split up with one of them, I'd think, *Maybe now. Maybe he'll see me now.* But you never did. And then you married Grace, and . . . it broke my heart."

He put his forehead against mine. "I am so sorry, Beth . . ."

I pulled in a ragged breath, continuing on because it all had to be said. "Then, last Christmas . . . I thought you were using me. For comfort. To feel better. And . . . and . . ." I pulled my breath in on a sob. "I couldn't bear it."

Mark shook his head, his face close to mine, tears in his eyes. "I would never do that to you, Beth. Never. Look, when we kissed, it was like waking up from a sleep. That's the only way I can describe it. I'm so sorry it's taken me so long to realise how I feel. But it isn't too late, is it? If you still feel the same way? You do, don't you? Tell me you do."

He kissed me then, and I melted into his kiss, desire and love thrilling through my entire body, my heart soaring.

I drew away only when I felt something wet and cold flutter onto my face. "Look!" I said, gazing up at the sky. "It's snowing!"

"So it is. How magical." Mark put his head back and poked his tongue out to catch the snowflakes, exactly as he'd done as a boy.

I laughed and did the same thing. Then he pulled me close again, the snowflakes melting in the heat between our lips as we kissed.

"Shall we get an Uber?" Mark suggested, his voice husky against my mouth.

I nodded. "Yes please."

We kissed all the way back to my flat. We kissed in my hallway, our coats slipping from our shoulders to pool on the floor. We kissed as we stumbled into the bedroom. I could have kissed Mark forever, except that I wanted to do more than kissing.

We fell onto the bed, still kissing, and I reached down for his belt buckle.

Mark pulled back slightly to look at me. "Oh no. No, no, no. There's no way we're going to rush this, Beth Bailey. We're going to savour it. Every last delicious second of it."

I wasn't about to argue.

~

"Did you see stars?" I asked him a long time later, lying in bed next to him, feeling as liquid and boneless as if I'd been filleted.

He sounded slightly breathless, as well he might. "About two hundred billion trillion and one of them, yes. And numbers. A long, beautiful line of numbers stretching on into infinity."

I made a sound.

"What? You've got to remember numbers are my nirvana."

"Something definitely went wrong with your wiring when you were put together. Except for just now. Your wires are in exactly all the right places just now. I didn't know it could be like that, did you?"

He stroked my hair back from my face, laying a line of kisses down along my collarbone. "Absolutely no clue, no." Then he sighed. "Think of all the time we've wasted."

"Maybe not. Maybe we needed all that wrong stuff, all that life, to get to this perfect moment."

"Maybe. You know, I think I first got an inkling of my feelings at the folk festival, watching you fall in love with that song."

"'Carrickfergus'?"

He nodded. "Yes. Your mouth was hanging slightly open. You looked as if you'd been slapped."

"It really spoke to me. The tune. That guy's voice. The words."

"The man saying he'd swim over the deepest ocean to be with his love?"

"Yes." Just thinking about it, I was coming over all swoony again.

"That's me, you know now. I'd do anything for you, Beth. I love you so much. I know I joke around, but half the time it's to give me something to hide behind. I adore you. You make me feel . . . I don't know. *Seen.*"

"Like you have permission to be wholly you?"

"Yes."

"That you don't need to change a thing about yourself?"

"*Yes.*"

"Me too. I feel that too."

"Of course you do. You're perfect."

He kissed me, pressing me to him, and it started up all over again, that great tumbling washing machine of passion which—for the moment—blocked out thoughts of absolutely anything else.

A long time later, Mark pulled the bedroom curtain aside to look out. "It's really snowing hard now. It must have settled, I think. Fancy making some snow angels?"

"I'm not sure there's enough space for snow angels in my garden."

"Come on, let's go and see."

His excitement was contagious. We pulled on our clothes as quickly as we'd taken them off and rushed outside. The snow had covered the paths, the branches of the plane tree, and the shrubs in the borders. Everything was coated in a glittering, sparkling, magical blanket, as if someone had waved a wand over it. But the only possible space to make snow angels was on the patio, which was sheltered slightly by the house and therefore had a lot less snow. So when we threw ourselves down on the paving slabs and moved our arms and legs up and down, we were actually moving as many bits of stick and old leaves as we were snow.

"Scarecrows are the new snow angels," joked Mark.

He looked ridiculous with leaves and bits of old twigs in his hair. Gorgeous, though. Happy too. Definitely happy.

"Did you know," Mark said from the paving slabs, "experts estimate that Mount Everest weighs three hundred and fifty trillion pounds?"

There were snowflakes on his eyelashes. I had no idea whatsoever why he was spouting random facts about Mount bloody Everest, but God, he was beautiful.

My stomach gave an unromantic lurch. Well, I hadn't even had breakfast. The croissants I'd bought to share with Rosie were still in their packet on the kitchen table.

"Wait a minute," he said, looking at me. "Was that cement-mixer sound your stomach?"

"Might have been," I said cagily.

He laughed, pushing himself off the ground, holding out a hand to pull me up. "Come on, I'll cook you some lunch."

Indoors, we took our wet jackets off.

"The snow's gone right through my jacket," Mark said, pulling his damp jumper away from his skin.

"Want to borrow some clothes? I've probably got something to fit you."

His gaze narrowed. "Not if it's that T-shirt you lent to Eagle Man last year."

"Eagle Man? Oh, you mean Jake," I said, transported straight back to that awkward encounter in the hallway with Jake, gorgeous and bare chested, holding the I'm not rude, I just have the balls to say what everyone else is thinking T-shirt.

"Did anything ever happen between you two?"

I shook my head. "It might have done."

"Only I ruined it by turning up when I did?"

I nodded. "That's what always happened. I'd meet someone, think, *This could be it at last. This could be something.* Then I'd see you, and suddenly . . . Nobody ever matched up, that's all."

"I'm sorry."

I shrugged. "Jake's in love with someone else now. It's fine. Anyway, are you going to cook me some lunch or what?"

He hung his sodden jacket up on a coat peg, suddenly becoming businesslike. "I am. Go and sit yourself down. Leave me to it."

I did as I was told, watching Mark move about the kitchen, pulling ingredients from the fridge and the store cupboards with a big, stupid grin on his face, which was no doubt echoed on my own. Tossing bell peppers into the air and catching them like a cocktail bar manager. Making me giggle when he held a leek suggestively low at the front of his jeans and twerked it playfully. Flipping the switch on the radio and breaking into a dance that involved a great deal of butt wiggling.

How many times had I seen Mark in full-on make-as-much-mess-as-you-can cooking mode? Many, many times. Only not so much lately. Not at all lately, in fact, because I had never once been invited over to eat in all the time he'd been with Grace. But even though I hadn't been over to their flat for dinner, I was pretty sure Grace would have put a cap on the number of saucepans Mark used and insisted on him doing the washing up as he went along, instead of leaving it all until the end.

Uh-oh—Grace. We were going to have to speak about Grace, weren't we? No matter if it would take some of the shine off this gleaming, glittering day. She was the elephant in the room. And elephants were big creatures capable of trampling and crushing things out of existence just by moving from place to place.

I waited until we'd eaten Mark's delicious stir-fry and he was smiling at me across the table in a way that made me think about the crumpled sheets on my bed.

"What happened between you and Grace? Why did it go wrong?"

"You mean apart from the fact that she was probably in love with Jaimie all along?"

"D'you think she was?"

"I do, yes. I think she spent our entire marriage trying to turn me into him."

"Did she try to get you interested in becoming a naturist?"

He flashed me a grin. "No. But then, I have a sneaky suspicion Jaimie won't be a naturist for very much longer. Grace may love him, but that doesn't mean she's going to do everything he wants. This is Grace, after all. She's very controlling."

A flicker of something crossed his face. Remembered hurt. Sadness. He reached for my hand across the table, turning it over so he could caress my wrist. Tingles of desire instantly shot right up my arm. I knew he didn't want to talk about any of this. That he'd much prefer we go to the bedroom to create some highly effective oblivion. But he took a deep breath, sighed, and pressed on.

"Grace controlled me right from the start," he said. "I thought I was the one making the moves, deciding it was high time I grew up and got married. But it was all her. She was beautiful. Successful. She wanted me. To be married to me. But then we were together, and nothing I did measured up. *I* didn't measure up. I'd spend my whole damn time trying to change." He ran a hand through his hair, remembering. "If we'd had a child together, I bet I still wouldn't have been good enough for her. She'd have criticised every little thing I did. *Don't hold him like that. He doesn't need that. That's not the right way to change a nappy.* I'd have spent my whole time trying to be the type of father she wanted me to be." He shuddered. Then he said, "God, I can't tell you how happy I am that I'm not a father."

I can't tell you how happy I am that I'm not a father.

The words reverberated around my head. On and on, like the gong bath Rosie had dragged me to once. I'd hated it with a passion, emerging afterwards feeling as if my brain had been chewed up by a tiger rather than soothed and unblocked, the way it was supposed to have been.

"What?" Mark asked, instantly sensing something was wrong.

I don't suppose it was very difficult to sense it. My heart and my mind and my body had all done a sort of emergency stop, turning me rigid, inside and out.

I withdrew my wrist from his grasp, putting my hand on my lap, out of his reach. I looked down at the table, away from his anxious, probing gaze.

If Mark had constantly tried to change himself to be what Grace had wanted him to be, then I had spent an inordinately large amount of my life waiting for him to notice me. And now he was doing just that— noticing me and apparently loving all that he saw. Only he couldn't see all of me, could he? Because there were still things about me he didn't know. Huge things. Things I wasn't prepared to change.

I couldn't become the person he'd been with Grace, constantly doing my best to adapt, leaving myself and all that I was behind in the process. I couldn't let anyone—even Mark—stop me from pursuing my dreams.

"You're crying," he said. "Please don't cry. What did I say? What's wrong? Tell me. Please, Beth. What is it?"

"It's your timing," I said viciously. "It completely sucks."

He frowned. "My timing?"

"Yes, your bloody timing! Why couldn't you have waited until next year to tell me all this?"

He shook his head. "I don't know. Maybe because I've already waited *thirty* years to tell you, and that feels plenty long enough?" He reached across the table to take my chin between his fingers, lifting my head up to look at him. "Maybe because I felt like I was going to explode? Because I was so scared another Tom or Jake or Jaimie might pop out of the woodwork? Pick your reason. Look, what's this all about, Beth? Please tell me."

I pulled my face away from his hand, swiping the tears away from my cheeks. "You should have waited until next February to say something."

He frowned. "Why February?"

I met his eyes. "Because by February, I'll be pregnant. Hopefully. If all goes to plan. And when I presented you with a fait accompli, you'd have thought, *Well, that's not ideal, but I love Beth, so I'll love her child too.*"

Mark was still frowning. "Why might you be pregnant by February?"

"Because I've got an appointment at a fertility clinic in the New Year. To be . . . inseminated with sperm from a carefully chosen sperm donor. And now you're going to want me to change my mind, aren't you? And I just can't, Mark, all right? I've waited to be a mother practically as long as I've waited for you."

I took a deep breath. Faced him. "I love you. I do. More than Mount Everest and the second- and third-highest mountains put together."

"K2 and Kanchenjunga," Mark supplied, looking gutted and baffled at the same time. "They're the second- and third-highest mountains."

"Thank you. Mount Everest, K2, and Kanchen whatever you said. Look, I'm really sorry, but I have to do this. I have to. No matter what. I've waited so long. And nothing and nobody is going to stop me. Not even you."

WINTER FIVE

❄❄❄❄❄

33

"I now pronounce you husband and wife. You may kiss the bride."

Mark smiled at me. I smiled back, pulling him in for a long, sweet, loving kiss.

There was applause. We drew apart to join in, Mark putting two fingers in his mouth to produce a long, drawn-out wolf whistle that had his sister mock scowling at him in a manner quite inappropriate for a bride dressed in lacy, low-backed satin finery.

Mark laughed, throwing his head right back, his hand finding mine.

"She looks so beautiful," I said emotionally. "Doesn't she look beautiful?"

"Stunning."

But I wasn't listening. I was too busy trying not to sob at the gorgeousness of the parade of flower girls following Rosie and Giorgio down the aisle. Giorgio's three nieces—who had flown in from Rome the day before with the rest of his family—all utterly adorable with their dark hair, dark eyes, and frothy pink dresses. Delicate, graceful. Touchingly proud of the role they were playing.

Far better than the lumbering cart horse of a bridesmaid I'd have made, what with being almost nine months pregnant.

"You don't want me ruining your wedding photos," I'd told Rosie when she'd broached the subject.

"You wouldn't spoil the photos."

"I would. People would look at them in years to come and say, *Didn't you look lovely? What a wonderful dress. But goodness, whoever's that? She looks about to pop!* No, sweetie, it's your day, not mine. Let Giorgio's nieces do the honours."

"Oh, all right," Rosie said. "But don't think you're getting out of organising my hen do."

"Better have it soon, then," I said. "Unless you want to make it a hen do–cum–baby shower?"

In the church, I was suddenly overcome by emotion. I'd been ultra-emotional those past few weeks anyway, but what with the occasion and being in church, my feelings were suddenly even more heightened.

"I wish . . ." I began to say to Mark, and as usual, he read my mind.

"I know," he said, handing me a tissue. "He would have been so fucking proud, wouldn't he?"

I blew my nose. "He would. He really would."

"Think I did an okay job standing in for him?"

"You did an amazing job."

"Good." He kissed me again, putting out his hands to haul me up from the pew seat.

Only I didn't take them straightaway.

"Beth?" he said, noticing my frozen expression.

"I think . . . I think we'd better wait until everyone else has left the church before we leave," I said.

He frowned. "Why? Won't they be waiting for us for the photographs?"

"I think I might have"—I lowered my voice—"wet myself."

Mark sat back down again. "Wet yourself?" he repeated, far too loudly for my liking. "What d'you mean, you've wet yourself?"

"Well, I'm sitting in a pool of water. So either I've wet myself or my waters have just broken."

"Christ. Really?"

"Trust me, this is not something I'd lie about."

"Isn't it too soon?"

"It's only a week early, so no."

"Well, come on, then, we need to get you to hospital."

"I'm sure there's no rush," I said, just as a wave of pain spasmed through my belly. "Ow! Shit! Ow!"

"Jesus Christ." Mark ran a hand through his hair, making it stand on end. "Come on, you need to get up. Here, wear my jacket." He shrugged his suit jacket off, helping me on with it and pulling it down as far as it would go over my wet patch, guiding me carefully from the pew.

"We need to cause as little disruption as possible," I said. "Go and discreetly tell your mum why we're putting in a disappearing act while I slip off to the car."

"Will you be all right on your own?"

"Yes, of course. Go on."

Mark viewed me doubtfully. "Okay," he said and hurried over to Sylvia.

Unfortunately, the news he had to impart caused Sylvia to squeal loudly enough to draw the gaze of the entire wedding party in her direction and Rosie to say, "Whatever is it, Mum?" So Mark ended up having to make an announcement, and the next minute, Rosie was jogging across the churchyard towards me with Sylvia and a baffled Giorgio in her wake, the hem of her wedding dress dragging across the soggy grass.

She arrived, breathless and emotional. "You just had to upstage me, didn't you?" she joked. "Couldn't help yourself."

"Sorry," I said, sniffing to try and hold back the tears.

She hugged me, and I did my very best not to get snot down the embroidered beading of her bodice.

"I can't believe you're going to do this huge thing without me," she said, sniffing herself.

"You just did a huge thing without me," I reminded her. "Congratulations, kiddo." Then a fresh wave of pain gripped me, and I cried out.

Rosie backed off sharply. "What are you waiting for?" she asked her brother. "Get my best friend to hospital pronto!"

Being laid-back was kind of Mark's trademark—the reason for the success of his first term as a qualified maths teacher. But I doubted whether his students would have recognised this version of him as we made our way to the hospital. The nostril-flaring, wide-eyed, hand-on-the-horn, sweating man in the driver's seat beside me wasn't the cool, wisecracking, make-maths-interesting-for-everyone man they were used to. Hell, he wasn't the man *I* was used to.

But he was the only one I'd got to get me to the hospital safely.

"Please, Mark, can you slow down a bit?" I said. "I don't want to puke on top of everything else. I'm sure we'll get there in plenty of time."

"Sorry. Yes, okay."

For about a millisecond Mark drove at the speed limit. But then I had another contraction and couldn't help crying out.

"Jesus," Mark said, pressing down even harder on the accelerator.

We were almost there when the traffic came to a complete stand-still. A bus had stopped at a bus stop on the other side of the road, and a fleet of taxis was parked outside a restaurant on our side, blocking the road. Absolutely nothing could get past in either direction.

"Come on!" shouted Mark, hooting just as a group of what looked like drunken work colleagues—all wearing Santa hats—congaed out of the restaurant, kicking first their left legs and then their right, singing and screaming at the top of their voices.

"Buffoons!" shrieked Mark hysterically, but I burst out laughing. Especially when I caught sight of two of the Santas locked in a passionate embrace they were bound to regret when they went back to work in the morning.

Mark was oblivious. "Why do all the significant events of my life happen at Christmas?" he lamented.

I had no answer for him to that, but fortunately, the bus pulled away from the stop just then, and we were back on our way.

At the hospital, there was a wheelchair bay in the car park, which was just as well because the car park was packed, and we had to leave the car a long way from the entrance. Mark nabbed a wheelchair. I sat in it, and we set off like a steam train. But just before we reached the entrance, I spotted a familiar face on her way out of the building. It was Clare, the social worker. And she was carrying . . . a *baby*.

"Stop!" I yelled to Mark.

"What d'you mean?" he asked, puffing onwards. "I hate to break it to you, but there's no way to stop this thing now."

Realising he was speaking about childbirth, not the wheelchair, I said it again. "Stop, Mark. Stop!"

He stopped. A matter of feet from Clare. I couldn't take my eyes off that bundle in her arms.

"Clare. Hi."

"Oh, hello, Beth." Clare's gaze swept over my baby bump and my hands clutching at it. "It looks as if congratulations might soon be in order."

"Yes," I said vaguely, aware of Mark pawing the ground like a stallion behind me. "This is my partner, Mark. Mark, this is Clare, my social worker."

The baby was a girl. I could tell that from the pink hat and booties emerging from the white blanket she was swaddled in. She was fast asleep, her eyes and rosebud mouth closed. Completely perfect.

I could guess why Clare had her. Somewhere inside the hospital— possibly somewhere close to where I was about to end up—a woman had most likely just given birth. A woman deemed unsuitable to be a mother. Clare had just removed her child—very possibly right from her arms—and now she was taking her into care. Sometime soon, the baby would be adopted.

Another contraction arrived. I gasped and clutched my belly harder.

"Looks as if you'd better get inside," Clare said. "I'm so glad it's worked out for you, Beth."

"Thank you," I managed to grind out. Then Mark was pushing me through the doors, and Clare and the baby were gone.

I hadn't expected to see Clare again after our last meeting. I'd *hoped* not to see her, in fact. Not because I had anything against her but because if I did see her, it would mean my fertility treatment had failed.

It had been so scary waiting for my final appointment with her. I'd made my decision, and I was confident fertility treatment was the right choice for me. But I still had to tell Clare about it, and the finality of speaking those words provoked a myriad of fretful questions in my mind. What if it didn't work out? What if I had the treatment but didn't get pregnant? Would I still be able to adopt? Or would my rejection of adoption now be a rejection of adoption forever?

All those weeks of scrutiny and questioning while Clare made up her mind whether I was right for adoption. She was hardly going to be impressed by someone who thought of adoption as a consolation prize, was she?

I could have sworn that woman was psychic. She knew something was wrong the second she came in through my front door. She'd barely got her coat off before she said, "I can sense a change in you today, Beth. Has something happened?"

I swallowed. Nodded. Then, feeling as if I were jumping off the edge of a cliff, I told her about my plans.

She could have put her coat straight back on, collected her files, and left right away, I suppose. But being the dedicated professional who cared deeply about children that she was, she didn't. Instead, she quizzed me for ten minutes on my childcare choices, my strategies for managing my work as a single parent, and what I planned to tell the child about its origins. And because I'd done my research and thinking, I answered all her questions with a confidence that gave me hope.

Finally, she pushed back her chair and got to her feet. "You need to know that should your fertility treatment be unsuccessful, you'd need to take a six-month break before you restarted the adoption process," she said, holding her hand out to me. "That's our policy for everyone undertaking fertility treatment. But I wish you good luck, Beth."

I shook her hand. "Thank you, Clare. For everything."

"Are you all right?" Mark asked as we waited for the lift to arrive to take us to the maternity unit.

I nodded, sending a tear spilling down my cheek. I couldn't stop thinking about that perfect baby, so completely innocent of what was to come and what had just happened.

Good luck, I whispered to her inside my head. *Good luck.*

Then another contraction arrived, punching away thoughts about anything else but my own baby's imminent arrival.

~

"Push, Beth, push."

"I am bloody pushing!"

"Push harder, darling."

"I can't . . . bloody . . . push . . . any . . . Oh Christ! Argh!"

"That's it, you're doing so well," said the midwife. "He's almost here."

"I can see him. I can see him! Our little boy's coming, Beth. He's coming!"

I had stopped being a woman and become a ball of fiery pain instead. A ball of fiery pain that was going to explode at any moment.

But then there was a sudden slippery feeling. A gush. And I caught sight of Mark's face at the exact moment it transformed from anxious to ecstatic.

"He's here," he said, tears running down his face. "Our baby's here."

Right on cue, our son took his first breath and began to cry. Seconds later, I was cradling him, a perfect tiny weight that my arms had never truly dared to believe they would hold.

"Hello there. Hello, little one." I couldn't stop smiling. Couldn't stop gazing and gazing down at his perfect face. "He's beautiful," I whispered. "So beautiful."

Mark was still crying. "He is. Oh, he is."

"Do you want to hold him?"

"Can I?"

"Of course. He's your son."

Awkwardly, so carefully, Mark took the precious bundle from me and held him in his arms. I watched them. Saw Mark's beaming smile as our baby's fingers curled around his thumb. Noticed the similarities in their features. Rejoiced in them.

It was Rosie who'd dissuaded me from going down the whole sperm-donor route in the end, although I'm sure I would have changed my mind anyway, even if it had happened on my way to the fertility clinic.

Mark was far too afraid of upsetting me to have said anything to stop me going through with it, I'm sure. But Rosie was having none of that.

"Look," she said. "I know my brother can be remarkably slow on the uptake, and I know he was hurtfully deluded for a while when he thought Grace was a better marriage bet than you. But actually, beneath it all, he's all right, you know? I'm just saying I think you ought to give it a try naturally. You know, just do it, and see what happens. And if it turns out you do need a turkey-baster job, why not use Mark's sperm? If he's firing blanks, you can always go back to the sperm donor. Just my two pennies' worth of advice."

"But he told me he was relieved he wasn't a father," I said.

"He'll have been talking about Grace, dimwit," Rosie told me. "About being relieved he and Grace hadn't had a child. Not that he doesn't want one with you. Of course he wants to have one with you. The man's besotted. He'd give you ten babies if you asked him to. Go on, speak to him. Try it. See what happens."

I'd taken her advice. All of it. I spoke to Mark, and he reassured me that Rosie was right. He did want my babies. Very much. So we took some very pleasurable action to do something about it. And now here was the result: gorgeous Alfie, our son.

I like to think I'd have loved any baby I'd given birth to. In fact, I was certain of it. But I was very happy Alfie came from both me and Mark.

"Would you have loved him as much if he'd been conceived via a sperm donor?" I asked Mark now.

He looked up at me. "Of course," he said. "No question."

I nodded, satisfied. But a little later, when Alfie was lying on my chest, skin to skin, I thought of another question.

"And if we were ever to adopt, the two of us, maybe an older child who really needs a home with a loving family, do you think you'd be able to love him or her too?"

Just for a fraction of a second, a look of pure panic crossed Mark's face. But then he rallied and smiled. "I'm sure I would. But is it all right if we focus on this little one first?"

I nodded, lying back against the pillows and closing my eyes. Just for a moment, though, because I had the marvel that was Alfie to gaze at. The rest of my life as a mother to live.

When Alfie was an hour old, his aunt and uncle came to meet him.

"Blimey," said Rosie. "He's tiny."

"*Che bel bambino,*" cooed Giorgio, a smile splitting his face in two. "Can I hold him, please?"

"Of course."

I watched Mark carefully place Alfie into Giorgio's arms. Saw Rosie watching the two of them. Reached for her hand, feeling her brand-new golden wedding band against my fingers.

"He looks like Dad, doesn't he?" she said, and tears filled my eyes.

"I think he does a little, yes."

Giorgio was holding Alfie to his chest now, still cooing to him. "*Bel ragazzo. Bel bambino.*" He was going to be a fabulous uncle.

"I suppose," said Rosie, "that now I'm an aunt, I'd better start liking children a bit more. Just for Alfie's sake, you understand."

I swallowed. "Think you're up to it?"

She pulled my wrist to her lips and kissed it. "For this little treasure? I reckon so."

"Good. Now for goodness' sake, go and have your honeymoon, the pair of you."

Then it was Sylvia's turn. Sylvia, still dressed in her wedding finery, her large-brimmed green hat drawing glances that she was entirely oblivious to as she entered the maternity ward.

"Oh," she said as Mark placed her grandson into her arms. "Oh."

"Mum," he said, "I'd like you to meet Alfie Richard Groves."

I watched Sylvia's expression move from ecstatically happy to sad to happy again in a heartbeat, a single tear sliding down her cheek. Alfie stirred slightly, opening navy-blue eyes to peer at his grandmother.

"I'm so very pleased to meet you, Alfie," Sylvia said, her voice quavering. "We are going to have such good times together. Such good times." She glanced up at me and Mark. "Oh, thank you, you two. Thank you for giving me such a wonderful gift."

"Ma, you do know he's coming home with us, right?" Mark said. "Don't go signing him up for any agility sessions, will you?"

Then our visitors were all gone, and it was just me, Mark, and Alfie again.

"Want me to go off somewhere so you can get some sleep?" Mark asked me.

I shook my head. "Nah. May as well get used to sleep deprivation straightaway. Besides, there's too much gazing at our beautiful son to be done. You'll never catch up if you stop now."

"He is beautiful, isn't he?"

"He's perfect."

"Like you. I love you, Beth."

"I love you too. There's no one else on this planet I'd want to go on this roller coaster ride with."

We smiled at each other. I knew he was remembering—as I was—Richard's speech in the garden at his parents' ruby wedding celebration. *I'm so glad I've been strapped into that roller coaster next to you,* he'd said to Sylvia, the love of his life. I knew exactly how that felt.

Alfie stirred, opening his eyes and starting to wail. Very loudly.

Mark grinned. "Buckle up, kiddo. The ride's about to start."

I laughed and lifted our son from his crib. "Ready," I said.

ACKNOWLEDGMENTS

This book wouldn't exist if I'd never had my heart broken or grieved for loved ones. So thank you, heartbreakers! You know who you are. Thanks also to my parents—I know you won't mind me drawing on my experience of saying goodbye to you and accepting your passing. I think of you every day.

I also need to give thanks to my fierce craving for a child of my own—for my determination to do whatever it took to make that happen. The struggle and ultimate joy of that quest runs throughout this story, and I'm so blessed that my very own Alfie is the result. Alfie, you are a constant joy. I'm so impressed with the man you're becoming.

My thanks to my agent, Carly Watters, who didn't give up on me and who helped to bring out the very best in my characters and this story. To my editor Alicia Clancy, for her heartwarming enthusiasm for my words, and to Danielle Marshall, Jen Bentham, Adrienne Krogh, Rachael Clark, and the whole team at Lake Union. To Ann Warner, my talented writer friend and the person to whom I entrust my early drafts. I value your continued insight and advice so much. To all the friends who have passed through my life, both online and in person—thank you for the good times and the laughter, and for listening to me in times of struggle.

To my readers—your support means so much and gives what I do meaning. Thank you so much.

Lastly, to Graham, my rock. Love you always.

ABOUT THE AUTHOR

Kitty Johnson lives in Norwich, Norfolk, in the UK, with her partner and teenage son. She has an MA in creative writing from the University of East Anglia and teaches creative writing part-time. A nature lover, Kitty enjoys walking in the local woods and by the sea in Norfolk with her dog. Also an artist, she paints and makes collages in her studio when she has time. Kitty enjoys a challenge and once performed stand-up comedy as research for a book—an experience she found very scary but hugely empowering.